OCEAN'S
GODORI

OCEAN'S GODORI

ELAINE U. CHO

HILLMAN GRAD BOOKS
A **zando** IMPRINT

NEW YORK

Hillman Grad Books is an imprint of Zando.
zandoprojects.com

First Edition: April 2024

Text design by Aubrey Khan, Neuwirth & Associates, Inc.
Cover design by Evan Gaffney
Cover illustrations by Jee-ook Choi

The publisher does not have control over and is not responsible for author or other third-party websites (or their content).

Library of Congress Control Number: 2023948981

978-1-63893-059-4 (Hardcover)
978-1-63893-060-0 (ebook)

10 9 8 7 6 5 4 3 2 1
Manufactured in the United States of America

The first one was always going to be for my 엄마.

Thank you for everything, Mom.

Did my mother only give birth to me

so I'd have hands made hard from rowing?

–TRADITIONAL HAENYEO SONG

OCEAN'S
GODORI

PROLOGUE

HADRIAN SITS at the bar, gagging down a drink he hates.

The screen overhead plays a popular Icelandic holo-soap whose characters seem to peel off clothing at every available opportunity. A customer yells for a freeze-frame, and the people lined up on barstools hoot as the bartender angles the scene so they can ogle the actress on-screen.

Hadrian idly envisions smashing their mouths in. First the gaping boy sitting at the end of the counter, drool practically dribbling from his mouth, all the way down the line to the man waving his football scarf in time with an anthem sounding from another screen. Hadrian shivers at the thought of their teeth cutting his fists, blood dripping, pain flaring in their eyes. He composes himself so the thoughts stay submerged, but like a crocodile, they're lurking in wait.

"Councilman Einarson?"

Hadrian turns toward the hand on his shoulder and shapes his mouth into a lopsided smile, feeling the pinch of the dimple on his right cheek that tells him he's done it correctly. The spindly man behind him is of the uncomfortable type, as if he never adjusted to the growth spurt of his limbs shooting out like Alice's after fisting her prescriptions. He squints at Hadrian, who keeps from tensing under the scrutiny. The man unwinds his scarf, shrugging off his coat as he takes in the bar.

"Unusual meeting place, isn't it?"

"One of my favorite haunts, Councilman Rawls."

Hadrian scratches at the thick beard at his neck in an idle gesture Einarson does as a nervous tic. Rawls frowns.

"Why have you called me here, Einarson?" he asks. "To gloat? The ecological referendum is as good as passed. You've won." He raises his hand to order.

"Perhaps." Hadrian keeps his voice low, affecting the slight accent he has been practicing for the last week. He's counting on the noise of the bar to cover up any weaknesses in his performance. "But let's not talk shop while we're here, yes?"

Rawls pauses in his futile efforts to nab the bartender's attention. He squinches his eyes at Hadrian again. Rawls is the perfect target. He has never been close with Einarson. They're technically political enemies, but Rawls has never been popular with anyone. He's a weaselly politician who doesn't get asked out to drinks much—or at all really.

"Bartender!" Hadrian raps his knuckles on the wood grain of the bar, and the bartender finally comes over. "Your usual is an old-fashioned, isn't it, Rawls? An old-fashioned for my friend here."

Hadrian registers Rawls's pleased flush in the gloomy bar. He's taken the first step in easing his suspicion. Alcohol will take care of the rest. It's not difficult to keep the conversation going, and Hadrian asks the bartender repeatedly for refills. He excuses himself once for the restroom, tripping into a nearby table in a drunken caricature. For good measure, he knocks over several drinks as he straightens, drawing jeers.

At the end of the night, after he's made sure Rawls is drunk but not so swozzled he won't remember anything, he pays for their drinks, concealing his disgust at the total. He hoists Rawls up, and they stagger out front. Without hesitation, Hadrian shuffles them down a dark side alley.

"Einarson? My car . . . is the other way."

Hadrian drops Rawls in a heap on the snow-scraped ground. His breath comes out in frosted huffs, luminescent in the dark. He crouches down and grabs Rawls by the face, tilting it upward.

"I need you to pay attention."

"Einarson?" Rawls blinks at him. That ugly stupid gape. "Grimur, help me up, will you?"

"You're a sorry excuse for a councilman," Hadrian says easily. And still, he holds on to Einarson's Icelandic accent, the lilt in Common. He no longer has ambient noise to cover his tracks, but it shouldn't matter too much at this point.

"Excuse me?"

That crocodile, his lethal bundle of thoughts, presses against the surface of Hadrian's mind, and this time he lets it emerge. He smashes Rawls's face in. Over and over. Blood flies in ribbons, the hot viscosity painting his face, the messy gush of it a contrast to the bitter cold.

"Grimur! Stop! Grimur!"

Rawls howls the name over and over, though it won't do him much good. It's not even the right one. His screams burble as he skids across the icy ground, his feet scrabbling for purchase. Hadrian keeps pounding. His hands ache, but the pain ricocheting through his body lights him up like a pinball machine. That pain connects him to Rawls. He keeps alert for any sounds from the bar but can hear only cheering from the football game. The easily subdued sheep are deaf to the violence on the other side of the wall.

Hadrian deliberately pivots so the nearest street camera has an unobstructed view of his face as he grits his teeth and rains down blows. Reykjavík, a land rich in renewable energy and reliably outfitted with unwavering streetlights and cameras.

Chest heaving, Hadrian idly scratches his throat again. Then, he runs.

When they scan the camera footage later, they'll follow the trail as he loses his coat and uses his scarf to wipe down his face, cupping snow from the road to scrub it down. They'll track him into the marketplace where Einarson will get lost in the crowd.

And when Hadrian appears on the cameras later, it'll be as an innocent, inconsequential Mercurian.

ONE

OCEAN WONDERS how long he's been cheating on her.

Adama and the rest of the *Fafnir* crew clamor around the noisy restaurant table. It's a throwback to the BBQ restaurants of old, even if the charcoal heating the grill is a hologram. The smooth glass walls flash soju ads, the fresh-faced celebrities looking as if they've never even heard of a hangover.

Oori Da is a riot of languages and the universal sizzle of pork belly on the grill. People enter the restaurant from all over, but they'll ascend to the street wreathed in the same carnivorous incense. Ajumma step to the rhythm of clinked glasses and a harmony of voices raised in drunken cheer or heartbreak. Ocean loves the crisp snap of lettuce wrapped around meat nestled against steaming rice, pungent doenjang, and piquant kimchi. There's nothing like sharing food with people around a table—serving personal-sized pieces of meat or receiving the offering like a benevolent god.

Early in their relationship, Ocean introduced Adama to Oori Da as a flex, and she regrets it now. She returned from Marado early to join his crew for dinner before they went to the Alliance gala together the next day. It's hard finding the time when they belong to different crews, but they've always made the best of their situation. She never considered it a problem, but clearly Adama has a different opinion.

"Ocean! Let me top you off!" Robert, the *Fafnir*'s captain, waves a green bottle at her. "Aish, sorry," he says when liquid overflows the soju glass she's held out to him with two hands. He clinks his glass with hers. "Skål!"

"Geonbae!" She twists to the side to down her glass while turned away from him.

"Another?" he asks, and she holds out her glass again, but this time she puts it down on the table after a perfunctory sip. "You're not really a drinker, are you?"

Ocean's never gotten more than pleasantly buzzed, but Adama answers for her from across the table.

"Ocean can't stand soju."

His easy grin flashes impossibly white teeth. He reaches a long dark arm across the table to nab Ocean's drink and downs it easily. His crewmates playfully heckle him as he winks at Ocean and places the now empty glass in front of her. The wink should annoy Ocean, but it's his supposedly chivalrous gesture that irks her more than anything else. And the fact that while most of the people around the table are laughing and egging on Adama, the woman next to him, Liesl, is studiously quiet. She's deliberating the grill as if her life depends on the shade of the pork belly.

"Shouldn't you have soju flowing through your veins?" Robert teases.

Ocean slides her empty glass closer. "Soju's only good in context: with beer, mixed in a cocktail, or with a jjigae chaser."

Adama's right; she's never been huge on alcohol, doesn't see the appeal of the clear, burning liquid. Except here, followed by a steaming, sharp mouthful of jjigae or a sliver of fresh pickle delivered by metal chopsticks. She grabs the soju bottle and pours herself another glass, her face now pointedly blank, her eyes trapping Adama's.

For the first time that night, his smile falters. But just for a moment. He hunches a shoulder against her and dives back into the conversation with verve. Beside him, Liesl doesn't even have to participate to belong. Delicate Liesl only joined the *Fafnir* a half year ago, but she's always easily flitted around the boisterous group. She's pretty and petite, with dark lashes and an oval face. Her fine black hair flows like a waterfall over her shoulder. They're both Korean, but unlike Ocean, if you cut Liesl open, soju would probably spill out.

Adama and Liesl have carefully avoided touching each other all night, even casually. Some people give themselves away with their eyes, but Ocean's always known to pay attention to what people don't look at. Anyone else might have dismissed it as a bit of paranoia or assumed that Adama and Liesl had some argument earlier they hadn't yet gotten over. It's so little to go on, but Ocean knows that feeling well—overly aware of another person's presence, sensing them in your periphery like the honey glow of light on your skin at the end of the day. Ocean hasn't experienced it for a long time, but that doesn't mean she can't recognize it in someone else.

Characters in Von's serials always have a cup handily nearby to fling when someone insults their family's honor. But soju glasses don't hold enough alcohol to drench a kitten, and ice cubes cluster her water glass. She keeps thinking about the hard cubes smacking his face. Does everyone in serials drink room temperature water?

The table's rehashing stories of their latest mission. Adama's speaking over Liesl, and he drapes an arm over the back of her seat, while she almost imperceptibly moves forward. The table cracks up at Adama's joke. The Ocean of several years ago, still attending Savoir-Faire, would have pasted on a smile. The worst thing wasn't being ignored; it was having people notice you being ignored. But Ocean's life already has too many meaningless smiles she wishes she could rescind. She tilts her head back. The ad on the wall shifts from a winking Korean idol to a low-Q pic of an actor posing with the restaurant owner, the picture distorted because the file size is incorrect. Noise presses in on all sides, opposing waves competing to swallow her whole.

She drops her chin down in time to see Liesl knock over the red-hot metal tongs and give a dainty, startled *oh* as they hit Adama's bare arm. He bolts upright, banging his head against the low-hanging BBQ exhaust pipe. Liesl shoots up, too, hands flurrying while she figures out whether to cradle his head or arm first, and in her panic, she looks at Ocean. She doesn't wear the stricken expression of someone caught being overly concerned for someone else's steady but rather an uncertain *Shouldn't you be worried?* look.

Instead of bothering to act like a caring steady—no, a caring person—Ocean lets her face go slack. Liesl and Adama freeze as if she's hissed at them. Ocean neatly knocks back her soju. She places it down and hears the glass connect with the wood even in the overloud restaurant.

"How long have you two been sleeping together?" she asks.

The whole table goes deathly silent, but Ocean concentrates on Adama and Liesl. Liars react one of two ways when confronted. Adama takes the first route: outright denial.

"What are you talking about? Who? Us? Are you crazy?"

His eyebrows shoot straight up, stretching his eyes wide. Adama doesn't push his incredulity too hard as he goes on to ask how Ocean could suspect anything between him and Liesl—they're crewmates. But as he pivots the conversation to Ocean's being insecure, misinterpreting their relationship, she moves on to scrutinizing Liesl, who takes route number two: avoidance. She's gone pale. Her eyes flicker to the ceiling, as if searching for an answer there, and then down among the myriad of banchan. If Ocean ever has to bury a body, she's not asking Liesl for help.

They haven't been together long based on how awkwardly they're acting around each other, but Ocean finds she doesn't care. She just doesn't. She reaches under her bench and presses her palm against the bin there. It slides open after identifying her palm print and she pulls out her overnight bag. She stands and pats Robert on the shoulder.

"You're a solid captain, Robert."

His round baby blue eyes match the O of his mouth. He probably didn't suspect a thing; if he had that kind of noonchi, he wouldn't keep forcing alcohol on her at every gathering. She casts a cursory glance around the table, but although she's tried to imprint these faces on her brain for the past year, they already look like strangers on the street.

"Ajumma!" Ocean turns and calls, ducking her head while raising a hand as she weaves between crowded tables. At the register, she pushes back her sleeve to expose her wristband and scans for her share even though she didn't have more than a few bites. She absently pulls at a handful of her short hair, but it barely reaches her nose. She probably wasn't there long enough to absorb the smoke.

Ocean climbs the stairs from the BBQ restaurant that's a herald to centuries past and into the hyper-bright nightlife of Seoul. The humidity and oppressive street odor hit her like a wet slap of sewage across her face. Ocean pulls her nimbus from her bag and positions it over her head, pulling it down as she taps the side over her right ear. Kim Yongim's voice warbles about lost love, set to a fast beat in two. Ocean immediately flicks her gaze to the left and the song cuts. As she scrolls her library, two girls on hoverskids race past her in a whir, their long hair and long trench coats floating behind them as they dart through the lively street.

"Ocean!" Adama steps from the stairway.

She shouldn't have dithered over her personal soundtrack. Adama drops his hand on his opposite shoulder, his arm muscles bunched. For a moment, Ocean lets herself remember how that arm felt curled around her when she was pressed into him during the liminal space between oblivion and waking. But he's only here now because in front of his friends, he can't be an asshole who would let her go like that.

"Where are you going?" he asks.

"Namisa." It's childish, but she means it too.

He roughly rubs his closely shorn hair. "Is that it, then? We're not going to talk about it?"

Ocean faces him. "What's there to talk about?" she asks mildly. Adama said everything he needed to say with what he did.

"Don't you want to know why? Or when? Or . . . anything?"

"So you're not denying it anymore?"

Adama's mouth tightens. "Can you . . . can you forgive me?"

What he's really asking is this: If they got back together, could she forget what he did? When she kissed Adama, would she think about his lips kissing Liesl's? When he was inside her, would she suddenly think about whether he compares the two of them? Could she get over it?

"Sure," Ocean says.

Adama's face twists. "What's wrong with you?"

"Are you really asking me that?"

Adama sighs noisily, as if she's the unreasonable one, and finally, a red-hot lick curls around Ocean's chest. "Do you actually want to be with me?" she asks. "What about Liesl?"

"It was a mistake. I . . . You . . ." His eyes scatter around, but no one in the bustling streets is interested in another lovers' spat unfolding in public. "You left me alone."

"Alone?" she repeats. "You can't be trusted alone? Is that what you're saying?"

"No!" he bites out. "You left me *alone*. All the time!" The neon lights shine on the sweat-sheen of his skin, the flash of his teeth as he grimaces, and, suddenly, the wetness of his eyes. She realizes what he means. She knows it's the truth too. He jams the back of his hand up to his brow, which he only does when he's trying to fight the crease there, and she notices the pink of his palms. She's traced those palms, pressed her own against them as if in a prayer. "I should have listened to what they said about you. There were all sorts of rumors from Yong School."

The words snuff out her empathy. She's not going to indulge his last-act monologuing. Adama should know that provoking her has never worked. But he has no clue, and that's probably as much her fault as it is his. Ocean puts a hand up to her nimbus again, and his face stiffens.

"You were always looking for an excuse to break up." His words are brasher than his searching gaze. "Why did you even go out with me if you were always looking for a reason to get away?"

"You just gave me that reason, didn't you?" Ocean lowers the nimbus over her forehead. She puts a hand over her right ear. It would probably ease him, vindicate him somehow, if she met his anger with her own. But she doesn't owe him any more fabricated emotion, if she ever did. Her next words are gentle. "We're done, Adama."

She taps her nimbus and the soft blue glow of it blinks as she slings her bag over her shoulder. The first touches of the piano drown out whatever else he might be saying, and they're followed by the rising hush of brushes scraping a cymbal. Even before the unmistakable fuzzy timbre of a trumpet enters, she knows the song. It's too melancholy for her mood, but it happened to be where her visual scroller landed when Adama interrupted her.

She folds herself into the wave of people. Ocean lets her feet lead the way, while her uptilted chin cuts a path through the crowds. A cluster of students in uniform, probably on their way home from hakwon, pass by her, heads together as they share steaming ribbons of skewered odeng. She catches the fishy whiff as they go by and her stomach shifts in response.

Well, she can at least take care of that.

· · ● · ·

Haven hears the chime as he swipes the dial to turn off the shower. Not the doorbell—this cascade of notes indicates someone's at his window. He stumbles out, bare feet skidding on the tile while he grabs his underwear. He wrests it on over wet skin. The window chime rings again. The hawker is early. Or Haven completely lost track of time while under the endless spray of hot water that he didn't have to worry would suddenly blast ice cold while he was still soaped up. Hopping across his small dorm room, Haven towels himself off with one hand while pulling his pants up his legs. He reaches the window just as he wrenches the pants over his hips and slams his palm on the plate next to his window.

The window panels fold up with a whir to reveal a smiling old Korean man. Immediately, a bevy of aromas waft in from the tiny food-packed kitchen behind him.

"I apologize," Haven says. "I must have lost track of time."

"Oh, don't hurry on my account. I'm always happy to make a trip to the Alliance." The old man spreads his mouth wide to show off a row of perfectly straight, perfectly white teeth. His heavily accented Common is easy enough for Haven to understand. "Thank you for your service."

He taps the counter and the menu springs to life, the display lighting up with an array of the best street food Seoul has to offer. Haven examines the pictures, his mouth watering. The old man reaches out to zoom in, and Haven automatically skitters his hand away to avoid the touch.

"I'm surprised you're not out on the town tonight. Seoul's probably half lit up with Alliance members flying in for the gala tomorrow. You need a guide? Tips for where the best noraebang are?" The old man pulls out a worn pamphlet from underneath the counter, leans forward, and winks. "Where the prettiest Koreans gather? How about—"

Water from Haven's hair drips onto his bare skin. He's still shirtless. He clears his throat. "Would you mind if I grabbed . . ."

"Euh, geurae geurae. Such a polite boy!" The old man bobs his head. "Please take your time! I am at your disposal."

Haven bends to pick up his dropped towel from the floor. He grabs the clean tunic lying on his bed and pulls it over his head, the canvas folds settling over his body. Much better. He turns back to the flyby, toweling his hair, but stops short at the man's expression. His face is screwed up in disgust.

"You . . ." He trails off, pointing at Haven's shoulder.

Haven realizes his mistake. He hasn't been too concerned with hiding his skin thus far, but he's at least tried to keep track of what's exposed.

"Yes," Haven confirms his unspoken question.

"Vulture." The man spits and Haven hides his wince as the spittle lands on the wood floor of his room. The man slaps a button and his aeroship disengages from Haven's window with a *skrrchh* of metal. As he hovers in the night sky, he gingerly pinches the pamphlet—which Haven grazed his fingers against—and flings it at him. "I don't serve Death Hands. Don't you know what that would do for my business?"

With a jerk of his wheel, he's gone, zooming away.

Haven stares out his window at the now unobstructed view of Seoul at night. One of his admonished death hands hits the plate again to shutter the window. He scrubs his towel over the spittle on the ground and then recycles the pamphlet. His stomach gurgles as the compactor identifies and sorts the trash with a series of beeps. A quick glance in the mirror reveals the etched feather grazing the exposed skin at the back of his neck. He grabs a jacket, telling himself that he doesn't care if anyone else sees it. He just doesn't want any more drama. Then he pulls on shoes and leaves the room.

The hallway's quieter tonight than on any of the other nights he's been here. The old man was right—everyone else is enjoying the Seoul nightlife. He enters the elevator, pressing the button for the sublevel connected directly to the metro. The bank of elevators empties out onto a floor with several exits and escalators leading to different levels. The signs would be helpful if he knew where he was going, but when drunken shouting bubbles up from one escalator, he quickly swerves toward another random one. It glides down to the platform for the metro to Apgujeong.

The platform's empty, and a blast of recycled air is the only thing greeting him when he enters the train. All good signs, as far as he's concerned. His sub car compartment is lit by fluorescents, with the ever-constant zip of UV sanitizer sweeping the seats. A display lets him know that outside it's still a balmy night with 97 percent humidity, but that reality is just a minor inconvenience. He's found that people on Earth tend to scurry from one building to another like cockroaches avoiding light.

The automated voice, a perfectly engineered contralto, announces an upcoming station in Korean, then Common. The ads that scroll along the overhead compartment above him also flash in both languages. A beautiful Korean man caresses his face with one hand, holding out a small container with the other, as if to say, *You, too, can have this flawless white skin.* Even if he's been only half paying attention since he arrived in Seoul, Haven recognizes him as the same person plastered in almost all the ads.

He leaves the train, and it races away. As he's deciding between labeled exits, he sees her.

On the opposite platform, waiting for a train back to the Alliance dorms, is a young woman. Either a Corps or maybe visiting one, judging by the duffel bag dropped on the bench behind her. She has short black hair and pale skin that looks like it bene-fited from that advertised face cream. Haven would guess that she's Korean, but it's hard to tell for sure at this distance. She has a glowing electronic halo around her forehead and her eyes are closed.

She's also dancing.

Given the time and place, Haven might have thought her inebriated, but her movements are too controlled. He can tell almost immediately that she's classically trained as her soutenu twists into an arabesque. The slow, sensual stretch conveys a strength under the softness, her face angled in an épaulement, which Balanchine described as the movement of a tilted cheek asking for a kiss. Her technique's Vaganova though, if he has to guess, not Balanchine. Here, the woman's cheek is kissed by the light of the subway station.

As she spins again, her arms swooping up and down in an arc, he sees the halo's anchored to earbuds. She raises her arms wide, her wrists held loosely, her fingers pointed outward, as if she's spreading her wings. Her right leg lifts in a straight line and, simultaneously, Haven's own leg lifts in a sympathetic gesture.

A train skims in front of her, coasting on a whoosh of warm air that breaks the spell. Haven drops his leg and casts a quick peek around. Still no one. He hastens toward the closest escalator, but as he ascends, he glances back across the tracks behind him.

The train's gone, the platform empty again.

TWO

KIM MINWOO is saying something, but Teo's distracted by his slightly crooked, entirely endearing bottom row of teeth. Anyone can get fixed in the "right" way—double eyelids, perfect veneers, or even a slitted belly button to make the stomach appear thinner. But lately, Korea's trended toward the kind of natural beauty that no amount of money can fabricate. So, tiny defects like an upturned nose, a few crooked teeth, or weirdly creased ears are all the rage. And freckles. Koreans go *wild* over freckles. It's in vogue now to surgically add a strategic mole, and Teo's partial to a well-placed beauty mark near the mouth.

But the desire for natural blemishes only goes so far. Minwoo still has perfect skin, carries a parasol, and does anti-grav Pilates and jjimjil yoga for two hours each day to beat any flaws out of his body. He's watched—no, experienced—from every angle on serials. Rumor is he's had his neck lines filled in, and Teo can tell that his jawline has been skimmed to create a more angular face.

Minwoo blows his bangs off his forehead. He's too polite to directly call out Teo, second son of the Anand Tech empire, for not listening, but the tug of his lips says everything. Not that many people can call him out for anything.

He can still picture Captain Hong's face after he told him that he needed the *Shadowfax* to dock in Seoul a day earlier specifically to accommodate this date. The Alliance gala isn't until later tonight, and the *Shadowfax* needed to burn extra energy to make it happen. Captain Hong's automatic outrage of "You're telling me what now?" was followed instantly by his swallowing that frustration when he remembered exactly who Teo's father is. Teo could see it went down just as easily as a mouthful of ginseng health drink.

"Who's the date with?" Captain Hong asked politely. Teo just flashed a smile.

"I don't kiss and tell, Captain. You'll find out with the rest of the solar soon enough."

But only if he plays his cards correctly now. Teo's here as a favor to his father, but that doesn't mean he has to be rude. And he has never been accused of showing his date a bad time.

He clears his throat. "I'm sorry. You were saying about *Cemetery Venus*?" He refills their teacups, Minwoo's first, of course. "Had you been to Venus before?"

"It was my first time."

"I'm certain you're well aware, but I would take stronger sunscreen. Preserve your skin," Teo says. "Lasers do wonders these days, but I know you work hard to maintain yours."

Minwoo reaches over the table. "Why don't you use them to clear your scar?"

"Careful." Teo catches his hand before it reaches his cheek. He briefly presses Minwoo's soft fingers to his lips. "You haven't earned the right to touch that yet."

Minwoo flushes and pulls his hand back to fiddle with his cup. It takes another minute until his blush subsides. "You reserved this private space." He gestures around them. "But I was wondering . . ."

The huge room is the most coveted area of Han Oak, an exclusive restaurant that sources its ingredients directly from the garden next door. It's the best of the haute cuisine restaurants that line the street next to Bongeunsa Temple. The chef apparently trained for years with Buddhist monks and then opened a restaurant espousing the philosophy of connecting to nature. He's met great acclaim and profit. Teo's not sure how that all fits with the Buddhist teachings, but no one seems to be complaining.

It's hard enough to get a seat here, but he's reserved the whole area bordered by the floor-to-ceiling glass windows facing the main road. You can see the temple grounds by day, and by night, Seoul serves as the backdrop to a lit-up Maitreya Buddha, which Teo vaguely remembers is due for its regular maintenance soon. Usually, the room opens into another dining area, but today the doors are shut tight, ensuring the common rabble won't even get a whiff of sunlight. Let them glare enviously at the small slit of natural light that peeks out from underneath the closed doors.

"You don't like the intimacy?" Teo asks.

Minwoo hesitates. "It's very nice."

"Nice is a banal word," Teo says. He doesn't know why Minwoo's bothering to soft-foot. "It seems innocuous, but it's one of the most damning descriptors that exist." He tilts his head over at one of the waitstaff, whose sole role has been to stand unobtrusively in the corner. The server bends once they reach Teo's side. "Can you put the whole restaurant on my tab? And add a 40 percent tip on top of that. Feel free to let everyone know now, so they can add to their meals and order extra drinks on me. But please, keep it anonymous."

Minwoo gawks. Teo can almost hear him mentally calculating the number of tables on the other side of the door, all the nine-course meals and alcohol that will pad the bill.

"Koreans don't tip," he says faintly.

"But I do," Teo replies. The server is too well trained to let anything slip. They bow again with a "Nae, gamsahamnida" and exit the room. Teo's father taught him the importance of tipping. His generosity will benefit not only the diners but also the people working back of house. It means word will spread even further. "I am not *nice*, Minwoo-ssi." He delicately lifts a lightly fried squash blossom with his chopsticks. "Shinjeong Co. made a deal with my father. You need exposure. The *Cemetery Venus* premiere didn't do as well as they had hoped, and they want us to give the numbers a helping hand. In return, Shinjeong will air two of my father's ad campaigns at a future date. We are, it seems, at the behest of our fathers, literal or not. Why not enjoy ourselves while we do it?" Teo pops the plant into his mouth and swallows. He hasn't seen the show, but it's hard to avoid its incessant promo vids. Shinjeong is trying a little too hard, and people instinctively shy away from desperation. "Obviously, we Alliance Corps don't get paid well enough to buy out a whole restaurant, but it's all in a day's work for my father."

Teo has sat in on the multiple dinners his father hosted for Mars dignitaries.

"You say you want Anand Tech to produce augmented suits for you and that you'll pay handsomely. But have you thought about the price our image will pay for supplying such weapons?" Ajay Anand once asked, smiling as he poured the tea for Anthony Chau with the pot held up high to showcase the graceful arc of golden water. "Oh, pardon me. It appears I've oversteeped the Brentaris."

Brentaris, a Martian plant coveted because the backbreaking labor of harvesting it has made its price skyrocket, costs upward of thirty marks a gram. Teo watched his father call over the servant. "I've done it again, Dana. Could you throw out this pot and bring us a fresh one?"

Chau understood.

At another dinner with an embassy from Mercury, Teo sat front row to his father's handling of people who hated him.

"You say that your miners are protesting the conditions and refusing to work? I suppose the problem will solve itself soon enough because if the Alliance learns that there's no more to be gained from Anand Tech's partnership with your mines, they'll ask us to take our business elsewhere. But believe me, I sympathize with your plight."

Translation: It's your plight, not mine.

Teo has barhopped with his brother, Declan, while he gladhanded businessmen from Tokyo, Ceres, and New York.

"Drink up! This might be the end of whiskey as we know it! Mercurians are commissioning to terraform bogland on their planet so they can make their own. Can you imagine?"

The next week, when a Mercurian Diplomat petitioned to terraform the planet, the request was met with a somehow preprepared counterreform.

And Teo? Well, he goes on dates and spends his family's money. Earth is his playground. The server's out of the room though, so he's free to expound a little.

"It might seem paradoxical that we're closed off from prying eyes since, well, the whole point of today is exposure," Teo says. "But I like cultivating an air of mystery. People hate being left out. Conversations, secrets, birthday parties. By now, enough word has spread throughout the kitchen, among the waitstaff, and to the other diners that their meal is being paid for with gratuity involved."

"But you told the server to keep it anonymous. Are you expecting them to talk?"

"They're very discreet at Han Oak," Teo says. "But the request for anonymity is never more than a humble brag. People are going to be paying even more attention to our closed doors now. A few people saw us come in—that's inevitable. I want our exit to be even more focused." The doors from the kitchen open. "On that note, here comes dessert."

More than that, though, when people are being paid off, either directly or with a free meal, they expect a catch. They'll assume that because an anonymous benefactor is paying for their meals, he's asking for discretion. About a half hour later, after their dessert and post-meal coffee, Teo opens the door to the main dining room and knows every eye is on him. He steps to the side and holds the door open for Minwoo. As they're framed in the doorway, he leans over as if whispering a secret into the actor's ear.

"Do you think Shinjeong will be satisfied with this exposure?" he murmurs, making sure every comm and palmite zooming in for a picture is benefiting from the curve of his long lashes. Minwoo's no fool either. He pouts up at him with those strategically barely parted lips and places a hand on Teo's chest before drawing it back bashfully.

"Quite," he says.

Teo drapes Minwoo's hand around his arm, and they leave the restaurant together. Minwoo has a car waiting for him outside, and Teo opens the door for him and helps him inside like the gallant gentleman he is. After he shuts the door, the window slides down and Minwoo leans out.

"If you ever want to go on a real date, call me. I think it could be interesting."

Teo reassesses. He *is* pretty. And charming. And . . . nice.

"Go on a date without strings attached? I'm not sure I know how to do that."

"I can always teach you."

The window rolls up and Teo adjusts his cuff links as the car drives off. Today's his first time wearing them, but now that pictures have been taken, they'll have to be retired. He's not sure what will happen when he's outlived his own usefulness as a sparkling accessory.

· · • · ·

Ocean's fussing with the tie on her jeogori when her nimbus rings. She checks the display and answers.

"Don't worry, Dae. I'm on my way."

On her way meaning that she's almost ready to leave, of course. She adjusts her jeogori for the fifth time.

"Yeah, about that," her captain's voice blares too loudly. "I need you to do something first." Ocean waits, listening to the bursts of laughter on the other end. "Can you move the *Ohneul*? I'd do it, but I'm already at Coex. They're holding a separate event for higher-ups."

One where the alcohol's flowing, judging by Dae's voice.

"Where do you need me to move it?" Ocean asks.

"Alliance's Seoul dock. It'll be more convenient for when we leave tomorrow." Dae's voice raises in pitch. "Dangyeol, Lieutenant Seo! Yes, yes, I'm speaking with my pilot now." When Dae's responding to a superior, she has a particular laugh calibrated to warmly flatter. She launches into it now, and Ocean rechecks her jeogori tie. Maybe she should watch the instructional video again. Dae's tone drops. "I think it might be dicey tonight, with all the Alliance ships in the parking hangar because of the gala."

"If you're worried about the ship, I wouldn't mind staying with it—"

"You need to make an appearance at the party," Dae says. "It reflects badly on me for you to always skip out."

As if Ocean needs another reminder of what's waiting for her at the gala, some inevitable trotting out in front of Dae's superiors as a reminder that she's been the one keeping Ocean in line all these years. The problem with begging off every social event of the year is that Ocean has to make an appearance to one at least, and Dae chose the biggest. Everyone's flown back for it. The only upside is that there are so many people, she might not even see Adama and the rest of his crew.

"I'll be there," Ocean says.

"If you show up after 1900, I'm requiring you to attend the next Alliance event too."

"You want me to be there by *1900*? That's impossible!"

"You better book it then, don't you think?" Dae hangs up abruptly.

Ocean leaves her room, and in the elevator she jabs the P2 button more energetically than she needs to. After presenting her palm for a scan and inputting the *Ohneul*'s ship ID, an illuminated map offers directions to where it's parked. When the doors slide open, lighted blue arrows on the ground point the way. Her heels click on the concrete, echoing in the massive hangar. As she follows the arrows, she hears low voices. She can't place exactly where they're coming from—the noises are ricocheting off the ceiling and the gargantuan ships lined up in rows—until she gets to the *Ohneul* and finds two huddled figures nearby. One of them, a large Asian man with a buzzed head, crouches on the ground keeping watch while the other, a Black woman with braids gathered into a high bun, pulls back her fist, ready to punch open the side door. She's wearing large gloves that are glowing bright green. Power gloves, if Ocean had to guess. All three of them freeze.

"Well, this is awkward," Ocean says.

The woman slowly lowers her fists, and the man says completely unconvincingly, "Oh no. This isn't our ship?"

The woman puts her hand up to her ear. "Lupus, you were supposed to be on watch!" she hisses, and then after a pause, she snaps into her comm, "What do you *mean* it was your favorite scene?"

"I told you not to count on Lupus while they had on *Midnight in Europa*," the man says, straightening. "Every scene is their favorite scene."

Ocean thinks over her options. Her gun is somewhere in a closet about eight floors up. She hates having it with her even if it is regulation; the weight of it on her hip is all wrong. She sighs. It looks like Dae did have something to worry about after all. The raiders' idea was not a bad one—the garage is packed tonight, and with the party going until the morning hours, they'd only need to take out the cameras to have free rein.

"Were you planning on punching your way into every ship?" Ocean asks.

"The configurations for this one weren't quite what we were expecting," the man explains.

"Aries!"

"Cass," the man replies mildly.

"Ocean." Ocean points to herself and then to the *Ohneul*. "And this is a 180-Han. An older model. Nothing fancy and usually easy to break into. But we have a mechanic who upgraded its security settings." Maggie will be pleased to hear she kept two raiders out. Ocean checks the time on her comm. If she's going to make Dae's ludicrous deadline, she has to leave now. "If you're looking for Han-series ships, there are three in the next row," Ocean says. "The Narae ships have similar entry doors too. They have that distinctive scalloped fletching on their tails."

"Damn, that's cold." Cass narrows her eyes. "I thought you Alliance kids were at least loyal to one another."

"I'm kind of on a tight schedule," Ocean says, ignoring how that comment stings.

"Oh, I'm sorry," Cass sneers at Ocean, taking in the silk jeogori, the black Sav-Faire dress underneath that's seen better days, and the heels that are too high to be of any use in this situation. "Are we keeping you from your party?"

"I'm supposed to move the ship for my boss," Ocean says. "I have to get it to the Alliance Seoul dock and be back at Coex by 1900."

Aries checks his comm while Cass scoffs, "There's no way."

"It's becoming less likely by the minute," Ocean agrees.

Aries remarks, "You don't seem too concerned to catch us breaking into your ship."

"Trying to break in. You don't seem too bad on the raider scale," Ocean says. They're calm for one thing; if they were skittish, she'd have a problem. "You must be pretty low grade if you're rifling through Alliance ships for loot."

"Low grade?" Cass sputters. "I'll have you know—"

"So you *are* raiders?" Ocean asks. From Ocean's experience, the more defensive a raider is, the more they feel they have to prove. Ocean has no gun and no way in hell of beating someone in a fist fight, especially not someone wearing power gloves. "It doesn't matter to me either way, but I'd rather avoid the delay."

Aries eyes her without any of his partner's judgment. After his once-over, he nods. He steps onto the walkway, tugging Cass along by the elbow, and gestures for Ocean to go ahead. "We'd rather avoid that too."

"Seriously?" Cass asks. "You can't trust Alliance trash, Aries."

Ocean slips past them, but she waits until they're far enough away before entering the passcode and pressing her palm to the panel.

"Oh, I don't know about that," Aries says breezily as the hatch door opens with a metal creak. "But I do know he's going to be disappointed if you attract any unnecessary attention. You promised we'd keep a low profile." He touches his ear. "Lupus, will you actually keep an eye out this time?"

"Thanks," Ocean says to them as she pulls the door closed.

"You're never going to make it!" Cass yells at her as the door seals.

All the lights blink on in the hallway, except the one at the far end that always flickers a few times with a buzzy zap before giving up. Ocean cocks an ear; she half expected Gremio to be here, asleep in his room by the infirmary, but the ship has an unmistakably empty feeling. Good. She can very clearly picture a disgruntled Gremio bursting out of the ship to knock his cane on the heads of the hapless raiders. He would also definitely not approve of the ride she's about to take the ship on.

Ocean checks the time again as she strides to the cockpit. Aish. She really might not make it. She slides into her pilot seat and flicks switches with one hand while undoing the straps of her heels with the other. She kicks them off and settles her feet against the pedals.

Immediately, all the tension eases out of her body. Her right hand takes the wheel, and her left one rests on the shift. This feeling may have been the real reason she agreed to Dae's order.

The metro leaves every five minutes from the Seoul dock. It takes about twelve minutes to get to Coex from there, including all the stops. So that gives her about six minutes to move the *Ohneul* and find parking. Just for kicks, Ocean connects her nimbus to the console and opens up Gilla maps to check what it thinks. Seventeen minutes. Marv. She shifts right and down on the lever, and the satisfying weight of the mechanics confirms her existence. The ship lifts into the air, and from the left display, she sees the two raiders heading over to the next row where she pointed out the Han ships. The closest one is the *Samjogo*, piloted by Kim Seunghoon, who once roughed up Von outside A-Mart.

"Good luck," she says, although she's not sure whether she's speaking to Cass or herself.

Ocean jabs in the code to open the garage's entryway, and she follows the slow slope of the hangar floor out. Then she's streaming through the Seoul air. The sun's just setting now, and she admires the purple hue of the sky behind the city lights.

Another memory comes to mind, of hands on the wheel, of wind streaming in through an open window. She allows herself a brief moment, then she pushes the clutch, her right foot ready to supply gas to the thrusters, her left hand on the gear lever, all moving in smooth synchronization. The *Ohneul* zooms forward.

"Five minutes," she says to herself as she angles around the Lotte World Tower and over the World Peace Gate. She knows Seoul better by air than by foot and is making good time; the air's free of traffic tonight, probably because she's the only one being sent on an errand by her commanding officer. At least that's what she thinks until she spots blinking lights out of the corner of her eye. Her console beeps, and she squints at it before reluctantly opening the transmission. If it's an Alliance officer, word will get back to Dae that she ignored it.

"Dae swore you started from the Alliance dorms."

The transmission's coming from the *Flying Cloud*, which means the pilot is Lim Yeri.

"I did," Ocean says.

"Liar. No way you got here that fast. Still, keeps things interesting, yeah?"

"What do you mean?"

"Didn't they tell you? There's one parking spot left at the Seoul docks. Our captains made a wager to see which one of us would get to it first."

Ocean remembers Dae's drunken glee. "Marv," she mutters.

"We're subject to the whims of our seonbae, I guess."

"You can take the spot." Ocean couldn't be less interested in Dae's latest pissing match.

"Oh, come on." Lim laughs. "I was kinda interested in seeing what the famous Crane had to offer, but I guess that was all talk?"

Despite herself, Ocean stiffens. She reflexively looks down at the tattoo on her right hand. The profile of a crane in flight stretches its beak up to her index knuckle, its wings spreading up the back of her hand, legs pointing toward her wrist.

The *Flying Cloud*'s drifted close enough for Ocean to see the cloud pattern etched on its hull. This one's a Byeol-10X, an actual racer. It's last year's model, the X-wing an homage to space fighters of old, the layered divots in its shield an aerodynamic dream. Ocean flexes her fingers against her wheel. Truthfully, she doesn't want to have to go to another party.

"Don't say I didn't give you a chance," she says as she punches her feet down.

The display flashes blue then green. The *Ohneul* spirals out, jetting forward amid a cloud of profanity from Lim. A rush of pure pleasure floods Ocean, and she can't remember the last time she felt this focused, this awake. Lim catches up easily. Byeol-10X models are built for speed, and the *Ohneul* is barely keeping it together as it is. If their route was a straightaway with nothing but sky, Ocean wouldn't have a prayer. But Lim doesn't dare go high enough to gain that advantage because of how close the Alliance dock is, and Ocean knows Seoul like the back of her right hand. Lim swerves in front of Ocean, cutting off her path. Ocean veers right, then left, but Lim blocks her each time.

"You think you can pass me in that clunker?" Lim yells.

Ocean doesn't need to. Lim's flown the *Flying Cloud* far enough to the left now that the *Ohneul* can't edge between it and the fast-approaching Shinjeong Tower with its distinctive crescent moon top. Ocean fakes right, and when Lim moves to cut her off again, Ocean hits the brakes. She loves feeling the lurch in her body as the ship reacts. She's piloted the *Ohneul* for five years, and even if she's never raced it, she still knows each clank, every fluctuation, and the exact resistance of its wheel. At the perfect moment, she spins the wheel in the opposite direction, fighting its inertia, and the *Ohneul*'s back slides out. Ocean turns the ship sideways and up so that it cradles in the curve of Shinjeong's crescent before completing its somersault.

Ocean predicts the *Flying Cloud*'s brake lights flashing even before Lim stops short. She knows there's that new apartment development just ahead. Ocean's already calibrated her landing, so once she flips in front of the *Flying Cloud*, she's ready to corner sharply around the stalled ship, cutting Lim off. As if on cue, the panel pings at Ocean to complain, telling her this ship is not equipped to travel at these speeds. She smiles as she curves around a block of hotels. At this point, she's not even worried about Lim; she's just following the best line. The gates to the Seoul dock are in front of her, and she's home free.

"Injeong halggeh." Lim laughs over the transmission. "I'm not even mad. What the hell are you doing piloting a Class 4?"

Just like that, the thrill running through Ocean's veins dries up.

"You can take the parking spot," she says.

"Wait, what? Really?"

Ocean turns off the transmission and drops her head back on the seat, putting the *Ohneul* on coast. The console beeps and Ocean slaps the button to respond. "I'm serious, just take—"

"Ocean-ah." Damn. It isn't Lim. Too late, Ocean realizes that the alert was a different tone than the internal calls between ships.

She slumps forward over the wheel. "Why didn't you call? You said you would call last night when you got to Seoul. You're too busy with your friend to call your umma?"

Her mother's insistence on calling all her steadies "friends" is, at least, consistent. She'll probably be happy to hear they're not *friends* anymore.

"I'm sorry, Umma. I forgot."

Her umma has an unerring instinct to call at the absolute worst times. Then again, it's not like Ocean's taken the opportunity to create her own battlegrounds. Ocean pulls the ship up higher so she can idly guide the *Ohneul* through the clouds with one hand on the wheel.

Her umma exhales heavily. "Babeun meogeoseo?"

"Not yet, Umma." A wave of guilt always accompanies this response, but she can't lie. Her mom's able to sniff out a lie quicker than a priest in a confessional box. "I'm on my way to the Alliance gala. They'll have food there."

"Alliance gala?"

"You know, Umma. The party they throw every year."

"Euh, the gala. Where they gave Hajoon that award?"

"Yes. That one." It was years before Ocean's time at the Alliance, but the memory is painfully bright. She remembers the crisp rustle of her mother's brand-new hanbok. Even more palpable is the pride her parents wore that night, the tears glistening in her mother's eyes as her older brother waved to them from the stage.

The silence gapes so widely that if Ocean sighs, her mother will hear it, no matter how much she stifles the reaction. "I was going to call, Umma. I'm sorry I didn't. But I'm flying now, and I need to park the ship."

Ocean holds her breath.

"How long are you going to live like this?" The weariness in her mother's voice sucks all the air out of the cockpit.

"I should go. I'll call you later, Umma."

Ocean hangs up. Her nimbus display clocks the call in at barely over a minute. The sun has fully set now, but Seoul is still spread out in vivid color below. Ocean rests her hand on the shift. She still has a party to get to.

THREE

COEX'S CONVENTION SPACE has been adapted for the gala, and the hall teems with people. The lights are dim enough to cloak the gyrating people on the dance floor, the music loud enough to render conversations impossible. Not that Haven has anyone to talk to.

Captain Song insisted that he attend even though the only time he's stepped on her ship so far was for his interview. According to her, it'd be a fun way to launch his "illustrious Alliance career." Haven's only planning on staying with the Alliance until his father is satisfied. Not a mission longer. But it's never a good idea to tell that to the person who hired you. His face must have conveyed some of the sentiment, though, because Captain Song quickly broke off with a forced laugh and an "I don't know why it's so hard to get my crew to come to these parties."

It's a different sort of force than what Haven experienced at Alliance space training, where teachers and seonbae trainees all but said, "You'll eat this dirt, and you'll thank me for it." But it's force nonetheless. She is his captain. Though, right now, it's hard to tell whether he'll even be able to find her. He takes an offered drink from a server to be polite and then is left with the awkwardness of proffering it around because he doesn't want to waste it. The music buffets him over to the far side of the room where a long table, crammed with food, stretches across the wall.

His stomach is too tight, his senses a little too raw, but scanning the table gives him something to do. The array is as extravagant as this whole event; it might be the most food Haven's ever seen in one place. It reminds him of the first time he sat down for a meal in a Korean restaurant, the ajumma shoving more side dishes onto a table that couldn't possibly fit another. He tried to tidily finish everything, but the plates kept getting refilled, leaving him to wonder what happened to the inevitable leftovers. He hardly recognizes any of the dishes here, but a touch panel at the edge of the table glows faintly, indicating where he can press if he has food allergies, prompting the trays to move forward or back.

The crowd at his back is a similarly organized chaos: Alliance students in their trainee suits and officers who puff out their chests when talking to one another to show off their decorated stars. Alliance members in between, and civilians, dress in a range of formal attire. Haven strokes a hand down the embroidered trim of his brocade chuba, one of his father's from his time in Tibet, which he pressed into Haven's hands when he left for the Alliance.

A chorus of squeals rises above the music and Haven twists to see the tall, attractive man causing the commotion. He's wearing a maroon velvet suit and his coarse black hair is styled back from his forehead. He moves through the flurrying group of admirers with an enviable ease. Moses in the Red Sea of people who part for him before pressing forward in his wake. Haven vaguely recognizes him, maybe from an ad or a serial. He can see the long streak of an old scar on his cheek, the line standing out against his brown skin. When the man flashes an ostentatious grin, an Alliance student swoons, collapsing into their friend's arms. A disbelieving chuff escapes Haven's mouth.

"Oh, Haven! You made it!"

The bright voice cuts through the din, unmistakably blurred from alcohol. A flushed Captain Song strides toward him, expertly lifting two glasses.

"Dangyeol, Captain Song," Haven says as he salutes, the movement still awkward when he tries it.

"Oh, no need for that. We're here to have *fun*. Isn't this wonderful? They really spare no expense every year." She holds out one of the glasses for him and then notices he already has one. "More for me, I guess."

Captain Song laughs and downs one of her glasses. She sets it on a side table, the rim red from her lipstick. She wears an officer's uniform with four diamonds set above the CAP SONG stitched over her heart. The diamonds are buffed bright, their gleam poking sharper than their points.

"Drink with your captain," she says as she holds out her second glass for him to clink. When he obliges, she toasts, "To your future with the *Ohneul*." Haven winces inwardly as he drinks to that, the champagne as warm as his sweat-slicked palms. "I would love for you to meet your crew members while you're here. Let's see if I can track them down."

Haven's spine straightens. "Are they here?"

"One might be coming in later than I wanted." Captain Song's face darkens momentarily. "But she'll be here." He wants to know why that sounds threatening, but she's replastered a smile on her face. "Until then, maybe I can introduce you to the other Alliance officers. They were particularly fascinated to hear—" Captain Song looks past him, and he doesn't know what would be worse: her seeking out another tray of drinks or a pack of Alliance officers, but her face freezes.

"Captain Song?" he prompts.

Haven checks over his shoulder, and Captain Song grabs his arm. He stiffens, removing himself from her grasp before considering how it might offend her.

She doesn't seem to notice and instead rasps, "How did you get in here?"

A man in a tuxedo sidles up to them. He also holds a drink in his hand, and as he waves it in front of him, Haven sees that the top button of his dress shirt is misaligned, setting the fabric askew.

"That's rude, Dae," the man says.

Captain Song touches her tightly woven braid as her eyes dart to Haven and then back to the man. "Excuse me, Haven. This is . . . well, he's a client. We need to talk business."

"Oh, certainly," Haven says. "Sir, my name is Haven Sasani and I'm the *Ohneul's*—"

"That's fine, Haven," Captain Song interrupts. "No need to . . . I mean . . ."

Haven's ears burn as Captain Song fumbles over herself.

"I understand," he says politely. "I overstepped."

The man's amused disdain slides over Haven, who resists the urge to check the edges of his collar. The instinct makes him hot in a nauseating flush.

"Oh, Haven, don't worry your head about it." Captain Song's lips spread into a trembling, wide smile. "Why don't you enjoy the party? It's not a night you should be thinking about business. Excuse us."

She ushers the man away as if she can't get him out of Haven's earshot soon enough. They park in an alcove, half-hidden, although Haven catches Captain Song's serious demeanor, now abruptly woken from her convivial stupor. He should shake it off, move on, and actually eat something, but he keeps glancing over instead. After a few minutes, someone else joins them. Haven angles himself to see whether Captain Song will also wave away the newcomer, but stops.

His hand lowers the drink to the table and his feet propel him forward. Even in profile, there's something about her posture, her hair, the way she lifts her hand to salute Captain Song. He barely even notices the man slink away, or how dark Captain Song's face looks again, as he approaches. He's not aware of how close he's drifted toward them until he hears Captain Song's voice.

"Haven! What good timing! I'd like you to meet—"

The woman turns and just as Haven thought, it's her, the woman he caught dancing on the subway platform. But as she faces him head-on, another recognition, another realization, jars him.

"*You're* Ocean Yoon?"

Her picture had been included in the classified Alliance report he read covertly. It was an old photo taken when she graduated from flight school years ago, her hair longer then. Perhaps it was that or the distance that stopped him from making the connection last night. She also has a scar across her right eyebrow that he hadn't seen in the picture. Yoon's black hair is tied back now, exposing her long, graceful neck. The years have sharpened her angles, but her uptilted chin and full upper lip are the same.

"Sorry to disappoint you."

Her eyes are even harder than her words, and they puncture him. But she's already focusing her attention elsewhere. He quickly scans in the direction of her gaze and spots a retreating maroon suit, soon swallowed by the crowd.

He whips back. "I—"

Yoon salutes Captain Song. "Dangyeol, Captain Song. Enjoy the rest of the party."

She slips away, rendering him insignificant without another word. He can't even be upset because he's always wished he had that kind of incisiveness himself.

"I can't believe—Haven, I'm so sorry! Listen, Ocean may be the *Ohneul*'s XO, but she's rude to everyone. I promise I'll talk to her."

Haven doesn't know how to respond to Captain Song. He tries to swallow a few times, but his mouth is too dry. That wasn't how he wanted to meet Yoon.

The music cuts abruptly and the stage in the middle of the room lights up. Haven can't concentrate at first and only snaps to when the emcee approaching the microphone says, "Please join me in welcoming to the stage Ajay Anand, one of our generous sponsors for tonight's event and the upcoming Seonbi Embassy to Mars."

The room erupts in applause as a tall, confident man with a healthy mustache strides up to the platform followed by his team, none in Alliance uniform. Ajay Anand, head of Anand Tech. Haven's seen the name stamped on all the Alliance's equipment.

"Thank you so much. I'm especially proud to be here tonight since—"

A woman standing behind him hurries forward and Ajay pauses, putting a hand over the mic as she whispers in his ear.

Ajay frowns and glances behind him before squinting out into the crowd. He says something to a handsome man standing beside him, who could just be a younger version of himself. The same charisma links Ajay with the person he's speaking to now and the man in the maroon suit whom Haven assumed to be a serial star earlier—the three must be family. In response to whatever Ajay is saying, the man frowns and puts two fingers to his forehead, rubbing in irritation.

Ajay Anand turns back to the microphone. "As I was saying, thank you for the warm welcome. We've upheld a close partnership over the years, Anand Tech and the Alliance, and I'm especially pleased to support this next visit to Mars, where the Alliance will escort the Seonbi. To maintain good relations we should meet and share ideas often, and I'm happy that the Seonbi Embassy will represent us just as honorably as they represent Korea's past alongside its future."

Haven's always appreciated that in order to understand where we're going, we first need to understand where we've been. The Seonbi hold a neutral status within Korea, above politics or self-gain. As scholars dedicated to preserving Korea's rich history and leading lives of integrity, the idea of studying with them once greatly appealed to Haven. Unfortunately, he found out that they were technically a separate entity from the Alliance. And nothing but the Alliance was going to satisfy his father.

Ajay Anand, having recovered from the interruption quickly, continues his prepared speech, but Haven returns to his expression before he smoothed it over. It's one he's all too familiar with—well-worn disappointment, not only in his son, but also in himself for expecting something different.

• • • • •

Teo barely escapes undetected, and he takes a circuitous route to the A-Mart. She's already waiting by the time he arrives, standing in front of the shifting ads on the convenience store's facade: Alliance class announcements, sign-ups for intramural football, a two-for-one green onion sale. The display blinks and then features a full-page poster of Phoenix. No one would ever guess it's a mug shot meant to advertise the bounty on the raider's head. He poses with a roguish grin, his tousled golden-blond hair striking a note between devil-may-care and please-won't-you-fix-it-for-me? Donna, the *Shadowfax*'s XO, has a poster-size printout of this exact same photo hanging up in her room aboard the ship. There's something too brash, too aware of his own good looks about that smile though. Not that Teo is one to talk.

The screen shifts to a smaller ad of Kim Minwoo beseeching Teo. He sighs, and she looks back.

"You're late," Ocean says. "And it was your idea to ditch the party."

"You were dying for an excuse to leave, Hummingbird."

Ocean can usually be drawn using only straight lines: impeccable posture, scar through her eyebrow, flapper-style haircut. Even her monolid eyes could be cut from stone. But as he speaks, those dark-brown eyes soften and the left corner of her mouth lifts, complicating her usual symmetry.

"Was it that obvious?" she asks.

"Your disgust was palpable from across the room."

"I'm surprised you noticed anything other than your cloud of consorts."

Other than that scar, she has perfect skin, due to a strict nightly regimen he's witnessed several times. She'll probably look the same until some day in her sixties when she wakes up a wizened sorceress who forgot her daily dose of virgin blood. It'd be charitable to call her dress last season, though. It's obviously from her Sav-Faire years, where she trained to be unobtrusively charming rather than fashionable. Teo's drawn up multiple outfit drafts for Ocean, any of which he would love to make, but she's rather unfairly claimed that his designs are too showy.

"I really wish—" he starts.

"Nope." She's seen where his eyes drifted, and cuts him off.

She steps up to the door and presses her palm against the panel at waist level. It identifies her as YOON OCEAN before allowing her entrance. Teo follows suit and ANAND TEOPHILUS flashes at him. He grabs a cart. As he suspected, and hoped, the only sound in the abandoned A-Mart is its soft Muzak.

"Shopping for anything specific?" Ocean asks as she pushes her own cart forward.

"Just travel snacks. We're heading out next week for the launch ceremony at Artemis."

"Launch ceremony?"

"We're escorting the Seonbi Embassy to Mars?" Teo prompts Ocean. "For interplanetary relations?"

"Are we having trouble with Mars?"

Teo halts his cart in the middle of the aisle and Ocean takes the opportunity to survey the cereal packets in front of them. He sucks in a deep breath, ready to explain Mars's fraught history and maybe even reference that think piece in AllianceVision last week titled "Mars: A Polite Independence," but Ocean has adopted an expression that says, *I will pretend to listen, but only because I am your friend.*

"You brat." He bonks her on the head. "Are you sure you were ever training to be a Diplomat?"

"There's a reason I dropped out of Sav-Faire." Ocean carefully checks the packets. Like him, she prefers them flawless, often reaching straight for the boxes in the back.

Teo more than suspects his father pulled some strings to get his crew assigned to the mission. It will probably be mentioned in his speech tonight, making it doubly mortifying for him that Teo isn't in the audience to bat his eyes. Teo doesn't do the humbled and bashful thing.

"It's all a huge publicity stunt, you know. A big hullabaloo that we're escorting Seonbi for the invite. More importantly, though, they had space suits designed by Yi Jeong and this will be their inaugural trip wearing them."

"Ah, there it is."

Teo ignores her interjection. "They're white neoprene and harken back to the Joseon period of *your* country's history." Teo's seen mock-ups and pictures. The way Yi Jeong integrated the traditional understated grace of flowing Seonbi robes into the space suits is truly remarkable. She even designed their helmets in the shape of semitranslucent heungnip. "Are you paying attention?"

"Of course."

Ocean drops what she was examining into Teo's cart, and he's momentarily mollified by the pristine packages of his favorite cereals, Saturn-O's and Asteroid Belt with marshmallows. He pushes the cart forward to catch up to her again and drapes his body over it while they amble down the aisle.

"How was home?"

"Home was . . . fine. Same as ever."

Fine. Jake. Sure. Back when they first met, he nicknamed Ocean "Finesure" since that was how she answered every question. Not particularly inspired, but it's not the worst nickname he's come up with for her either.

But they don't talk about that. Handling Ocean is like trying to pet a cat. You have to feign complete disinterest and leave the door ajar for her to nudge open on her own.

"I visited Hajoon though," Ocean says. "Poured him some soju. He listens a lot better than my parents."

"I'm sure he appreciated it. Did you go swimming?"

Ocean's shoulders bunch before she curtly forces them down. "No."

Teo grabs a pack of banana milk from the top shelf for Ocean. Then he places a carton of 2% in her cart as well.

"Osteoporosis is more severe in women than men," he says offhandedly when she glowers at it. "You should take the pills your mom gave you too."

Ocean grimaces. "How did you know?"

"Your mom always sends you back with a drawerful of supplements." Ocean's bags are usually rattling when she returns from her home in Marado. Other people might trade affection in hugs or kisses; Ocean's mother's love language is vitamin D pills. "Are you going to grab Choco Pies for Vonderbar?"

"I should get a few boxes."

They walk up and down the aisles in a companionable silence, their pace barely faster than a crawl. It isn't until they've reached a spot a couple rows over, after Teo squats down to mentally debate fusilli or ziti, that he says casually, "Do you want to talk about it? About Adama?" He shakes a box haphazardly, as if testing it, but really, he's giving Ocean an excuse to pretend she didn't hear him if she wants.

Ocean taps her shoulder and, after a moment, responds, "I felt bad for Liesl. Is that weird?"

Teo contemplates the box of angel-hair. "It's only weird if you think too hard about whether it's weird."

Teo finds out about Ocean's life through the Alliance rumor mill faster and more easily than by asking her directly. Ocean's relationships often last a while, but not due to any commitment on her part. He understands Adama's desire to spark something in her—anger, passion—anything stronger than a fine, jake, sure. Not that he condones Adama's actions or anything. But, not for the first time, Teo wonders how long Ocean is for the Alliance. How long she'll stay in the limbo of her fallen state. As always, that thought burns like a hot coal in his chest. Ocean could easily get a job with some other spaceflight program, even with her record. The Russians would fall over themselves to accept her, but nothing else would be the Alliance.

He reaches up a hand and she takes it to hoist him back to his feet. He's going to do ravioli anyway; it's a lot more filling.

"I got an earful from Declan about you skipping out on your father's speech," Ocean says.

"My old man will get over it." Teo doesn't ask how his older brother predicted it; Declan's always had a sixth sense for his mischief. Teo can hear Ocean's burgeoning next thought. It's not just that he's absent, but whom he's absent *with*. He shakes his head at her. "Who's around to see? Everyone's at the party, including my father's favorite child."

Ocean wrinkles her nose. "I hope you're right because unlike you, *I* have a reputation to uphold." He swats at her, but she perches up on her cart to push off with her foot, coasting forward like she's on a hoverskid. "Do *you* want to talk about it?" Her voice sails back to him.

"Dear diary," he intones. "It's me again, the solar's favorite ne'er-do-well son." He drops the act and scratches his temple. "Sometimes, it's easier to create new problems for my old man to worry about rather than beg forgiveness for something long past." Ocean's cart rolls to a stop and she hops off it again, waiting for Teo to catch up. "I can't be like this forever," he says when he does.

Ocean glances at him and smiles. "Why not? I like you how you are."

He feels a scorching squeeze in his chest like he might cry, but instead grabs a Jolly Pong bag off the shelf and lobs it into her cart. They stop by the soft drink aisle, but, as always, a blank spot only teases where the lychee soda should be.

"They're sold out. Again."

"Give it up," Teo says. "There's only one place you can get it."

"Why won't you tell me?"

"I'll go to my grave with that intel."

They pay for their groceries with the store's lone cashier. It's a world, a solar really, in which almost all transactions are contactless, automated. Except Korea. In Korea, there have always been people at the door to greet you, people running to fill your gas tank, and even here, in a small mart that only serves the Alliance dorm, a sleepy human rings them up. *Honor in service.* The Alliance motto.

They take their groceries out back, to a small balcony behind the mart. Teo directs them to a specific bench between two cameras, in what he calls a "blind white noise" spot. The small light above their bench buzzes steadily like an insistent insect, and they're out of both security cameras' frames. Warm air brushes his face. The rest of the balcony is empty, plastic chairs resting upside down on the tables. Ocean and Teo pierce their tiny straws through the foil tops of their Yakults and then knock them together with a geonbae.

"Do you know why they'll always keep these containers?" Teo asks.

"Hmm?"

"Cans. Bottles. These tiny Yakult containers. Do you know why these will always stay the same?" He holds it up. "It's because of the sound of the straw going through the top. The little *jik*. It's the most refreshing noise in the world and there's something . . . visceral about it. Like some memory handed down to us through the generations to trigger a pleasure point in the brain." Teo bumps Ocean's head with his Yakult for emphasis. "It's like when you smell someone's perfume and think, *Ah*, and there's something nostalgic or bittersweet about it. You know?"

"Someone you loved in a former life? Someone you can't remember?" Ocean asks. She has her legs folded up on the bench as they look out on Seoul together.

"Or someone from this life I can't remember."

"It's still another life. You're a different person now than you were then."

"Injeong." They're quiet for a while. Ocean shakes another Yakult and spears the top of it.

"Ocean?"

"Hmm?"

"This is so much better than listening to my father's speech."

"Is that supposed to be a compliment?"

"Yeah, I think so."

FOUR

THE *OHNEUL'S* DISTINCT MUSTY SMELL is a mixture of recycled air and persistent biological funk. Unlike the last time she was here, though, the lights are already on when Ocean enters.

To Ocean's left, a clank and Dae's muttered *shibal* drifts from the cockpit, but she sidles past it down the sloping floor. The ship curves so that the large room in the front, the greenhouse, is the meeting point between the two floors. She heads there now but notices light spilling into the hallway from the infirmary. She pulls out the bag of tangerines from her bag, then stops short at the doorway.

Stepping into the infirmary always felt like slipping into a sideways dimension, with its scent of acrid herbs and shelves overflowing with knickknacks. But now, the whole area has been swept clear, leaving only a mat and a pair of boots in front of her, along with a room divider that separates the entrance from the main area. A brand-new infirmary cot has sheets folded so sharply they could cut.

Next to it, a stranger sits at a long table. Someone thirty or forty years shy of being Gremio. He's perched on the bench with bare feet. They're lithe feet, with strong lines. Dancer's feet. He lifts his head, and she recognizes his double-lidded dark eyes against pale skin. His inky black hair falls over his forehead. This is the man she talked to briefly at the gala. He's wearing *Ohneul* coveralls with the name SASANI stitched across his chest, but that doesn't illuminate anything for Ocean. He clears his throat and stands. If she hadn't already placed him, his unselfconscious grace would have given him away. She'd never forget his elegant, theatrical way of spreading his fingers. She has to tilt her head back as he comes closer. In response, his chin comes up as a challenge.

"XO Yoon," he says. His voice is quiet, his Common accented enough that her brain tries to place the particulars of it. "Can I help you?"

She struggles to catch up. The door that connects to Gremio's bedroom is open and the space inside has also been completely altered.

"Are you new?" she manages. He frowns, his eyebrows drawing together. They create a perfect vertical line, so solid she's surprised a divot hasn't formed in his forehead.

"I believe Captain Song attempted to introduce us last night."

"Right," she says, drawing out the word.

Gremio's still a couple years off from retirement, and surely he would have let Ocean know if he got sick or something. But then the new guy looks off to the side, and he rubs what she now sees is a shaved undercut. Beneath the dip the delicate bones make at the back of his neck, two feathers embellish his skin, peeking out from underneath the curve of his shirt.

She's going to strangle Dae with her bare hands. Ocean can't stop her expression from going dead, can't change it before the man sees. His face tightens and he drops his hand. It's not his fault, and Ocean swallows the anger. The bitter lodge in her throat dissolves painfully as she blinks at the bag of Jejudo tangerines hanging from her hand. They were for Gremio since he loves the sweet fruit, but he won't be enjoying them anytime soon. She holds out the bag as a peace offering.

"Would you like some tangerines? It's one of the things Jejudo is famous for."

He coldly regards them. "I don't like citrus."

Ocean finds her eyebrows shooting up. "Sure. Fine. So . . . you're our new medic?"

"Yes," he says. "Haven Sasani."

"Sasani, have you gotten a tour of the *Ohneul* yet?"

She's able to count the seconds it takes for her to receive his monotone answer and wonders if soliciting responses from him will always feel like pulling teeth.

"No."

"Well, come on then, Haven Sasani who doesn't like citrus. I'll show you around before the *Ohneul* embarks."

⬤ ⬤ ⬤ ⬤ ⬤

Haven can't believe he just denounced citrus.

But Yoon's face betrayed her disgust when she caught a glimpse of his tattoo. She *knows*. And she loathes him already. Did she really expect him to say "Yes, thank you" and to reach for her tangerines only to have her recoil so she wouldn't have to touch his skin? He'll have to remember that he doesn't like citrus for the rest of his time here now. As he mentally catalogues which fruits count as citrus, he sneaks a peek at Yoon. The *Ohneul*'s XO and pilot. She seems so . . . unassuming, maybe because she isn't in uniform yet. The only time she even seemed awake was when she reached that hard point of anger that had speared him through the chest earlier, but she tucked that away too.

"Let's start at the greenhouse." Yoon pushes open the door and immediately Haven can smell life. The sharp soothing scent of eucalyptus washes over him, soaking into his pores. One second in here and his hands are sweaty. He brushes aside soft leafy greens to make himself a path. The shades haven't yet been drawn in this room, and light streams in through the glass ceiling and walls. Yoon leans over the platform railing. Glassware crowds the table in the middle of the room, jockeying for space with microscopes and an open tabula. A figure sprawls across the cot next to the table, his eyes closed and a book tented over his chest. "Sleeping in the greenhouse again, Von?" Yoon calls down.

The slender Black man sits upright, his hair springing with him. "Ocean!"

Yoon's clambering down the ladder, and the man scrambles to his feet. He's dressed in the bright-blue *Ohneul* coveralls and has a patch with KENT stitched over his heart. He trips forward to wrap his spindly arms around her. After adhering to what seems to be an internal timer, Yoon gently but firmly extricates herself.

"Von, this is our new medic, Haven Sasani. Sasani, this is Von Kent. He's our xenobotanist."

Kent's shorter than Haven, less so if he didn't stoop. "Haven Sasani? New medic?" His tightly curled hair is frazzled in the humidity and skews to one side. He takes in Haven over Yoon's shoulder. The scene unfolds as if in slow motion: Kent's face lights up, and he throws his arms wide. "Welcome!"

Haven only has time to let out a dismayed *oh* before Yoon tosses two tangerines at Kent, who catches them with a fumble.

"Heads up, Von," she says.

"Ocean! You say heads up *before* you throw." Kent's twin moon eyes fixate on the tangerines. "Souvenirs?"

Yoon deposits the bag of tangerines on Kent's workstation. She opens the bag at her side and draws out a large packet. "This one's for you, actually. From Osulloc."

"Oh, you shouldn't have." Kent, if possible, brightens even further.

"It's nothing," she says dismissively. "This, on the other hand—"

"Wow! For me?" Kent claps his hands.

Yoon's pulling out boxes of Choco Pies from her bag as Kent eagerly grasps for them. He drops a box and the top pops open, scattering individually wrapped Choco Pies everywhere. One of them skitters across the floor and bumps against Haven's foot. Both Kent and Yoon are kneeling to gather up the Choco Pies. Haven starts to bend down, too, but stops himself. If he picks it up, they might throw it out because he touched it. If he doesn't, they'll think him rude for not helping. He's weighing the pros and cons of hiding the packet and destroying the evidence, but Kent's already crawled over to him. He stands with it in hand, a sunny smile on his face.

"Wasn't that so nice of her, Haven? I promise, Ocean is *much* softer than she appears. I thought she was scary, too, when I first met her on the *Hadouken*."

"The *Hadouken*?"

Yoon frowns when Haven's voice cracks, and he schools his face back into what he hopes reads as appropriately polite.

Kent chuckles. "Yeah, weird name, isn't it? Our captain was into vintage video games. We even had an arcade set up in the common room."

Kent's name wasn't in the report Haven read about the *Hadouken*, but most of the names had been redacted. Really, the only one left was Yoon's. And that tiny little report, buried out of sight, had been the reason Haven applied to the *Ohneul* in the first place.

"Shall we have some tea?" Kent holds up the packet Yoon brought him, and Haven can see loose-leaf tea in the semitranslucent bag. "Haven, Osulloc is this gorgeous tea farm on Jejudo. Their volcanic rock tea is divine. After we finish, if you want, I can tell you all about my *algae*."

Kent infuses so much pride and hope in that last word, refusing him would be like snapping a child's kite into pieces right in front of them, but fortunately Yoon reaches between them into the bag of tangerines.

"I think later, Von. I should finish showing Sasani around." Yoon holds up a handful of tangerines. "I'm taking these for Maggie, jake?" When they're up the ladder and outside the greenhouse, Yoon says, "Von would be thrilled to have tea with you anytime. And I promise you don't actually have to talk about algae. The whole time, at least."

Haven studies Yoon, searching for any sign of her earlier disgust. "I don't need any favors," he says stiffly.

"Suit yourself, Sasani." Yoon's eyes are light brown and mocking. They walk past the infirmary and Yoon bangs on a door on the opposite side of the hall before pushing it open. If it was smell that assaulted Haven before, this time it's sound. Loud clangs riff around and a chorus of voices blasts from the speakers overhead, reverberating in the space like an amphitheater. Various vehicles and gadgets in wildly different stages of dismemberment litter the huge spread-out area. "Maggie!" Yoon yells.

The clanking halts and a head pops up from behind a small machine. Behind the head, pokes a . . . tail? She shoves away from the machine, her body dipping and pivoting around on glowing hoverskates. As she glides closer, Haven sees that the tail bobbing behind her is some sort of machine appendage attached to her hips.

"Yo!" she says.

"What's it today?" Yoon points up.

"Gregorian chant." The mechanic tilts her head as they listen for a moment to the call and response between a tenor and the choir. She's stocky with tanned skin and messy blond hair drawn back into a topknot. The sleeves of her uniform are rolled up, showing off streaks and burns across her arms. She wears black knee guards, and goggles perch on top of her head. "Who are you?" she asks Haven.

"New medic," Yoon explains. "Haven Sasani. This is our mechanic, engineer, occasional cook, Maggie Thierry."

"New medic? What happened to Gremio?" She stretches her hand out for Haven.

He hesitates, but before he can decide what to do, Yoon's put herself in between them, intercepting the handshake as if it's meant for her. So, he didn't imagine it, after all; she's deliberately keeping her crew from touching him. He should have expected it, but just because he's familiar with the taste of shame in his mouth doesn't mean he likes it. Thierry bemusedly regards Yoon as they shake hands.

"Uh . . . Ocean?" She peers over at Haven and pulls her hand out of Yoon's grip, circling him on her hoverskates. Haven has to stop himself from hiding his neck, and she says, "Aw shit. Mea culpa. You're Mortemian?"

Haven's muscles solidify even as he tries to keep from tensing. He waits for Thierry to back away, to wipe down hands that didn't even have the chance to touch his. Haven glances at Yoon, but she's not looking his way.

"Maggie," she warns.

"What's that *like*?" Thierry skates in front of Haven again, her face full of open curiosity. "Where are you from?"

"Prometheus," he manages.

She stops midskate and peers at him. Haven finds himself stiffening again, an instinctive reaction no matter how conditioned he is to this response. When he was very young, he laid under the sun, willing it to bake him into a different color, as if that was all it took. It only turned his skin a bright, painful red. Later, his father tutted as he smoothed aloe over his skin. He said, "You have your mother's skin," as if not realizing those words stung even more than the sunburn.

"Ooh, you must have been in deep. What are you doing here? Oh! Are you in the middle of your rumspringa?"

"Rum—what?"

"You know like, your journeyman stage? Or are you *out* out? I'd love to pick your brain sometime. Will you show me your tattoo? Why'd you put it on your back? How far does it extend?"

Haven reflexively grips his shoulder.

"Maggie," Yoon says. "Generally, you should know a person for longer than five minutes before asking them to take off their shirt."

"Injeong. Unless there's money involved." Thierry ignores Haven's dropped jaw and moves on. "I'll have you know though, Haven, that I have three wives and a husband back on Venus. We're opening a restaurant when I return from my stint with the Alliance. That's why I joined as a contractor, you know. I wanted to experience different cuisines and cultures all around the solar."

"Ah, that reminds me." Yoon swings her bag forward again and removes a couple glass jars filled with a bright-red substance. She hands them over to Thierry, along with the remaining tangerines.

"Ah-ssah!" Thierry crows. "Your mom's kimchi?"

"She made it specifically for you."

Yoon's bag is deflated now, and Haven recalls how surprised she was when they met at the infirmary, the bag of tangerines drooping from her hand. She'd brought back something for everyone on the ship. Haven had been under the impression that, other than the Captain and XO, the ship's positions changed hands regularly. But Gremio must have been the former medic, and everyone seems so surprised that he's gone. It's unlikely he was fired for a specific incident, then, so why . . . Haven dismisses that line of thought, his insides curdling. *He* was the incident. He chased someone else out of their job.

"So," Yoon says. "Maggie here can handle anything electronic or mechanical, or you know, if you want someone to compose a playlist, she's got you covered there too. She'll show you around the kitchen later. It's kind of her domain." Yoon pauses. "That is, unless you think it's beneath you to accept a favor."

His cheeks prickle hotly, but Thierry spins around unconcernedly, her skates glowing. "You can drop by anytime."

"I'm taking him to the cockpit next."

"You've met Dae, right?" Thierry asks Haven.

"Captain Song?"

"Oh, I bet she loves hearing that." Thierry whizzes back to her station and ducks behind the twisting tubes of metal. "Don't forget, Haven! I want to hear all about your life!"

When they're back in the hallway, the door closes, completely sealing the noise behind it. Haven resists the urge to slump back against it.

Yoon's several paces away before he's gathered himself enough to speak. "You knew. That I was Mortemian?"

"I saw your tattoo."

That much had been obvious. "And you kept your crewmates from touching me."

His voice comes out flat, and he wonders why he's pushing this. He's never done this, not when the vendor called him Death Hands, not on that first day of the Alliance's space training when his dormmate's expression fell when their rooms were assigned. Yoon's face is unreadable.

"Everyone has boundaries, Sasani. I was trying to respect yours."

"I see." But he doesn't. "I noticed your tattoo too."

Yoon's right hand spasms, and the slight movement would have been lost if she hadn't otherwise been so still. "It's an old one."

"What does it mean?"

"Do tattoos always have to mean something?" she asks tiredly. A cold rime frosts everything around him. She taps her shoulder with her right hand. "Crane was my call sign back at Yong."

Yong, the Alliance's flight school. There's also Bangpae Corps and Horangi Command School. The hundreds of ships that form the Alliance are all divided into separate designations, some more militaristic and others, like the *Ohneul*, that serve as transporters. This system allows people like Thierry and Haven to attach on to a crew or mission, even if they've never trained with the Alliance. Haven himself only endured the minimum few months of space training to receive the certification that qualified him to apply. The pay's decent, the experience stands out on your résumé, and you end up seeing a lot of space. Although that's not really why he's here.

"Keep up. Next is the cockpit."

Yoon's down the hall, disappearing into the next room. Inside the cockpit, Captain Song stands behind one of the chairs at the front panel. Her long black hair is styled into what must be its customary coil, a braid wrapped across the crown of her head.

"Oh, Haven. Did Ocean finally find her manners?"

Like Thierry, she heartily stretches a hand forward to shake Haven's. Haven half expects Yoon to intervene again. If he wasn't watching for it, he would have missed her slight hesitation before she deliberately tucks her chin to her chest, leaving Haven to smoothly put up his hands. He places one hand over his chest and bows over it instead, turning it into a movement of subservience that allows him to hide his confusion: Yoon said she respected his boundaries, but then left him to fend for himself in front of their captain. Captain Song, fortunately, has moved on.

"Ocean." The word wavers, just like the captain's smile. "Thanks for bringing Haven to my cockpit. I can take it from here."

After the merest pause, Yoon, in a perfect imitation of Haven's gesture, bends her head over a hand she places on her chest. She doesn't bother saying anything to him, but as she turns, he catches the mockery in her eyes. Only after she leaves does he realize that he didn't thank her at all for showing him around.

"Are you settling in all right so far, Haven?" Captain Song sits at the front seat and gestures to the one next to her. When Haven sits, his feet bump into something, and he peers underneath the panel to find three pedals beneath the wheel. The captain doesn't have anything extra under hers, just the standard wheel in front. "Oh yes. Ocean had Maggie retrofit those." Captain Song taps her right shoulder. "But don't be intimidated; the ship pretty much flies itself."

"It does?"

Captain Song snorts. "We're a Class 4 Transporter. We attach to small teams and transport them to and from their destinations. We're not maneuvering against enemy pilots or dipping through asteroid belts. I could put this on autopilot, and it would do the job just as well." She frowns and mutters, "And clearly all that talk about her skill is overblown. I lost a lot of money because of her."

A storm cloud has settled on Captain Song's brow, and Haven prompts politely, "Captain Song?"

"I hope she didn't force you on a tour after I already gave you one. You've seen how rude she can be."

Yoon hadn't exactly twisted his arm. He just found himself saying no when she asked if he'd had a tour already. Captain Song showed him all the spaces, including the rooms downstairs and the dining and kitchen area that's supposedly Thierry's domain. She told him what to do in case of an emergency, where to find supplies and the escape pods. She even showed him around this room, pointing out a piece of paper—astonishingly, affixed with peeling Scotch tape to the side of the panel—with numbers for the Alliance HQ, Alliance IT, and the ship's ten-digit ID number, which other ships need to connect or dock. But Yoon's tour consisted of other components entirely.

"I thought as a novice, it wouldn't hurt to get another review of the ship," he says blandly. "She was polite."

Captain Song relaxes back into her seat. "Good, good. Ocean's been my second for a few years now, but you'll have to forgive her. Some things can't be taught, you know?"

Haven studies the unfamiliar pedals at his feet again. Most vehicles are automated these days. Even on a backwater moon like Prometheus, you just punch in your destination on your scooter panel, and it takes care of the rest. When he looks back at Captain Song, he finds her waiting expectantly.

"Sir?"

She waves a hand. "You don't need to call me that. You'll find this is a very relaxed ship, Haven. You don't have to call me captain either. You may call me your noona. Dae noona is fine."

Noona is a respectful Korean address for older women and girls used by speakers who identify as male, but Haven's found it often used around the Alliance as a term of affection. He initially thought such words were used only among family members, but apparently that's not the case. He's never had any desire to call someone noona or hyeong or reunsaeng, though.

Captain Song's hand is about to grasp his shoulder and Haven's whole body stiffens as if an electric current has passed through it. She's too close now for him to avoid her touch, but her hand halts in midair when she sees his expression.

"Or not. I would never force that on you." She withdraws her hand to smooth the front of her suit. "As I was saying, don't be surprised if you find Ocean to be cold. I think it's from all her years at Savoir-Faire."

"The Diplomat school?" Haven asks, surprised.

"That's right. She dropped out a year before graduating. Isn't that crazy? She could have just stuck it out one more year and . . . well, that's beside the point. Anyway, she was there too long, I think. They breed ambition there. And diminish compassion. It's a bad combination." Captain Song clears her throat. "But Ocean is a valuable part of this team. We all are. I hope you'll consider staying on with the *Ohneul* after this mission."

There's no way she could be sincere. Unless she wants him to stay because of the monetary incentive.

"Thank you," he manages stiffly.

"No thanks needed. Be back for our crew meeting by 1300. We'll leave not too long after, so make sure you have everything you require."

"Is there . . . is there anything you would like me to do now?"

"Hmm?" Captain Song's face dissolves into another smile. Her lips curve into the pliant shape. "No, don't worry about me. Just do whatever you think you need to do."

Her vague response is clearly meant to put him at ease, but it does the opposite. He stands and bows again over his hand. This is ridiculous. At this rate, she'll think this is how everyone from Prometheus enters and exits a room.

"Thank you, Captain."

"You don't have to call me that."

Haven straightens and tries, really tries, to say what she wants. Dae noona. They're just words and for some reason, they'll make her happy. She certainly affects the sort of ease that would invite others to call her that. But the words are like wooden blocks in his mouth, and he can hear how insincere they'd sound. He bows curtly and leaves the room.

FIVE

TEO NURSES A COCKTAIL as he sits in the back corner of Donggam. It's where he comes to drink alone, a quiet bar you have to enter through the freezer door of a convenience store. The *Shadowfax* leaves for the Moon tomorrow, and he's skipping the orientation. He wants to be in that room even less after the gala. He'll catch jansori from Captain Hong later, but he doesn't need another lesson on the Seonbi, their history, and their antiquated etiquette. Basically, they'll need to be treated like one of Korea's national treasures, which they are.

Donggam's small tables fan out to discourage large groups and the menu specializes in bite-sized individual plates. Neon signs flashing hangeul words dot the walls, but Teo's favorite feature might be the pink-lit vending machine near the restrooms that features the retro snacks of childhoods a solar over. He's not sure how they keep it stocked and he's sure most are years past their expiration dates, but no one has ever eaten Novadips with sprinkles for the health benefits anyway. He has a soft spot for the idiosyncratic vending machines that hide in alcoves.

The low murmur of voices comforts him. He exchanges a few words with Kevin at the bar, but takes a seat at his own table. Kevin, with his good noonchi, leaves him to his own devices for the most part. Which is why it's unpleasant when someone sits directly across from him. Teo sips his drink, a concoction of Kevin's that uses, of all things, coconut curry. The man before him says nothing, lounging back against the seat, arms spread on either side. He's a few years older than Teo, and pale enough that even in the shadows, he exudes an inner light. His eyes are similarly washed of color, and he has an angular face, cheekbones like carved plateaus. A smile tugs at his lips as he looks Teo over.

"Well?" Teo says.

"I heard this was a frequent hangout of yours," the man says.

His voice has had its roughness sanded away, its sibilance contrived to seduce. More than the words, the voice puts Teo on alert, even if he maintains his outwardly relaxed posture.

"Oh?" Teo says.

"Aren't you going to ask how I know who you are?"

"Darling," Teo drawls and sips his drink. He sets it down and slowly licks his upper lip. "Everyone knows who I am."

The man's distaste flashes across his face. Teo's able to identify the emotion all too easily. Apparently, he's done his research, and Teo doubts he's a mere stalker. Who knows how long he's been coming here, or if he's had this place watched. The manner in which he approached Teo suggests salacious intent. Several love hotels dot the neighborhood and maybe that's his angle. But even if Teo is familiar with scandal, he's an Anand son, and it wouldn't do to be caught at a sleazy motel.

"Teophilus Anand," the man says.

"Bravo," Teo says. "Now what?"

"I have a proposal for you."

"So soon?" Teo asks. "Do you even know my ring size?"

The man hides his displeasure better now, but not enough to conceal it from Teo. He contemplates Teo's face, then his shoulders. Teo languorously rolls them. He doesn't like anyone who can't meet his eyes.

"Are you happy in your role as the Anand whore?"

Teo feels his eyes flare wide before he can control his reaction. "That's a bit strong," he says, and his voice comes out steadily enough.

But the man has seen the chink in his armor and presses into it. "Is it? They keep you sated with money, with sex, with . . ." The man gestures to the drink on the table.

"What else do people live for?" Teo asks.

The man caught him off guard, but Teo recognizes the glint in his eyes as he pushes what he thinks is his advantage. But far more telling is the way he scans Teo's face, his body, for tells. Teo casually threads his hands together and leans his elbows down on the table, resting his chin on his tented fingers. It's enough to hide their tremor.

"Power. Respect," the man says. "All things your brother has in abundance, I've noticed."

The brother card, huh? Teo blinks slowly at the man. "Of course Declan does. What would I do with all that? I'm lucky that they haven't cut me out of my inheritance."

The man weighs his response. "Haven't you ever wanted more?"

"More?" Teo scoffs. "I'm one of the richest men in the solar. What would I do with more?"

The man's eyes rove over Teo, but he's perfected his fatuous mien. People have been underestimating him for years, and it's easier to let them.

"Your family gave you up as a sacrificial lamb to the Alliance," the man says. "But wouldn't you rather be free from them, to even rise above them?"

"No one's above Koreans," Teo says. "Where have you been for the last century? They're more confident than ever. If they could survive reunification, they can overcome anything." Everyone always assumes that his parents shipped him off to the Alliance to get him in line, but Teo enrolled on his own. Anand Tech has been linked to the Alliance in a symbiotic relationship for almost as long as Teo's been alive. What better way to symbolize and cement that relationship? But even that attempt had fallen flat. And now it was just another embarrassment for his father, another thing for him to fix. "They're not such a bad bunch," he continues. "And they're great drinkers."

"Are you really this vapid?"

Teo's tired; he came to the bar to enjoy a drink alone, not to get accosted.

"What would you know about it?" Teo asks lazily. "You've come down to this bar, but you haven't ordered a drink because you don't have the money, do you? You sit there in an expensive suit, but you don't know how to wear it. The hemline of your pants goes too far down, and the front pocket of your jacket is still sewn shut. And you think you can offer me something?"

Something hot and dangerous scrapes across the man's face. Teo's stomach knots. But his exterior maintains that arrogance, that foppish ignorance that is his signature.

"Thank you, Teophilus," the man says and stands. "You've confirmed my opinion of you."

"My pleasure."

The man walks away, leaving Teo unsettled. He picks up his drink again and sips from it. Yes, his family uses him. But that is not this stranger's business. After all, the man planned on doing the exact same thing. Teo's in no mood to be used by anyone except himself tonight.

* * * * *

"It'll take us two days to get to Sinis-x. We're traveling to warp gate Archimedes, and we'll exit at Galileo, which is closest to our destination. Sinis-x is a small, terraformed moon."

Dae's gesturing at their open screens, but Ocean doesn't bother. Dae sent them the info a while ago, not that Ocean read it then either. Maggie's not even pretending to pay attention, instead softly chortling at what's probably an animal compilation video on AV. It momentarily distracts Sasani, too, although deciphering his non-reaction would be useless. Dae snaps her fingers at Maggie, who blinks up at her and pauses the video.

"Um, Dae?" Von speaks up and pokes Ocean's elbow. "Did you say that it'll take two days?"

"That's shaving a day off the typical ETA," Maggie says, suddenly interested.

"That'll be up to Ocean, won't it?"

Ocean checks the route Von's showing her. "I can do it. We'll just have to burn a little extra energy," she says, figuring that will be the end of it.

"That's fine. I want to keep to this schedule," Dae says offhandedly. Ocean exchanges glances with Maggie and Von. Maggie gives an exaggerated shrug, and Von only crinkles his brow. "Sinis-x is part of the Sinis Series, as you may have surmised," Dae continues. "It was known as their rain planet." Across from Ocean, Sasani flinches but quickly hides it, flicking his fingers across the tabula keyboard. It's hard to tell if he's offended by what Dae just said or by whatever video Maggie's gone back to watching. "We'll be collecting data, as well as performing routine maintenance to the robot facilities. We're an eclectic team, but I've been creative in obtaining jobs that fit us." Dae clears her throat. "I'm required by Alliance regulations to remind you that this is a Grade E mission, but regardless of the grade, A or F, we always apply the same amount of care and professionalism. Understood?"

The *Ohneul* isn't cleared to handle anything above Grade D, but Dae never bothers to mention that in her sign-off.

"Dangyeol, sir, Captain Song, sir!" They chorus back to her. They all salute and, as always, Dae's mouth twitches with pleasure. She nods solemnly back at them.

"Dismissed. We take off promptly at 1330."

They file out, but Ocean waits until everyone else has exited. Then she gets up, too, folding her arms as she stands in front of Dae, who tilts her head, an uncertain smile wavering on her face.

"Ocean, if you want to apologize about yesterday, I understand. Listen, it was too much to—"

"Tell me it wasn't for the kickback," Ocean says quietly but lethally.

Dae's eyes widen, but she composes her face into the picture of innocence. "What are you talking about?"

"The kickback. Tell me you didn't fire Gremio and replace him with Sasani because the Alliance gave you a nice monetary incentive for employing a *Mortemian*."

"I don't know why you're so outraged," Dae says. "Gremio was on his way out anyway."

"Gremio was two years shy of retiring. You booted him out? Just so you could pad your bank account?"

Dae makes a noise like Ocean chopped her throat. "Open your eyes, Ocean. We're *Class 4*." She stops and takes a breath, continuing through her teeth, "Gremio's answer for everything was to slap a pa-seu on it. The rest of the time, he was holed up in his room playing go-stop on the tabula and smoking. What value did he add to the ship? Yes, I took the Vulture because of the bonus. But you're not in any position to question *my* decision." Her eyes burn into Ocean. "You have no idea how lucky you are to even be here. Do you realize how close you are to being thrown out of the Alliance for good?"

Dae holds up her fingers to show Ocean just how small that margin is, the motion overblown and performative.

"I perform my duties," Ocean says.

"Barely," Dae says. "But you don't really understand what it means to be a part of the Alliance, Ocean. Even when I ask you to do something simple like move the *Ohneul—*"

"If this is about your stupid bet—"

"Ocean!" Dae cuts her off. "You don't get it! Do you think you'd be able to talk to your commanding officer like that anywhere else? If it wasn't for Hajoon oppa—" She clamps her mouth shut.

"If it wasn't for Hajoon oppa, what?" Ocean asks icily.

"He would have wanted a place for you." She pauses as if magnanimously allowing Ocean the chance to respond, as if they both don't already know that Ocean can't. "But I can't keep this spot open for you unconditionally, Ocean," Dae continues. "I need you to do your job."

They both know there's nowhere else for Ocean to go within the Alliance. Ocean walks stiffly to her seat. Her hand floats before her, as if against her will, mechanically entering the code to connect to the Seoul station. Distantly, she hears Dae taking deep breaths behind her. In through the nose, out through the mouth.

"Alliance Seoul, this is Yoon Ocean of the *Ohneul*, ship ID seven-three-four-three-one-eight-four-five-nine-seven. Requesting permission to take off."

Dae shoves into the seat next to Ocean. She takes one more calming breath and then punches on the intercom.

"Hi everyone, this is your captain, Dae." Dae's voice is upbeat, and its perkiness hurts Ocean's teeth like she's just gulped ice-cold water. "We are now disengaging from the Seoul port and heading into deeper skies. Once we've hit space, I'll check in again."

Ocean disconnects from their dock, then steers the ship toward the launching pad. She has to force herself to unclench her jaw. Instead, she concentrates on the wheel in her hands, the comfortable feel of the pedals beneath her feet. Something always locks into place here. As she relaxes, Dae sighs.

"You know," Dae says. And Ocean hears a softness in her voice that isn't meant for her. "When you're behind the wheel, you look like . . ." she trails off, as if it wasn't clear what she was going to say. Her words disrupt any pleasure Ocean felt from settling into the ship. "Listen, I know you were fond of Gremio."

"Captain," Ocean says. "I'm trying to do my job."

Dae draws a breath, and Ocean half expects her to launch into another tirade about how to properly speak to a *commanding officer*, but Dae falls silent instead. Ocean shifts gears with her left hand. She maneuvers to the Seoul launchpad and then shoots vertically into the sky. As the earth falls away, and the darkness comes to greet them, Ocean moves her feet and she can hear the ship breathe in response to what she asks of it. The vastness of space opens before her. Dae moves to flip on the intercom again.

"In case you couldn't tell, we're up in the air, kiddos." Her tone turns reverent. "Only in space do we realize how lucky we are to be Korean." Dae repeats it every time they fly, but today, her dramatics irk Ocean more than usual. As she shifts gears, she fumbles the connection, and the ship grinds a complaint before she quickly corrects her movement. The mistake immediately draws Dae's scrutiny. "Do you even know why I say that?"

"Should I?" Ocean asks, before adding flatly, "Captain?"

Dae clears her throat. "It's something Yi Soyeon said. The first Korean astronaut? 'Only in space did I realize how lucky I am to be Korean.' She's a big deal." Dae pauses, and her voice is drenched in pity. "To Koreans."

"Got it."

Dae fidgets noisily behind Ocean, who hears her open her mouth and then close it again before finally announcing, "I'm going to do the rounds, check up on everyone."

After Dae leaves, Ocean transfers the coordinates for Archimedes and then sets the *Ohneul* to coast. She settles back into her seat and rests a hand in the curve of the wheel.

"A big deal to Koreans," she says to herself.

Unbidden, she thinks of Hajoon oppa. It was a summer night, the windows of Hajoon's car rolled down and the stereo turned up high. Ocean can't remember what was playing—the radio or an album streaming from Hajoon's nimbus—but someday, she thinks she'll be in a café or walking down the street while a car drives by and she'll hear it again. Even if she doesn't immediately recognize the song, a pang will pierce through her sternum. Kind of like Teo's mysterious nostalgia for a forgotten love. Back then, though, it was the soundtrack of their freedom, her brother winding around the isolated road as if they were the only two left on Earth.

"Jjohljimah," Hajoon said.

Ocean didn't have the chance to ask Hajoon what he meant before he flicked the headlights off. It lasted only the space between breaths, but for a thrilling, terrifying moment, they hurtled through pitch darkness. If Ocean could have produced a scream, it would have caught in her throat. They were in free fall together, suspended in oblivion. Then Hajoon threw the headlights back on to reveal that they'd never left the road and were still coasting with the summer night's breeze flowing through the window.

It was the kind of stupid stunt that gets you killed in a flash. An animal could have been crossing the road or, god forbid, a person. He could have misjudged the road and sent the car twisting around a tree or careening off a ledge. But when you're younger, you take the risks that seem impossibly dangerous now. We court death as children, not understanding how close it already is. Ocean would jump off cliffs into the water below, bolstered only by the proof that the kid before her did it and lived. That was how Ocean would always picture Hajoon: laughing widely, wind ruffling his hair as he drove with one relaxed hand on the wheel, a gleam in his eye that welcomed danger even as he told her not to be scared. She'd never been afraid in his passenger seat.

But for all the stupid stunts Hajoon pulled, a freak accident got him in the end. Ocean didn't cry much—not then, not at the funeral, not during her years at the Yong flight school afterward. She drove around at night alone, stumbled numbly around the same halls her brother had wrestled through years earlier. But then she flew her first ship out of Earth's atmosphere and into the vast, black space, and the sobs finally wrenched out of her chest as hot tears gushed from her eyes. She shoved the heels of her hands into them, trying to stem their flow, trying to stifle her shuddered gasps. Her teacher and other classmates stood behind her, bewildered.

When the teacher pulled her aside later to ask what had happened, Ocean kept saying "I don't know." She didn't want to seem insolent, but how could she put into words something that large in her throat and tangled up inside? If she tried to explain, it would have cheapened it.

She kept saying "I don't know," but somewhere along the way, the repeated words turned into "I don't care." I don't care I don't care I don't care.

Sometimes floating in space brings her closer to her brother than she ever was while he was alive. But sometimes, she's just floating in a void, not closer to anyone or anything.

SIX

HAVEN CAN SCARCELY BELIEVE they're in space after hearing Captain Song's announcement. He was unconsciously bracing for the jolt, the squealing mechanics that he's come to associate with takeoff. He had been certain that with an older ship like the *Ohneul*, it would be even worse. Halfway thinking it's a prank of some sort, he slips on his shoes to pad out into the hallway. A peek into the cockpit reveals the black oblivion of space on the display, and Yoon behind the wheel. Her posture is as rigid as ever. He mentally mulls over a few greetings and conversation starters, but nothing sounds right, so Haven retreats back to the infirmary. After checking the time difference, he closes the door, sets up his screen, and dials the home number to Prometheus. The line rings a few times, and then the screen opens to his father's brown, wrinkled face.

"Haven!" His father's black eyes shine brightly. "You have time to talk to your father? This is why you are my most beloved pesar."

"Your only pesar," Haven says. "Drod, Pedar."

"As far as you know. Your father was quite the charmer back in the day." He laughs.

His father is still young, not that you'd know it from his appearance. The sun has aged his skin, and his rumpled hair is completely white now, matching the white and brown feathers etched around his neck, imitating the ruff of a Himalayan vulture. The tattoo etched on Haven's back is of the black and silver feathers of a white-rumped vulture.

"Did you try cutting your own hair again, Pedar?" Haven doubts the unevenness of it is a stylistic choice.

"Well, I don't have my usual barber on call, do I?" His father rubs his hands together. "Come, tell me. Your first mission. Your crew. How are they?"

"It's . . . they're . . . interesting."

"Tell me more!" He leans forward into the screen. "When I think back to my first days . . ." Haven doesn't need another retread of his father reliving his Alliance glory days. As if his father can hear his thoughts souring, he shakes his head in a nod. "Now, my beloved son. Has anyone caught your fancy?"

"What?" Haven stops scanning the backdrop of his father's video, the bookshelves of his study, the dust-speckled light he can almost smell.

"Come, come, don't be shy. I won't tell Esfir."

All the warmth vanishes from Haven's body. "No. Don't be ridiculous. I'm not here to do that. I'm not like—" He bites off the end of the sentence.

His father's smile fades. "You can't always help who catches your eye, Haven." Before Haven can respond, he surges onward, his brightness coming back in full force in a way that's too chipped. "You don't need to stress. Ease your way into the missions."

Haven knuckles his forehead. "I don't want to *ease* into it. How long do I have to be out here, Pedar?"

"It's only your first mission and you're already asking me that?" He coughs. "You'll no longer have to ask when it's time for you to come home. *If* you want to come home."

"Of course I'm coming back," Haven snaps. "Why do you keep saying that?"

"I never wanted you to neglect yourself in some attempt to protect me," his father says. Always so gentle, as if Haven's anger only rubs him smooth.

Haven says helplessly, "I've never thought I was missing out on anything."

Thierry had eagerly asked Haven if he was "out," as if Prometheus was some kind of prison. But an outsider could never understand the close-knit community of Mortemians, the sacred ceremony in learning the death arts. They're all free to leave at any point, and most are even encouraged to take a few years outside the community to gain perspective. And sure, some never return. But that's not Haven. He misses the ritual of quiet mornings with his father, the aromatic inhalation of rose water and cardamom from their morning tea. He misses the press of the sun against his skin. And it's not that he misses being around people he can touch; he misses not having to *think* about the touching or not touching.

"I know," his father says. "But I am your father. I still know a little more than you do. It is important that you try some time away from home. You'll learn so much that you wouldn't back here."

Deep down, his father is afraid of losing him, so he pushed him away. How typical of him, so like a Mortemian. Centuries ago, considered unclean, no one wanted to touch them. So what had they done? They turned it around, claiming *themselves* superior and saying that *they* didn't want to be touched. And as a culture, they chose not to engage in physical touch outside their community. So what if the Saturnians banished Mortemians to a moon because they didn't even want to occupy the same planet? Fine. Mortemians didn't want to live with them anyway. They thought of themselves as pilgrims instead of exiles, claiming the moon as a holy space. His father has always expressed his love for others by granting them freedom. He's a man who hides his fears and won't speak his doubts. And the only way Haven could assuage him was to leave. So here he is.

"It doesn't look like I'll gain a lot of medical experience. Class 4s don't see a lot of action. I might work on some research instead." Or something. He can only read up on the stats of Sinis-x so many times. He'll go stir-crazy if he just sits around.

"Class 4?" His father frowns for the first time. "I'm sure you could have ended up on a better ship, if you wanted."

It's true. Haven could have. But he simply wants to complete his time and return safely. Back to his father, back to his home, back to his real life.

"This suits me."

"I hope they appreciate you."

"They appreciate the extra money from hiring a Mortemian."

His father's face falls. Haven regrets how caustic his words are, but can't bring himself to apologize either, as if by acknowledging it, he'll somehow add to the hurt he's caused.

"Have they been friendly?" his father asks finally. Haven wants to laugh. It's like he's being sent off for his first day of school. Is Haven the type to play well with others? He doesn't think so, but nobody wants to hear that about their own child.

"They are very friendly," he assures him. "They're watching a serial tonight and invited me to join."

Kent had come timidly to Haven's door, letting him know that the crew were watching a serial together in the garage and telling him how nice it would be if he came by, no pressure of course. Oddly, he advised Haven to wash his face beforehand. His father perks up right away.

"Ah! Which one?"

"*Cemetery Venus?*"

"Oh, even your pedar has heard about that one." His attention isn't on Haven anymore but off-screen as he types, scanning another screen. "I'll watch it, too, so we can talk about it!"

"Ah, sure."

"You should go. Be with your new friends. We can talk later."

"Sure." Fatigue hits Haven all of a sudden. "Bye, Pedar."

The screen freezes on the image of his father waving, as if he's in a huge hurry to get Haven off the call. Haven checks the clock. It's almost 1900; they'll probably be gathering across the hall soon, although he's uncertain whether the whole crew will be there. He remembers how earnestly Kent's doe eyes shone as he apologized for trying to hug Haven earlier and shoulders the thought away. Instead, he pulls down the glowing keyboard from the screen and types *Cemetery Venus* into the search bar. He plugs in his headphones and hugs his knees up to his chest as the first episode starts to play.

After all, his father will be asking him about it later.

SEVEN

AS EXPECTED, the rain has been unceasing since Ocean landed them on Sinis-x last night. The lush forests are amply fed by the constant rain, but she landed the *Ohneul* in a clear space next to a large lake. Ocean can see the hulking shape of it far off to the right, a lone mammoth rising from the wilderness. Any establishments have long been dismantled, their parts carted away and frames taken over by greenery. Flying over the moon, Ocean had seen only the occasional vestige of a road, metal bridge, or isolated streetlamp.

Sinis-x was host to a robot AI facility once, which was summarily given up, leaving behind ghostly shapes of white metalloid robots all over. Rows and rows of frozen bodies, limbs stiff in the air. The weather contributes to a gloaming atmosphere, like it's some sort of purgatory or a Greek sculpture garden, and the air is slightly sweet smelling, which Von attributed to the rain's mixing with the soil. The *Ohneul* was hired to pick up some research samples from the area and perform a status report on the robots so

Anand Tech can assess what can be repurposed for future projects. It's inconvenient, out-of-the-way work that might as well have been done by other bots.

Von's taking care of the first part, and while Maggie and Ocean were suiting up to leave the *Ohneul* this morning to take care of the second, Sasani wordlessly joined them, zipping on his Alliance gear.

"Oh, Sasani," Dae said when she strolled by holding a bowl of oatmeal. "You don't have to do that. It's not your job."

Dae was freshly scrubbed, and Ocean had heard her leave and return to the ship early that morning before the others awoke. Sasani, on the other hand, could have just rolled out of bed; a thatch of his hair was floppily trying its utmost to defy gravity.

"I'd like to," he said simply, checking the seal on his suit.

"Well, don't strain yourself," Dae said, ducking back into the cockpit. "It's cold out there. And don't stay out too long."

"Wow, she *really* likes you," Maggie said.

Ocean didn't say anything aloud, but Sasani slid his eyes over to her, as if he could hear her uncharitable thoughts about marks and bank accounts. They'd stood under the stinging spray of the disinfectant shower and heat dryer that ridded them of possible contaminants, but it wasn't until after they exited the *Ohneul* that Ocean thought Sasani might be regretting his decision. At the garage opening, he stared balefully out at the rain.

"What's wrong, Sasani?" Maggie asked as she propped up a scooter.

"Nothing." He frowned and combed his fingers through his hair. "It's just . . . it's raining."

After waiting a beat, Maggie responded, "Riight. You do know it's going to be like this every day?"

Maggie cheerfully hopped onto the scooter and vroomed out into the rain, sending back a spray of drizzle. Sasani stepped backward and brushed off his suit, his movements strangely sluggish.

"You don't have to come," Ocean said. "Maggie and I can handle it."

"I want to be of some use," he said, then added quietly, "but if you'd prefer that I wasn't . . . if you would rather I wasn't there, I can stay behind."

His lips thinned and he clutched his elbows. For the first time, Ocean wondered what he was getting out of this. As a Mortemian, his skills as a medic far outclassed anything a Class 4 needed.

"You have steady hands, right?" Ocean asked. "They must come with the territory. I'm sure we can find some use for you."

He looked at her, eyes widened and suddenly awake. But when their eyes met, he careened away, almost stumbling right into a scooter. She grabbed the scooter handles before it fell over and decided to ignore his fumble. They stayed silent on the ride out.

At the first site, Maggie gave them a primer, opening up a humanoid robot for Sasani and Ocean. Now they're working through the rows of the robots, opening panels, running start-up tests, and organizing wire tangles.

After a while, Maggie says, "Huh, that's weird."

"What is?" Ocean asks.

"This robot's been tampered with. It's missing some of its parts," Maggie explains, standing. "I'm going to check down the line."

As she moves away, Ocean pulls on her nimbus to play music— "Alice in Wonderland" off the Bill Evans Trio's album *Sunday at the Village Vanguard*, back when they still had Scott LaFaro on bass. She hums along with the music, and at each robot, she waits for the light to flash green three times before moving to the next. On the album's third replay, she rolls her neck and checks to see where Sasani and Maggie are. Sasani has his head tilted up to the overhang, which is clear and sparks with a faint light every time a raindrop hits the surface. At her look, he says something, and she pauses the music and pulls down her nimbus to hear better.

"What was that?"

He points up. "What's the light coming from?"

"It's kinetic energy. The panels are Anand Tech, so they store the energy emitted by the raindrops hitting the panels," Ocean explains. Everything energy saving and energy converting on their ship is Anand Tech, allowing them to recycle almost everything to be used as power. It's why Teo and his family are one of the richest in the solar. "We have the same ones on our ship."

Sasani bends his head over his hands, exhaling a white cloud onto them. Maggie packed heat lamps to keep the chill at bay, but they've been working for a couple hours now.

"Maggie," Ocean calls down the line. "Time for break?"

Maggie's head pops out a few rows down. "Oh yeah! Time to eat!"

Ocean stands and stretches. Gloves only get in the way of the wire work, so her hands are red and sore. She massages her fingers.

"You didn't even eat breakfast, did you?" Ocean asks Sasani.

She noticed earlier that along with the portable heat lamps, Maggie brought her distinctive square rollaway bag. Maggie trundles up with it now, so excited that the bag skips behind her. She rolls it around and unzips it, pulling out a metal cooker, a hot plate, gas canisters, and other supplies. It's all terribly primitive, but Maggie derives a certain pleasure from old tech.

"You're not going back to the ship to eat?" Sasani asks.

"Sasani," Maggie says solemnly as she connects the pieces of machinery together. "The food would taste completely different on the ship. This meal is about vibes." She wiggles her fingers at him.

"I'm calling Von." Ocean presses her comm.

"Ooh, tell him to pick up ramen for round two. I forgot." Maggie's dumping a bag of dumplings into the golden pot and quickly adds water and a gochujang sauce packet that'll dissolve once the water boils.

Von's face pops up from Ocean's wrist. He's standing knee-deep in the lake, the water lapping around him. His eyes flick past her. "Wait for me!"

"Maggie says to bring ramen from the ship."

"How many?"

Maggie drops ddeokbokki into the mix with a wave of her wrist. As she does, she scans Sasani up and down. "Hmm . . . four?"

"I don't think four will fit into the pot, Maggie," Ocean says with amusement.

Steam rises from the boiling concoction, and Maggie pours in fish cakes and an alchemical mixture of spices.

"Use your judgment then!" she exclaims and upends a container of quail eggs, hardboiled and peeled. At this point, the pot is so full, she couldn't cram in anything else if she wanted. She stops short and looks up at Sasani with round eyes. "Um, do you have any food preferences or allergies?"

Sasani shakes his head. He's crouched as he watches Maggie's proceedings with a cautious yet inquisitive air, as if she's a wizard concocting potions. She pokes at the ddeokbokki with a chopstick.

"It's almost ready."

"Wait for me!" Von yells, and the video closes.

"Ddeok waits for no man," Maggie says. She pulls out bowls and starts ladling the soupy mixture, holding out the first one for Sasani. "Here."

"Me?" Sasani only reaches for it when Maggie shakes the bowl at him again.

Maggie blinks. "Oh shit, you're right. I should have offered it to Ocean first since she's the XO?" She shrugs. "Oh well."

Maggie's too busy ladling the next bowl to notice Sasani dubiously eyeing his ddeokbokki. Ocean doesn't think Sasani's reply had anything to do with Alliance hierarchy, and something in her chest hitches at how he stares at his bowl. She takes the next bowl from Maggie and hands Sasani a pair of chopsticks. He dazedly takes that as well, and Ocean plops down on the ground next to Maggie.

"Jal meokkesseumnida," Ocean says. She picks up the first piece of ddeok and bites. Maggie and Sasani echo her.

The first mouthful is just hot air, but then Ocean can taste the undertone of sweetness in the spicy sauce. Maggie likes to fold in a little brown sugar to the gochujang, adding depth to the red pepper paste. But Ocean's favorite part is the chewy consistency of the rice cakes. As it yields for her teeth, she tilts her head back to exhale the hot air like a dragon expounding a jet of flame. Maggie waves her hand in front of her mouth as she puffs a few rapid *hahs* and Sasani purses his lips to breathe out a stream of white smoke. He tucks back into his food, eating steadily. His face is flushed from the heat of his bowl, and he's pushed his hair back from his forehead so it's ruffled again. For a few moments, the only sound punctuating the patter of rain is their chewing.

"Is it that good, Sasani?" Maggie asks suddenly. "Your eyes are like . . . so sparkly." Sasani freezes mid-bite. Ocean can't help but laugh and he abruptly swivels to face her. As Sasani's eyes trace her mouth and the side of her face, she finds her laugh dying. "Von!" Maggie says excitedly.

Sasani flinches and wipes his mouth with the back of his hand, hunching his shoulders. When Ocean turns, she sees Von standing at the clearing, studying Sasani with a thoughtful air before he notices the simmering golden pot in the middle.

"You started without me?" he asks plaintively.

"This last bit is for you! And then we'll add some more water and, oh good, you brought the ramen! Let's get that started." Maggie pushes herself off the ground. In her haste, her elbow knocks into Ocean's side and clips her gun belt. "Ow!" Maggie rubs her elbow. "Do you have to wear that everywhere?"

"It's regulation," Ocean says mildly.

Maggie kneels as she takes the ramen packs from Von. "Does Dae carry a gun too?"

"Yeah, and a bonguk geom." Ocean tries to pick up a slippery quail egg, but it evades her chopsticks. Is it cheating if she spears it?

"What's that?" Maggie ladles the last bit of the ddeokbokki for Von and adds more water into the pot afterward.

"It's the national sword from the Joseon era."

Maggie breaks a ramen block in half with a satisfying crackle. "Wow, she's such an Alliance kid."

In other words, such a Korean. Dae with her Alliance-grade sword that opens and folds only when you say the correct Korean words aloud. Rumor is that if you ask it to yeolyeora with the wrong accent, it'll open in reverse to cut the user. Not that Ocean's ever tried.

"My gun wouldn't be of much use if we were in trouble anyway," Ocean says. "My aim makes people uneasy."

Von's leg jiggles a rapid staccato on the ground, and she's surprised to find Sasani narrowed his black eyes at her as well. However, she's soon distracted by a much more serious problem.

"Maggie, no!" she yells. But it's too late. Maggie's dropped a handful of cheese into the ramen.

"Don't be such a snob, Ocean," Maggie says with a sniff.

• • • • •

The connecting hallway from the *Shadowfax*'s common room to the kitchen is a media gauntlet. The walls run with displays of Alliance announcements, news from around the solar, mission debriefings, and the occasional classifieds ad. The *Shadowfax* is more like a luxury cruise than a serious Alliance ship with its extensive entertainment center in the common room, expansive quarters, and sauna. The crew is mostly made of Teo's ilk: kids whose influence comes from former generations. Though, admittedly, they look good for the cameras, as they proved when they dropped by the Moon to pick up the Seonbi Embassy for a heavily televised launch ceremony at Artemis. It won't be long until they reach the gate leading to Mars.

Teo glimpses Councilman Einarson on one of the screens and pauses. They have nothing new to say about him, other than a brief mention of his envirocampaign to reassess the solar's rampant terraforming. To no one's surprise, his project has lost support. No one wants to side with a man known for smashing another politician's face in beyond all recognition.

Teo kneads his own pounding head as he continues down the hall. His palmite rings as he opens the fridge door, and he automatically answers the personalized tone. Teo always picks up when it's his amma. Not only because he likes talking with her, but also to avoid the grief he'll get later if he doesn't. It never crosses his mother's mind that he might be on a date, watching a movie, or, you know, working. And it's such a double standard; if she keeps her palmite on her, she must keep it on silent. He lets the video slide out from his palmite as he arranges ingredients in the *Shadowfax*'s kitchen. If he's going to be 100 percent honest, the ship's large kitchen was one of its main selling points. That, and the fact that his father was able to maneuver him onto it after Teo disgraced himself on his last one.

"Amma," he says. "You ever make bugeo soup?"

"What soup? Why don't you try something I know how to make?" His mother squints on the screen.

But whenever he tries to make one of his mom's specialties, it never tastes quite right. If he asks her for recipes, she usually instructs him to "add enough" of something "until it tastes right." Also, he *really* needs bugeo soup. He opens the fridge and rummages around until he finds a container labeled LEE YOONCHAN 이윤찬 anchovy stock 6/21, TEO NO. The last two words are underlined several times. He pours a hefty amount of its liquid into a pot and adds dried pollack strips to it. He turns on the heat.

"We saw you on the news for the Artemis ceremony," his mother says. "You were so handsome."

"I'm always handsome," Teo says absently as he chops onions, radishes, and garlic. How much garlic should he use? More is always the answer. "I have your genes, Amma."

"Your father was so proud," she says and Teo frowns. "Weren't you, Ajay?"

Teo straightens and brings up his palmite to eye level. His father always seems too large for the screen, with his broad shoulders, thick mustache, and piercing Amrish Puri eyes that could wither powerful solar leaders, and who is Teo in the face of that?

"Teo, I hope you're taking the opportunity to get to know the members of the Seonbi Embassy."

Teo makes a noncommittal noise. The *Shadowfax* crew and Seonbi Embassy share dinner together, but it's been a rather polite affair so far. They're all quite reserved and . . . pretty. They mostly give off the air that etiquette is forcing them to be there and mingle with the crew. Also, they mostly speak in Korean.

"It's the *Shadowfax*'s responsibility to take care of them, you know. And you represent not only the Alliance but also Anand Tech."

"An enviable position," Teo says dryly. "Baba, you do remember that I'm a lowly soldier, not like a commander or—"

"But you *could* be. With a little more ambition. Consider all the good your brother is doing."

"Declan does so much good that you don't really need me to add on to it, do you? That's an embarrassment of riches."

"I was hoping that the ceremony would feature you more."

"Baba," Teo says. "As if I needed *more* attention."

Teo's already had a sensational Alliance career, and his entry into the *Shadowfax*'s crew was far from orthodox. To top it off, his father had insisted on outfitting his room, and his room alone, with an escape pod. He puts his palmite to the side as the soup begins to boil. He lowers the heat and adds the vegetables. His mother has conveniently slipped away, but Teo can imagine her just off-screen, scowling at her husband.

"Attention is a privilege," his father says. "And it's a tool. Rather than be embarrassed of your entitlement, why aren't you grateful for it?"

As the soup simmers, Teo cracks an egg into a bowl and beats it more vigorously than he probably needs to. His father sighs, and that breath holds the weight of Teo's past failures. It's all the reproach he needs. His father's disappointment is as easily parsed as a line of Shakespeare.

"Let me meet with Chau on Mars, then," Teo says suddenly.

"Chau? Anthony Chau?"

"Einarson's still denying he beat up Rawls. You need to pivot to someone else to champion your ecological referendum," Teo says. "Chau's not the obvious choice, but he's the right one."

His father's silent, which means Teo correctly guessed his father's next move. His father crafted the envirocampaign Einarson was supposed to lead. Outside all the work Anand Tech does to create sustainable technology, his father is a fierce supporter of ethical space exploration. Sure, Anand Tech got its start in the terraforming business, but Teo's father is against it now and passionately advocates for planets to be respected and left as they are.

"Chau requires a delicate hand," his father says.

"Right," Teo says. He tosses bean sprouts in the soup for a refreshing crunch. But it's still missing something.

"Teo," his father says tolerantly. "Why are you always thinking about what you can't do? You can do so much good in your current position."

Teo rubs his forehead. He has a raging headache, and this isn't helping. "What good am I doing with my position, Baba?"

"Teo," his father says, "being in a position of power means we have to take care of the people below us. I wish I had learned that earlier in my life."

"Yeah, I know," Teo says. He picks up a pair of chopsticks and halfheartedly pokes at the radish in the soup to see if it's soft enough yet. "I get it."

"I wish you would take this time to talk with some Seonbi," his father says.

Teo can't imagine how that would help his father. There's no political leverage to be had there, but maybe he hopes that their discipline will rub off on Teo. Or, ugh, perhaps he's hoping Teo will join their ranks. Teo ponders the years of training and asceticism involved, but also the uniforms Yi Jeong designed for them. Yi Jeong tailored the collar of their space suits to resemble a dopo's straight-lined one, and their sleeves are wide, long, and flexible. A cut in the back gives the illusion of a slit. The white neoprene is slashed with light blue.

During the launch ceremony, Teo's hands itched to sketch all of it. Back at Bangpae, one of Teo's favorite classes was about Alliance uniforms and the history of Korean style. He knows that Yi Jeong specifically modeled everything—down to the lapels and colors—after a style that lower classes were forbidden from wearing during the Joseon dynasty. She designed uniforms that are not only beautiful but also signify superiority. Teo would consider joining the Seonbi Embassy if Yi Jeong designed more clothes like that for them. Or, better yet, if he could try his own hand at it. He imagines telling his father that, and the words dry up. He'll send his sketches to Ocean instead.

"Talking with the Seonbi helped me gain perspective during an important juncture in my life," his father is saying. "I wouldn't be where I am today without them."

"I'm sure they're grateful to have helped you achieve your status as one of the most powerful men in the solar," Teo says. Even as the words leave his mouth, he's anticipating his father's glower. A cold lump forms in the pit of his stomach. When he dares to peek at the screen, he sees something even worse: his father's expression is disappointed. It's not that they aren't on the same page; they don't even belong to the same genre most of the time.

"Baba, if you keep hijacking Amma's calls, Teo's going to stop picking up," a familiar voice says off-screen. Teo goes hot.

His father harrumphs. "I have a few more calls to make before dinner anyway."

He's replaced shortly by Declan, who's watching his left, clearly waiting until their parents are out of the room.

"Don't take it too hard," Declan says. "Baba's still working on Einarson. The guy's denying he did it up and down the wall, but cameras and eyewitnesses place him at the bar where it happened. Baba is trying to convince him to plead guilty and issue an official apology . . . claim that he was under some sort of emotional pressure, or even that he's an angry drunk. But he won't do it."

Teo resists saying that he was trying to help, that his offer was supposed to alleviate his father's stress. "I know that."

"Right. Sure you do." Declan smiles that politician's smile they all share. Teo's not sure whom he hates seeing it on the most. "I'm sure it's not that interesting to you anyway."

"Of course not."

"Babu, don't take it like that."

Teo's stomach clenches. He rarely hears his brother call him that.

"Thanks for ushering Baba away." He pokes at the radish again.

"You don't need him telling you what to do. You've never had a problem knowing right from wrong."

Declan sighs as he rubs his forehead with two fingers. Teo's apology is at the tip of his tongue, but he holds it there. There's no use apologizing for something you're only going to do again. Declan drops his hand.

"What are you making?" he asks. "Amma said she didn't recognize it."

"Bugeo soup." Teo swipes to show Declan. "I think it's done."

"Isn't that . . ." Declan frowns when Teo switches the screen back to his face. "Hangover soup?"

"Maybe!"

Declan bursts out laughing. "I can't believe you. Asking Amma how to make hangover soup while Baba lectures you!"

"Not so loud, please." Teo winces.

"Sure, sure," Declan says. "Next time you're Earthside, come visit our parents, won't you? Ask Amma for her own hangover recipe. Yours could use some jalapeños."

"Really?"

"Trust me," Declan says.

The screen then goes blank. Declan, rudely, always signs off like that. No warning, just an instant disconnect when he decides the conversation's over. Teo opens the fridge again. After he finds what he's looking for, he slices up the jalapeños and adds them to the soup. He stirs and lets it simmer a bit before trying a sip.

Declan, as always, was right.

· · • · ·

After they've finished their ramen, Thierry packs up her metal cooker. Haven is overfull, content even in the rain. It doesn't smell much like the rain at home, and he's grateful for that. He hears whispering and although he should ignore it, he can't help but check over his shoulder. Kent is hissing something at Yoon and elbowing her away from her work of gathering up the utensils. When Kent notices Haven, he freezes. Haven immediately shifts away and then feels a sick swoop envelope his body.

"Sasani, let me handle that!" Kent hurries forward, holding out his hands for the bowls Haven was collecting.

"It's fine," Haven says roughly, but Kent tugs the bowls away from him.

"Maggie and I will take everything back to the *Ohneul*. Would you and Ocean finish up here?"

Yoon has her face tilted up to the overhang with an air of exasperation, and all those warm feelings from the food curdle.

"I can manage by myself," he says. "You all can go ahead."

"We'll finish up together," Yoon says as she rolls up her sleeves, stepping back toward the robot rows.

"Ocean, can I borrow your nimbus?" Kent reaches for the nimbus around her neck.

Yoon chops Kent's hand. "No, don't touch—"

Thierry's squinting at the robots. "You know what? I think we can just call it a d—"

Kent drops the bowls on Thierry's foot, cutting her off. He claps his hands, punctuating Thierry's yelps. "Fantastic. Thank you *so much*. Maggie, let's go! I'll make you some tea, which we can all agree is the superior drink to coffee."

"How dare you," Thierry sputters as Kent takes her by the elbow.

They noisily shuffle off together, and Haven hides a yawn behind his hand as he squats at the robot next to Yoon's. He organizes the wires methodically, getting back into the repetitive motions. It takes his mind off Kent's whispers. He stifles another yawn. Yoon closes the panel and moves to the robot on the other side of Haven. She successfully kept ahold of her nimbus, but leaves it hanging around her neck.

"Sleepy from the food?"

Even though the question's for him, she seems more concerned with the robot's innards. He has no idea of his footing around her. On the trip out to Sinis-x, Captain Song, Kent, and Thierry all came by his infirmary to chat or invite him to one thing or another, but he hasn't interacted much with her.

"It's mostly the rain," he admits. "I'm groggy whenever it rains."

She rotates her arm. "My right shoulder gets sore sometimes when it's raining."

"From your injury?"

"How do you know about that?" Her eyes snap to him.

"I've noticed you favoring it," Haven says as blandly as he can, reaching into the robot. He could bite off his own tongue. Thankfully, she doesn't press him.

"Have you ever been to Japan?"

Haven tenses at the question. "No." He winces at how tersely the word comes out.

"I went on a trip there with a steady once," she says. "We stayed at a ryokan in Kyoto for a bit. That first night, we were in separate onsens. Outdoors. I was alone out there in the rain. It was light, like this." She closes the panel and flexes her fingers. "The air was cold, but the water was steaming, and I felt . . . at peace. Like everything in me was loosening." Haven tries his best to move softly around her. She tucks a lock of hair behind her ear, and Haven notices an earring, a silver wing. As he's staring at it, she glances at him. "It's probably a bad sign that being alone was my favorite part of the trip, right?" Haven catches something swimming below the surface of her mocking gaze before she turns away and says, "I don't know why I went out with him."

"You didn't have feelings for him?" Haven asks cautiously.

She doesn't answer for a long time, and he doesn't know if she will. She switches robots, and it's like they're performing a dance, rotating around each other while they move down the line of white metalloid shapes.

"I did," she says. "But I'm not sure they were the right ones."

Haven's throat tightens. "Do you think you shouldn't have been with him at all, then?"

He likes the way she thinks over his questions carefully as if weighing them. The silence between them, which he had thought would be suffocating, is filled by the tapping on the overhang. The rain's coming down more steadily now, but he barely notices anything beyond the sound of Yoon's voice, the slight flush of red on the tip of her nose.

"I think that depends on whether I like who I am now," she says. "I don't think I liked who I was with him. I don't like who I am when I'm dating." She tilts her head. "Are you dating someone?"

Haven scrapes his hand on the robot's metal edge. "What? Why do you want to know?"

"That's a strong reaction." Her voice, on the other hand, is mild. "It was a natural follow-up."

From a distance, he hears himself say, "I'm betrothed."

What an old-fashioned word. Haven laces his fingers together and breathes on them. They're so cold they're going numb. He darts a look over at Yoon, but she's composed. It's calming, how unflappable she is. No matter what he says, she'll respond matter-of-factly. She reaches into her pocket and holds something out for him.

"Someone you know?"

"Yes." His response is curt as he automatically reaches for her, accepting the item. He feels the heat of it first. He can't read the hangeul on the pack, but there's a cartoon of a person printed on it, squiggly lines radiating outward from their clasped hands.

"Someone you have feelings for?" Yoon asks and slaps her panel shut, the bang too loud between them.

"That's not your business."

"No, of course not," she replies gently. "I didn't mean to offend you."

"You didn't offend me," he says. He doesn't know what it is, but her smoothness, much like his father's, bristles him like someone petting a hedgehog the wrong way. He bites his lip as he wraps his fingers around the heat pack's warmth. She studies him as if judging whether he means it.

"You should chat with Von. He's engaged, too, you know."

"He is?"

"Yes, and he's dying to get to know you better." Yoon raises her left hand and waggles her fingers. "Have you seen his ring? It's a good story. I'll let him tell you about her."

"You know her?"

"Yeah. Sumi. She's an Alliance Corps on the *Queen Seondeok*. She's very sweet, very headstrong. They're a good match, I think."

"What do you think makes a good match?"

The robot's green light flashes three times on Yoon's face. "Someone who makes you more, not less."

When their eyes meet, his flush is immediate, involuntary in the most unwelcome way, as if he's put the heat pack to his face. He opens his mouth to say something before he's decided what.

A loud chiming slices between them.

Yoon lifts her wrist, sliding open a holoscreen with the push of a button. Immediately, gunshots ring out. Haven stands as bright lights flash across the lake. Captain Song is on-screen.

"Ocean! I need backup!"

"Where?"

Yoon's on her feet. Haven looks up to see the blaze on the other side of the lake and back down at its reproduction on the screen.

"Follow the explosions! It's raiders. They're—"

The line cuts and the screen fizzles out.

"Get inside," Yoon instructs Haven brusquely "We might need you soon."

Haven hears it again, gunfire. Yoon runs for one of their scooters, leaps on, and pushes off the ground with a kick.

EIGHT

"ARE YOU AFRAID?"

"I am not afraid."

Haven watched as large wings descended on the bodies. His father clutched his hand firmly.

"Do you fear?"

Haven looked up at his father, who had just been abandoned by his mother. He squeezed his hand.

"I do not fear."

The spiritual exists within a thin veil over a mundane world. Death elides in life's curves. Haven has always taken Prometheus's values to heart. This is what he honors: a holy fire, a sacred earth, both of which would be desecrated by a dead body. So instead, they prepare and carry bodies for sky burials.

"Are you afraid?"

To condemn their way of life is to never see his father stretch his limbs skyward in supplication as he performs the ritual dance to coax vultures into descending. To accept that condemnation is to deny the grace of his own body as he dances with his father, imagining his tattooed wings unfurling across his back. To turn your back on the past is to be uncertain of your footing in the future.

"Do you fear?"

To fear death is to deny the equalizer of life.

But as Yoon speeds away on the scooter, Haven knows he doesn't want to die. Not today, not like this, not while his father is waiting for him. But if he only lives to protect his own life, if he lives in fear of death, then he has learned nothing at all from his father. Yoon wanted him to get ready to receive people in the infirmary, but people might be hurt already, and gunshot wounds don't have the luxury of time. Haven mentally confirms the contents of the emergency pack nestled inside his med officer's uniform. Then he grabs the handles of another scooter. He revs the right bar and pushes off after Yoon. She's already far ahead of him, her blue suit flashing. The rain pelts down even harder, the water stinging into his skin. He shudders. His wrist lights up and an alert beeps all around. Yoon's voice comes through the communicator.

"*Ohneul*, this is Ocean. There's been an attack on the west side of the lake. Dae says it's raiders. Stay away and take cover. I'll update you all when I can."

As Haven gets closer and the gunshots sound louder, he sees Captain Song sprinting. She ducks behind the white robot forms, hunching around a metal suitcase. Four hoverbikes weave in and out of the robot lines, the raiders aiming and hooting at her. Three have helmets on, but the one leading them crows in exaltation as he swerves on his bike, tossing glorious blond hair entirely unhampered by the Sinisian rain. Phoenix. Even Haven knows of him. One of the most notorious raiders. Here, on a backwater moon.

"Get down!"

Something collides with him, and he's tumbling, narrowly avoiding the gunshots that blow his scooter to pieces. Warm arms and the warm body they belong to wrap around his. Together they roll from the dirt onto a platform, out of the rain. Haven's palms slap wetly against the cold metal floor.

A hot breath fans his face. "I'm sorry."

Yoon pushes herself off him, her palm against his back a final warning to stay down. Her gun's out and she skids behind a contorted robot body, leaving him sprawled against the ground with a racing heart that has little to do with the bullets whizzing overhead. One of those bullets hits the robot directly above him, ricocheting off in a spray of sparks and dragging him back to reality. He gulps in a few lungfuls of air and forces himself up into a crouch, hiding behind the blasted robot as best he can while peeking through the negative space between its bent arm and torso.

"No!" Captain Song shrieks as a body hits the ground. Haven flinches and then scrambles to see who fell. Not Yoon, but a raider she hit. Captain Song screamed because Phoenix wrenched something out of her arms.

"Sorry, sweetheart. Better luck next time!" Phoenix yells and then uses the box to block Yoon's shot. "Aries! Gem! Let's go!"

He tosses the case to one of the other raiders and then races off on his hoverbike. Yoon raises her gun in his direction, but Captain Song stops her.

"No! Not him!" Captain Song snaps. The other two raiders fly in the opposite direction of Phoenix, leaving behind their fallen comrade. "I've got the one on the right."

The raider on the right holds the case. And Haven sees, with painful clarity, how Yoon hesitates at Captain Song's command.

She had the same barely perceptible grimace when Captain Song first reached for Haven's hand and Yoon paused before choosing not to interfere. Not to embarrass him or Captain Song. To defer to her.

Words he read on the confidential report come back to him: *For insubordination and reckless behavior, Yoon Ocean is hereby demoted, no longer fit to serve on the* Hadouken *or any ship above Class 4, and suspended for a month as of 34.10.01.*

Yoon adjusts her aim to the raider on the left. Haven can barely make out the hoverbike's bright lights under the rain and gloom, but Yoon hitches her injured shoulder up and it rocks back only slightly when she pulls the trigger. The raider on the left goes down like a stone. Captain Song fires two shots. The raider with the box flies away. Yoon lowers her gun, face blank.

"Shibal saekki nom," Captain Song curses to the sky. The raider's too far away now.

"Ocean! You jake?" Kent runs up, panting. He stops when he reaches them, bending his body over.

"I thought I told you to stay away," Yoon says.

Captain Song grabs Yoon's arm. "I need that case back."

Yoon glances at the raider speeding out of sight. "What's in the case, Dae?" she asks flatly.

"That's not important."

"Oh, I don't think that's true," Yoon says. "What's in it?"

Kent's puzzlement matches Haven's, but Captain Song's face contorts. Haven has to strain to hear the captain's words over the roar of the rain on the roof above them.

"I needed the money. I need that box," Captain Song repeats more loudly. "I . . ." She stops, then says abruptly, "Hajoon oppa would have done it for me."

Kent sucks in a breath through his teeth. Yoon's chin drops to her chest before she nods. She stalks up to Captain Song, who stiffens as she approaches, but Yoon brushes past her to the glowing hoverbike belonging to the raider she shot down. She steps over the raider's body. There's no blood. Haven doesn't even see any bullet holes in his suit, but the man lies completely still.

"Wait," Haven blurts out. "You can't—"

The words die in his throat as Yoon slides into the seat. Her feet move fluidly, her right heel punching down as her left comes up. There's the sound of a catch and the hoverbike beeps and rises in the air. Yoon looks back at Captain Song, her mouth tight.

"You could have just said please."

"Give her your gun, Dae." Kent's words are clipped and angry. "At least give her your gun."

Captain Song touches her gun, but hesitates. "I can't. It's against protocol."

"You can't be serious." Kent gapes. Captain Song cringes, but Yoon only pumps the pedal again and turns her bike around. "Ocean! Put on a helmet at least!"

Maybe Yoon doesn't hear Kent over the bike's engine because she only leans forward in her seat. The high-pitched whine of the hoverbike surges in volume as she shoots off like a cannonball, leaving a twin trail of red lights behind her.

"Be careful!" Kent yells uselessly. She's already gone. Her hoverbike skirts the brace of robots and then zooms away.

"We should tie this one up," Captain Song says dully. "And the one out there too." She walks over to her discarded weapon, a red glowing bonguk geom. "Ggeut," she says, and the sword folds up. She jabs it into her belt.

It takes Haven a moment to figure out what she means. He kneels at the body of the raider before him and pulls off the helmet. She's dark skinned with braided hair. He'd guess maybe around his age or younger. He puts two fingers to her neck and registers a slow pulse.

"I don't understand," he says.

"Ocean's weapon only stuns," Kent forces out. "She hasn't been allowed to carry a regular gun for years."

"Because of what happened on the *Hadouken*?"

Kent looks at him sharply. "How do you know about that?"

"She's going to get killed." Haven stands in a rush. "How could you send her out there?"

Captain Song scoffs, but her face is pale and pinched. "A stun gun works just fine. It still incapacitates."

"Only if she shoots her target in the heart," Kent retorts. Captain Song frowns uncomprehendingly at him, and he laughs disbelievingly. "You didn't know that? How could you not? You're her *captain*. A stun gun only works if she shoots the laser straight through the heart. Otherwise, it's completely useless," Kent spits out viciously. "And why was Ocean the one who warned us? Isn't that your job?"

"I lost my comm." Captain Song holds up her wrist, showing a bleeding red slash where her communicator should be.

Kent is shaking. It could be from the cold, but Haven notices his narrowed eyes, his hands that clench and unclench. "She's not some tool, some *weapon* for you to use and throw away, Dae."

"No one forced her to go."

"You did. After you said what you did, she had to."

As Haven gingerly arranges the limbs of the raider on the ground, he tries to remember any mention of a Hajoon in the report he read.

During his space training, he hacked into AllianceVision and riffled through some of their more confidential files. Bored, but perhaps more accurately, searching for something. Everyone at the Alliance space training had specific ships, specific roles, in mind that they were actively working toward. But Haven's goals for the future didn't include the Alliance. As a skilled medic, he'd normally have many options, but it was impossible to know who, if anyone, would welcome a Mortemian. The instructors were meant to guide and mentor trainees but mostly sorted them according to invisible social guidelines and some political agenda that was too specific for Haven to really understand. It hadn't escaped him that his peers from richer, more influential families were recommended to prestigious, big-name ships. No one offered him any help, and Haven purposefully sought out what the instructors purposefully held back.

During his late-night investigations, he found a report labeled *Class 1* Hadouken // *Incident 0913.xdsp*. It detailed an altercation on the *Hadouken* after it had been boarded by raiders. Several firsthand accounts and testimonials were recorded, but the ones that intrigued him most involved a pilot named Ocean Yoon.

One of the raiders took a Corps member hostage, their name redacted like most others. The raider ordered everyone to drop their weapons, and the *Hadouken's* captain commanded the crew to comply. But Yoon didn't obey. Eyewitness accounts were muddied. A slow-motion capture from the ship's cameras also failed to fully clear up the events, although Haven was unable to hack into *that* file. But the outcome was agreed. In the space of three seconds, the raider and his hostage were on the ground, the former very much dead and the latter alive, even if no one could tell at the time because of all the blood. Yoon took a shot to the shoulder, but that didn't stop her from decimating the remaining raiders.

The coroner's report afterward detailed two precise shots to the raider's body: one neatly severing his trigger finger and one through his heart. The accuracy would have been impressive on its own, but the *Hadouken's* captain, Casey Han, deemed it nearly impossible given that the hostage had been in the way. Perhaps that was the reason for the punishment Yoon received. *For insubordination and reckless behavior, Yoon Ocean is hereby demoted, no longer fit to serve on the* Hadouken *or any ship above Class 4, and suspended for a month as of 34.10.01.*

Haven knew about the Alliance's love of authority, but the punishment seemed to far outweigh the crime. Several reports corroborated, often begrudgingly, Yoon's skill at taking down the raiders, but always condemned her for endangering lives. Over and over again, the reports said that she had been lucky. Her behavior didn't exhibit the necessary deference and revealed a dangerous pride and nonconformity. She probably would have been expelled from the Alliance altogether if not for an entreaty from the Corps soldier who'd been taken hostage. He adamantly stuck by Yoon, claiming he wouldn't be alive if not for her. Haven found it all fascinating. Especially Yoon's testimony.

> **Q:** *Why didn't you lay down your weapon after Captain Han ordered you to? Why did you disobey your captain?*
>
> **YOON:** (Long pause.) *There wasn't a lot of time to think. I wasn't rationalizing it at the time.* ▬▬▬ *was going to die. I could see it in that raider's eyes. We'd drop our weapons and*

then he'd shoot ▇▇▇ *in the head. Some people play fair, but you can't expect that. I saw the opening and I took it.*

Q: *You deliberately disobeyed your superior's orders.*

YOON: *Is that a question? Captain Han was thinking about the well-being of the crew. I was thinking about* ▇▇▇*. There was just . . . There was no way I was going to let* ▇▇▇ *die like that.*

Q: *Your reckless decision could have killed everyone. It could have resulted in* ▇▇▇*'s death too.*

YOON: *I saw the shot. I wasn't going to miss.*

Yoon's unequivocal actions proved that her words weren't empty. For all of Haven's convictions, he doesn't know if he could move as Yoon did, even to save a life. She risked her position, her safety, and her soul. She had killed. How could she have accepted such a cost? He followed up to see where she'd landed and was surprised to find that she joined a Class 4 Transporter. Why stay in an organization where she was not supported or understood? Finding the answer seemed as good a reason as any to apply to the same ship. Maybe Yoon understood something, had learned something. Perhaps it was the same thing that still sparked stars in his father's eyes, something Haven had been sorely lacking while training.

It was easy to connect the dots, to deduce Kent was the redacted hostage Yoon saved. He originally suspected their relationship to be of the romantic sort, but seeing Kent and Yoon's interactions on the *Ohneul* dispelled that notion. Since joining the crew, he had been unable to match the woman he read about with the one he met. At times, he thought of her as a ghost, inexplicably bound to the ship instead of asserting the type of agency he'd been so drawn to in the first place. He even speculated whether the report had been about a different Ocean Yoon altogether. At least until he saw Ocean shoot her gun, until she tackled him off his scooter, shielding his body with her own.

"Where are you going?" Kent asks when he spots Captain Song rushing away.

"I have to . . . I'm going to check the other sites," she says over her shoulder. "They might have left something behind."

"Are you serious?" Kent yells after Captain Song.

Haven kneels at the raider's body and after a quick scan, he carefully rolls her onto her side, folding her top leg up.

"Are you going to tie her up?" Kent asks dubiously.

"No," Haven says. Even if he had rope, he wouldn't do it. He tilts her head slightly back. "We're going to keep her warm. Can you bring that heat lamp closer?"

Haven strides out into the rain to check on the other raider. This one's much larger; he'll need Kent's help to carry him back to the other. As he waves Kent over, he looks back over his shoulder to where Yoon flew off, but he can hear only the distant roar of the hoverbikes.

· · · · ·

The *Shadowfax*'s common room has screens set up all over, and Teo settles onto the couch in front of one showing a football match. He doesn't care much about it, but the other options are a serial he doesn't recognize or the news, and he's not in the mood for either. Teo plops down between Donna and Yoonchan, perfunctorily saluting the former. She rolls her eyes but scootches over so he can spread out, and holds out a bowl of popcorn to him.

"Who are we cheering for?" He takes the bowl and grabs a handful. Marv—M&M's peek out colorfully from his bunch.

"The team that's winning."

Teo points at the score, set at a dead 0–0. "So . . ."

Donna grips his arm to shush him. A player approaches the far end, dribbling. She stands, still clutching Teo's arm. This must be the team they're rooting for then. He hands the bowl over to Yoonchan, easily the calmer spectator, and inspects his handful.

"You know what would make this better—"

"No, ugh," Yoonchan says.

"You didn't even let me finish!" Teo protests.

"I don't want to hear about another one of your weird snack combos, Teophilus."

"Injeong, but hear me out. Furikake, the Zia brand of course, and tuna—" The player kicks and Donna yells, throwing her fists in the air. The goalie makes a fantastic leap, batting the ball away. Donna swears up and down a blue streak and only halts when her wrist comm beeps. She frowns down at it. "Everything jake?" Teo asks.

"Yeah, I have to go to the bridge. Captain Hong hailed me," she says, giving one last regretful glance at the screen. "Don't change the channel!"

"As if you would know," Yoonchan scoffs, cramming a handful of popcorn into his mouth.

"Don't do it!"

Teo and Yoonchan wave at her as she leaves the room.

"Wanna change the channel?" Teo asks.

"Nah."

They keep watching the game, but Yoonchan's buzzed head is bent over the popcorn bowl, brow furrowed as he composes the perfect chocolate to popcorn ratio during a penalty kick. He's about as into the game as Teo is.

"No!"

Teo cranes his head back toward the other side of the room, where the screen closest to the door to the bridge is showing the serial. It's a kiss scene and the camera is doing that zoom-circle thing around the couple. Finn, Haditoshi, and Dayeon are all reacting very strongly to it, although not in the same way.

"You have any plans for Mars?" Teo asks Yoonchan.

"Not really. I'll pick up some souvenirs for my family though."

Teo doesn't know Yoonchan's parents, but he's met all three of his younger sisters, who take every opportunity to attack Yoonchan, each going for a different limb so he can lift them all with a Herculean yell.

"How are your sisters doing?" he asks, and Yoonchan brightens. "Isn't Yoonji starting godeung hakgyo next year?"

"Yeah, but she says she wants to join the Alliance when she's done with schooling, like me. Yoonha entered a violin competition and came in second, even if my umma calls it first loser. And Yoonseon wants to quit ballet and take tae kwon do." He laughs loudly.

"Cute."

"How's your brother?"

"Busy," he says.

"Really?" Yoonchan asks. "I forgot to tell you, I saw him the night before we left."

"Is that so?"

"Yeah, at Psy/Cho."

That seedy nightclub in Gangnam? Teo clicks his tongue sympathetically. "Who was he with?"

"Huh? No one. He was by himself."

Teo shakes his head. "No way he'd be caught dead there. Not unless it was for business."

"Hey!" Yoonchan protests. "I like that place."

"It's just . . . not his vibe. Especially not alone," Teo says dismissively.

"Hmm," Yoonchan says, unconvinced. "I'm pretty sure that was him. You kind of look alike."

Teo flutters his lashes. "Is that your way of acknowledging how uncommonly dashing I am?"

Yoonchan gives a noncommittal grunt, and Teo decides to count that as affirmation. They watch the game some more, but after a bit, Teo checks the time. He can take a shower now and then read for a while in bed. He doesn't think anyone is back in the sleeping quarters. He has first watch tomorrow morning before breakfast, but he can still get a good six hours in. He stands and bids Yoonchan good night.

He's on his way out the door, across from the exit leading to the bridge, when an alarm blares overhead. Captain Hong's voice blazes over the intercom as Teo's comm beeps crazily.

"*Shadowfax*, shut down immediately. We have intruders. Seonbi Embassy, disengage. *Shadowfax*, whatever you do, protect the Seonbi. Repeat, we have int—"

The announcement cuts off, and Teo turns as the bridge door opens. A group dressed in unfamiliar space suits enters. Dayeon, whip-fast as always, has her gun up, but somehow, one of them is even faster. Dayeon's in their hands. Her back cracks over a thigh, body thrown to the ground. Teo scrutinizes the faces behind their helmets, the flags sewn onto their suits, but he has time only to think *Martians?* before they're shooting everyone down. Teo ducks and checks for the ever-present gun at his hip, but when he looks back up to take aim, he sees that no one has fallen. His team have all been shot, but not by regular bullets. Darts protrude from their bodies.

In front of him, Finn assumes a dazed, beatific face. He drops his gun. Haditoshi drops his too. One by one, a patter of thumps sounds as everyone drops their weapons while standing in place. Only Teo is on the ground, gawking at them. The Martian in front of the pack pulls out another device. When he pulls its trigger, a viscous liquid sprays out, covering everyone in gunk. But the *Shadowfax* crew maintain their sheep-eyed, glazed expressions. Some even smile.

The second Martian steps forward and Teo recognizes the weapon in his hand. Teo snaps up his gun, but the Martian pulls the trigger first, and flames engulf everyone around him. Each person who was doused in the liquid goes up in flames. The fire devours everything immediately, leaping from one body to the next in the blink of a thought. The heat sears him, but it's the smell that overwhelms. Teo gags at the sickly sweet aroma. Haditoshi's body slip-slides to the floor as it collapses in on itself. Larkin, who was watching the news, has fallen to his knees. Yoonchan rotates halfway toward Teo as if he can hear Teo's retching from a far-off place. But as he's turned to face Teo, his eerily placid countenance melts and glops to the floor. The sprinklers turn on, but it's far too little too late.

"There's one left over there!"

"It's him! Get him!"

Teo scrambles back. Scrapes the skin clear off one hand against the threshold. He reaches up and slaps at the door panel before a sharp prick nips the back of his hand. Then, a shocking spray of liquid drenches him. The door shuts, leaving him trembling on its other side. He pulls the emergency lock and it seals as he hears the torch of a flamethrower against it.

A dart's sticking out of his hand. He yanks it out and hurls it across the hallway. He frantically shakes out the hand, slapping it against the floor just to feel sensation. Then he fumbles over the zip of his uniform. It's heavy and slippery, drenched in whatever it was they were spraying. He undoes his belt, and the buckle chatters. He wraps the belt around his arm and clamps his tremoring teeth down on the leather, pulling it tight. But he can't stop the litany of words that come out as muffled screams.

The door shudders, and a huge dent punches inward. Teo falls back. Something slams into the door again, and this time, the crater is distinctly foot shaped. Teo could laugh because of course, *of course* now he's witnessing an actual augmented suit, only it's not so funny when you're the target and realize the tech allowed your attackers to break your crewmate's back like the spine of a brand-new book. He tries to move and slips. He needs to . . . he needs to get away. But everything is taking on a fuzzy filter. Softly muted like a bumblebee's buzz.

The door bangs again. A whirring revs on the other side. They're going to cut their way in. And maybe Teo should wait for them here. He can take down a few, at least go out fighting. But in response to that thought, he sees something else reflected in the closed door, red hot from the flames licking against it. Ocean's gun pointed at him. His past blurs with the present. He's lying on the ground with blood pooling around him, shots from Ocean's gun ringing in his ears.

Teo snaps out of it. He's fighting his drunken lethargy, hurtling forward. He thinks he's walking straight until he runs into the wall. He pushes off from it and trips over to his room, then shuts that door behind him as he shakes his head, trying to clear it. At the far end of his room is the smaller door to his escape pod. Well, he guesses he owes his old man an apology now. A half-full bag sits next to the pod's entrance. His emergency pack. He grabs it and hugs it to his chest. His vision skates around the room, the walls lined with bookshelves crammed full of titles that will probably go up in flames. He practically falls into the pod after punching the button to open the door. It slides shut after him, and the prompt is thankfully immediate.

DESTINATION?

The darkness threatens to overtake him, flickering at the edges of his mind. His fingers are sluggish, but he doesn't have to think about the numbers, a mercy. He squints at his swollen right hand and tugs at the belt around his arm to loosen it as the navigation system calibrates.

CONFIRM?

Teo reaches toward the screen to do just that, and it's the last thing he remembers before he's gone.

NINE

F OCEAN GETS THROUGH THIS, she's keeping the hoverbike.

The rain's blowing practically sideways with the wind as she races through it. She leans forward in her seat, her leg muscles tensed underneath her as the other hoverbike's lights get closer. She pumps the two right pedals and anchors her foot swivel using her heel as she skids around a curve. The pitch of the hoverbike's engine goes up a half octave as she urges it forward. She can't see the path, but concentrates on following the other raider, his bike a flash of aqua blue in the gloom, his lights a stream of ruby. She has to catch up with him first; she'll figure out the rest after.

The bike kicks and she controls the clutch release into the next gear. It's been years since she's ridden, but it's all coming back to her, proving that adage true. Ocean's lucky. The raider's crew, Phoenix's crew, if her eyes can be believed, must have chosen these hoverbikes because they're cheap and difficult as hell to drive—less likely to be stolen. This gen of hoverbike was built for drift-car fanatics and doesn't include the brake-lever mechanism along its handlebars. Hajoon specialized in cars, including the Nissan 240SX that he rebuilt, but he taught her everything she needed to know about clutches, pedals, and gears. It's all in the feet, and Hajoon always said her sensitive feet were her greatest asset. All those years of ballet training were the only useful part of her time at Sav-Faire.

The raider in front of her isn't bad. She's just better. Even with his head start, he's losing time on the curves. She drifts through them faster, instinctively carving the best line. As she rounds the next corner, her bike tilts sideways, and she dips down. The road races by her cheek, spitting water and gravel. As she straightens, the helmeted head briefly swivels back to her. She's glad she didn't take Von's advice to don one herself, even if the rain flicks her skin like a shivery spray of stinging nettle. It's hard enough to see out here and she doesn't know the terrain well. She should have read Dae's info packet. The raider revs up a steep climb and she closes in on him, pressuring him from the back. When the path opens up he cuts an abrupt left onto a bridge that stretches over the lake. She turns sharply after him, and the hoverbike whines in response.

Wherever he's leading them, it'll be better to force him to a stand before they arrive. The bridge is metal and slick with rain, the water sloughing off the edges in sheets. There aren't any railings, and that's what gives Ocean the idea. She speeds forward, kissing her front wheel against his hoverbike. It's not enough to throw him off balance, but he peers back again, just as she was hoping. Ocean twists her handlebars to the side and then punches the button on the front panel. Her hoverbike goes dead and slams downward. Ocean's ready for it, though, and uses the momentum to launch herself from the bike. The bike's still turning from her initial twist and as it hits the slick bridge surface, it careens into the raider. Ocean hits the ground hard and the air collapses out of her lungs like a popped paper bag. The raider leaps from his bike as hers takes it out. Both hoverbikes fly over the edge of the bridge into the water below.

There goes that dream.

But there's no time to mourn the loss because the raider has recovered a lot more quickly than she expected. He slides over to her, kicking her square in the stomach. Ocean's body slaps the ground with a splash. She tries to get up but slips, her boot squealing across the ground. She reaches for her gun. His gloved hand punches it out of her grasp. Pain arcs rocket hot in her face where he follows up with another fist. Stars explode in Ocean's vision. She should have kept up with her PT, but *raiders?* Again? What are the chances? She tastes the blood dripping down her throat and when she spits, red mixes with the phlegm. He rips his helmet off and swings it around to hit her. She catches the blow with crossed arms. Rain's pouring down and when she falls backward, it sloshes around her body. She quickly pushes herself up onto one knee but he's already waiting. She lunges forward to tackle him. He throws his helmet away and grapples his arms around her. Then she's flipped through the air, rolling again.

Ocean sees where she's heading and scrabbles against the ground, trying to get purchase. Her fingers lock into the grate at the edge of the road, just as her body falls off the bridge. She holds fast against the wrench in her arms. She's never come this close to having them torn out of their sockets. Agony rips through her right shoulder. Her scream erupts from her whole chest.

The raider looms over her. He could stomp on her fingers and that'd be it. Instead, he crouches down above her, pulling off his gloves as he does. She blinks water out of her eyes. He's a lot younger than she expected. Olive skin and catlike eyes. He has a hard, appraising gaze and dark, wavy hair that's being flattened by the raindrops.

"Phoenix is going to be pissed that you destroyed those bikes," he says flatly. "But I'm the one who'll catch hell for it. Thanks a lot."

Ocean grits her teeth as her muscles strain. "You shouldn't have let me catch up with you then."

He looks back at the way they came. "It was good riding."

"Thanks." She should enjoy the last compliment she might ever receive.

His eyes flicker back over her face and then at the name stitched on her uniform. "Yoon, huh? We didn't expect any Alliance kids out here."

"I think the feeling is mutual," Ocean manages. Her fingers are numb. She doesn't even want to think about pulling herself up. She *really* shouldn't have given up on that PT.

"The Alliance doesn't pay you enough? You have to work a side hustle?"

"What do you mean? We're out here on Alliance business."

"Sure you are." He points back at the box a meter away from them, which he apparently thought to save as he jumped from the bike. "That's why you're so desperate to get this back." Ocean doesn't answer. Dae's the desperate one. Desperate enough to rely on Ocean, to pull the brother card. "You really have no idea, do you? You Alliance sheep. Your captain says jump, and you ask off what bridge. Literally this time, I guess." He leans back and picks the case up by the handle. He clicks his tongue, more a twitch of his mouth than a sound under the rain, as he sets the box back down behind him. "Most of the AI bots here have been mined for their prime parts, unless you know how to pick them apart. That's where the money is."

Ocean hears a clink. The rainwater's pushed her gun down into the gutter, the same one she's laced her fingers through. It's not too far from them. Much good it does her, though. It might as well be on the other side of the moon.

The raider continues, "Your captain's the real bastard, but you're so conveniently *here*." His lip curls in contempt. He pulls his own gun out from his holster and leans the barrel against his temple. A dull throb of fear pulses through her body. Her arms would have started shaking if they weren't already quivering with fatigue. "And, well. You blindly obeyed her. To the point of murder, even."

"I didn't kill them," Ocean says.

"Liar." He barks a laugh. "I saw them go down. One. Two. Why didn't you shoot me?" When she doesn't answer, he laughs again. "Seriously? Because your boss told you not to?"

"Namisa," Ocean spits out.

She could have shot him. But for Dac it had been a matter of pride, and no one goes against an Alliance officer's orders. At least, Ocean doesn't anymore. He mouths her word as if tasting it, then wipes the rain from his brow and flicks it at her. He holsters his weapon, but before she can relax, he reaches for her gun in the gutter.

"You say you didn't kill them. That you didn't shoot them with this gun right here. Well, let's see how you feel when—" He lifts the weapon and frowns. His face goes blank. And then he's laughing so hard he's practically rolling on the ground. He takes his time with it, too, letting the last dregs of laughter sputter out of him before he winds up and sends her gun sailing into the air. "You came after me with just a stun gun?"

Her fingers slip and a white-hot pain gasps jaggedly through her right shoulder. She bites back a yelp as her hand loosens, and she tries to clench it tighter through the stiff cold. The water below is probably not toxic—Von's been traipsing through its shallows all day. But she doesn't dare shift her position to try to gauge how high she is. Again, she wishes she had read through those reports. Hindsight.

"I guess I can't murder you in cold blood then." He leans forward and clamps his fingers around her right wrist, pulling hard enough that he takes some of her weight off her fingers. He jabs at her comm. It rings, connecting straight to the number saved as priority. But when the screen pops up, it's not Dae, but Sasani. His black eyes narrow. The raider salutes him jauntily. "I thought I was going to reach the captain, but you'll have to do."

"I picked up the captain's communicator from the ground," he says.

"If you hurry, you might be able to get here before Yoon loses her grip." The raider tilts Ocean's wrist back toward the water below them. The vertigo sends Ocean's thoughts in a spin. The raider lets go, and Ocean grapples wildly at the grate again with her right hand. "Or you can fish her from the water."

"I don't like getting wet," Sasani says. His face is so still that the screen might as well be frozen. "You know how cold that lake is? Probably ten degrees."

"Don't bother," Ocean says. "You won't get here in time."

"I don't swim either," Sasani says in the same unconcerned tone. "The last time I was in a pool, it was only two meters deep, and this lake is easily ten times that." He looks off to the side. "I need to go."

He hangs up unceremoniously and the screen disappears. All Ocean can hear is her own labored breathing.

"You need better friends," the raider says.

"He's not my friend," Ocean replies automatically.

"Obviously. A captain who sends you on a suicide mission and keeps you in the dark. A crewmate who cares more about staying dry than saving your life." He cocks his head. "You could do better with a crew that had your back."

A sick lurch shivers through her body. "You offering?" Ocean asks acidly, but the raider doesn't laugh in response as she expected.

He rocks back on his heels. "You're a crack shot. And a wicked rider. You interest me, to say the least. And Phoenix would take care of you. He's good at that."

"Are you . . . are you trying to recruit me?"

He pushes his hair off his forehead and his answering smile dazzles her. She stares at him, completely speechless. He leans forward and tucks her hair behind her ear before holding out his hand. "'If I profane with my unworthiest hand.'"

Teo claims that *Romeo and Juliet* is a prosaic choice, but she recognizes the quote because he's dragged her to see it multiple times in London anyway. The raider's gray-green eyes are strangely luminescent, even in the gloom, his hand ghostly pale in the rain.

"'These violent delights have violent ends,'" she responds.

She lets go of the bridge and hurtles through the air.

TEN

THE WIND SNATCHES AWAY any fragment of Ocean's breath. If she doesn't fill her lungs, she'll be dead. But she's so cold. So, so cold. Mechanically, she points her toes down. Locks her knees. Folds her—

Ocean hits the water, and shock obliterates all thought. Ice replaces the blood in her veins. Her body plummets through the depths like a hand is dragging her down by the ankle. Her Alliance uniform might as well be a shroud. Voices rise inside her, overpowering her struggle. A chorus of women singing a Korean song with a lilting rhythm that rises and falls like waves.

"*Ieodo sana, ieodo sana.*"

"*Row, row your boat hard.*"

Ocean shakes her head to clear it.

"*Ieodo sana, ieodo sana.*"

"*Whether we're eating or starving, we dive in the sea.*"

"*Ieodo sana, ieodo sana.*"

"*Every coin I save goes into my husband's pockets.*"

Distant laughter greets the refrain. Ocean closes her eyes and sinks deep into the memory of the last time she dove into frigid waters.

Women in bright-pink goggles and black-and-orange wet suits burst from the surface of the water. As they did, the piercing sumbisori escaped from their lips, the whistles a release of excess air from their deep dives. Neon orange taewak bobbed in the water, holding the catches of the haenyeo. These fabled women divers of Jejudo, mermaids of Korea, call the surface of the water the line between death and life, and as Ocean broke through it, the refreshing air kissed her skin. She tried to produce her own sumbisori but just spit up seawater and dipped back to float on the waves. The water cradled her as boisterous yells volleyed back and forth. Each gulp of cold air stabbed her lungs, reminding her that she was alive. Each gulp of cold air reminded her that Hajoon wasn't.

On the boat ride back, the haenyeo chattered as they took turns at the oars. Even after all these centuries, they've foregone fancy boats and diving equipment. Part of it is pride, but mostly it's a surrender to the natural order of things. They never harvest too much, and nothing out of season. Otherwise, they'll disrupt the delicate ecosystem that sustains them.

"You're a good daughter." The older woman slapped Ocean's back hard enough to separate soul from body. She continued in Korean, "Having you close will be good for your mother." Ocean glanced at the boat's helm to her mother, the head of the Marado haenyeo clan. Her mother's back remained straight even as her body swayed with the waves. Her face was solemn and wrinkled, a map that Ocean's never had the legend to. "Such a shame."

Whatever else the woman might have said was interrupted by a chorus of heads shaking and tongues clicking. At the other end of the boat, an ieodo sana rose, starting another call and response that carried over the choppy waves. The ieodo sana's rhythm was suited to the boat's rowing pattern, but this round took on an extra poignance. The women around Ocean sang about reaching ieodo, the utopian island that awaits a haenyeo after death. Ocean heard the song many times before, but still she closely studied her mother's reaction. They didn't resemble each other much, but then again, her mother started training as a haenyeo when she was eleven years old, and this was Ocean's first time out in the water with them. When she was a child, her mother forbade her from going out in the sun, into the water, kneading sunblock into her skin every day until she was sent off to Sav-Faire at age eight.

"Ieodo sana, ieodo sana."

"Row your boat, and go where?"

"Ieodo sana, ieodo sana."

"Go deeper and deeper, it seems like the way to hell."

Her mother's face stiffened at the sudden sea spray. Every day, the haenyeo dive deep into the water. The women will dive no matter the circumstance: rain or shine, during pregnancy, often right up until the day they give birth. Sometimes, right after they've experienced the death of a loved one.

An hour later, they were gathered in a circle in the meeting room of the bulteok. Evolved from the fire pits of old, the new bulteok are equipped with central heating, shower rooms, and changing facilities. Haenyeo gather there before and after a dive to change their clothes and attend meetings.

And today, they were meeting about Ocean.

"We take a vote. We cannot accept Yoon Ocean unless every single member agrees. All in favor of accepting Ocean as a member of our clan?"

Hands went up, one by one, around the room. Even though the vote bordered on perfunctory, each uplifted hand was like a thread in a lifeline for Ocean. It felt like coming home. No, not like. It *was*. All these years, she had been away from Korea, from Marado. She saw these women during her holiday breaks, only in passing and with her mother. But this past week, she put names to faces. These were the faces of women who put their hands on her ribs, indicating where she should fill her body with breath to prepare it for diving. The faces of women who picked through shells as the taste of fish thickly coated Ocean's throat. Faces of women who conveyed their empathy with wind-roughened voices, whose hands were gentle as they tried to mend more than just the fishing nets in front of them. Today was Ocean's first dive after completing her training, the first of many with them. She couldn't wait to leave Sav-Faire behind, to—

Then, she saw one hand that wasn't raised. One hand held firmly down in a lap, unmoving.

Her mother's.

"Ocean-ah."

"Wae, Umma?"

Her mother didn't flinch. "This isn't your life."

Her reply in Common dug into Ocean's body like a bullet.

"It could be," Ocean tried.

Her mother turned to address her haenyeo, in Korean. "We haenyeo die every day, and we bring one another back to life. We rely on one another. The sea is dangerous and ever changing, but we survive because we share everything, together."

"But Umma, I—"

"We are not merely Jejudo haenyeo. We live on Marado, with the most dangerous waters." She put a fist to her chest. "Our haenyeo are the toughest, are we not?"

All around her, murmurs agreed and eyes avoided Ocean's.

"Umma, please. Give me a chance."

"This was your chance," her umma replied.

"How have I failed?" Ocean asked. "It was my first dive, Umma. I wasn't supposed to go too deep. I wasn't supposed to harvest anything. How have I already failed?"

The other hagun are young girls, not even a decade old. Ocean wasn't even asking to start as a junggun, didn't expect any special treatment for being the clan leader's daughter.

"I worked so hard to send you to Savoir-Faire, Ocean-ah," she said. "It's not too late if you go back now. You've only missed a few weeks."

"I can't go back there, Umma."

"In the sea, selfishness leads to death," her mother said. "You don't become a haenyeo on a childish whim."

"I'm not a child." But her words were strained and high. "I'm not a child," Ocean repeated in Korean, but her clunky pronunciation made it even worse.

"You're only a year from graduation," her mother said.

"I can't go back there," Ocean repeated desperately. "Not after Hajoon oppa—"

Her mother's face closed up. "Don't."

Ocean wakes violently, catapulted out of the memory, as water gushes from her mouth. That same cold air kisses her face, as if she's just broken the surface of the water. Coughs wrack her body, the air bruising her throat as she gasps repeatedly, her fingers digging into the sand grains beneath her. She's fine, but her body keeps convulsing. She's fine, but her body's convinced that it still needs to rid itself of something. Blurry hands, white forms move in her line of vision.

"Ocean, you're all right. You're good." The soothing voice repeats, "You're good."

Ocean welcomes the black void when it swallows her up.

ELEVEN

SOFT FABRIC RUBS against Ocean's skin, its many layers radiating warmth.

"She's up!" Von flaps his hands from his spot next to her cot. She must be in the infirmary. Maggie straddles the bench at a table nearby, tinkering away at a small device that has multi-colored wires poking out of it. Von reaches his hands for Ocean, then thinks better of it. He sits on them instead, bouncing up and down. "Ocean! I was so worried!"

"I wasn't," Maggie says. "Sasani said you'd be fine . . . but still, I'm glad you're jake."

"How long was I out?" Ocean's voice scratches painfully in her throat.

"A cycle." Von checks the hallway door. "We'll probably hit Galileo soon."

"We left Sinis-x?"

"If you're asking how, don't. I almost threw up with Dae behind the controls," Maggie pipes up. "Boy, did you miss out on a lot."

Ocean gingerly touches her face. "Did I?"

"Raider got you good," Maggie says. "I hope he looks worse."

"He doesn't." Close combat fighting has never been her strength. She carefully sits up in the bed. "What happened after I left?"

"Dae left, but Phoenix came back not long after."

"He did?" Ocean asks sharply and then puts a hand against her ribs. She has the feeling that over the next few days, she'll start remembering exactly how the fight unfolded.

"He was swinging back around to pick up the two raiders you shot. Good thing they weren't dead." Von frowns. "Though, I think he still might have done something to us, but he got a call that made him change his mind."

"I shouldn't have left you back there. It was stupid."

Von's eyes suddenly brim with tears. "That's *not* what you should care about!"

"You followed me here. I'm responsible for you," she says. "I take care of you. Not the other way around."

"Apparently, Dae was pocketing some robot parts for extra cash." Maggie rubs her fingers together. "Do you think she would have shared a cut with us?"

"Unlikely," Ocean says.

"She shouldn't have sent you out there." Von says. "You could have died! Over some stupid robot parts!"

"I didn't have to go," Ocean says. Those stupid robot parts had apparently been the solution to whatever money problems Dae was having. And that's all she needed to say. But instead, she pulled out that groin-puncher about Hajoon. Ocean had almost decided not to help after Dae provoked her, invoking *Hajoon oppa*. Exhaustion hits her, and she leans back on her pillow. "How did you find me anyway?"

"We tracked you through your comm."

"You fished me out?"

"No, you were already on the shore when we arrived." Von shakes his head. "You got yourself out of the water. You don't remember?"

What Ocean remembers is her mother saying "In the sea, selfishness leads to death." She covers her face with her hand. Von lets out a ragged sob and tears stream down his face. Ocean pats his head awkwardly as Maggie blinks at them, nonplussed.

"Of course you swam to shore. You're descended from a long line of haenyeo, aren't you?" Maggie confirms.

"I don't like swimming," Ocean answers curtly.

"Oh, what's that about?" Maggie puts down her gadget. "Family drama thing?"

"I think Yoon needs some rest." A voice skips into their conversation, not from the hallway door but from Sasani's bedroom. Sasani leans against the doorway, and for a moment, Ocean catches a keen relief in his eyes before his expression shutters into his ever-polite facade.

"Right. Doctor's orders. Of course." Von sniffs as he rubs at his eyes, now swollen and bright red.

"Can I rest in my own room?" Ocean asks Sasani.

"If you let Kent help you back," Sasani says. "And if you agree to stay put. Most of your injuries are cosmetic, but you have some bruised ribs I want to keep an eye on. I'll come by with ice for your shoulder later too. I'd also advise against laughing too hard at anything."

"Are those doctor's orders too?" Ocean asks.

"Maybe general life advice," Sasani counters.

Ocean smiles at the mild bite to his tone. He turns away at that, and the deliberate movement reminds her of his sign-off during their call earlier. It must have happened right before Phoenix arrived.

"She can still watch *Cemetery Venus* though, right?" Maggie asks. "It's not a funny show or anything. And we've been saving the next episode for so long."

"Maggie!"

"What? Aren't *you* curious about which of Rian's half siblings betrayed him?" Maggie retorts. Ocean's touched that Maggie waited to watch the next episode. The last one ended on a cliff-hanger, and it's never easy to avoid spoilers when you're behind. "But if you ask me, it's Naomi. It's always the steady. Or the ex-wife. You can tell she doesn't actually want to find him. She's just pretending."

"I think she really loves him."

The comment is almost whispered, but it still stops them all short. As one, they rotate toward Sasani. His skin goes bright red.

"Have you been watching *Cemetery Venus*?" Von asks.

"Without us?" Maggie adds.

"My father is really into it," he says quietly, looking anywhere but at them. He rubs the back of his neck. This time, Ocean can't help the laugh that spills over at Sasani's bashful expression. But, true to his word, she immediately regrets it. Von's hands are on her shoulders, and Sasani jerks forward a step. "I warned you."

Ocean waves a hand, whether in response to Sasani's comment or to reassure Von, she's not certain. She pushes back the covers and Von kneels in front of the bed.

"Ocean, get on my back."

"Don't be ridiculous," she says.

"*You're* the ridiculous one!" he cries. "I carried you back to the ship, I can carry you a little farther!"

"My room is next door, Von." Ocean is about to slide from the bed, but Sasani steps forward again, folding his arms. "I'll lean on your shoulder," she concedes.

Back in her own bed, she lets Von arrange her blanket and fuss around the room.

"Here," Von says as he puts something on her bedside table.

It's one of the lychee soda cans that magically appeared outside Ocean's Alliance dorm room the morning after her grocery jaunt with Teo. She automatically reaches for it, but Von parries it out of her reach.

"Don't drink it," he says. "I don't think it's good for your throat."

"Are you taunting me?"

"Doesn't it make you happy just to see it?"

She'd answer with a retort, but her lids droop before she can, her body weighed down into the mattress. Her last thought is about how nicely Von's tucked her in.

 · · • · ·

Godsdamn his curiosity. Or his latent shame at being found out. Haven doesn't know what exactly prompted him to come, but here he is, pushing open the garage door, face damp and freshly scrubbed. A large couch sits in front of a projector, which has been pulled down in the middle of the room. Classical music streams over the speakers, and Thierry bobs her head as she circles a table in her hoverskates.

"Sasani! You came!" Kent's happiness blossoms as if Haven is his long-lost brother. "I *told* you he would."

Yoon still has a starburst of broken blood vessels on her right cheek, and her bottom lip's cut. She raises her piled plate in greeting.

"Oh bon, you washed your face." Thierry pops up at his elbow and he jumps. She's wearing a white sheet mask. "Take one. Use these bobby pins if you want to pin your hair back."

"Maggie picked these up in Seoul." Kent also plucks a face mask.

Haven grabs a couple bobby pins to pin back his hair from his forehead. He then takes a face mask. He holds it out, both ends pinched gingerly, until he notices Yoon observing him.

"You're making a mess," she says, pointing to the sheet mask dripping on the ground.

Haven hastens to the mirror at the table, using it to align the mask correctly, which he judges using the eye holes. Covertly imitating the others, he smooths the cold, wet mask down, easing out the wrinkles. As he does so, he recognizes the music playing on the speakers.

"This is the *Cemetery Venus* theme song, isn't it?" Haven asks.

"So, you *have* been watching," Yoon mutters as she takes the last face mask. Haven's grateful that his sheet mask hides his burning face.

"Close!" Thierry responds eagerly. "It's Holst's *The Planets* suite. They use the *Venus* theme as a motif in the serial! Isn't that clever? Holst is popular, but some people argue that Haori Nakada's composition is the definitive space opera—"

Kent passes Haven a plate and loudly whispers, "Better prepare your plate now or she'll never stop."

A chattering Thierry trails behind Haven as he fills a plate with Turtle Chips, a Choco Pie, and a glorious mess that Thierry interrupts her stream of music talk to explain is gourmet kimchi nachos. Kent and Yoon are seated on the squashed couch and completely evade his aggrieved, albeit silent, pleas for help. After his plate has been filled an acceptable amount, Thierry breaks away from him to take her own place, sprawling across the ground. Haven takes the last seat on the couch, to Yoon's right.

"Is Captain Song coming?" he asks.

Captain Song has been conspicuously holed up in her room since they left Sinis-x. Her ramshackle takeoff from the moon had taken Haven straight back to Alliance training simulations. He had been in the infirmary with Yoon by then and couldn't help but compare the turbulence to the smooth glass of her flying, how she coasted through the atmospheric changes seamlessly. Thierry spent so much time retching into the toilet while adjusting to Captain Song's flying that they were already in the air by the time she heard about what happened with the raiders. And besides that, they'd all been distracted by Yoon's recovery. Captain Song has offered no explanation or apology since.

Kent scowls. "She never joins us, but after what happened, she's not invited."

"Batshit captain could've gotten us killed." Thierry cringes guiltily at Kent. "Sorry."

Kent raises his eyebrows. "For what?"

"For swearing. I mean, I know you've said you don't care. But for some reason, I don't like cussing around you. Anyway, I've been asking around about openings on other Alliance ships, but pickings are slim."

"Choose wisely." Kent unwraps his Choco Pie with a rustle and crams it into his mouth. He chews angrily. "Life's short enough without having to work for someone so selfish."

"Yikes. I never thought I'd hear you speak about someone so badly," Thierry says.

"I know Dae's always pinching marks, but I never thought she'd go this far." Kent delicately wipes the corners of his mouth free of crumbs while avoiding the edges of the face mask. "Do you think you'll stay on with the Alliance, Sasani?"

"Me? I don't know . . ." After a beat, he deflects, "XO Yoon?"

"That's Mr. XO Yoon," Thierry corrects.

"Please. Mr. XO Yoon is my father," Yoon says. Then, she adds, "I might stay here, actually."

"I'm sorry, what?" Kent coughs and crumbs fly through the air. He leaps to his feet, plate gripped haphazardly in hand. "Ocean, she almost got you *killed*. There were raiders! *Why*—"

"Von," Yoon says. Kent's still standing, his plate pointed at Yoon's face. "You don't have to follow me. I'll be jake."

Haven's not sure what falls faster, Kent's plate or his face.

"Yikes," Thierry says again nonchalantly, catching the congealing cheese from falling off her chip. She shoves the whole mess into her mouth. "Ocean, have you even seen your face? That is not jake. It's messed up."

Kent deflates and flops on the couch. "The whole situation is messed up," he mutters.

Thierry turns off the overhead music and lights and starts the episode. It picks up right where the previous one left off, with Rian waking up in a laboratory, tied down to a cot. He spends a lot of time in this serial getting tied up and finding a way out of it. Venusians swarm around him. A few have the same extra mechanical limb Thierry uses. They mumble technical jargon Haven can't decipher.

"In Common, please?" a non-Venusian character says tartly.

"Such a stupid stereotype," Thierry scoffs. "Just because they live on Venus doesn't mean they're all tech geniuses."

"Shh."

Thierry swivels her head to Haven and stage-whispers, "Von's very serious about his serials."

"Shh!"

About ten minutes in, Rian's broken free and is fighting a handful of Venusians single-handedly. Haven leans forward, enthralled. He has no idea when this series suddenly morphed from soapy drama to action-thriller, but he's definitely not complaining.

"Want one?"

He automatically closes his hand over the fruit Yoon offers. On-screen, Rian does a flying kick. He is hurled to the floor and quickly throws himself back on his feet. Haven peels the fruit while keeping his eyes glued to the action. His mouth waters at the bright, juicy aroma, and he pops a slice in his mouth, savoring the burst of freshness. It's surprisingly sweet. The whole thing disappears all too soon and when Yoon holds out another, he takes that one as well, easily peeling while Rian throws a Venusian over his shoulder.

"So, you do like citrus?"

Haven gawks at his hands, at the spiral of two peeled tangerines, the frayed whites he unconsciously tore off the slices. The piths. His mouth goes dry as he thinks, ridiculously, of how he's always loved the way the soft fuzziness of the name accurately describes the piths' tactile reality. His head snaps to Yoon, all Rian's acrobatics forgotten, but she's watching the screen, sipping from her drink. She holds out another tangerine. He takes it and settles into his seat, doubly grateful for the sheet mask and the darkness now.

At about the halfway mark, when *Cemetery Venus* hits a transition point, Thierry pauses the show and turns on the lights. She picks up the bin next to her and extends it to them. Both Yoon and Kent pull off their masks. Thierry holds up a hand when Haven starts to do the same.

"Make sure you peel the mask from the bottom up," she instructs.

Kent freezes while in the middle of patting down his face. "Really? I thought it was from top down?"

Everyone looks at Yoon, and she taps her shoulder. "Does it matter?"

"*Yes*," Thierry says with a scandalized tone. "Just uh . . . I don't know which way is the right way."

Haven has his hands on the edge of his sheet mask, waiting.

"Maybe you should alternate," Kent suggests.

"Cover all your bases." Thierry nods sagely.

Yoon sighs up at the ceiling. Haven strips off his mask top down, as he was originally planning to do, and places it into the bin. Everyone is massaging their own faces.

Kent notices his confusion and explains, "We have to make sure our skin properly absorbs what the face mask left behind. Use your fingertips and make circular motions, like this. Or pat down."

Thierry slaps her own cheeks with more enthusiasm than is probably warranted.

"And what's the purpose of this?" Haven asks.

"Dewy skin, obviously," Yoon says.

"It depends on the mask." Kent frowns at the packaging. "This one's specifically for hydration."

"Glow, baby, glow!" Thierry says enthusiastically. "You can't leave the mask on for too long either. That's a rookie error."

Haven imitates their movements, rubbing the mask's residue into his skin.

"No, no." Thierry stretches out her hands. "Listen, it might absorb better if you pat it in. Want me to do it for you?"

"No!" Kent exclaims. Haven draws backward reflexively. Kent's halfway across Yoon, about to tackle Thierry.

"It was a nongdam!" Thierry rubs vigorously at her face. "You have *the* scariest expressions, Sasani. I thought Ocean was bad, but you gave me daksal." She points at her arm to show him the actual bumps. "Do they teach you that at Vulture school?"

"Maggie!" Kent's mouth drops open.

Thierry wrinkles her face before she says to Haven, "Dae's always saying I need more noonchi." She bends over the remote control.

"What does that mean?" Haven asks.

"Noonchi?" Kent puzzles over it. "How would you describe it, Ocean? It's like . . . awareness?" Then he blinks and flaps his hands frantically in Thierry's direction. "I mean, not saying that you don't . . . that is—"

"Huh?" Thierry goggles at them, distracted from fiddling with the control. "I think there was a slight delay with the audio, don't you think?"

"It's about being able to read the situation," Yoon says. "The literal translation is eye feeling? Eye measure? Like, if you asked someone out on a date and they said, 'Wow that sounds like so much fun, let's invite all our friends.' Someone with noonchi would take the hint."

"But some activities are more fun as a group," Thierry protests.

"Not if you like the person asking," Yoon says.

"People say circle when they mean triangle. But if it's a triangle, why wouldn't they just say triangle?" Thierry scowls.

"Because sometimes people can't see the shape of their feelings clearly," Haven says.

"Sasani, I really like that." Kent's eyes might as well have sparkles in them, and try as he might, Haven can't take his comment as patronizing.

"I bet you have *great* noonchi," Thierry says glumly.

Haven's not so sure about that. Even if he can tell that a circle is sometimes code for a triangle, he has no idea where to go from there.

"I'm sure it takes a lot of EQ to be a good Mortemian," Kent says thoughtfully.

"I have plenty of emotional intelligence!" Thierry protests.

"You do," Yoon agrees. "More importantly, you're honest. I like that."

"Yeah. Besides, Gremio used to say you have *too much* noonchi. He said that's worse."

Kent's eyes dart to Haven at the mention of Gremio, but Yoon diffuses the moment by saluting Thierry with her lychee soda can. "And there's that honesty."

"How can someone have too much noonchi?" Haven asks.

"At our first *Cemetery Venus* session, Ocean told Von and me that we should call you by your last name instead of your first. When I asked her why, she just said that you'd probably prefer it. But I know she didn't ask. Is that a Vulture thing too?"

"Maggie!" Kent hisses.

"What?" Thierry asks.

"Sasani called us by our last names, so I assumed he'd want the same. It was just an assumption . . . and that's probably why having too much noonchi is bad."

"But it's true." Haven resists the urge to rub at the back of his neck, where the heat's inching up his skin. "It's not a Mortemian thing, though."

"I wouldn't burden Sasani by assuming he's representative of the whole culture," Yoon says dryly.

Haven's never wanted to represent Mortemians as a whole, as if everything he does is emblematic of his culture. But at the same time, why shouldn't he? Is he such a poor example?

The door slams open. Captain Song strides in. She's dressed in her coveralls, but her hair is down. She halts in the middle of the room, and her eyes skate over the group assembled, the snacks strewn about. She points at the projector.

"Turn on the news," she says.

"Dae, what —" Kent starts.

"Turn it on," she says.

Thierry fumbles for the remote. "Which channel?"

"It doesn't matter."

Thierry flicks on the TV and Haven barely glimpses the headline splashed across the bottom, ALLIANCE SHIP *SHADOWFAX* DESTROYED WHILE ESCORTING SEONBI EMBASSY, before Yoon's on her feet, blocking the screen.

"No." Kent raises his hands to his mouth.

"What? How?" Thierry asks.

"They sent out the announcement over AV. Weren't any of you paying attention?"

"Von always makes us shut off our comms before we watch *Cemetery Venus*."

Thierry reaches for her wrist comm along with the rest of them. Haven swipes open the flashing bulletin and scans through the report, catching snippets of information. They lost contact with the *Shadowfax* and haven't yet found any survivors, but he's more concerned with Yoon, whose face has gone completely pale. She's moving through the article on her nimbus so quickly, she can't possibly be reading. She's searching for a name, he realizes.

"We have to go out there, Dae," she says.

Captain Song blinks. "Out where? To do what? The Alliance already sent ships to salvage the wreckage. I don't want to get in the middle of that mess, Ocean. It's just pieces of an exploded ship. And any bodies they're finding aren't exactly . . ."

If possible, Yoon goes even paler.

"Dae," Von interrupts sharply.

"What?" Captain Song snaps back. "I knew people on that ship, all right? Donna Shim was in my graduating class. But what can we possibly do to help out there?"

"I can't do nothing," Yoon says.

"Why do you even care?" Captain Song stares at Yoon, baffled and somehow unable to put the pieces together, even though it's so clear to Haven. Yoon flinches. Captain Song lets out a big breath and starts braiding her hair. "It's not worth talking about. We're en route back to Seoul."

"You owe me," Yoon says.

Captain Song pauses mid-braid. "Excuse me?"

"You owe me," Yoon repeats, enunciating the words as if Captain Song is hard of hearing.

"I am your commanding officer, Ocean," Captain Song bites out. "You do *not* talk to me like that." She steps forward and jabs a finger into Yoon's shoulder. "I owe *you*? I gave you this position when no one else would *touch* you." Captain Song pushes farther into Yoon's space, the words spilling out of her. "And what have you done to thank me? Nothing. Because you've just been handed everything your whole life. You don't know what it is like to have to fight for your position. You're selfish. You think I'm just going to hand over control of my ship? Have you even thought about the other people onboard? Do you think they'll want to fly along with you on an unpaid mission?" Captain Song spreads her arm out to indicate the room, as if to seal her point.

Kent stands up behind Yoon. "I go where Ocean goes," he says.

Captain Song falters and looks to Thierry, who's still cross-legged on the ground. Thierry shrugs. "I don't see why not, Dae," she says. "Ocean got a bad deal on Sinis-x. I mean, I don't know what all went down, but look at her face."

A flicker of desperation crosses Captain Song's face, and she says to Haven, "Haven—"

"I'd be happy to offer aid to our fellow Alliance members," he says. "What happened is a tragedy, and we should help where we can. And after our last mission, it wouldn't hurt to earn goodwill with your superiors. Don't you think, Captain Song?"

She seems to collapse in on herself, and in that moment, Haven almost pities her, with her posture and half-done braid unraveling.

"We don't have enough fuel to get there," she says.

"There's a refueling station on the way," Thierry says. She's typing away at her tabula. "Daltokki-5."

"All right," Captain Song says. She won't look at any of them, but continues more firmly, "We'll go. It's our duty as Alliance members. I'll check in with the Alliance to let them know."

"Good." Yoon squats down next to Thierry. "What's the best route? I can—"

"No," Captain Song interrupts.

Yoon raises her head, and Captain Song folds her arms, her mouth a straight line.

"No, what?" Yoon asks.

"You won't be flying us there, Yoon. In fact, after we land in Seoul, you'll never fly Alliance again."

"Dae, you can't—" Kent protests.

"I can," Captain Song says. "Maggie, send me the coordinates of Daltokki-5. I'll take it from here."

Yoon's expression as she watches Captain Song retreat cuts Haven to the quick.

"Ocean," Kent ventures. "Do you want to talk—"

"It's fine," she says. Yoon steps back from Kent's outstretched arms. She turns and leaves the room as well.

TWELVE

THE VIEWS on AV of extracted footage are already in the millions. A pod latched on to the *Shadowfax* and received permission to board. Then, in a ritualistic manner, the intruders went through the entire ship and on to the connecting Seonbi Embassy's ship, shooting, spraying, and lighting on fire. And as every single person burned, they bore it placidly. Stoic wasn't even the right word to describe their demeanors. A few grisly close-ups showed many faces smiling.

The reason the intruders were so readily granted access to the ship was soon ascertained. They were a group of Martians claiming to be the vanguard of the embassy's meeting.

Now the solar is in uproar. The Seonbi Embassy closed their borders on the Moon. Koreans are demanding retribution. Families are mourning. Martian Diplomats are saying lots of things, but mostly, they're denying everything. The *Shadowfax* and Seonbi ship were destroyed. Bodies are still being salvaged and identified, but progress has been slow. Ocean knows that going out there is selfish and pointless. But she still needs to be there.

There's been no news on Teo, and none of the retrieved footage showed sign of him. And stupidly, as if no one else has tried it, Ocean's been sending message after message to him. She's even pulled up Declan's number, but . . . she has nothing to offer him.

It's going to be jake.

Let me know how I can help.

As if what Declan needs is yet another empty promise or person to tell what to do, someone else to reassure that he's fine when he's not.

Ocean can't keep refreshing her Alliance inbox and watching the news. So, she's mopping. After Dae barred her from the cockpit, she told Ocean to make herself useful and clean the ship. In response, Von muttered something impolite and distinctly un-Von-like under his breath, but Ocean had honestly been glad for the distraction. While mopping, she tried listening to Nam Jin—there's nothing like the Seoul Playboy to drive away anxious thoughts—but felt the noise pushing her closer to some sort of edge and pulled off the nimbus. The only thing that would help, the only thing that could make her feel *something* else, was taken away from her.

You'll never fly Alliance again.

When Ocean first got behind the Alliance controls in her cockpit, it went against everything she learned from Hajoon. The automation protected the ship from sliding, from drifting in the air, from crashing, but it also made the ship impossible to drive the way she'd been taught. She had spent countless nights locked in flight simulators to relearn the basics, but she kept failing and failing until Captain Lee, one of her instructors, found out about her nightly study sessions. When she learned that Ocean was Hajoon's sister, she told her about the pedals her brother had self-installed in his own cockpits. Captain Lee found one of the ships her brother had remodeled for Ocean to try instead. After that, Ocean was still staying up all night, every night, but for the sheer exhilaration of it. She still wanted, no, needed, to get better, to be better. Something she'd never had the chance to do in the water.

Ocean can still see the smug face Dae bore as she condemned her: no more pedals beneath her feet, hands on the wheel, oblivion of space before her.

"Do you want some help cleaning the engine room?"

The voice, although soft, startles Ocean. Sasani leans his long form against the doorway. He has some sort of cloth folded over his shoulder.

"It doesn't really need much cleaning," Ocean admits. Von also came by to help, but she chased him out. The floor still has the slick reflectiveness of a new mopping from her second time going over the room.

"In that case," he says. "Would you do me a favor?"

"What?"

He steps into the room on the balls of his feet, with an over-exaggerated care so as not to mar her work. Ocean is about to tell him not to bother, but she's silenced by the graceful way he moves. He pulls down the cloth from his shoulder. As he unfolds, its shape becomes familiar.

"Can you teach me how to play go-stop?"

• • • • •

Haven spreads out the mat on the infirmary table between them, and Yoon organizes the cards into groups of four.

"These are the cards organized by month."

The cards are small, thick, and red backed. The front sides display bright pictures of animals, leaves, and other landscape imagery. Haven can parse out some similarities between them, but he's not confident that he'll be able to keep them straight.

"All right," he says cautiously.

"But then you have the gwang cards." Yoon pulls out five cards from the assorted groups and points to a red circle on each with a Chinese character in it.

"Sure . . ."

"And then you have the ddi or ribbon cards." Yoon puts aside another group of nine cards that all have a short ribbon overlaid on the picture. "And these are split into hong dan, cho dan, and cheong dan."

"I'm never going to remember that."

"You don't have to remember what they're called, just that you're always grouping the ones that look alike." She points to a red ribbon with writing on it, a blank red ribbon, and a blue ribbon.

"You also have animal cards." Yoon sets aside yet another group of cards, all with animal pictures. "And the godori." From that set she puts aside the three cards that have birds on them.

That part seems straightforward enough. Haven places a finger on another card, a crane with its head tilted up to a red sun. He asks, "Why isn't this a godori card?"

"Because it's a gwang," Yoon says.

"Should I be taking notes?" Haven reaches for his tabula.

"Sasani, it's easy once you start playing."

"I don't believe you," he says flatly.

Yoon laughs and he relaxes. He had initially doubted that she would agree to his request, but like everyone else in the Alliance, and in the solar perhaps, he'd been watching the news. Everyone onboard those two ships is dead or missing. Whoever Yoon is anxiously awaiting news about is likely dead too. He couldn't stop thinking about her pale face in the garage, and the next thing he knew, he was leaving his infirmary.

Yoon flips the cards over and jumbles them, the cards going *schk* as they slide over one another. Then she gathers up the cards and shuffles them in her hands, her movements as casual and well worn as the cards.

"Have you ever played hwatu?" she asks as she deals their cards.

"No, but my father always said I should learn from an Alliance member."

"I guess that's true," Yoon says. "Although I didn't learn until I was in the Alliance for a while."

Haven knows this already. Kent told him that she used to play with their former medic, Gremio. They don't discuss anything that doesn't have to do with the game for a while. Yoon directs him as they trade turns. She demonstrates how to throw down the cards to claim matches, reexplaining the rules from time to time.

A few rounds later, Yoon throws a card down and says, "I don't know if I'm the best person to learn from. I've heard that I don't play like a Korean."

That surprises Haven, but she says it quietly enough that it would be easy for him to ignore.

"No?" He frowns at the cards in his hands. There are red leaves on this card. Does that mean it doesn't go with the black leaves on the mat? They *are* the same shape. "What does that mean?"

"I never know."

Haven thinks he might understand. Promethean Mortemians almost all share the same brown skin, thick hair, and large brown-black eyes, but Haven's always stuck out.

His mom abandoned him because of how ugly he is.

Ironically, he takes after his mother, always has. He could've passed as fully Japanese, having barely taken anything of his dad's. His appearance sprouted a lot of talk when he was younger, a badge of dishonor that he couldn't shed no matter how fervently he adopted Mortemian culture or how many feathers he inked onto his skin. He's always been aware of how he's been set apart. Shunned by the public as a Mortemian. Shunned by other Mortemians on Prometheus for being mixed.

"I was born in Korea, but I'm pretty much a foreigner," Yoon says. "My parents shipped me off to a boarding school on Neptune when I was eight. I visited Korea only once a year until I turned eighteen. And now it sounds like I won't be in the Alliance much longer either."

"You're a good pilot though," he says.

"That's never been the problem." A smile flitters across her face, stilling the follow-up question in his mouth. "What about you, Sasani? Do you think you'll stay with the Alliance?"

He's combed through openings on AV but has no idea where to go. He wants to ask her for advice but it wouldn't be fair, especially since she already, albeit unknowingly, guided his path to the *Ohneul*. And next time, he'll be careful not to take someone else's spot.

"Another ship might not take me on after they see I only stayed with the *Ohneul* for one mission," he admits.

"I can't say it'll be worth much after this, but I'd be happy to write you a recommendation."

Haven grimaces against his will and throws down his next card with more force than necessary. "Would you?"

"I don't say anything I don't mean," Yoon says.

"What would you even write?"

"That you don't like getting wet." Her mouth quirks into a smile, the one that lifts the left side of her mouth higher than her right.

Of course she would remember that. He only said it to her emphatically while she was hanging off a bridge. He closes his eyes, mortified.

"It doesn't rain much on Prometheus, but I read that occasionally you get downpours," she says, her sentence punctuated by the slap of the card she throws down. "And when it does rain, the vultures stay away, so the bodies soak up all the water. They get heavier and if you try to move them, they sometimes rupture." Haven clenches his eyes more tightly, fighting sickness at the memory. "It's understandable why you don't like the rain. I wouldn't have expected you to come save me."

"That's not why I said that," Haven blurts, his eyes flying open.

"I know," Yoon says. "You told me everything I needed to know over the comm. How cold the water was. How deep the lake. Everything I needed to know to safely drop into it." She cocks her head. "And all while Phoenix was doubling back on his hoverbike, right?"

Haven can't answer, but a surprisingly sharp pain throbs in his chest. He folds over himself, pretending to focus on the cards again. When he ran to the shore with Kent, he thought he made the wrong call after seeing her body curled up on the ground, the water lapping around her.

He says finally, "I'm sorry I couldn't do more to help you. Even after you saved me."

"I'm sorry I laid hands on you. I didn't have time to ask for permission."

"In the future," he says, "you don't need to worry about permission." She doesn't answer right away, and Haven hastens to explain. "I mean—if you're saving my life!"

"I gathered," she says. "Thanks. And thank you for agreeing to come along to the *Shadowfax*."

"It was the right thing to do." He shrugs. Their next few rounds are quick and silent except for the sounds of the cards hitting the mat. "Do you want to talk about it?"

Haven keeps his eyes fixed on the cards between them. It's her turn, but she doesn't respond or make a move. When he looks up, her face is so vulnerable he wants to apologize immediately for asking.

"No," she says.

They turn their heads away from each other at the same time, and all Haven's breath slams back into his lungs at once. He tries to softly take it in, but his body trembles. He clears his throat, waiting until he can trust his voice.

"My father is the one who wanted me to join the Alliance. You know, the one who said I should learn go-stop from an Alliance member."

Yoon tucks her hair behind her ear, and Haven notices that she's missing an earring. "Your father served in the Alliance?"

"He did. It's where he met my mother."

"Double legacy? Dae is, you know—her parents met at the Alliance too."

"No, he was like me, joined up with the Alliance for a few years during his exploration period. My mother was an actual member though. Bangpae." He shrugs. "He wanted me to experience it. Experience . . ." Haven waves his hand around.

"You must be close."

"Why do you say that?"

Yoon considers. "He wanted you to experience something that he loved. And you did it because what he wants is important to you. At least that's how it sounds to me." She draws a card and purses her lips. "Also, you talk about serials together. It doesn't mean everything, but it's something."

"We've always . . ." Haven pauses. An ache has hooked into his chest, and he can't allow it to grow. "We've always tried to make up for what we thought the other was lacking."

"That sounds tough."

Yes, he wants to say. No, not at all, he also wants to insist.

One of the godori cards is face up between them, and he finds himself tracing the minute details of the nightingale and plum blossoms. He inspects his cards and then the godori again. If he takes it, he'll have all three godori cards, giving him five points. He can claim it with his February plum card, but only if Yoon doesn't also have a plum.

When he glances up, he's startled to see Yoon studying him instead of the cards. He's become familiar with that, though— how she's always observing others. He opens his mouth to ask her what she's looking at, then clamps it shut again. But her eyes travel to his mouth because she notices that, too, of course. A flush creeps up his neck and the thought of her spotting it only makes the prickle more insistent.

Yoon sits back in her seat and slaps a card down. As she rearranges her pairs on her side, Haven lets out a long breath. Then he throws his plum card to take the last godori.

"You win," Yoon says without looking up. "Go or stop?"

Since he's won, he can declare go or stop. They can keep playing, and he can accrue more points, though there's always the risk of losing it all. Or he can secure his win and end the game here. Haven examines the godori he's claimed, and a suspicion sneaks into him.

"You let me win," he says.

"Hmm?"

"You knew I wanted that nightingale."

"You can't prove anything," Yoon says.

"Let me see your cards."

Haven holds out his hand, but Yoon swiftly jumbles her remaining cards into the middle, expertly and instantly mixing them with the pile. Haven gapes at her. He dives into it as well, as if he can possibly retrieve her exact cards.

"Sasani." Yoon places her hand on top of the pile, stopping Haven mid-scramble. They're both leaning over the table, and he's close enough to Yoon to see how light her brown eyes are, to notice the way her scar cuts through her eyebrow before its arch. "Take your win," she says. "They say you're not Alliance until you've won your first hwatu game."

He swallows and looks down at the mess of cards to see that his hands are framing hers, a parenthetical statement. He holds that position, feeling the tension in his arms all the way up to his shoulders.

"Well," he says. "Thank you, then." He slowly pulls his hands away. Yoon continues shuffling the cards together, the motions like choreographed circles, as she spreads them around the mat. Tentatively, he asks, "Another round?"

"Are you up for it?" she asks, her eyebrow arching.

"Winner deals the next round, right?" He takes over her shuffling. As he gathers the cards in a pile, he adds, "I don't say anything I don't mean either." When he looks up, he finds Yoon staring at him. "Are you—" He stops himself. "Are you ready to lose again, Yoon?"

He almost asked if she was all right, as if she wanted any reminder of the very thing he's been trying to distract her from. Yoon smiles, and any thought he had flies out of his head like a flock of birds ascending in a flurry of dark wings.

"Sasani, you have no idea what you're getting into."

THIRTEEN

THE SHIP SHUDDERS and Haven's stylus skitters across his tabula. He waits and the water in his cup shivers with another vibration. As he walks to the door, Kent scurries by and disappears into the cockpit.

He hears Kent ask, "Do you want me to get Ocean?" followed by an emphatic no.

Haven puts on his shoes so he can peek inside the cockpit as well. At the controls, Captain Song sits before a view of space littered with debris. He's never seen such a large cluster, but it's not uncommon around fueling stations. Captain Song's glower is glued to the window, her knuckles white as she maneuvers the wheel. Haven winces at another scrape.

"Are you sure?" Kent tries again.

"Yes, Von! I'm sure!" Captain Song whirls in her seat to glare at Kent. "Can you *please*—" A loud bang interrupts her and immediately, an alarm beeps. Captain Song takes a calming breath. "Aish." She turns back to the panel. "Von, come here and find out what happened."

Captain Song scowls out the window as Kent inches forward, his fingers darting over the panel as he pulls up the ship schematic.

"Our wing was dinged."

"Go get Maggie."

Kent rushes out of the room. He nods jerkily at Haven before running down the hall. Captain Song hunches over the control panel, her body creating painful angles. Haven has the distinct impression that if he enters her space, he'll get pecked on the head like a hapless pedestrian dive-bombed by a murder of crows. Doors bang behind him, and the sound is followed by running footsteps. Thierry and Kent hurry down the hallway.

"What's up, boss?" Thierry asks.

"Shut up for a second," Captain Song hisses.

They all fall silent as the ship inches forward through the rest of the floating debris. When they're through, Captain Song huffs and falls back against her seat.

"Can I talk now?" Thierry asks.

Captain Song turns around. "I need you to suit up and get out there. Our wing was hit."

Thierry staggers backward toward Haven. Kent's forehead wrinkles at whatever he sees on Thierry's face.

"Dae, maybe I can . . ." Kent ventures.

"Do you know how to fix a control panel?"

"Maggie could talk me through it."

"No. She needs to go out there and fix it. It's her job."

Thierry clears her throat. "Is it crucial?"

"We won't know until you're out there, will we?"

"You know I . . ." Thierry's shoulder twitches. Her voice cracks when she continues in a low voice, "You know I don't like it out there."

For a moment, Captain Song seems to soften, but just as quickly, her expression firms. "Maggie, why would you sign up for a space mission if you're afraid of space?" she asks. "I'm not going to repeat myself. Suit up and get out there."

"Dae," Kent says, "what if I asked—"

"If you suggest one more time, Von, getting Ocean, I'm going to lose it."

Kent clamps his mouth shut.

"Von, can you help me suit up?" Thierry asks shakily.

"Maggie, you don't have to do this," Kent says, then turns to Captain Song. "Don't we have bots we can send out there?"

"What kind of ship do you think this is?" Captain Song asks. She swivels back to the wheel, but Haven hears the tremor in her voice. She smooths down the sheet of paper listing emergency numbers and tries to flatten the peeling Scotch tape holding it in place. It curls up, and she presses again and again until finally she tears it off the panel and faces Thierry. "Maggie, did you think you could apply to different Alliance transporters without it getting back to me? How do you think your chances will fare if I file a bad report?"

Kent shrinks back from the onslaught, and Thierry sucks in a deep breath and pivots around woodenly. Her face is gray and covered under a growth of sweat. She and Kent walk past Haven to the room that leads into the air lock. It shuts behind them, closing on Haven's offer to help. He still hasn't entered the cockpit. He has no desire to get any closer to Captain Song. After a few minutes, Captain Song turns on her mic.

"How's it going in there?" she asks.

Kent's voice replies after a burst of crackle. "We're making sure the suit is good and that the anchor line is solid."

"I check those regularly. They should be fine."

"It doesn't hurt to double-check."

"Sure. Turn on the video feed when you get a chance, will you?" The panel beeps and Captain Song swipes up the screen. The sound of heavy breathing fills the room, Thierry's from inside her helmet, but Haven can't make out much else. Just the void of space. She's already outside. "Talk to me, Maggie," Captain Song says easily, leaning back in her seat. "You're over the hardest part, getting outside."

A brief detestation for Captain Song glances through Haven. The door behind him opens and closes again as Kent dashes into the cockpit.

"I'm . . ." Thierry doesn't finish the sentence.

"Keep your mind off it. And show me what you're up to."

The camera tilts downward to better display the body of Thierry's white neoprene space suit. A colorful belt trails out into the air, floating in space. Thierry moves ponderously across the ship's body, making her way toward the wing in question.

"You jake, Maggie?" Kent asks.

"I just . . . I need this to be done."

Pity washes over Haven at Thierry's rigid words. It's so still in the cockpit, he can count his heartbeats until Thierry reaches her destination. She plants her feet against the surface. From her camera feed, Haven sees a ripped open panel exposing colorful wires.

Captain Song asks, "Can you fix it?"

"I can seal it."

"Confirm everything in there's operational first."

Thierry pulls the belt toward her, each of its colored panels a separate compartment. At her touch, one unfolds and the tool inside magnetizes to her shaking hand. She leans into the panel after flicking on her helmet light. Her gloves steady as she works. Captain Song and Kent are so intent on the screen that they aren't keeping an eye on the window. But Haven, standing farther back, notices a piece of floating debris skimming by. Captain Song's head jerks up but it's gone.

"Aish," she says.

"What is it?" Thierry squeaks, immediately on high alert. Her camera goes wild with her erratic movements. "What?" The word catches and she wheezes.

"It's nothing. Don't worry about it."

But Thierry whips around, bumping her floating tool belt. She knocks the tools from the open compartment, some of them spinning in the air. Thierry grabs at them, but misses, and the camera skeeves wildly as she gasps.

"Maggie! Calm down! You're anchored! You're jake!"

Thierry is sobbing. "Oh god, oh god."

Kent stands and runs out of the room. Haven assumes he's rushing to the air lock to suit up and retrieve Thierry himself, but he heads down the hall instead. His shoes skid when he almost falls while rounding the corner.

"Should I go out there to get Thierry?" Haven asks. He's only suited up in simulations, but that should be enough.

"We only have one suit," Captain Song says.

"Only one suit?"

"I sold our extra," she snaps at him. She barks into the mic, "Maggie! You just need to seal it up and come back in. It's easy. You can do it."

The camera feed is fully white. Thierry is doubled over on herself. "I can't I can't I can't. Don't make me. I can't."

"You can!"

Haven can't watch this. He turns from the window, pained, in time to witness Yoon entering the cockpit. Kent follows her in, panting.

"What is she doing out there, Dae?" Yoon's words aren't loud, but they're as severe as whiplash. Even Captain Song stiffens.

"She needed to fix up our wing. One little thing out of place in space can be catastrophic, Ocean. You should know that."

As Thierry sobs in the background, Yoon's face blanches white. If Captain Song had taken a literal knife to Yoon's stomach, Haven doesn't think she'd look as distraught as she does now. When Yoon speaks again, it isn't to Captain Song.

"Von, I need you to pump some music into Maggie's helmet."

"Right. What should I play?"

Yoon takes a breath, considering. "Beethoven. Archduke Trio."

Kent quickly scoots over to the panel and as Captain Song stumbles out of the way, her hands graze the buttons, opening a few windows on her screen. Kent immediately mutes them, not bothering to fully close the applications as his fingers fly over the panel. Not too long after, the light strains of a piano fill the room, flowing like a stream. Yoon walks forward and sits in the seat next to Kent. Her seat. She doesn't say anything for a moment as the music plays. She doesn't speak until after the violin and cello join the piano and create an interplay of three instruments.

"Hey, Maggie," she says, her tone surprisingly gentle. Thierry only gulps in response. "You know what I hate most when I go to restaurants?" Yoon waits a couple beats before she pushes on. "When I'm with a group of people and everyone's getting through their obligatory catch-up and then the server comes around to take our order." Over the video, Thierry's sobs are quieting down. "And, of course, nobody knows what they want yet. They've spent the whole time talking while I've been studying the menu. Like why can't we get the food going first? They're wasting my time, they're wasting the restaurant's time, they're wasting the server's time. I think it's the most annoying thing." Thierry hiccups. "Do you remember when we went to that diner while we were visiting Von? That all-night pancake place. What was it called?"

"Stacks on Stacks." Thierry's pronouncement wobbles.

"Right! And you and Von had a contest to see who could eat the most banana chocolate chip pancakes."

Yoon pauses for so long, Haven wonders if she's reached the end of the story, but then Thierry speaks.

"It was blueberry pancakes."

"Oh right. Mea culpa," Yoon says easily. "Anyway, I told you two it was a bad idea, but like children, you got excited about how they take pictures of everyone who eats more than twenty, you remember? It's a scam to make people buy more pancakes. But you went for it anyway, and told everyone really loudly that the best method is dousing every pancake in butter and maple syrup before squeezing it into your mouth." Haven's stomach turns. But he's more fascinated with the casual tilt of Yoon's head. Kent watches her with his mouth ajar. Captain Song is in the back, her face unreadable. "Von had a different method. He liked to roll them up and cram them into his mouth," Yoon says. "Isn't that right, Von?"

"Yeah," he says, his smile slowly spreading. "You were smart about it though, Ocean."

"I kept out of it. I think I ordered an omelet."

"No, you didn't," Thierry corrects, sounding a bit more like herself. "You had french toast. With a side of bacon, which wasn't crispy enough."

"Right. And you and Von kept on getting more and more pancakes."

"Stacks on stacks," Kent says.

"Now . . . I don't remember exactly what happened after that. I feel like there was some sort of dispute. Didn't Von win?"

"No!" Thierry's interjection is so immediate, Haven jumps. "That cheater! You think I didn't see how he added one of his pancakes to my stack? I could tell my stack was larger after I turned around! I have witnesses!"

"You did have many witnesses," Yoon agrees. "To the fact that you turned around and vomited all over Von. All. Over. Him."

Haven's not sure if it's wise for Yoon to bring up a past memory of Thierry's nausea, but Thierry's voice rises in protest.

"I still won!" Thierry yells.

"In more ways than one," Yoon says.

"Ugh," Kent says.

"So, Maggie. How about getting back into the ship with the rest of us?"

Thierry dives into silence again, and they all hear her shaky breath. "I—"

"She still has to seal up the panel," Captain Song argues. A hiss escapes Kent's lips, and Captain Song meets Haven's icy stare with her hands held up. "If we don't seal it up, we'll be right back where we started!"

"I'll take care of it," Yoon says, not even turning around. "Maggie, all you have to do is come back inside. Reach behind you to the cord there. The one that connects you to us. Can you put your hand around it?"

"I . . . I think so."

"Good, hold on to that. You don't have to tug it so hard. Just hold on to it firmly. Now you can disengage your foot anchors."

"I don't—"

"How about one step at a time? Disengage one, take a step, and anchor it again. Then take the next one. And keep holding on to that cord. It's going to bring you home," Yoon says calmly. "Jake? Good. Next step. Take your time. Do you want me to change the music to the *Rocky* theme? Or a moonwalk exercise video?"

"Beethoven is the superior choice."

"I figured you'd say that."

Haven can hear the smile in Yoon's voice, and he relaxes. But even as he does, he notices that Captain Song has been edging forward all this time. When she's close enough, she squeezes Yoon's shoulder.

"Nice job, Headshot."

Her words are low, but her eyes are stone cold. Kent sucks in a sharp breath through his teeth. Yoon's shoulder hardens under Captain Song's touch. Yoon leans forward to the intercom, and though her words are pleasant, the tone of them scrapes like rusted metal. Haven has to stop himself from ducking behind the doorway.

"So, tell me, Maggie, why do you like the Archduke Trio so much?"

The nuance of her voice apparently doesn't carry over the intercom, or maybe Thierry is just otherwise occupied.

She happily explains, "Oh, Ocean, you have no idea. Bon, listen, it marks the end of his heroic period, one of the last pieces he performed. And, oh! Did you know he probably wrote it while he was nursing his wounds from a failed love? Add to that the pathos of his encroaching deafness . . ."

While Thierry waxes on about Beethoven and how her favorite recording of this work is *obviously* by du Pré, Barenboim, and Zukerman, Yoon presses the mute button.

"Don't call me that," she says. She tilts her chin up to Captain Song, and the captain stumbles backward. "Von, can you receive Maggie in the air lock?"

"Yeah, of course," he replies.

Kent's head whips back and forth between Yoon and Captain Song. As he scrambles past, Kent shoots Haven a frantic look that he can't decipher. There's no way to ask what he means before he's gone, the door to the air lock opening and closing behind him.

"Why did you do it?" Yoon asks.

"It was just a nong—"

"No, why did you send her out there?"

Captain Song's eyes flicker to Haven. "She's our mechanic, Ocean. She should do her job."

"She'd do her job more effectively if I went out there, aimed a camera inside, and let her walk me through it," Yoon says evenly. "And you'd do your job more effectively if you didn't act out of anger."

Captain Song pales. "How dare you—"

Yoon laughs. "Me? How dare I? You were angry and you took it out on her!"

"I was trying to teach her a lesson! If she can't perform in a low-risk situation like this, she's a liability out in space. I thought it was a good opportunity for her. And *I'm* the captain, Ocean. Not you."

"As the captain, Dae," Yoon says, "you're supposed to take care of us."

Captain Song's face twists. "You always paint me as the bad guy. That's what you tell yourself, right? And the others? They're supposed to be on *my* side, Ocean! Even back on Sinis-x, everyone—"

"Ocean," Kent interjects.

He stands arm in arm with Thierry, and at first, Haven thinks Kent's stunned expression is in reaction to the tense conversation happening between Yoon and Captain Song, but then Kent lifts his arm and points. He's indicating one of the muted screens Captain Song accidentally activated earlier—a news station. The tail end of some confused footage shows a body being removed from a small escape pod. Whoever it is has attracted a lot of attention. Haven reads the scrolling caption on the bottom. *Breaking news from Seoul: Teophilus Anand, sole survivor of the* Shadowfax. Yoon runs out of the room.

"Where's Ocean going?" Thierry asks. She untangles herself from Kent and sits heavily at the table.

Captain Song's fixated on the screen and doesn't answer, but Kent looks down the hall, his eyebrows knit together in concern.

"Teophilus Anand?" Haven asks. The man who made people swoon at the gala, but couldn't deign to stay present for his own father's speech? Haven remembers Yoon looking past him when they were first introduced, at Anand in the crowd.

"Kim Minwoo's steady?" Thierry perks up. "Is he the only one they've found?"

Haven half listens to them and half listens down the hall.

". . . me when you know more?" Yoon's voice carries in from just outside the room. She emerges and Haven leans toward the cockpit again, fixing his attention back on the news screens. He hears her footsteps approaching. "Right."

"Is he . . . ?" Kent asks, low enough that Captain Song and Thierry can't hear.

"Unconscious. But stable," Yoon answers quickly. "And—"

A loud siren knifes through the room and a red light flashes overhead.

"Aish," Yoon says, a hand to her chest.

Thierry has her hands over her ears. "Did we get hit again? I'm not going back out there."

"Requesting permission to board."

The voice comes from the cockpit's main control panel, the obvious automation of its syllables irrationally sinister. They all turn toward the sound as if it has answers. A floating hologram invites them to open a video feed. Next to it, lines of code stream down the screen. Captain Song frowns at the text, obviously understanding more than Haven can.

"What the fuck?" Thierry whispers.

"Who is it?" Haven asks.

Captain Song seems more confused than perturbed. "It's . . . an escape pod."

"Escape pod?" Kent repeats. "How?"

"That's what I don't understand. It's connected to our air lock. It knew our ID code."

"Requesting permission to board," the robotic voice intones again.

"Where did it come from?" Yoon asks.

Captain Song taps the attached video file, a live feed from inside the escape pod. A man is sprawled across the screen, and Haven thinks at first that Captain Song's opened the wrong file, that it's the news again.

In a strangled voice, Captain Song asks, "Teophilus Anand? That's Teophilus Anand, isn't it?"

FOURTEEN

THE BODY lies too still. Ocean white-knuckles the seat as she tries to clinically inspect all the details, but her attention ping-pongs around the screen.

Von asks hesitantly, "*Is* it Teo?"

"*Teo?*" Dae repeats incredulously.

"It can't be," Ocean says. "They recovered Teo from an escape pod in Seoul. He hasn't woken up, but his family is with him. I think they'd know if it wasn't him."

"Then who is that?"

Maybe the video feed is faulty. Maybe it's looping and the escape pod is either empty or hiding something else.

"We won't know unless we let him in."

"No way." Dae runs diagnostics on the pod. "Whoever he is, he's covered in some sort of weird goop. It's like what they sprayed the *Shadowfax* crew with. We can't bring that in here. We have no idea what it is."

"They said it's not toxic," Von says. "If it's the same stuff that was on the *Shadowfax*, the Alliance reports have determined it nontoxic."

"We can't leave him out there," Ocean says.

"Why not? We'll be at Daltokki-5 in a cycle. He can wait until then. Whoever he is."

"He could be hurt." Ocean struggles to keep her composure, but each word feels like venom being spat out of her mouth. "He came to us. We have to save him."

Dae's eyes squint into slits. "No. That's my final word."

Anger has been mounting inside Ocean since Von came to get her. Once the tide rises high enough—

"Requesting permission to board."

"Dae—" she starts, but then Sasani's calm voice folds over hers.

"We have to retrieve him, especially if he may require medical attention," Sasani says. "Captain Song, this person needs help. As your medical officer, I'm honor bound to assist him. I can assure you we'll take every precaution to clean and isolate him once he's inside. I have a duty toward the ship I serve, after all. We'll be careful." Dae draws back at Sasani's poise. He puts a hand to his chest and bows his head. "Captain Song?" he prompts again.

Dae folds her arms painstakingly slow. Then, she nods. Ocean's already turning to rush out of the room.

"You listen to Haven, Ocean!" Dae shouts after her.

Ocean runs to the infirmary. She grabs one of the hazmat suits next to the door and tosses the other at Sasani. They both suit up. Von flits around, hovering, double-checking their seals. Ocean steps to the side to defer to Sasani, but she's right behind him as he strides to the connector door. He palms the door open to the transition room and then pauses at the next one leading straight into the mystery escape pod.

"Ready?" he asks.

Ocean can barely hear him through the double seal of their suits. She feels like they're on the edge of a precipice about to hurtle into something beyond her comprehension. She doesn't even have a gun on her. There was nothing to replace the one that raider tossed. But then she thinks about Teo's prone form on the ground.

"Ready," she says.

Sasani punches the door lock. The door hisses open and a rush of frigid air escapes. Lights flood in.

Teo lies in a fetal position, his knees bent up to encircle a bag he holds with one arm. His other arm is flung above him à la flamenco. She'd recognize him anywhere, even from the bare line of his back. A gelatinous fluid covers him, and a belt loosely circles his arm. His open eyes are unseeing, his mouth curved up in an uncanny suggestion of a smile. His chest rises and falls slowly, but steadily. Ocean kneels but resists the urge to touch the scar on his cheek.

"It's him."

· · ● ● ·

"I don't know how, Declan. But he's here."

Yoon's on her nimbus, her voice urgent but low, not that it matters because Teophilus Anand isn't going to be easily roused from his sleep.

They sprayed him down, disinfected and scanned him. He's clean. But still heavily sedated. Whatever he was injected with is keeping him unconscious and . . . eerily peaceful. His eyes still blink, but he doesn't seem to register anything around him. When Haven moves his limbs, they stay in place, hanging in the air, until they're rearranged again. Haven can't do more extensive tests using the ship's limited equipment. He took a sample of the liquid covering his body and placed it in a vial to study later. If this is indeed Teophilus Anand, then it's likely that the solution is some sort of highly flammable formula. He scanned the news and AV to see if they released anything more concrete about the substance, but unsurprisingly, he didn't find anything. The more concerning question is: If they have Teophilus Anand, then who's back in Seoul?

"I can't say for certain until I talk with him. But one of them . . ." Yoon nods, even though she isn't on video. "Yes. I'll let you know. And you do the same. We're on our way to fuel up, so if you can't reach me, it'll be because we've hit an MF."

Since Yoon made her first call, Haven discreetly searched the net. Despite all the details of Anand's fashion evolution through the years, salacious headlines, and paparazzi pictures of him doing the inanest things, Haven can't find one glimpse, one mention, of Yoon. But when Yoon knelt down before him in the escape pod, Haven knew exactly what she would say even before she opened her mouth.

"You should get some rest," Haven says once she pushes up the nimbus again. "We don't know when he'll wake up."

She rubs her face. "I can't."

"Then I'll go ask Kent to brew us some tea." Haven stands from the bench. She nods vacantly. At the door, he puts his shoes on, tugging up the heels with his finger. "Who is he to you?"

"A friend." Her answer seems wildly inadequate. At the same time, it tells Haven exactly where he stands with her. "Sasani?" His body automatically responds to her voice, and he stops short. "Thank you for stepping in earlier. And insisting that we retrieve Anand."

He stops himself from giving her his usual canned response about it being the right thing to do. He doesn't want to tell her a partial truth. He steps into the hallway, and almost directly into Captain Song, who pounces on Haven. Captain Song, Thierry, and Kent had all been crowded inside the infirmary earlier, and though Kent ushered them out, the captain's apparently been hovering.

"Is it really him?"

Haven shrugs. "Barring a DNA test, which we can't complete right now, I don't know how we'd be able to definitively identify him. He's not responding to stimuli, but he seems otherwise unhurt."

"How does she know him? Shouldn't we contact someone? The government? Alliance?"

"Hmm," he manages. Declan Anand asked to talk with Captain Song, requesting that they sit tight with the information until they better understand what is going on, but clearly that instruction hasn't hampered Captain Song's anxiety. He chooses to answer the easiest of her questions. "I don't know how they know each other."

Captain Song trails after Haven as he walks to the greenhouse, but then peels off before he arrives, perhaps to hover outside the infirmary again. Inside the greenhouse, Kent's already boiling water in his kettle.

"This is the only thing I could think of doing," he admits as Haven climbs down the ladder.

"It's very helpful."

Kent's shrug is a spasm. "I'd slip a soporific into Ocean's tea to get her to sleep, but she'd never forgive me."

"Do you know him as well?"

"Teo? Only in passing. It's Ocean who knows him."

Haven clears his throat. "Are they . . ."

Kent pauses while pouring hot water into the waiting mugs to blink at Haven. Then he laughs. "Oh lord, no." He musses his hair, which is the messiest Haven's seen it yet. "Never that. But their relationship has always been special."

"I see," Haven says, though he doesn't.

"The only real friends they have are each other."

"What about you?"

"Well . . . I know how Ocean likes her Earl Grey. How do you take yours, by the way? Sugar? Milk?"

"Two sugars. No milk," Haven answers. At home, he places sugar cubes in his mouth before sipping hot tea, but he sees that Kent has only dissolving sugar packs.

"Like Ocean." Kent smiles. "It's not the only similarity I've found between the two of you."

"What do you mean?"

"Talking to either of you is like trying to climb up an ice wall." Kent smiles brightly at Haven, taking the sting out of his statement. "But, you know, I've been meaning to thank you."

"Thank me?"

"For taking care of Ocean."

"It's my job," Haven says automatically.

"It's been good for her, I think," Kent says. "Someone being there for her without obligation, without anything she can interpret as pity."

"It is my job," Haven repeats a little more loudly.

"The other day, you came here to ask me about what might offer her comfort. Surely that's outside your job description." Haven shrivels with each sentence. "Well!" Kent drops two sugar packs into each mug. "Wherever we all end up after this, I'm very thankful that you joined this crew and that we could meet. And that you call me Kent! That's been nice. Like we're in boarding school together."

Haven doesn't feel deserving of Kent's generosity, not after constantly rebuffing his attempts at friendship. He rubs the back of his neck as he grasps for something to say in return, thinking about what Yoon told him about the xenobotanist.

"I heard you're engaged," Haven says finally. His voice comes out strained.

Kent lights up like the sun. He holds up his left hand and points to its fourth finger. "Did you see my ring? Yes! Sumi proposed to me. I had a whole thing planned, but she beat me to it. Got down on one knee, and oh just look at this ring. She designed it herself." Kent extends his hand to let Haven admire its intricate leaf design. After Haven has finished inspecting the engagement ring, Kent picks up the mugs and indicates the ladder with his elbow. "If you climb up, I'll pass the drinks to you."

Kent gingerly hands him the mugs, holding the bodies so Haven can grip the handles without burning himself. He appreciates the small gesture.

"Thank you," he says.

"Yours is black tea, too, so don't drink it if you're susceptible to that kind of thing and want to sleep soon," Kent warns.

Back in the infirmary, Yoon is still bunched up in the chair, staring fixedly at Anand.

"Here's the tea," Haven says. He places the two mugs on the table and sits on the bench, also facing Anand. "Kent made it for you." Yoon makes a little noise in response. He picks up her mug and holds it out to her, stopping himself from folding her hands around it. "You should drink it."

The tea's a diuretic, but he wants her to drink something, or at the very least hold something warm against her. Yoon absently grasps for the mug, but then Anand gasps in a huge breath. She slides out of her seat, and Haven puts her mug down. Anand blinks rapidly at the ceiling and for the first time, actually seems to understand what he's looking at. He bolts upright.

"Ocean?" His eyebrows press together in confusion. "Where . . ." Horror seeps into his expression. "Ocean?"

"I'm right here."

"I couldn't save them."

Anand grabs blindly and Yoon immediately catches his hand. His face crumples and his body bends as he starts sobbing, pressing Yoon's hands into his face. To Haven's astonishment, Yoon climbs into the bed with Anand and wraps her arms around his head.

"It's all right," she says. "You saved yourself."

"I didn't even try to save them."

He weeps and Yoon sits still, holding him. Haven has never felt so strongly like an intruder. He wants to back away and leave the room, but Yoon looks up, nailing him to the spot. She carefully pulls off her nimbus and hands it to Haven.

"Can you call the last number on there? Tell Declan I have him."

Haven leaves the room to give them some privacy. He paces the hallway as he hurriedly brings the nimbus up, adjusting it for his head size. His eyes flick through the call history, and his finger presses to call Declan Anand's number. It rings and rings. He's never wanted someone to pick up a call this badly. Each unanswered ring jangles his nerves. The door to the garage opens and Thierry exits.

"Heads up. We're about to enter the MF around Daltokki-5," she says. "Can you let Ocean know? I'm going to tell Von."

Daltokki's magnetic field, artificially created since the moon doesn't have its own, is a dead zone. It protects the station's atmosphere from solar wind but also means they'll have no access to comms while passing through. Most ships have an adaptor onboard to make up for the deficiency, but Haven doubts it's been a priority for the *Ohneul*. The line keeps ringing. Haven is not sure exactly what's going on, but he knows it's important to convey that they have the real Teophilus Anand as quickly as possible. The other end clicks and Haven melts against the wall with relief.

"Hello?"

"Hello, is this Declan Anand?"

"Yes, of course. Who is this? Ocean?"

"Yoon's with your brother. She wanted me to call you right away. She said to tell you that we have him."

A long pause ensues. Haven lets the man process the information.

"You have him? So, what you're saying is . . ."

"She's certain of it."

"Can you give me video confirmation?"

"Of course." Haven hesitates. "He's not . . . he's not in great condition. His vitals are stable, but he's just woken up and—"

"I understand. I just want to conf—"

A sizzle and a keen high-pitched tone slices Haven's ear. He tears off the nimbus with a groan.

"I warned you," Thierry says, walking back down the hallway from the greenhouse.

"How long will we be in the dead zone?"

"Two, maybe three, hours? Why?"

Haven hastens back to the infirmary. Yoon's holding Anand, who, amazingly, is fast asleep. As Haven tiptoes closer, he notices Anand's hand is wrapped around her wrist.

"Did you reach him?" she asks.

"I did, but our conversation was cut short." He points up.

"But you got the message across?"

"Yes. He wanted video confirmation, but I didn't get back here in time. Should I ask Captain Song to turn the ship around?"

"If you told Declan that I said we have Teo, it should be enough." She frowns. "He's not going to wait for video confirmation to secure the other one."

Haven shivers. "Who do you think the other one is?"

Yoon peers down at Anand, but his breathing remains steady, moisture trembling on his thick eyelashes. "That concerns me, but Declan will know what to do."

Her calmness steadies Haven. He's not sure if it stems from her faith in the older Anand or having Teophilus Anand safely beside her, but anything's better than her earlier hollow-eyed vigil. Anand flinches in his sleep, and the movement jars him so much that his eyes fly open. His hand around Yoon's arm clenches more firmly, but he doesn't otherwise move.

"Hey, Red?" he asks after a few moments.

"Yeah?"

The tension leaves his body, and he slowly straightens, letting Yoon go. "I brought a bag with me, didn't I? You didn't throw it out, did you?"

"Would you like it?" Haven asks. "I think we may have to throw out the bag itself to be careful, but I wanted to check with you first."

After all, Anand had protected it with his whole body. Anand rotates slowly toward Haven, as if it's just now occurring to him that someone else exists besides Yoon. Then, he simply stares.

"Wow," he says finally. "You're pretty." Haven's eyebrows shoot up against his will. "Don't worry, I'm not flirting. Just stating facts. Don't you think so, Ocean? Even you can't be immune to . . . never mind, why would I even ask you? As if you have any taste at all."

Haven shoots a look at Yoon, who has her head tilted up to the ceiling. After a moment, she sends an apologetic grimace his way. He rubs the back of his neck, trying to ward off the red he can feel creeping up there.

"Innnteresting. You're Haven Sasani, right?" Anand doesn't even give Haven time to sputter a response before he bows from his seated position. "My name is Teophilus Anand. You can call me Teophilus. Or Teo. All my friends call me Teo."

Haven's next words come curtly before he can stop them. "Are we friends?"

Anand laughs, and Haven can hardly believe the contrast in his demeanor from just a few minutes ago.

"Injeong, I guess not. And to answer your earlier question, Sasani, the bag's not important. It's what's inside that's important. That's safe, right?"

"Of course. I didn't look through its contents, but I saw that the bag was doubly insulated, so it should be fine."

"Good, good. Where is it now? Sorry to be a bother, but could you bring it to me?"

Haven pulls out a drawer from the wall. He removes the sterilized bags that had been inside Anand's bag and brings them to Anand, who promptly hands them over to Yoon.

"What is this?" Yoon asks.

"The contents of my emergency pack."

"Aren't you supposed to keep . . . emergency things in your emergency pack? Rations, first aid?" Yoon asks as she flips the bags over. Her hands go still.

"You're supposed to keep the things that are most important to you," Anand says. Yoon opens one of the bags and pulls out a red leather flight suit. From the other bag she retrieves a gun. As she holds the gun in her hands, Haven catches a glimpse of the white crane painted on the handle. "It's high time I returned these to you, anyway."

"This . . . this is what you were keeping in your escape bag?" She puts the gun down. "How did you get these? I thought—"

"I squirreled them away." Anand reaches out to touch Yoon's ear as she unfolds the flight suit. Each smoothed-out layer reveals a different expression: dazedness, a harsh downward tug at her mouth, her eyes softening. "You're missing an earring, Hummingbird."

Yoon puts a hand up to her earlobe. "It's been missing for a while."

It's casual and yet too intimate. Haven wants to turn away again, and a less charitable sensation spreads in his chest.

"So," Anand says brightly. "How long have I been out? I should probably call my parents, right? Did anyone . . . was anyone from . . ." His face falls.

Haven sits in the chair Yoon abandoned. "The reports say you're the sole survivor of the attack. Even the ships were destroyed," he says gently.

"Right." Anand says. "But my family knows I'm alive?"

"I talked with your brother." Haven hesitates. He doesn't want to depend on Yoon, to foist this burden onto her, but he doesn't know how to field this situation himself. "But . . ."

"What is it?" Anand asks sharply.

"A *Shadowfax* escape pod landed back on Earth." Yoon pauses. "You were in it. Or someone who looks exactly like you."

"What?" Anand's face goes blank. He shakes his head and then raises his hand. "I'm sorry. Let me try that again. *What?*"

"Your family knows you're alive, but they think you're back on Earth, in a coma. Or, they did. Now, Declan knows you're aboard the *Ohneul.*"

Anand tries to lift himself up, but Yoon grabs his shoulders. He throws his hands up.

"What? What does that mean? I have a clone? This isn't fucking *Cemetery Venus!*" Anand entreats Yoon, his words pitching high. "You know I'm me, right? I mean—" He holds up his hands for inspection and Haven can see the existential crisis unraveling before his eyes. "*I* know I'm me, right?"

"I know." Yoon's voice stops Anand's spiraling. "I thought I would have to do more to confirm it. I was even planning on asking you what Captain Han's log-in was—"

"Up up down down left right left right B A Start."

"Or where you get the lychee sodas—"

"I'm *not* telling you that!"

"But I knew right away," Yoon continues, nonplussed, silencing Anand. She touches her right shoulder. "I just . . . did. And your family will know too."

"I should call them."

"We just hit an MF," Haven says apologetically.

Anand gapes at him and then at Yoon. "Don't tell me you don't have an adaptor? Isn't that an Alliance requirement now?"

"So are a lot of expensive things."

"Aish. Then turn around!" Anand says. "If you just entered it, we can turn around! Where are we headed?"

"We're refueling at Daltokki, then we're heading back to Earth," Yoon says and slips from the bed. "But we probably have enough fuel to reverse course momentarily so you can contact your family. I'll talk to Dae."

She places a hand on the red suit and then touches Anand's head lightly. Haven wants to know if Anand feels the weight of that brief gesture but finds, instead, that Anand is watching him. Yoon stops by Haven's chair, and he tears himself from Anand's uncomfortable scrutiny. She holds out her hand and *oh*, oh right. He pulls her nimbus from his head and fumbles to adjust its sizing back to her settings.

"I can do it." Her fingers close around it, a carefully measured distance from his, and then she's out the door.

"She likes you," Anand says once she's gone.

"What?"

He stands too quickly and the chair skids backward. He walks to the drawer with as much dignity as he can muster and takes out a pair of gloves as well as the diagnostic wand. He should have checked Anand's vitals sooner.

"You know, as a person," Anand says pleasantly. "And I have to say, I like how you look at her." Haven isn't going to flatter that comment with a response. He gestures for Anand to sit up straight and waves the wand over his body. Blood pressure. Temperature. Heart rate. All of them appear normal. "Most people don't look at her like that," Anand says. "They find her standoffish."

"It's a good thing you loosened your tourniquet," Haven replies. "It could have caused permanent damage if you had kept the belt tightened around your arm for so long."

"I don't even remember doing that," Anand says as he absently strokes the red suit at his side. The vibrant red leather seems well cared for.

"Are those hers?" Haven asks as he grabs his tabula to input Anand's vitals.

"I modeled it after the jacket from *Akira*. She's so badass in it."

"You made it?"

Anand smiles, and it's less abrasive than his previously brandished grin. "It's probably my favorite thing I've ever made. When she's flying a ship . . . Have you seen her fly?" Haven thinks back to whether he's actually seen Yoon handle the wheel, but Anand laughs softly. "No, I guess you haven't."

Haven gestures to the suit. "Is that why you nicknamed her Red?"

"One of the reasons," Anand says. "You know, she's never asked me why I call her anything? Usually, people are curious about the nicknames you give them, if the reason isn't readily apparent. She's never seemed to care. Or . . ." He drops his voice. "Or maybe she's scared. Not all my nicknames have been kind."

Haven recalls her knee-jerk reaction to the moniker Captain Song gave her. "Are you the one who came up with Headshot?"

Anand's head snaps up. "Where did you hear that?"

"Captain Song called her that."

Anand's eyes become black slits. "Did she?"

The ship turns. Nothing in the room moves, and Haven doesn't have a window in the infirmary, but he hears a barely perceptible shift in the mechanics underneath their feet.

Anand cocks his ear. "It's been a while since I was on an older ship like this," he says thoughtfully.

Haven lets a few beats go by as he stares at the information on his pad without reading it. "So what was the reasoning behind that name then?"

Anand busies himself with rearranging the pillows behind him. When he settles back against them, he seems surprised that Haven's still looking to him for an answer. "I came up with that before I met her. I was trained over at Bangpae, but I heard things about her from my friends at Yong. She's an incredibly good shot."

"But that's not why."

"No." Anand shakes his head. He considers Haven, then says, "She had a reputation back then. The rumor was she tended to go off during simulations."

"Go off?"

"It's not worth getting into." Anand mouth twists. "But the joke was that she'd be the best and worst person to have on your team in the event of a zombie apocalypse. The joke I made, I mean. I might as well own up to it. The best because she'd make the head-shot every time. And the worst because once you were bitten, she wouldn't hesitate to turn on you and deliver that same headshot. So . . . Headshot."

"That . . ." Haven feels his expression harden.

"I didn't think it would catch on. But it did. And I didn't think it would bother her either." Anand stops and smiles ruefully. "That's not true. None of that is. I knew it would catch on. I'm clever like that. And I didn't think it would bother her because I didn't stop to think about her at all." He inspects Haven before he continues, "She doesn't play nice, and at the time she had just . . .

ah . . . do you know about her brother?" Haven shakes his head. "Well, never mind then." Anand scrubs his face. "I've regretted it a thousand times over. I don't think I'll stop regretting it."

"But you still call her nicknames."

"To atone? To cancel out past transgressions? To try to prove my undying ardor and appreciation?" Anand shakes his head. "I don't know. She's never asked me about them." Anand waves his hand as if trying to dispel the seriousness of his words. "And now she's stuck with me."

"How's that?" Haven asks, despite himself.

Anand peeks over at him. "They say when you save a person's life, you're bound to them afterward."

"You saved Yoon's life?"

"No, she saved mine. In a rather dramatic fashion." Anand taps his cheek, where a long thin scar cuts across his skin. And Haven realizes the truth.

"You're the one. The redacted name. The *Hadouken* incident?" he blurts. "It wasn't Kent?"

"You know about that, huh?" Anand picks up the gun from his escape bag. "This is the gun that did it." He tests its weight, then sets it down again. "I'm not all for glorifying weapons of violence, but she did save my life with it. They took it from her after she was demoted, but I stole it back. She left behind her flight suit on purpose, but I saved that too."

"Do you feel like you owe her?"

"No. And yes. I mean, I'm always going to owe her. My father stripped her of everything when he covered up the incident, to ensure that it didn't squelch the family name. He made it so that we'd never serve on the same ship again. Sure, she saved my life, but he still wanted to separate me from that sensational story."

Haven had puzzled over Yoon's harsh punishment, exacted just as swiftly and forcefully as Zeus would mete out a thunderbolt. "I suppose he was trying to protect you."

Haven can't imagine his father reacting the same way. If anything, he would have been on his knees thanking Yoon. Maybe he still will be, since Yoon kept Haven from getting shot not so long ago. Oddly enough, he has that in common with Anand.

"He thought she would try to use the situation. Use me." Anand tilts his head, searching Haven's face.

"What is it?"

"You're not going to ask me if she does?" Haven slowly shakes his head, and Anand says, "A lot of people said that at the time. I don't think anyone thought either of us was capable of real friendship. For different reasons." Anand's mouth wrenches to the side. "My father is always maneuvering my life. I think he would forgive me for anything, but sometimes I wish he would just think better of me."

Haven thinks of his own father. "I might know a little about what you mean."

"'How sharper than a serpent's tooth it is to have a thankless child,'" Anand says. "My father made it very clear that anything I did would only make things worse for Ocean." He lets out a long breath. "But sometimes I wonder what worse would even look like. Ocean's never said anything, never blamed me. But I don't love Ocean because I owe her. And I'd never want her to think I'm friends with her just because she saved my sorry ass." He frowns. "Yet I worry that she does."

A knock at the infirmary entrance punctuates the end of Anand's sentence.

"Am I interrupting?" Kent asks, poised at the doorway.

"Vonderbar!" Anand throws his arms open. His whole demeanor transforms, immediately pivoting him from his serious conversation with Haven. "Come here! Aren't you a sight for sore eyes! I mean, not that Sasani here isn't lovely too."

Kent shucks off his shoes and ducks in. "I don't want to exhaust the patient," he says apologetically to Haven, as if he expects to be ushered out.

"I'm fit as anything, right, Sasani? Soon you can call me a crew member and add my name to the chore chart."

"You two met on the *Hadouken?*" Haven asks.

"Kind of," Kent says. "I mean, I knew of Teo. He was above my tier. Most Alliance ships are pretty segregated. Alliance members don't mingle with non-Alliance members."

"You're not part of the Alliance," Haven says, clarifying aloud for himself. He assumed but hadn't known for certain. "Why did you follow Yoon after she left the *Hadouken?*"

"Von's a good egg." Anand ruffles Kent's hair.

"We didn't really know each other back on the *Hadouken,*" Kent says. "But what they did to her was wrong. It was easy to take her side." He dashes an embarrassed look at Anand. "I mean, I know it wasn't your fault—"

"Oh, stop dithering. I'm glad she's had you all this time. It was more than I could do." Anand throws an arm around Kent's neck. "I'd buy you allll the Choco Pies in the world if I could!"

Kent squirms ineffectually under Anand's arm. "Should you be moving around this much?" He squeaks over at Sasani, "I mean, should he?"

"His vitals are fine."

"Good because this infirmary cot is cramping my style. Can I move to a real bed tonight?" Anand asks.

"All of our rooms are occupied," Kent answers thoughtfully.

"Oh, I know that," Anand says with an evil glint in his eye. "I figured I could share Ocean's bed."

A strangled noise Haven has never made before escapes his throat. Immediately, he wishes the floor would open and swallow him up.

"I was going to say, you can have my bed, since I sleep in the greenhouse all the time anyway," Kent finishes.

"That works too." Anand winks at Haven, whose blood pressure is through the roof. He closes his eyes.

"Teo?" Yoon calls. Haven's shoulders stiffen. But when he turns around, Yoon's attention isn't on him at all, and she has her nimbus out. "Your brother's on the line." A mess of emotions cross Anand's face, some too quickly for Haven to make out. He thinks he recognizes relief, but also anxiety. "You good?"

Anand squares his shoulders. "Yeah."

Yoon flicks up and a large video opens from her nimbus. She places it on the table and steps to the side. The video stabilizes on Declan Anand. He and Teophilus are very much alike, each with the same sloping noses and dark eyes. And across Declan Anand's face is another complicated tangle of emotions. Relief and concern dance in his eyes as he leans forward, his regard raking across his brother's features.

"I'm so glad you're all right, Babu," he says in a rush. "When Ocean called, I didn't believe it. How did you end up there? Are you on the *Ohneul*?"

"Yeah, this is where I directed my escape pod," Anand says.

"Why didn't you come home?"

"It was home, for me," Anand says hesitantly. "I mean, my fingers automatically punched in the ship's ID code to direct me here."

Declan Anand puts two fingers up to his forehead and rubs. "Teo . . ."

Even Haven can recognize that well-worn gesture of exasperation. But at the motion, Anand goes very still. He glances at Yoon, who immediately reaches over and cuts the feed. The video disappears.

"Ocean, did you just hang up on him?" Kent says in a hushed tone.

"What is it, Teo?" Yoon asks.

Anand shakes his head, and when he speaks, his voice trembles. "That wasn't him. That wasn't my brother."

FIFTEEN

"**W**HAT?" Von asks, but Ocean thinks she has an inkling.

"How do you know?" she asks.

"You said someone crash-landed on Earth in a *Shadowfax* pod. Someone who looked like me? Someone even my family thought was me? That wasn't my brother. That wasn't Declan. This thing?" Teo imitates the gesture they saw, two fingers to the forehead. "It's like his patent gesture for me." He drops his hand. "But whoever answered the call did it with his left hand." Von holds his hands out, as if trying to figure out what Teo's saying. "Declan always does it with his right hand. Why would he switch hands?" Teo's own hands are shaking uncontrollably, in what Ocean recognizes as full-blown panic mode. "Am I crazy? It looked just like him, didn't it?"

Her nimbus lights up and rings. They all jump. Ocean sees the caller ID.

"It's him."

"Don't answer it!" Von says.

"You can't not answer it," Ocean says automatically. "He'll be suspicious enough that I hung up on him. What do you want to do, Teo?"

"I . . . we . . . I need to talk to him, right? I have to find out . . . oh god. He has Declan's *palmite*. What if something happened to Declan?"

The nimbus rings again loudly.

"You have to answer," Ocean says firmly. Teo's not in a position to rationally decide anything. "Don't let on that we know anything. But try to figure out who he is, where he is. And Von, go call Teo's parents. Teo, what's a number for your mom or dad?"

"567-1367-01," Teo rattles off automatically. "That's a direct line to my dad's palmite."

"Von, call him and tell him what's happening. Whatever you do, keep him on the line until Teo can get there."

"Me?" Von squeaks. "What was the number again?"

"567-1367-01," Sasani answers.

He holds out his palmite for Von, the number already entered. His response is so measured that Ocean almost asks him to go with Von, who runs out into the hallway. But her nimbus rings unceasingly, seeming to grow in volume. His gaze steadies her, somehow muffling the shrill tone and allowing her to take a breath.

She reaches out to her nimbus, but waits. "Jake?" she asks Teo.

"Yes," he lies.

"Hide your hands, then," Ocean instructs before connecting them.

The screen pops up to reveal Declan's frowning face. Ocean, off to the side, inspects him.

"I'm sorry, Declan. We lost reception all of a sudden."

Teo's put his hands under the blanket, although they're probably not even in the frame. His voice has none of its earlier tremor as he lies to the man posing as his brother. But Declan grimaces immediately.

"What gave me away, Teo?"

"What do you mean?"

"It was this thing, wasn't it?" Declan puts his hand up to his forehead as if to rub it. His voice sounds like Declan's, but now with a distinct accent Ocean struggles to place. "I didn't want to show you my other hand. But I guess it doesn't matter now."

He raises his right hand to the screen, and it drips blood so red, it's like someone's upped the saturation of the video. Cartoonishly red.

Teo gapes. "What . . . whose blood is that?"

"Mine, technically," the stranger says. "It's Declan's blood and now I'm Declan."

"You're lying," Teo snarls.

"Why would I? But then again, I don't care whether you believe me or not." A languid smile crosses his face, and if Ocean had any lingering doubts, they're wiped clean by the malevolent expression.

"Stop," Teo says tightly. "Stop it. Where is he? Where's Declan?"

"Declan only exists through me now," the man says.

"No. No, you didn't."

He's about to answer Teo, but then he cocks his ear. It's only then that Ocean scans his backdrop. The lighting is fluorescent, the walls white. His words echo vaguely. Then they hear a jangling ringtone, an upbeat song. Teo bites his lip, pulling it pale and taut against his teeth. The man glances off-screen and bares a grin. The screen moves with him as he walks. When he stops, it lands on a splatter of blood on the ground. Teo groans. The man reaches forward to grab a lit-up wristband from around a hand on the ground. He lifts it to read the number before carelessly dropping the hand.

"Someone's trying to call your father. An unknown number. You wouldn't know anything about that, would you?"

"No. No no no. This is some sort of sick joke. What did you do?"

"The question everyone is going to be asking soon is what did *you* do?" he says. "Your beloved parents and your devoted brother were visiting you when a shocking turn of events occurred. You awoke from your coma, obviously crazed. Using Declan's knife, you stabbed your parents to death. You stabbed your brother and only then in your disturbed state did you think about the cameras. You took them out so no one would see how you escaped." The man taps his chin. "Of course, you weren't you. My colleague has gone by now and shed your identity. You haven't been you since they rescued your body from the pod in Seoul. Just like Declan is no longer Declan. I killed him not too long ago. It was easy to get to him in the hospital."

Ocean doesn't know when, exactly, this conversation took on a tilt of unreality. She wants him to rewind, as if having prepared for the gut punch would make it any better.

"You *liar*." The guttural words tear out of Teo. "I'm going to find you and I'm going to rip you apart."

"Such harsh words from my adored babu."

"You're not going to get away with this," Sasani says from the back.

The man posing as Declan perks his ear. "I know that voice. I talked with you just now, didn't I? Well, whoever you are, yes, I will. The hospital cameras have it from every possible angle.

Every single knife plunge. Every blood splatter. It's going to be hard to dispute. And then there's me, the lone survivor. The tragic heir left for dead by his younger ne'er-do-well brother. I'll testify to it too."

"You can't possibly think this will work," Sasani bursts out. "We have Anand here. We know he wasn't at the hospital!"

"*Do you have him?*" the man on-screen asks. "What is Teo going to do? Say an evil clone is running amok? Some imposter with his face?"

"Why? Why would you do this?" Teo asks brokenly.

"Do you really not know?" The man shrugs. "I'm not going to waste my time enlightening you. It's not like your father gave us any answers before ruining our lives." He grins. "Now if you'll excuse me, I've been losing blood this whole time, so I think I'll heroically drag myself out to the hallway to be found by the staff."

The screen closes. Teo is sallow. He's staring at the space where the imposter's face floated a moment ago.

"This . . . this isn't right. Is it, Ocean? He can't be telling the truth. That wasn't my baba's hand. They can't be—"

He doesn't finish the sentence. The word he can't say doesn't only hang in the air, unspoken. It expands in Ocean's ears, her brain, until the throb of it has taken over her body. Nothing is going to make this right. And whatever she does or doesn't do is going to be the exact wrong thing.

"Ocean, he's not picking up!" Von shouts from outside before he gives a big "Oof."

He stumbles into the infirmary, palmite in hand. Out in the hallway, Dae pushes herself off the ground, hastening away.

"What are you doing?" Ocean asks, and the way Dae doesn't even acknowledge her question is a clear response. "Dae, stop."

"They can't be gone. I can still feel them here. I would know, wouldn't I?" Teo asks as Ocean strides to the door. Dae's already tripping into the cockpit.

While Ocean shoves her shoes on, Von crawls onto the bed with Teo. He grips Teo's hand and says gently, "I'll keep trying to call, Teo."

Dae's voice sounds clearly from the cockpit, "This is Captain Song requesting the Alliance. Ship ID seven-three-four-three-one-eight-four-five-nine-seven. We have a situation."

Ocean bursts into the room as someone picks up the line.

"Captain Song, how may we direct your call?"

"We currently have onboard—"

Ocean slams her hand down on the panel, cutting off the call.

"Yah," Dae snarls. "I could write you up for that."

Ocean laughs, and she wishes it was merely incredulous instead of laced with an edge of hysteria. "What are you doing?"

"What I should have done when we first found Teophilus Anand in that escape pod. I shouldn't have listened to his brother. I can't believe I withheld this from the Alliance for so long. It could be my neck on the line for this."

"You're throwing Teo to the wolves?"

This time Dae gives the disbelieving laugh. "Why am I always the bad guy to you, Ocean? We're in over our heads. Clearly Declan Anand has gone insane. They need to contain him right away."

"That wasn't Declan. Didn't you hear anything he said, anything Teo said? He *murdered* Teo's family."

Dae shakes her head. "I don't know anything, and neither do you. All I know is we have a Teophilus look-alike either here or on Earth. If the Alliance is going to clear up the situation, they'll need this Teophilus in their hands. This is the safest thing for him, too, don't you think?"

"You think they'll keep him safe?"

"Don't you?" Dae asks, and Ocean's gut reaction to her question surprises her. "Why are you with the Alliance if you don't believe in it? This is bigger than us, Ocean. The *Anands* are involved. If that really is Teophilus, then we can testify that he's been on our ship, and we can give them our ship ID so they can confirm our location."

It makes all the sense in the solar. But even as Ocean tells herself that, her hand won't lift off the panel.

Her decision is taken from her when an explosion rocks the ship. She stumbles to the side as alarms shriek overhead and a door down the hall bangs open.

"Requesting permission to board," the voice intones from the intercom.

"Again?" Maggie shouts.

"Requesting permission to board."

Ocean goes out to the hallway. Everyone's gawking at the air lock door that leads to the anteroom, previously connected to Teo's escape pod.

"This is Captain Song of the *Ohneul*. Who is this?" Radio silence. Dae lets out her usual epithet of *shibal saekki*. A craft much larger than Teo's tiny pod veers into the viewpoint. Whoever it is came around the *Ohneul*'s blind spot as if they'd known where it was. "They're not answering! And they're blocking visual. What the hell is happening here?"

"Don't open it!" Maggie yells helpfully down the hallway.

Dae rolls her eyes. "*Why* would I—"

The anteroom door clicks and slides open.

"What are you doing!" Maggie yelps.

"It wasn't me!" Dae snarls back.

A tall person in a space suit poses in the doorway. He tosses a head full of golden hair that somehow captures even the dingy hallway light. His space suit is the standard white, but a red phoenix is painted across his puffed-out chest, its wings spread upward. He glares into the hallway and Ocean tenses at the sweep of his piercing blue eyes. He looms so large, he blocks the light from the anteroom. She reaches for her holster, only to grab at air. Her stomach drops, and as if he can hear it, he hones his predatory glower on her.

And then Phoenix, the most infamous raider of the modern age, steps forward to announce his presence.

"I thought our ship was bad, but this place is a dump."

"Manners, Phoenix."

Sprawled on the ground behind Phoenix, a familiar figure has his hands in a mess of wires coming out of the panel next to the door. His space suit has two sketched figures standing side by side. He winks at Ocean.

"C'mon, let me get a look," a woman says.

Phoenix sidesteps to reveal a third raider. She's tall with dark skin, and the braids of her hair are gathered back into a bun. Her suit is painted with the image of a woman in a gown sitting upon a throne. When she sees Ocean, she frowns.

"You?" she asks.

It takes a moment for Ocean to recall her. "The looter from the Alliance garage?"

"You've gotten yourself into a real mess this time, Ocean noona," the raider on the ground says.

"Noona?" Dae asks, as if that is what requires the most explanation.

"Did I get that right? I'm a year younger, so technically, noona."

Phoenix directs his hawklike visage at Ocean and clears his throat.

His voice booms. "'Let me have war, say I: it exceeds peace as far as day does night; it's spritely, waking, audible, and full of vent.'"

He waits expectantly for Ocean, as if he's extended a challenge. She looks bemusedly from Phoenix to the man on the floor.

"What are you doing on my ship? How did you find us?" Dae shoulders her way into the hallway.

"Gemini, you promised!" Phoenix exclaims, pointing at Ocean.

"We don't have time for this," the third raider grumbles. She glares at Ocean. "It's bad enough that we're risking our necks for Alliance trash. I can't believe we came all this way for her. She doesn't care about anyone except herself."

"Not low grade after all, I see," Ocean says. "You're working for Phoenix?"

"You've met, huh?" Gemini replies, amused. "Maybe you woulda caught on sooner if she hadn't conked you out so quickly on Sinis-x, Cass."

Cass furiously opens her mouth but is quickly interrupted.

"'Peace is a very apoplexy, lethargy; mulled, deaf, sleepy, insensible; a getter of more bastard children than war's a destroyer of men.' Coriolanus. Not exactly a prosaic choice." Everyone turns to Teo, who's stepped out of the infirmary. He raises his eyebrows at Ocean. "You met Phoenix, and you didn't tell me?"

If anything could draw Teo out of a stupor, it's someone reciting Shakespeare. Despite the craziness of the situation, relief washes over Ocean. He's got a hand up against the wall to steady himself, the other against his ribs.

"Holy shit, that's Teophilus Anand," Cass says. "He's . . . he's not supposed to be here."

"Ah. Job makes sense now," Gemini says, delicately untangling his fingers from the cat's cradle of wires. He turns toward Phoenix. "And for your information, I didn't break any promises. She quoted *Romeo and Juliet*. While hanging off the edge of a *bridge*."

Ocean wants to cover her face with her hand. Phoenix and Teo simultaneously erupt into exasperated noises.

"*Romeo and Juliet?*" Phoenix says derisively, throwing his hands in the air.

"Talk about a prosaic choice!" Teo says. "You might as well have asked her 'to be, or not to be'!"

"Good sir, let's not knock *Hamlet*. 'Tis a noble question whether asked by a spoiled Danish prince, an animated lion, or an AI coming into sentience," Phoenix points out.

"True, the Bard is timeless."

Phoenix grins at Gemini. "I like this one. Can we keep him instead?"

"We're wasting time," Cass warns.

In her periphery, Ocean notices Teo moving slowly but steadily down the hall toward them.

"Stop," Gemini says suddenly. He pulls out his gun and points it at Teo. "Right there is good. And put your hands up."

"'I doubt not then but innocence shall make false accusation blush'?" Teo ventures.

"Well, *I* doubt a man who only quotes other people," Gemini says. "It means he can't think for himself."

"Gasp," Phoenix says with mock offense.

"Hands up," Gemini repeats, motioning at Teo with his gun.

Teo tightens his grip on his ribs as if judging how much pain he'll be in if he cooperates.

"Certainly," he says.

True to his word, Teo snaps his hands up. His left hand reveals his gun. And out from his right, he flings another object into the air. Ocean's hand is already outstretched to receive her gun mid-flight. It's almost unsettling how easily it nestles into her hand as she flips it around and aims it at Gemini. Teo points his gun at Phoenix, Gemini's is still pointed at Teo, and Phoenix has reacted quickly enough to pull his gun on Ocean. Cass also has her gun pointed at Ocean. She probably should be flattered by the double mark.

"What. The. Fuck," Maggie says from down the hall.

Unlike Teo, Maggie has her hands stretched up high as if announcing a goal. Dae's ducked behind the door in the cockpit, and Ocean hopes Sasani and Von will stay out of sight.

Gemini allows himself a sideways peek at Ocean and her weapon. He asks, "You leveled up?"

"Something had to replace the one you threw away," Ocean answers evenly. She keeps her eyes on Gemini, whose arms are unwavering. "Now. What are you doing here?"

Gemini shrugs. "Phoenix?"

"Well," Phoenix harrumphs. "Not so long ago, our LP sent out a very intriguing job."

"LP?" Teo asks.

"It stands for long play," Maggie pipes up from down the hall. "A vinyl medium for storing music that first came about in the twentieth century, although its popularity—"

"Not this time," Phoenix interrupts. He presses his lips together and his mouth twitches before he continues, "Although, I commend you for that piece of trivia. LP, liaison-proxy. They act as middle-men between raiders and their clients. It protects both parties."

"What's the job?" Teo prompts.

Teo's buoying the conversation, effortlessly as always, letting Ocean's mind race. The situation in front of her is a chessboard, but it's hard to figure out which pieces are in play.

Gemini answers, "It's simple: Destroy an Alliance ship called the *Ohneul*. No contact, no survivors."

No one moves.

"Wait. That's not your MO," Teo says, breaking the silence. "You never take on mercenary contracts."

"Are you kidding?" Dae hisses from wherever she's hiding. "Don't you remember the Mercury Murders? That's why his bounty is so high!"

In one of Phoenix's most heinous exploits, a group of Mercurian government officials was found dead and sliced open, gutted. Ocean remembers the huge uproar it caused about a decade back.

"That wasn't him," Teo says. "Sure, they found his DNA at the scene, but any idiot could tell he didn't do it."

"We've got a fan, I see," Phoenix drawls. "But I can assure you, I've killed plenty."

"Not for money."

At this, Phoenix breaks his gaze from Ocean to assess Teo.

"Huh." A different tenor snakes through his voice. He straightens his shoulders and returns his laser-sharp focus to Ocean. "Well, this one did offer quite a bit of it. And Gemini recognized the ship ID."

"How?" Dae asks suspiciously. "Ship IDs are classified Alliance information."

"We have a kid who specializes in classified," Phoenix says. "Anyway, we didn't take the job. We hauled ass to get here before whoever did so we could gallantly bail you out. Lucky for you, we were close by."

"Wait." Dae holds up a hand. "I don't understand. Why would you do that?"

They could have easily blown the *Ohneul* out of space without boarding it, without ever making contact. Just as Gemini could have shot Teo before he pulled out his own guns. And they also brought only three of their crew onboard.

As Ocean's tabulating, Gemini answers, "Her."

He points to Ocean with a cock of his head, startling her. She keeps her gun on him; it could be a distraction. His lips curl up in a smile.

"Gemini's my talent scout," Phoenix says. "He's talented at finding talent, you might say. If he says someone will be a good fit for our team—" He's interrupted by a *tsk* from Cass, but finishes blithely, "then I take him at his word."

"I hate wasted potential," Gemini says. "I figured Ocean pissed someone off since I've seen how friendly she can be. But now it seems like the contract has more to do with Teophilus Anand."

"Destroying a Class 4 Transporter is much different from assassinating an Anand heir," Ocean says.

"Marv. I always wanted to be important enough to have my murder called an assassination," Teo mutters.

"I want to see the job posting," Ocean says.

"Are you always this suspicious, sweetheart?" Phoenix asks.

"My brother always said I shouldn't trust anyone who calls me sweetheart," she says.

"Your brother sounds like a real heartbreaker." Phoenix laughs. "I wouldn't mind meeting him."

Ocean catches Gemini's grimace: just the slightest downturn of his mouth.

"I can arrange that," she says. "Sooner than you might think."

"Is he on the ship?" Phoenix asks.

"He's dead."

A gun whirs as it warms up. Cass is carrying an old-school laser, one she wasn't planning on using before.

"Cass," Phoenix says in a warning lilt, stretching the name into two syllables. "Why don't we all take a step back? Be a dear and pull up the posting for Ocean here."

Cass slowly reaches into her back pocket, although really, what else could she pull out? Another gun to add to the party? As she does, her palmite beeps two tones.

"What did I do to draw your ire, Ocean?" Phoenix asks.

"You did threaten to kill her," Teo says.

"No," Gemini corrects. "It's because she thought we might kill *you*."

"Maybe we should," Cass says. She holds up her small palmite, the screen lit. "He's got a warrant out. Two hundred thousand marks. Dead or alive."

Phoenix gives a low whistle. "That's higher than *my* bounty. Should I be insulted?"

"Wanted for what?" Teo asks harshly.

Cass glances down at the palmite, then pockets it. And even if Ocean has been expecting them, the words hit like a blow.

"For murdering your parents and attempting to murder your brother."

SIXTEEN

TEO'S FACE fights to distort into a garish smile. He's still waiting for Declan to step off Phoenix's ship, to get a call that this has all been an elaborate setup to teach him a lesson. His family would never be so cruel, but it's easier to believe that than . . . His gun drops from nerveless fingers and he grasps blindly. He keeps his hand outstretched, not even sure for what, until other fingers grip his.

"My family—" The rest of his words are lost in a horrible noise that can't be coming from him. A tidal wave smashes through his head. "Ocean, my *family*."

Teo's knees hit floor. He needs to lash out, to fold in the pain, but all he can do is shove his face into Ocean's shoulder. Words ricochet around him, but they fly past his ears and float into the ether.

"This trip might be worth it if we hand the prince in for a payday."

"Whoever posted the job was counting on us not boarding, Phoenix. They *specifically* asked us not to."

"It's a lot of money."

Keeping her arms wrapped tightly around him, Ocean says, "Over my dead body. Step away."

"You think your dead body is a deterrent, sweetheart? That was part of the original job."

"What about the rest of us?"

"Well, well, the captain. At long last, huh?"

"If you take Teophilus and Ocean, will you let the rest of us go?"

"What did I say? Alliance trash."

"It's not my *MO*, as mentioned, to leave people hanging. That said, the sooner we split, the better. Your ship ID was on that job posting, and the reward is high enough that you'll be receiving other visitors very soon."

"We can call for reinforcements from the Alliance and make a run for it."

"You think you can outrun anyone in this second-rate junker?"

"It's not a junker."

"I'm guessing you don't even have guns outfitted since it's Class 4. How are you going to defend yourselves if someone shows up? Which, I repeat, they *will*."

"If they don't want to be saved, then let's not save them."

"Cass, you're not helping."

"Let's at least grab the murderer."

"I'm not," Teo says finally. "I'm not a murderer." Each word he says brings him closer—to the claustrophobic air of the ship, to Ocean's hands clutching him, to his smarting knees. He shoves everything down, like vomit in his throat, and struggles to stand. When he reaches out, Ocean's hand is already waiting for him, and he uses it to push himself up. He lifts his head and says coolly, "Five hundred thousand marks."

Phoenix's eyebrows shoot straight up.

Gemini challenges, "You sure you're that loaded?"

Teo's never amounted to much. But he has always had this.

"Consider it a thank-you for not blowing me up or turning me in," Teo says. "Plus another five hundred thousand if you agree to drop me off somewhere."

Phoenix's face smooths over. Completely. The poker face of someone who's received such a good hand, he has to hide it. But he's already revealed himself.

"Everything has a price," Teo says. "Everyone."

Phoenix frowns. "Can you even access your money right now? You're even more wanted than I am."

"I have offplanet accounts."

"Of course your father squirreled away his precious money in offplanet accounts."

"He didn't," Teo says. "I did, without his knowledge."

Teo can read how Phoenix quickly processes that.

"Ten minutes," Phoenix says briskly. "Aries is keeping an eye out on the horizon for us, but we're going to keep it under a tight ten for everyone to pack up and bid this ship adieu."

"What are you talking about?" Dae interrupts. "We still haven't agreed to go with you. What will happen to my ship?"

Phoenix tilts his head. "What do you mean? There's only one thing to do. Blow it to pieces."

· · • · ·

Ocean doesn't have much, even if she's been with the *Ohneul* for years. She's carefully packed away the flight suit and the gun Teo brought back for her. Maggie spends a precious minute tugging at the garage door until Ocean goes over and pushes it open for her. Ocean wants to help Von organize his research or to make sure Maggie doesn't forget any of the tools she's tucked away. A decent XO would check in with Dae or offer to help her pack. But then again, a captain wouldn't have tried to barter away a decent XO. Logically, Phoenix is right. If they blow up the ship, then everyone will assume the job's been taken care of and there's no need for pursuit. Leave the ship empty, and other raiders, and whoever ordered the hit, will correctly assume they've been rescued.

"You don't have anything else to pack up, Noona?" Gemini asks as he slides up to her. He flips a metal box up in the air and then another.

"Don't call me that," Ocean says automatically.

"Why not?"

He plants one of the devices on the wall above her and keeps his hand there.

"We're not that close."

"How close do we have to be?" he asks. He steps toward her, and she backs up and hits the wall. He moves forward almost simultaneously, as if the space was made for him. Now he's only a breath away, so she can measure their distance not by meters or arm's lengths but by how curved his lashes are. He's only a head taller than her. She notices a mole on his nose, as if someone's touched the tip of it with a black marker. "How's this?" Then Gemini stops suddenly and backs up, straightening. "And I thought *I* was stealthy."

To their side, Sasani slouches against the wall. He lifts his chin at Gemini's words, affecting an unbothered yet completely unbelievable *Who, me?* expression.

"Are you always going to be satisfied with just observing, Haven Sasani?" Gemini's mouth quirks. Sasani's back stiffens and Gemini laughs. "I'm looking forward to getting to know you."

In a blink, he's halfway down the hall, joining Phoenix and Cass.

"I am tired of strangers knowing my name," Sasani says heavily. He has a large pack on his back. Apparently, it didn't take him long to pack either.

"Coming to my rescue?" Ocean asks, somewhat amused.

"Given what just happened, it doesn't seem like you'd need my help."

Sasani pantomimes her hands coming up to cup her gun. He drops the pose and shrugs. The motion is far more elegant than anything Ocean could have done, and she's surprised to find she can manage a smile. Sasani rubs the back of his neck as he stares at her, then abruptly clears his throat.

He asks, "He's the one from the bridge, isn't he? On Sinis-x? I didn't think you had much time for conversation."

"It wasn't a very even exchange."

In more ways than one. Her bruises have faded by now, but she still remembers the crack of Gemini's helmet against her body and the wrench of her arms as she rolled off the bridge.

Phoenix is talking with Teo now, and it's surprising to find him not so different from those glossy wanted ads after all. All this time, she was certain that they edited the color of his eyes and hair. He grips Gemini's shoulder and slings an arm around Cass, drawing them both closer as they converse in low tones.

"Time's up!" Phoenix yells a few minutes later. "Let's go!"

Ocean notices his timer reads eight minutes and he lifts his brows at her.

"If we want to leave on time, we need to start exiting now," he explains.

On cue, Von staggers out of the greenhouse with a huge bag on his back and two others in his arms.

"What in the world—" Cass says.

"I'm not . . . leaving . . . without . . . my algae," Von pants.

Ocean's heart goes out to him. He wouldn't even be on this ship if it wasn't for her.

"How many people are you hiding on this ship?" Phoenix asks.

Gemini ticks on his fingers as he counts, "Ocean Yoon, Dae Song, Haven Sasani, Von Kent, Margaret Thierry. And Teophilus Anand."

"That's some party trick," Teo says.

Dae climbs up from below, saddled by bags. She touches the ship's wall reverentially, and when she turns her eyes on Ocean, the accusation cleaves into her. Maggie bustles out of the kitchen, momentarily blocking Dae.

"Stop. What is that?" Cass asks suspiciously. Her hands open and close at Maggie. "Everyone hands over their weapons to me before entering our ship."

Maggie immediately puts her hands up, one of which wields a silver object.

"It's my ice cream scoop," she says.

"Your . . . ice cream scoop?"

"It's the one item I would save if my house were burning down," Maggie babbles. "I mean. After my spouses. But they're not items, I guess, so that doesn't count. And it's not like the ice cream scoop could walk out on its own, you know?"

"Come on, let's go, ice cream scoop." Phoenix gestures them all forward. "Gemini will take you all in, and I'll bring up the rear."

Cass walks down the line, waving an instrument over their bodies and gear and collecting whatever weapons they've saved. Ocean flips her gun over handle-first, but Cass has to practically yank away Dae's bonguk geom. They wait for Gemini to open the door, and a fine tremor seizes Teo's back. Ocean places her hand against the divots of his spine, and Teo nods at her unspoken question. The door creaks open. The distinctly familiar raider behind it is Asian, with monolids like Ocean's and buzzed black hair. He's large and top heavy, and his thick brows crunch together like two fuzzy magnets.

"Well, this party just got larger, didn't it?" He spots Ocean. "Oh. You again?"

Teo's head swivels back to Ocean. "How is it that *everyone* knows you?"

"Go right in. Welcome to the *Pandia*," Phoenix says expansively.

They file in, and Ocean notices Phoenix transform as his foot crosses the threshold of his ship, as if he's walking through a force-field. His shoulders and chest relax, and he absently combs his hair with his fingers. When he speaks, it's without the pomp and bravado of his earlier welcome; like an actor no longer reaching for the theater's back row, his elocution is looser.

"And now," he says, "we'll take your comms."

Maggie's hand jerks to her chest pocket and Dae reflexively covers her wrist. Gemini's gray-green eyes catch every movement. Ocean doesn't think he misses a thing, but what she admires more is the clear implication that he and Phoenix work in tandem.

"Why should we?" Dae asks. She immediately lets go of her wrist, but her scowl says she realizes it's too late. "We've already given you our weapons."

"We're going to get real friendly here, all sleepaway camp–like," Phoenix says. "But you can't write home to tell people about it. In fact, I can't have any calls in or out."

"But," Von interjects, "if people hear the *Ohneul* was destroyed . . ."

"Exactly. People can't know you're alive until we're in the clear. Whoever ordered the hit on you is very powerful, and I don't want to get mixed up in that. And I can't have you contacting the Alliance while you're on my ship."

"It's bad enough we're risking ourselves to rescue you," Cass adds.

"Cass here thinks I'm too trusting, so let me make this clear. Once we part ways, you never talk about our ship. Got it? It'll be like your own Uranian bachelor party."

"We can have them sign NDAs," Aries suggests, disappearing into another room after receiving one more scathing glance from Cass.

"As you know, I've got a hefty bounty," Phoenix says, "and the only reason the law hasn't caught up to me is because they don't have my ship ID. I'd prefer to keep it that way. Consider it a small, a *very* small price for your lives."

The Alliance will send ships out here to salvage and investigate, and everyone will think the *Ohneul* crew perished. Sumi will think Von died, Maggie's spouses will be contacted, and Sasani's father will be devastated. They'll send an Alliance messenger to Dae's moms, to Ocean's home in Marado. The last time her parents opened their door to an Alliance courier was when Hajoon died.

"We need to do it," she says.

Dae says dully, "Easy for you to say."

Ocean ignores the sting of Dae's rebuke. She forces the next words out, steamrolling anything else, "Otherwise, we're back at square one. They'll just send someone else to destroy the *Pandia*."

Von pulls out his palmite, but he doesn't move. His anguished grimace almost sways Ocean to try to change Phoenix's mind. But it wouldn't accomplish anything. She knows that much.

"Screw that," Maggie says. "You're saying we can't send a message out to let them know we're alive? I can't—"

"You can," Phoenix says. "You will. We don't know if they're watching your families or tracing your attempts to contact them. You either hand over your comms, or you can die back on your ship. But this way you'll stay alive long enough to beg forgiveness later."

He holds out his hand. Ocean pulls out her nimbus, and her thumb smooths over an old divot in the curve. After a brief hesitation, she's the first to hand hers in. Surprisingly, Dae is next, followed by a trembling Von. Maggie has her comm out, but it's not until Cass tugs it that she lets go.

"This is bogus," she mutters.

"It's going to be crowded," Cass says as she takes Sasani's device.

"We can buy a new ship with the money Teophilus pays us." Phoenix mentally calculates. "One and a half new ships." He gestures to Teo. "And you?"

Teo listlessly raises his hands. Phoenix lifts his chin at Gemini, who pats Teo down.

"Clear," he announces.

"Nothing?" Phoenix asks. "I always pictured you attached to your palmite."

Teo wets his lips and Ocean is ready for the flirtation he always drops into as a defense mechanism, its opening already created by Phoenix. *Darling, you pictured me?* But he falters.

"I'm not—" He stops. "You've caught me at a very strange time." The words halt Phoenix, who's otherwise been all rapid-fire energy. He studies Teo, and Ocean almost expects to hear his appraising *huh* again. Teo continues, his voice firmer, "But I'm afraid you're going to have to make an exception for me."

"Oh, I can't wait to hear this," Phoenix mutters, his countenance shuttering again.

"I need to contact the Alliance to explain the situation. If we give them your ship's coordinates—"

"Were you listening to anything I said?" Phoenix laughs. "People do say your brother is the smart one."

Von sucks in a breath through his teeth.

Teo winces but pushes onward. "Nevertheless—"

Phoenix shoves Teo into the wall. Ocean immediately has her hands on him, but he doesn't pay her any mind. His forearm presses against Teo's chest. One more step would flatten their noses against each other.

"Phoenix." This time it's Cass who issues the warning, but he ignores her too.

"Sweetheart." Phoenix is so close that Teo's eyelashes tremble under his breath. "I don't care about your reputation. Not when it's put up against the safety of my crew. And right now, our arguing is endangering the *Ohneul*'s crew too. Can't you see beyond yourself for one moment?"

The door shuts behind them, startling Ocean. Phoenix steps away from Teo and holds up a hand just as Gemini tosses something to him.

"Right." Teo slumps down the wall. "You're right. I'm sorry."

Phoenix pauses, but just for a second. He strides down the hall. "Aries, get us ready to leave. Gemini, we set?"

"Ready on your word."

Only then does Ocean see that the item in Phoenix's palm is a detonation remote. She crouches in front of Teo.

"Was," he says. She doesn't have to ask him to clarify. "It's not about proving my innocence, Ocean. I swear. But who else is going to take care of them?"

"I know," Ocean says. It's the only thing she can say, really. She could say *you will*, but it's such a heavy burden.

"Can I . . ." Dae's voice breaks. She's still looking back at the door Gemini closed. "Is there somewhere I can watch my ship from when you do it?"

Sympathy flickers across Phoenix's face, and it unexpectedly softens Ocean too.

"Follow me to the cockpit, Captain," he says.

As Dae brushes past Ocean, she knows someone should be with her so she's not alone while she watches the *Ohneul* break into pieces. She wearily calibrates herself, not just to see if she's capable of it but also to gauge if she cares as much as she should. Ocean catches Von's eye. And Von, even though he's bewildered and scared, knows exactly what Ocean wants. Even if Ocean doesn't deserve to ask anything of him right now, Von is always generous, always giving.

"I'll go with you, Dae," he says. He places his bags on the ground and follows Dae, resting his hand on her shoulder.

"You're not going too?" Cass asks. She leans against the wall across from Ocean. "Aren't you her XO?"

"I've never measured up to what an XO should be," Ocean replies.

She should go anyway, she knows that. But she hates the thought of being there just because she *should* be.

"Gemini, can you get them sorted?" Phoenix asks. "Then you can join us."

Gemini sidles by, motioning them forward with a tilt of his head. Phoenix's ship is a larger, older model. There's a clear thoroughfare through the hallway, but the clutter along its sides is a hodgepodge. One pile has an old handheld gaming console precariously balanced on top. Gemini clambers up the ladder immediately next to the door. Sleeping quarters are probably upstairs, making it easier for the crew to slide down in the event of an emergency rather than climb up.

Teo turns back to Sasani before they follow Gemini. "Would you . . ."

"Yes?"

"I won't be there for my family. To . . ." Teo trails off. Then, briskly businesslike, he resumes, "I won't be there for their funeral. Can you help me make arrangements onboard?"

"Yes," Sasani assures him. "I will help you honor them."

Teo's shoulders deflate so completely, he staggers as he steadies himself against the hallway wall. "What should I do? What do you need from me?"

"I'll take care of it," Sasani says.

His gentle words aren't directed at her, but they brush up against Ocean too. A balm for an ache she didn't even know was there.

SEVENTEEN

THEY STAND before the makeshift altar Sasani made. He must have had help from Phoenix's crew, but Teo doesn't know how he arranged it. Sasani meant it when he said he'd take care of it. He brought Teo some white clothes to change into, and then took him to what was likely a common room on the ship, one side cleared out with a row of chairs facing an altar.

They don't have bodies to burn, and they don't have the proper food, but then again, what does Teo know about proper? He has only vague memories of the one funeral he went to as a kid. Sasani has the sacred texts ready on a tabula and patiently guides Teo through the lighting of the homa. When they read through the thousand names of Vishnu, Sasani's steady recitation joins Teo's faltering one. He's uncertain, and then numb, but through it all, Sasani's voice bolsters and envelops his.

Teo knows so little about how they died, and he has no idea what's going to happen next. Sasani selected an excerpt from the

Bhagavad Gita for him to read. He puts a finger on a line from the second chapter.

"'I can find no means to drive away this grief which is drying up my senses,'" Teo reads aloud.

He has to stop. His family ascribes to Hindu funeral rites: once a person dies, their soul departs, and their body holds nothing of them. Bodies are burned and cremated, the ashes spread in a sacred or meaningful place, usually a river. Is there another Mortemian overseeing his family's rites back on Earth? Should he know this about his father, his mother, his brother—where they would want their ashes to be scattered? He never learned these pockets, facets, of his family, and now he never will. And what of him? His family's souls have moved on, and it's not the point of this moment, but he can't stop thinking, *What about* me?

Their words eventually subside into the crackling of the fire. Although Sasani set up chairs, Teo chooses to sit on the ground instead, and Sasani joins him.

"I should have done better while they were alive." Teo bends his head down, but the tears were waiting for him there and now he's brought them that much closer. They threaten to convulse his face and he furiously clenches his jaw to keep them at bay. "*Been* better."

"You don't have to stop wanting to do better now in their death," Sasani says after a long pause.

"It's not worth anything now. It's not." He raises his head, expecting Sasani to contradict him. Mortemians must learn how to deal with people's grief, and Teo ponders that flowchart: *If griever does A, then B.* Sasani's probably dealt with people like him who have seen their loved ones die before they're ready. As if anyone could be ready. But no judgment meets him. No condescending manner or empty remark about understanding *just* how Teo is feeling. If Sasani's eyes betrayed any sentiment approaching *Poor guy*, Teo doesn't know how he would take it. Teo has never been, in any sense of the word, a *poor* guy. "I . . . I don't understand it." Pain blisters through Teo and he bites back a gasp. "Have you seen a lot of death?"

"Yes."

"But this . . . this isn't how you do it, is it?"

"No." He doesn't elaborate, but when Teo keeps his eyes fixed on him, he nods. "Fire is holy to us. That's why we offer our bodies to vultures. Like those of the Hindu faith, we believe that once a person dies, nothing is left in the body. We give our bodies with thanks and sacrifice."

"You must know everything there is to know about death."

"No, we specialize in different death rituals, but we respect all cultures. No one is inked with a vulture's feathers unless they vow to serve not only a proper death but also a well-lived life. To be a Mortemian is to affirm life and the living."

"And how . . ." Teo can't look at Sasani anymore, at his composed facade, his unwavering hands. "How do I do that? How do I live?"

Sasani speaks gently. "My father would say generously."

"My father would too."

Teo's breath catches, and he hunches over. *Whatever you do, protect the Seonbi.* They had been after *him.* The attack was entirely his fault. He pounds his leg with his fist. Once. Then over and over, faster and faster. A warmth on his back halts him, a strong pressure between his shoulder blades. If he didn't know better, he could have mistaken Sasani's hand for Ocean's. As Sasani firmly supports him, a sob claws out of his body. Then he surrenders to the tears, his grief rending out of his throat.

When he emerges on the other side, he's completely wiped out, but something has been purged, at least momentarily. He drags a hand over his face and opens his eyes to Sasani holding out a cup, as if he had some inner metric to decipher Teo's bodily desires. Teo takes the cup and scoots back to lean against a chair's legs.

As he gulps from the cup, he studies Sasani over the edge of it. He wasn't lying earlier when he called Sasani pretty. He has fair skin, black eyes, and dark hair. The lines of his jaw are defined, as if an artist drew them with a definitive stroke. He's probably taller than Teo too. The white clothes he wears are too small for him, the material not creasing correctly on his long legs and the sleeves pulling back to reveal the sharp bones of his wrists. Because of the ill-fitting clothes, Teo can now see where he has his tattoo, the barest peek of it from the back.

"You're clearly made for a Mortemian's work," Teo says. "What are you doing with the Alliance?"

Sasani's settled on the ground with his own cup of water, a few paces away. If he noticed Teo's scrutiny, he doesn't remark on it.

He grimaces. "I ask myself that often. It's only temporary."

Teo gulps down more water. "What are your plans for after?"

"Back home to Prometheus. With my father."

"Your father, huh," Teo says. He shuffles through his mental dossier, plucking out Sasani's information without difficulty; he's always kept tabs on the people around Ocean. Sasani's parents both served in the Alliance, but his mom must be out of the picture. "You don't have a pretty steady waiting for you back home?"

The question's meant to be facetious, but Sasani replies, "I'm engaged."

Teo coughs into his cup. "That's . . . surprising."

"Is it?"

"Did your father arrange your engagement?"

Sasani frowns. "Yes. I think he thought it would make me happy. I've known her since we were children."

"*Does* it make you happy?"

"Is marriage about happiness?" Sasani truly sounds curious.

"That's a revealing deflection if I've ever heard one." A knock at the door interrupts them, and Teo cocks his head. "Saved by the bell."

The door opens, and Teo's chest loosens at the sight of Ocean. She enters, followed by a hesitant Von. They're both wearing white as well. Ocean's pant legs are rolled up a few times, and her shirt is overbig and baggy. But before he can scrutinize her any further, Von dashes forward and tackles Teo in an embrace.

"I'm so sorry, Teo," he says. Teo wraps one arm around warm, little Von and hugs him tight.

"It's jake," he mutters into Von's hair. It is, apparently, the thing you say. Here, too, Teo's the imposter. The sympathy doesn't belong to him. He's not the one something terrible happened to. It happened to *them*.

A hand rests on top of his head. Ocean's. She sits next to him, her knee bumping his briefly. He lets go of Von.

"Sit with me for a while?" he asks them. Von takes the space on the other side of him. Teo moves his knee until it's touching Ocean's again. Sasani has stood, and Teo can hear him pouring more water into cups behind them. He hands one to each of them, replacing Teo's as well. "So, Ocean," Teo says. "Do you think your brother and mine are hanging out?"

She doesn't answer right away. But when she does, she faces him squarely. "Yeah."

Teo laughs. He can't help it. Ocean flinches.

"Liar," he says. "I know that you think death is the end. When you visit Hajoon, when you pour soju onto his grave, who are you doing it for?" He pictures Ocean visiting Hajoon's grave, offering her brother his favorite foods as she tells him things she won't tell anyone else. Regret immediately sickens his stomach. He should apologize, but instead he asks the cup, "Does it get better?"

"No. And yes," Ocean answers. "I don't know."

Her answer soothes him even as the makeshift pyre's flames flicker. They listen to the fire snap, and Teo finally wonders where Sasani found all the materials to compose the fire, whether they had to prepare the room for ventilation or deactivate the fire alarms to allow for this ceremony. And then the lick of flames brings another memory forward, one that makes him shudder.

"Do you remember when Declan caught you rolling out your father's car in the middle of the night?"

Ocean's question bulldozes all Teo's other thoughts. He's half amazed to hear himself chuckle.

"My ears do. He dragged me back into the house by them." He explains to Von and Sasani, "I used to sneak out of the house in the middle of the night to meet a girl, and I didn't want to wake anyone up, so I'd roll my father's car all the way up the street before turning it on. I'd have to wipe its history after every date. But it was worth it."

"You told me he got so mad."

"Yeah. But after he dragged me home, he rolled the car back so I wouldn't get in trouble. My baba woke up and caught him in the act." Teo shakes his head at the memory of his roaring father, the lights going on throughout the house, and Declan being thrown into the living room. Teo ran down to intervene, but Declan stood in front of him, dissuading him. His back had always seemed so massive. "He was always covering for me. He used to be bigger than me back then. Vaster. In experience, wisdom, age . . . I thought I might catch up when I got older. I just made bigger mistakes."

"I thought I'd have everything figured out by now," Von offers. "I think I'm more confused. Things that were black and white developed shades of gray, I guess."

Teo can't help but snort. "Hoddeok, you might think you're seeing shades of gray, but I assure you your outlook is more technicolor than anything else."

"It is not!"

"Ocean told me about the time you got mugged in Seoul."

"Mugged? When did—oh, no that was someone who needed directions to the subway station." Von pauses, then adds, "And needed the funds to use the subway too. I wanted to help him get home."

"He was lucky to have you to help him. Humanity is lucky to have you."

Someone knocks on the door again and when it opens, Teo's surprised by Phoenix and Gemini. Their white clothing must be their own because it fits much better. Frankly, Teo's astonished they found so many white garments to clothe everyone.

"If it's all right with you, we're here to pay our respects," Phoenix says to Teo.

His expression is neutral, containing none of the utter derision he had for Teo not so long ago. Phoenix has golden skin and golden hair, piercing blue eyes below what can only be described as a noble brow. If nothing else, he's been christened appropriately. His nose is crooked, probably been broken one or two times, but it accentuates the rest of his features. Teo has, of course, always been a fan of visual imperfections.

Teo opens his mouth to tell Phoenix to go to hell, but Gemini clears his throat. Teo checks himself. He swallows down his anger and folds it up small.

"Of course," Teo says with a smile. "Thank you. Although my family might have been scandalized."

"I never met them. I did meet their ships," Phoenix admits as he crosses the room to sit beside Von. He speaks Common with a familiar drawl that Teo can't quite pinpoint.

Gemini slides into a cross-legged position behind Ocean. Teo can't wait to hear that story, but rather than call attention to them, he directs his next words back to Phoenix.

"I know all about it," Teo says.

"You have a crush on me, Teophilus?" Phoenix asks. "I'm flattered."

Teo ignores him. "For instance, there's your fabled supply run five years back."

Phoenix's eyes light up. "Oh, that. Yeah, that was fun."

"I think you may have taken it a bit far on Saturn though. Did you have to leave the guards naked?"

"A hundred and twenty-five marks each. That's how much the uniforms got us. Do you know how long a family can live off that?" Phoenix shrugs.

"I can't complain," Teo says. "My father let me design their new uniforms. So, thanks, I guess."

Teo promised his father he could make better uniforms, for cheaper. It was the only reason his father had, as he emphasized, *indulged* Teo. He didn't hear a word of thanks afterward, though, for the much better cut and design. He swallows down a lump in his throat.

"You designed those?" Phoenix leans his elbows down on his thighs. "Think you could modify our space suits? They're lacking a . . . je ne sais quoi? Cass painted them beautifully, but she said there was only so much she could do."

Designing space suits for *the* Phoenix and his crew? You can't buy that publicity.

"Space suits are more limiting design-wise, but Yi Jeong did some amazing work for the Seonbi Embassy recently." Teo fumbles for his next words. "That is . . . they were . . ."

The whoosh of flames, the slip-slide of skin, the smell of burning flesh, overwhelm him. Phoenix waits, but humiliatingly, Teo has lost the thread.

"I'm sorry," Phoenix says. Those cursed words again, now from *Phoenix*. "And I'm sorry about your family. Your brother too."

"Me too," he says hoarsely. Teo's throat burns. "Do you know who would do this? Or why?"

"There are lots of possibilities. Your family had many enemies. And as for why . . . Well, that's a bit obvious, isn't it?"

Teo rears back at that as Gemini says warningly, "Phoenix."

"He asked," Phoenix says.

"You have a lot of nerve—" Teo starts.

"Trust me, I have plenty of nerve—"

"Oh, please don't fight!" Von squeaks from between the two of them.

"Who are *you* to judge my family?" Teo spits out.

"Who am I?" Phoenix lashes back. "You think you know me? Gutter trash, yeah? An uneducated, ignorant criminal?"

"You said it, not me."

"I've done far less harm than Anand Tech."

"Harm?" Teo repeats angrily. "My father—" Teo chokes but forces himself forward. "Anand Tech has served the people since its inception."

Phoenix stares at him. "Is that what you really believe? Are you that naive?"

This is familiar ground, and it should be so easy for Teo to take the comment in stride. But he sincerely hates Phoenix for one brief, black moment.

"Anand Tech represents the desire to do good for the solar," Teo says through gritted teeth.

"Good for the solar?" Phoenix asks, his face going pale. "Do you even hear yourself? What about the planets you keep in limbo, the people you drain of their resources and lives just so Anand Tech can collect its blood money?"

As he snarls, his accent becomes more pronounced, emphasizing the elongation of his vowels as if they have more substance. It clicks into place.

"You're from Mercury, aren't you?"

"Does that mean something to you, Teophilus?" Phoenix snipes. Red spots appear on his cheeks. "I don't know what would be worse—you actively covering for your father or just being that stupid." He shakes his head. "But then again, people in power don't usually have to work that hard to cover up anything, do they? You're just a rich little boy dumb enough to swallow his family's propaganda."

And just like that, Teo's anger is all used up.

"I knew my place," he says. "I was always a villain of necessity."

Phoenix scoffs.

"I thought you were here to be respectful." Sasani inserts himself like a cavalier asking for the next dance.

His quiet but firm voice brings Teo out of himself. Gemini has leaned forward to speak to Ocean, who's listening to him but watching Teo. She shakes her head once at him, some signal he's not able to receive right now. Von has since backed up rather than be caught in the cross fire. He has the eyes of a child whose parents are explaining to him what a divorce is. Phoenix blinks at Sasani. He pushes his hair off his forehead and rises to his feet.

"This was wrong of me," he says, subdued. He speaks in Teo's direction. "I'm sorry."

He leaves the room, Gemini rising silent as a shadow to follow him out.

·　·　●　·　·

Captain Song entered the common room after everyone else left. Haven remained to keep vigil. He'd also wondered whether Captain Song would show up at all. Everyone else from the *Ohneul* has been in, and even Aries dropped by to sit with Anand and Haven for a moment. Captain Song is still dressed in her Alliance jumpsuit, and when she approaches the pyre, she gives the traditional Korean jeol for funerals, hands to her forehead, forehead to the ground. She rises and repeats the motions. It's two bows for the deceased, one for the mourner. Anand's not here, though, so Haven receives that last one in his stead.

Haven has a cup of water ready in case she chooses to stay. She kneels in front of the altar. His father once said Haven would be surprised how far a cup of water can go. Many funerary rituals involve food, and part of what he meant was that it is important to tend to the physical body. But it went hand in hand with his father's imparting on Haven the significance of small details, learning to simply pay attention.

"Thank you for coming," he says.

"Teophilus Anand isn't here?" Captain Song asks.

"I convinced him to take a break," he says.

"Will you let him know I came by?"

"Of course." He hesitates, then asks, "Did you know his family well?"

"You mean, like Ocean seems to?" Captain Song chuffs out a laugh. "I would never even dream of breathing their same air." She flicks a glance to the altar. "But I know of them. Who doesn't? Anand Tech made space travel easier, cheaper. I don't think I'd be flying the *Ohneul* otherwise." She pauses. "Although those days are gone, I guess."

"I'm sorry about your ship," Haven says.

"Me too. My ummas helped with the down payment on that ship. I was almost done paying it off. And now, because of Ocean, it's gone."

"Because of XO Yoon?"

"XO, shibal," Captain Song sneers. "She brought Teophilus Anand to my ship and got it blown up."

That's an oversimplification, but he says, "You could also say she's the reason we're alive. We could have been on that ship when it was destroyed."

Captain Song says bitterly, "Why does everyone take her side?"

"Because she takes ours," Haven replies.

Because she brought treats for her fellow crew members. Because she talked Thierry down from a ledge, literally. Because she's fiercely protected Anand from the moment he arrived.

Because she tackled him from the scooter to save his life. How can Captain Song understand that when, on his very first day, she asked Haven to call her Dae noona? Despite what his father intended, the Alliance didn't end up being what he wanted for Haven, but maybe Yoon is.

"No," Captain Song says. "She always takes her own side. I'm the one who took your side. I'm the one who hired you."

"You hired me for the extra money," Haven says calmly.

"Sure, that was part of it. I won't lie." Captain Song gulps her water. "But why are you looking at it so narrowly? Most people wouldn't even consider taking on a Vulture. Plenty of captains would have given you a hard time or avoided shaking your hand. I bent over backward for you. I knew that space training at the Alliance couldn't have been easy for you."

"I don't know what you mean."

Haven's shoulders tense. He doesn't want to think about the microaggressions he experienced during Alliance training. The spit in his food, his clothes stolen while he was in the shower, the wiping down of any surface he touched. The idea that Captain Song hired Haven because she pitied him doesn't feel any better than her using him for a payout.

"I know you do," Captain Song says. "I'm *Korean* and it was impossible for me. I got into Horangi because I'm a double legacy. I was surrounded by golden-spoon Koreans who took every opportunity to look down on me." She crumples her paper cup. "It didn't end when I graduated either. Because when you're poor, when you're average, you don't get fancy ships, you don't get important assignments. But I thought that once I got my own crew, my own ship, it'd all be worth it. I'd finally be Alliance. That ship was my home, and I watched it blow into pieces. And the crew has never been *mine*. I don't know how it happened, but it's always been Ocean's. What am I supposed to do after this?"

Haven goes to pour another cup of water and returns to replace the crushed one in Captain Song's hand. He would ask why she's pursuing this, why now or here. But he's familiar with what a brush with death can bring out—compassion or long-simmering resentment.

"My father wanted me to join the Alliance, Captain Song. You could say that we were both led here by our parents, even if it wasn't necessarily what we would have chosen for ourselves . . ." Haven trails off. "You weren't wrong about my experience during Alliance training, but I'm coming to appreciate that my father wanted me to find what I've been missing for a lot of my life. The feeling of belonging without having to fight for it."

Haven rises to his feet and bows to Captain Song, a repeat of her jeol from earlier, but only once.

"What are you doing?" she asks sharply.

"Again, I'm sorry about your ship. And I'm sorry we didn't stand by you." He pauses, then says softly, "But maybe it's worth thinking about how your crew might have needed you to stand by them too."

Captain Song doesn't respond, and Haven can't say what exactly her twisted lips and downcast eyes mean. She leaves soon after finishing her cup of water, but Haven stays behind, rubbing his stinging eyes. He suddenly, fiercely, misses his father, who's going to blame himself for Haven's death. For the first time in a while, he lets himself think about his mother too. He's never bothered to ask if his father is still in contact with her. If not, will he get word to her about Haven?

The last time Haven saw her was decades earlier. She was packing her suitcase in the bedroom. It wasn't until she was struggling to zip it closed that she saw him in the doorway and stopped. She hadn't been much older than he is now. His parents got married so young, had him so young. In the photos his father has carefully preserved and hidden away, she looks even younger than her age. He wishes he could remember more of her face. But all the details have woven into the rough polyester of the suitcase against his legs as he sat down on it so she could zip it more easily.

He's nearing thirty years old now and is even more confused than he was a decade ago. He's spent so much of his life thinking about who he is, what he is, and perhaps thinking about that has pushed any answers even further away. So instead, he reaches for the moments when he felt close to peace. Listening to stories as worn as the pages of a well-loved book while gathered around the korsi at Esfir's, feeling sleepy and warm from more than just the heat. His father's deft hands over Haven's, guiding the scalpel on a model. Raindrops sparking light overhead while Yoon's voice answers anything he might ask of her.

EIGHTEEN

THE *PANDIA'S* WHEEL is standard issue, as are its controls. From what Ocean can tell from the doorway, their cockpit isn't unlike what you'd see in any Alliance ship ten years past.

Aries is at the main wheel, and without turning around, he pats the seat next to him and asks, "Want to take a look?"

Ocean's hands itch. She hasn't touched a wheel since the Sinis-x mission. But she doesn't move.

Aries turns his head. "Phoenix asked me to show you our flight controls, but from what Gemini tells me, you don't need a primer."

Ocean finally walks in to take the seat. "I've handled a Tumbler before."

The *Pandia* looks like a Pril-80. Anything earlier than the 70 is classified as a Carrier, fine for atmospheric flying and moving close to the ground, but ships like this one are affectionately called Tumblers among pilots.

"That's right. You're savvy with ship models, aren't you? Go ahead, if you want."

Ocean traces a hand over the wheel. The surface is smooth where hands usually grip it. The keyboard's most frequently used keys are also worn—the *e* and ⊏ faded to bare hints. But, as a whole, the panel isn't too different from what they had on the *Ohneul*.

"Are you the *Pandia*'s pilot?" she asks.

"By default," Aries says. "But I heard you might be up for the job."

"Gemini did make an offer, but I think he was just messing with me," Ocean says.

Aries unscrews the top of his canteen and pours out a translucent amber liquid. "Oolong. Want some?" He hands her the cup. "It's hard to tell with Gemini sometimes. But he's got good instincts when it comes to choosing whom to trust."

Ocean almost laughs. "You think you can trust me? I shot you down once."

"I don't take it personally," Aries says. "But I'd prefer if you didn't make a habit of it." He sips from the canteen as he leans back in his chair. "Although to be frank, I'm surprised he dipped into the Alliance well for you."

"What's wrong with the Alliance?"

Aries shoots a sidelong glance at her, a placid examination like the serene up-and-down he gave her in the Alliance garage. "In my opinion? Nothing. But some things about Korea won't change, no matter the millennium. I mean, your captain still uses the bonguk geom when she's fighting."

"You think I should leave?" Despite herself, she hears a challenge in her question.

Aries switches screens to pull up the ship's schema. Ocean scans the diagram, and again, it's more or less familiar. He clacks away at the keyboard before he answers. "It's never a bad idea to consider your options. I'm more of a stats and facts person, so normally I'd suggest a pros and cons list. But I've found in my line of work that numbers often require context."

"Your line of work?"

"I manage the *Pandia*'s finances. I used to be an accountant. Big Martian corporation."

Ocean sips from her drink. He's tied down the top of his faded green coveralls, and his sleeveless tank shows off a bulked-up trapezius and thick arms. He absentmindedly rubs his shaved head.

"Is that a common trajectory?" she asks. Accountant to raider. Alliance member to raider. She can't say which sounds more unlikely.

Aries smiles as he taps a file. It opens a large spreadsheet, far more foreign to Ocean. His cursor sweeps up and down the columns of numbers.

"I used to spend every day at a desk, taking the train to work, taking the same train back after, collapsing in bed. Time would just . . . pass." Aries fills her cup again. "I was sitting at my desk one day and thought, *I spend so much of my time wanting my day to be over.* Is that what you call a midlife crisis? I don't know. I'm not the type to mourn the loss of youth. But I didn't want to live like I was just crossing days off in a calendar anymore."

Aries sips from his canteen. He's describing his previous life as a purgatory, and Ocean finds that she needs to hear how he escaped.

"So, you became a raider," Ocean prompts.

"So," Aries concedes, "in my thirties, I answered a very peculiar classifieds ad."

Ocean does laugh this time. "A classifieds ad?"

"It was just for a consultation," Aries explains. "From the beginning, Gemini was upfront about what this job would entail. I told him that I didn't know how long I would work with them. But it's been five years since then." Aries tips the last of the liquid into Ocean's cup. "Maybe this isn't the place for you. But it could be a transition point, if not a landing." He closes the spreadsheet. "And not that it should sway you, but I'd be very happy to turn the wheel over to someone else."

Ocean waits for him to continue, but Aries only opens another file, this one with lines of code down one column and dates and numbers across others. He seems content to leave it at that.

She asks, "Do you ever want to go back to Mars?"

"It's a weird little place," he replies. "Stuck in its ways. I feel more like a Martian when I'm not there, if that makes sense."

Ocean thinks back to sitting in a boat rocking along the waves. She places the cup on the counter and peers under the panel.

"These ships aren't designed for finesse," she says. "Nothing automatic is. The fact is, I can't fly this ship as-is."

They'd probably have to land for Maggie to assess the ship's internal mechanisms. And the commitment of rewiring a ship, reconfiguring its pedals, isn't a small one. It would give them, and her, an easy out. She lifts her head, but Aries is unperturbed, highlighting a column of numbers on-screen.

"What do you need?"

The camera drifts from the mourners bowing at the altar to the Seonbi on the path. Rows and rows of food-filled baskets line the ground. The news segment cuts to another vantage, where a Mortemian dressed in red, pink, and green silk is dancing a gut. She's surrounded on all sides by Koreans banging on janggus, plucking on gayageums, and ringing kkwaenggwari. As a voice raises in lamented song, she waves a long tassel. Its papered layers flutter in the air as she dances. Teo would have asked Ocean to watch the Artemis broadcast with him, but he didn't know what memories it might have provoked; Jejudo and its surrounding islands still perform traditional funerals as well. He's curious, too, whether Sasani's learned this dance, whether the shamanic rituals of Korea are one of his specialties.

"And although not yet completely recovered, Declan Anand was adamant about paying his respects—"

Teo turns off the screen.

He's holding a sick feeling in his mouth, the moisture gathering in his palms, when he hears a rustle behind him.

"What are you doing here?" Teo asks.

"It's the common room," Phoenix says. "My ship's common room, by the way."

"Got it." Teo stands, putting his hands up. "I'll leave you to *your* ship's common room."

"Wait," Phoenix says, stepping in front of Teo. When Teo raises his eyebrows, Phoenix retreats a step, also putting his hands up, so that they're mirror images of each other. "I came to say sorry."

"You already apologized," Teo says. "What do you really want?"

Phoenix openly weighs Teo, as if he can figure out anything from a look.

"I'm trying to decide where to take you," he says.

"We had a deal," Teo says. "I don't pay you unless you drop me off somewhere safe."

"Venus is the closest planet with an Alliance base, so I could offload you and the Alliance kids there in one go. Lots of places to hide on Venus." Phoenix pauses. "Or . . ."

"Or?"

"We could go to Mercury."

"What's on Mercury?"

"Our LP. It's possible he could give us more information about who contracted the hit on the *Ohneul*. Truthfully, I'd like to check in on him as well. He isn't responding to us, which is . . . concerning."

Teo frowns. "Are you . . . are you offering to help me?"

Phoenix bites his thumb. "If you truly want answers, I don't think they should be kept from you."

"You think I don't want them?" He clenches his hands into fists tight enough for his nails to etch crescent-shaped blood beds into his skin. His words trip out, faster and faster. "They murdered my family. They set my team on fire. They stole my brother's face, after killing him. I can't *sleep*—"

Teo breaks off, doubling over. Everything has been a messy smear since the *Shadowfax* attack, but that hasn't stopped him from asking question after question while staring up at the ceiling each night. He sucks in a breath, but something's blocking the air from reaching his lungs. He wheezes again to no avail. A sharp pain stabs him in the heart, and he grabs at his chest.

"Teophilus, breathe," Phoenix instructs. Teo raises his head to see the raider crouched before him, his bright-blue eyes holding him. "Breathe." Phoenix puts his hand over Teo's on his chest. "It will pass."

"No." Teo squeezes the word out, shaking his head.

"It will pass," Phoenix says firmly. Teo is ice cold but he's sweating, his vision sparking, but he latches on to Phoenix's right eye, concentrating on the black within the blue within the white. "What do you need?" Phoenix asks.

Teo grips Phoenix's hand and even though he squeezes tightly, Phoenix holds his position. He doesn't know how long they crouch there, but Phoenix doesn't move a muscle as the minutes tick by. Slowly, Teo's own muscles loosen and his legs buckle. Phoenix helps ease him to the ground. Teo puts his head between his knees and allows the air to fill his lungs again. He breathes in and out a few times.

"What do you need, Teophilus?" Phoenix asks again.

In the smallest possible voice, Teo says, "Let's go to Mercury."

Phoenix stands and lets out a long slow breath. Loud enough for Teo to hear, soft enough for it to settle into his bones.

"All right. We'll go," Phoenix says. Gratitude floods Teo, the suddenness of it pricking his eyes. "But you should stay on the ship. You're a bit . . . high profile."

"And you're not?" Teo manages to raise his head.

"I guess I should add that you're not well liked on Mercury. Also, if you die, who's going to pay me?"

If the raider could get his money by breaking him open like a piggy bank, he probably would.

"I'm sorry," Teo says. It's almost a relief to be the one to say sorry this time. "About what just happened."

"You don't have to apologize for that," Phoenix says. He roughly runs a hand through his hair and looks down at Teo. They lock eyes and Phoenix opens his mouth, only to be interrupted by a knock.

"Teo." Ocean's standing at the doorway. When she sees his face, her countenance softens. She raises her eyebrows in an unvoiced question, and he shakes his head in response. "You two should come eat. Maggie made some food."

Ocean leaves them, and Teo scratches his temple as he looks up at Phoenix. The raider, for his part, runs his hands through his hair again. Then, as if with great reluctance, he holds out a hand for Teo. Phoenix's hand in Teo's is callused, a story bisected with cuts, a journey his thumb could climb. He hoists Teo up before hastily letting go. Teo rubs his own fingers together and then shoves his hands into his pockets.

"Come on, let's go eat," Teo says.

When he steps into the hall, the smell hits him all at once. His eyes well before he even registers what's caused the emotional reaction.

Home. It smells like home.

He rubs the back of his hand over his eyes as he follows the aroma, Phoenix behind him. Electronic music booms out of the room that serves as both mess hall and kitchen. Voices rise and fall as Teo approaches the doorway. Von is defending a pot on the stove from Aries while Maggie flips naan on the grill and passes them to Sasani. Everyone's crowded into the room, including someone Teo's only ever seen out of the corner of his eyes. They have pale skin and a pixie nose, their silvery-gray hair cut in a soft silky cap. They slouch in a corner next to Dae.

"Teophilus!" Maggie exclaims. "They didn't have the right kind of rice and I had to improvise on some of the spices, but improvisation is the spice of life, right?"

"How—" Teo gapes at the kitchen, and then spots Ocean perched on the counter. She shakes her head and jabs a thumb over at Maggie.

"Sit, sit!" Maggie commands.

Von holds a plate piled with rice, and he ladles red curry onto it. He hands it over to Ocean, who nabs a piece of naan off Sasani's platter then places the spread on the table. Teo sags into the seat before it. Steam envelopes his face, and he breathes in the scent of tomatoes and cream. Garam masala, turmeric, cumin. Despite what Maggie said, she hit the main spices, at least.

Von prepares other plates and passes them around the room. It's a large table, but there aren't nearly enough seats for everyone. Ocean stays on the counter, Sasani leaning up against the wall not far from her. Phoenix shoves Cass over on a chair to share it, and Maggie watches them all. She turns down the music with one hand and flings out a bunch of spoons with the other, like she's distributing seed for pigeons.

"Catch!" she cries.

Gemini snatches his midair, one of the few spoons that don't clatter to the ground. Teo snags one that landed on the table.

"Oops!" Maggie shrugs. "Bon appétit!"

"Jal meokkesseumnida," Ocean and Dae chorus.

"Buen provecho."

"Bon apeti."

"Daste shomâ dard nakone."

"Thanks for the meal!"

"Dhanyavaad," Teo says. He means it in every sense of the word.

Haven has always loved the silence of usually bustling spaces. Empty classrooms, the temple after dark when it's lit only by candles wreathed in layers of wax like laced shawls. Part of it is the solitude, and the rest is feeling like he's witnessing something that most others haven't. The ship is dark, humming a low melody he couldn't hear during the day, when he slips out of the room he's sharing with Anand and Gemini. The only other person awake is Lupus, tapping away at their keyboard in their control room. Haven saw them for the first time at the family dinner earlier, and tonight they're too busy watching a 2D movie on one of their monitors to really care about Haven briefly poking his head in the room.

In the *Pandia*'s common room, he sits on the ledge next to the window and pulls out his device, unwinding his earbuds. After a thorough check, Gemini let him keep it because it only plays music, an old cracked dinosaur of a model. He's scrolling through the music, uncertain of what to listen to, when he feels the particular weight of her attention.

"Will you come in?" he asks.

Haven's footing around her is still unsteady. Every time he thinks he's planted his feet, the sands shift. Yoon enters the room and pads over to him, sitting next to him on the ledge. Haven pulls out his earbuds and she reaches for him. He goes very still, but she stops short of touching him.

"You don't have to stop listening," she says. Then, she points to the device in his hands. "Is that yours?"

"My father passed it down to me."

"They don't make them to last like that anymore."

Yoon's voice sounds impressed, but Haven likes the nimbus that often hangs around her neck, the halo it creates when she has it on. He's long come to associate her with it. "Your nimbus isn't too common either."

"Ah," Yoon says. "It was my brother's."

Haven nods to himself, letting her answer stretch out. "How did he pass?"

Yoon assumes the brisk manner of someone used to glossing over a tragedy. "Freak accident. He was an Alliance pilot, but he wasn't even on a mission. He was flying some friends over to Venus. And Dae was right, one little mistake, one routine checkup missed, and . . ." She waves a hand. "The coolant seal on his ship had worn through and the ship exploded. My parents fell apart. He was their son, their eldest. And then, I joined the Alliance."

"You joined the Alliance because of him?" he asks.

"I thought it would bring me closer to him," Yoon says. She leans her head back against the window and shuts her eyes. Haven wonders if she's telling him this because he's Mortemian or because he's him.

"After a person's gone," he says slowly, "I think one of the hardest things to contend with is how there's still so much to learn about them. But maybe that's good. Like there's no end to them."

"I don't think I knew him at all," she says. "I never got to know him well enough beyond this ideal of a person. How do you compete—"

She stops. Again, Haven senses the simmering emotion beneath the surface of her words, Yoon always holding herself in check.

"Are you angry at him for leaving?"

"I can't be angry at him. He's dead."

"You can be angry at ghosts. Or someone's absence." Haven doesn't need or want to get into it. Yoon's still pressed against the window, eyes closed. Haven leans his head next to hers as his voice dips low. "Anand said that you didn't believe your brother was with his. What do you think happens after death?"

Yoon doesn't answer right away, but Haven's become familiar with this rhythm between them. Whatever she says won't merely be some effort to fill the silence.

"Maybe you ascend to some other existence and gain a new understanding," she says. "But when I'm dead, I'm pretty sure I'll be—" She waves her right hand in the air again.

"What?"

"Nothing. I'll be nothing."

Yoon opens her eyes, and it's only then that he realizes how close her words have drawn him to her. He swallows and tracks how her eyes travel down to his throat.

"I don't know what's beyond this life, not for certain, but I think it's more than nothing. I think if you were to die . . ." The soft light of the room cradles her skin. The world is still enough that he thinks he can hear her pulse. Haven sits abruptly forward and unravels the cord of his earbuds, which he'd been anxiously winding into a knot. "I don't think it would be nothing," he finishes. He concentrates on smoothing out the tangled wires and casually holds out an earbud. "Want to listen with me?"

Yoon takes it from him and their fingers touch. The brush is a hot spark, and he snaps his hand back.

"I'm sorry," she says immediately.

"No, I'm . . ." He shakes his head. "I wasn't . . ." Flustered, he jams the other earbud into his ear and clicks on the player. He blinks at the bright screen as he's faced, yet again, with the question of what to listen to. Yoon inches closer, the wire of the earbud forcing their proximity as she puts it into her left ear. He takes notice of how close she gets, and how far away she keeps herself. "I've wanted to ask you something for a while," he says.

"What's that?"

He knows her well enough to note the wariness in her tone.

"I saw you dancing once," he says. She jerks her head to stare at him, but he keeps his head bent over the player.

"What?"

"In the subway. The night before the gala."

"In the subway? How . . . oh."

"What were you listening to?" Haven asks. "Do you remember?" Yoon gestures and Haven carefully hands her his player. She opens the keyboard to type into the search bar. She finds the song and presses play. A piano riff leads and then the bass thrums its supporting lines. The sultry tone of a trumpet saunters in. "What is this?"

"'My Funny Valentine.' Miles Davis."

"This . . . this makes sense with what I saw."

"Does it? Dance was my elective at Sav-Faire." That would explain the Vaganova. Haven pictures Yoon, her arms spreading wide, her leg lifting, and her toes pointing to some far-off distance. "You're a dancer, too, aren't you?"

Haven fights the urge to rub his neck. "Sometimes the vultures have to be coaxed down." He extends his arm, his fingers unfurling. He stops himself mid-motion, dropping his hands back into his lap. "We have ritual dances to encourage them to land."

"Does it work?"

"To me, it's more an acknowledgment of the balance of things. Of our reliance on each other," Haven says. "Vultures and humans. Life and death."

The trumpet climbs up a scale and they both listen as it warbles its line, the song evolving into something more playful. He thinks that's the end of their conversation, but Yoon speaks again, and her voice reveals a surprising wistfulness.

"You seem so sure of things," she says.

He glances at her, but she's looking away. This is how he'll remember her—this looking and not looking, the barest moments when they can hold each other's gaze.

"Not everything," he says.

NINETEEN

"DO YOU WANT IT?"

Phoenix holds out the gun to Ocean. The white crane hasn't faded in all these years, the dash of bright-red paint a shimmery crown on its head.

"Do you think that's wise?"

Phoenix's hand doesn't waver. Gemini scans their surroundings, similarly unconcerned despite his history with her gun. Everyone else is back on the parked ship. Phoenix approached Ocean earlier, asking if she wanted to come along in lieu of Teo. Now, they're walking down the connecting tunnel between the aircraft garage and the mining town of Penelope.

"I don't want you to be a liability planetside," Phoenix says. "And I hardly think you're going to shoot Gemini or me, especially when we have your friends back on our ship."

"My crewmates," Ocean corrects.

Her comment momentarily draws Gemini's attention back to her.

"Right," Phoenix says slowly. "Crewmates."

"Shooting you isn't the only way I can mess things up," she says.

"Let's call this a trial run. Test our chemistry." Phoenix tosses her the gun. Again, like when Teo threw it to her, she's unnerved by the familiar weight of it in her hands when she catches it, how perfectly her hand fits into the grooves worn smooth into the handle. "Keep up."

Phoenix and Gemini are striding ahead, and Ocean has to run a few paces to catch up.

"Your jacket should have a holster in the inner lining," Gemini tells her.

Gemini said her civvies were too Korean, so Lupus lent Ocean their jacket. Lupus normally zips their jackets all the way up or dons snap-on hoods. Ocean tries to recall if she's ever seen Lupus's mouth, even though they've eaten together, as she closes the hood over the bottom half of her face. She might not be as recognizable as Teo, but it doesn't hurt to be cautious.

The Alliance doesn't have a base on Mercury, and missions requested from Mercurians are rare. Ocean watched with interest as Aries radioed in, signaling for them to open the port. No further security exists, no identification needed, just a dry entry. As far as Ocean knows, the planet's few landing ports are each connected to two or three towns. Mercurians can't expand beyond the pocket communities encased in glass polymer that protect them from the outside environment. The planet is rich in minerals, rich in resources, and life within these enclosures completely centers on mining. However, even the land that's been made habitable is barely that. The dry air itches at Ocean, threatening to mummify her on the spot. They landed during a day cycle, and she's not used to the sun looming so large.

"First time?" Gemini asks.

"You know I've never seen the sky here except through glass?" Phoenix tilts his head back. "Solar plasma storms, mercuryquakes, temperatures that range from negative 180 to 430 degrees. But that sounds habitable to the Alliance, no? Everything's fine as long as the mines keep producing." Phoenix glances back at Ocean. "Teophilus's father, of course, being the biggest consumer."

"Korea's always played technological leapfrog. But they never seem to remember that pulling ahead comes at a cost." Gemini ticks off items, holding up fingers. "Seongsu Bridge. Sampoong Department Store. The ironically named Haetae Launch. Penelope Mines."

"Penelope Mines?"

Phoenix's mouth twists. "You should ask Teophilus about that. Although maybe he knows less about Anand Tech's involvement than he should."

Ocean remains quiet while the tunnel opens to a wide expanse filled with rundown buildings. They trudge through the dirt roads, and the air sours in Ocean's mouth.

"Are you from Mercury?" Ocean asks Gemini.

"Cass and Phoenix are." Gemini points over to Phoenix. "He's a hometown hero. Cass begged us to recruit her because she grew up hearing stories about him. Phoenix picked me up on Earth."

"This fool tried to pick my pocket in Guatemala."

"Tried, he says. As if he doesn't remember."

"I only say tried because I didn't have anything to steal."

"I think a fly came out of your jacket pocket when I opened it," Gemini concedes. "Rookie mistake. Shoulda read my mark better."

"You were too dazzled by my charisma to notice."

Gemini and Phoenix banter back and forth, volleying words. They stroll down the streets, clearly familiar enough not to need directions. It's Ocean who's pretending to be relaxed, her chin tilted up as she eases down the street. She takes in how people react to their trio, guesses at what each abandoned building might be holding, and jumps at the chime of an electronic bell as a kid runs out of a convenience store across the street.

Phoenix ambles into a bar. As he steps in, he instantly transforms: his posture puffs out, he dramatically flicks his hair. The bartender straightens at the end of the room. The churn of his soda gun elongates a familiar noise that Ocean's always thought sounds like someone hawking up spit. He sets three sweating glasses on the bar in succession while they approach. Moisture drips down the glass in front of Ocean, mirroring the sweat on the bartender's face. Art imitating life.

"What'll it be?" the bartender asks. He inspects Ocean and the strip of face she's allowed to show.

Phoenix winks at the bartender. "Usual for me."

"Me as well," Gemini slouches in a corner seat, eyes on the entrance.

Ocean surveys the few people inside the bar, as lethargic as the ceiling fan, moving slowly enough to be extras in a film.

"And you?"

Ocean gestures at the water. "I'm good." She's not going to open her hood to drink anyway.

"Can you get her the same as me?" Gemini asks the bartender. "She's our designated driver."

Ocean opens her mouth to protest but Gemini shakes his head, the slightest gesture. "You need a drink in front of you. Blend in."

"You don't drink?" Phoenix asks as the bartender slides over his glass. He sips his drink, which has the amber glint of a whiskey.

"I don't like to."

"Neither do I," Gemini says. "It makes people sloppy."

The bartender places two identical glasses in front of her and Gemini. Gemini flips his drink up and downs it in one go. He lifts his eyebrows at Ocean and mouths *iced tea* at her.

Phoenix smiles to himself. "Should we tell our new friend here how you get when you've had a few tall glasses?"

"Please don't."

"New one, Phoenix?"

The bartender is gone, and another large mustachioed Mercurian has come out from the room behind the bar. Different model, same sheen of sweat. He firmly shakes hands with Phoenix and nods at Gemini and Ocean. He scratches at his throat, and the stubble there is bristly enough that she can hear his nails against it.

"She's on trial," Phoenix says easily.

The man shakes his head at Ocean. "Run as far as you can, girl. And don't look back."

"Come on," Phoenix says. "You're going to give her an entirely erroneous impression of me."

"Entirely?" Ocean says.

"Oh, but what's the fun in telling you that?" Phoenix replies with a laugh.

He peeks over at Gemini, who inclines his head a fraction. Only then does Phoenix bend forward over the counter, his voice low.

"How's our friend Portos? Haven't heard from him."

"No one has."

Phoenix frowns. "Anyone been over there?"

"Not as of late."

Phoenix's eyelids droop. "Thanks."

"Not a problem. You holler if you need anything else."

The man nods at the three of them and leaves again.

"If you have contacts here, why didn't you have them check on your LP?" Ocean asks.

"That's what I said," Gemini says. "But Phoenix prefers the personal touch."

Phoenix tips the rest of his whiskey back and hunkers over the bar, but worry etches his forehead. Gemini clicks his tongue as he pushes his hair off his forehead. Ocean suddenly notices the flash of silver at his lobe, an imprint of a wing stamped into the middle of the stud. She reaches out, but he catches her wrist lightning quick.

"You finally saw it, huh?" Gemini asks, his eyes mischievous and searching.

"My earring." She touches her ears. Same as before, one with an earring and one without. "When did you grab it?"

"Figure it out." He lifts his chin at Phoenix. "Heads up."

Ocean checks the mirror above the bar to examine a man swaggering up to them. The grime on his skin has layers, like you could check his age by counting how many rings of dirt he's accumulated. He sucks loudly at his white teeth. He's followed in by three others, two men and a woman, who creep into the gloom of the bar from outside.

"Aren't you the famous Phoenix?"

"Infamous," Phoenix corrects. "And yes. You're not going to find anyone else in the galaxy that looks close to this."

He swivels around in his seat and leans back against the bar, hooking his feet back into the stool's legs. Gemini still has a finger on the lip of his glass, considering the dregs of his iced tea. Ocean sits tight, too, taking her cue from them.

"There's a bounty on your head."

"Oh, is there? How kind of you to tip me off. I guess we better get hiding, Gemini."

Gemini takes Ocean's drink and downs it. All three of them stand, but the man holds up his hand.

"No, you misunderstand me."

"No, we get you," Gemini says coldly. "You're the slow one here."

The man glares at Gemini. "Who are you? Are you wanted as well? And this one too?" He pulls out his gun to tip it at Ocean.

Gemini enunciates clearly, "Namisa."

But when Ocean looks to him in surprise, he slips by her. In a flash, he rises behind the man, twisting his arm up and back. His movements are so silent, the pop of the man's joints and his agonized yelp are even more pronounced. There are clicks and whirs as immediately, three guns cock and aim at Gemini. Ocean's hand flies up to her jacket, but Phoenix catches her arm.

"Hold," he tells her.

Her muscles lock in place. Gemini's eyes have focused on her as well. He shouldn't be concerned with her at all; he has far more important things to attend to, but as he holds the other man against him, he raises his eyebrow at her. She relaxes and Phoenix drops her arm.

"Now," the man who's being held by Gemini attempts to sneer, but it's marred by his wince of pain. "You're going to—"

But they don't hear exactly what Gemini should do because there's an explosion, and the man convulses, blood squirting. The gunshot rings in Ocean's ears as Gemini uses the force to flip the man's body over behind him.

"Don't shoot!" the man cries out. He's upside down, his body slung along Gemini's back like a human shield. His three henchmen are already frozen, gawking at their friend's unexpected acrobatics.

"I don't allow guns in my bar." The mustached man from earlier stands at the bar. His shotgun is lazily hitched up, the end a whisp of gritty smoke. "Normally, I would tell you to take your dispute elsewhere," he continues, "but I think you need to have something explained to you, friend."

"You shot me!"

"Yes, in the arm. It'll heal," the man says unconcernedly. "This is Phoenix. You don't threaten him here." He inclines his head to Phoenix. "I apologize that this happened in my establishment."

"It could have happened anywhere, really," Phoenix says. "I happen to catch people's eyes, that's all." He walks over and squats before the upside-down man. "I'd appreciate it if you didn't bust up this place though. I don't abide anyone profiting off another person."

"You're a *raider*," the man sputters.

"If your problem is purely a financial one, then you need only ask. Gem?" Phoenix cocks his chin at Gemini, who sighs and reaches into his jacket to pull out a silvery translucent card. He flicks it down and it slides to a stop in front of the man's upside-down head. "My contact info. I can help you find a job and your way somewhere else," Phoenix says. "And . . . you should get that arm looked at. Hector here can refer you to someone."

"He's all yours," Gemini says to the three standing still. He drops the man, who has the countenance of a cartoon character with birds flying circles around his head, and dusts off his hands, gesturing expansively.

"Hector, I leave it to you," Phoenix says. He winks at Ocean and saunters out of the bar.

Gemini rolls his eyes and follows. "You're such a showboat," he says to Phoenix once they're back outside.

"Me? You're the one who decided to get all flashy and moonwalk over to him."

"Are you really going to help him if he contacts you?" Ocean asks as she catches up to them.

"Depends," Phoenix says. "We'll listen to what he has to say, at least. 'If you suffer your people to be ill-educated, and their manners to be corrupted from their infancy, and then punish them for those crimes to which their first education disposed them, what else is to be concluded from this, but that you first make thieves and then punish them?' Thomas More said that."

"It's a good sign he has friends who tried to help him," Gemini adds. "And that they didn't shoot after I used him as a shield."

"What if they had?" Ocean asks.

"Then I would have killed them," Gemini says easily. "You let people like that go, and they think they've earned it somehow. Inflates their ego. They'd lick their wounds and then come back to trash Hector's bar." He knees Phoenix in the back of the leg. "Goes without saying, but Phoenix won't be the one vetting him if he contacts us."

"Hey! What do you mean 'goes without saying'!"

"If it were up to you, we'd be helping every sob story that came our way and probably get our throats slit in the process," Gemini says. "And my neck is so pretty."

"Are you implying I'm too soft or that my neck isn't pretty enough to matter?"

"Both."

"Gasp. Take that back. I have an objectively attractive neck."

Gemini fondly pats the back of that neck as he says to Ocean over his shoulder, "Phoenix is why Hector was able to build his bar." Gemini had claimed that Phoenix would take care of Ocean, and she's coming to understand what he meant. "You're too soft, but I knew what I was getting into from the beginning."

Gemini pulls out a gun from underneath his shirt, and Ocean recognizes it as belonging to the man who threatened Phoenix. Gemini breaks it apart and tosses the pieces far away, pocketing the bullets.

"When did you have the chance to take that?"

"When did I not have the chance to?" he rebuts. Ocean's hand goes to her ear and Gemini smiles. He sidles up to Phoenix and digs an elbow into his rib. "Isn't Phoenix handsome, Ocean?" Gemini asks as Phoenix yelps.

"You're very eye-catching," she concedes.

"Be still, my heart," Phoenix says.

Eye-catching is the best description she could come up with, though. The Phoenix strutting beside her, the same person who monologued on the *Ohneul*, is wholly different from the Phoenix she's seen on his ship.

"He's more Teo's type," she says.

Phoenix doesn't turn around this time. "Isn't he going out with that actor?"

"I don't think that was ever a thing."

"There were pictures of them in the news. I heard."

"There are pictures of him with lots of people in the news."

"Not you." Gemini hangs back to walk next to Ocean. "In fact, if Lupus hadn't dug up that old footage from the *Hadouken* incident, I woulda never connected you two."

"You saw that?" Ocean studies Phoenix's back for a reaction too.

"Lupus pulled some files together for me. I'm not a fan of surprises in my relationships, whether they're business or pleasure. I scout, I vet, I extend invitations. Like I said, if it were up to Phoenix, we'd take in every stray."

"The solar holds plenty of good drivers." And probably more than a few who wouldn't further complicate their relationships with their mothers by joining Phoenix's crew.

"Not any I liked," Gemini says. "Until now."

He smiles, baring his teeth. He could have run with the wolves at Sav-Faire. Easily. But she's long tired of the slippery way people use words.

"What do you want from me?" she asks.

"I'm just wondering . . ." Gemini lifts an eyebrow. "If Phoenix is Teo's type, then who's yours?"

Ocean doesn't know if her type has ever figured into things. She'd say it's more that she's never been the right type, but then thinks about Sasani stretching his arm out the night before. It's the twenty-third century and Sasani still uses earbuds with wires that tangle, wires he patiently works through. He moves deliberately, certain and straightforward, in both his most casual steps and his long, elegant shrugs. Ocean squints up at the sky, and there it is again, that same exhaustion.

"I guess I'm looking for someone to break the type."

"We're close," Phoenix says, so casually that Ocean doesn't realize he's changed the subject until Gemini drops behind her.

Phoenix shifts into a practiced, loosely confident pace. It's not his usual ostentatious jaunt, and it definitely doesn't advertise that he has two guns holstered under his jacket. He takes a right around the next corner into a shadowy side alley. A pungent, ripe smell drenches the air. Ocean scans the windows, the concaved embrasures. Halfway down, Phoenix hops down the stone steps that lead to a recessed door. Gemini lounges on the ledge above, his eyes alert.

Phoenix knocks on the door, and they wait.

"Gem?" Phoenix says.

Gemini stands on the ledge and leaps, grabbing onto the window of the next floor and pulling himself up. He stretches out his legs to wedge himself in place. He pulls out a worn, leather pouch from his inner jacket, slides out one long tool, and tucks it behind his ear. Then he retrieves another L-shaped metal piece and hunches over the window, blocking it from Ocean's view.

"He was picking your pocket, huh," Ocean says as they watch.

"Every team needs a good thief." Phoenix grins. He says to Gemini, "Don't break the glass this time."

"Tell Portos to answer the door then. We're not all trying to share the good news."

The window opens and Gemini slithers in. An alarm siren wails, sliding up in pitch and volume from the inside. It blares short, harsh bleeps.

"That's new," Phoenix remarks. "I'd think it'd be too flamboyant for Portos's taste."

Although Ocean has to keep herself from checking the alley for signs that anyone else has heard the alarm, Phoenix whistles through his teeth. The alarm cuts and the front door opens from the inside.

"The alarm's new," Gemini offers.

"Portos isn't in?" Phoenix asks.

Gemini opens the door wider. "He is. But I don't think he can help us."

Phoenix enters immediately and Ocean runs down the stairs after him. Her eyes take a moment to adjust enough to realize that the aesthetic before her isn't intentional. The entire place has been ransacked, furniture torn to pieces, shelves shoved to the ground.

"Gemini, you didn't have to go *that* far to dismantle the alarm," Phoenix says mildly.

Ocean steps around the crushed glass. Phoenix and Gemini are on the other side of the room, walking down the hallway, and Ocean carefully follows them. Neither has their weapons drawn, but Ocean pulls out her gun just in case. When she reaches the room they've entered, she halts, her hand dropping to her side.

Computers fill the room, each monitor smashed, their wires stripped and torn to shreds. Blood is splattered everywhere, and a man's body lies prone on a chair in front of the largest monitor. He has pale skin and eyes that stare sightlessly, like a sickly fish in a dark cave pool gone belly-up. But it's the smell that stops her in her tracks, her hand covering her mouth reflexively as if it can blot out the rotting stench of decay.

"We don't have a lot of time, Phoenix." Gemini has gloves on and is using them to gingerly lift shards off the ground.

"Will the alarm alert the authorities?" Ocean asks.

"What authorities?" Gemini pulls open a cabinet drawer that's been partially smashed in. "That alarm wasn't Portos's. He'd rather not tip off an intruder. An alarm like that is to scare people away, or alert someone else nearby."

"Rest, my friend." Phoenix closes Portos's eyelids. Unlike Gemini, he isn't bothering to sift through the wreckage. He's crouched on the ground, his face serene as he gives his full attention to a Portos who can no longer appreciate that regard. Portos's insides spill out from a jagged tear through his stomach. Ocean holds out a hand over the body, but of course, it's long gone cold. Revulsion broils beneath her skin, but Ocean clamps down on it. The man's face is still contorted in pain even though Phoenix has closed his eyes.

"I'm ready, Gem. Let's go." Phoenix stands, pulling his guns out as he does. "Front door?"

"Any exit is as good as the other," Gemini says. "Or as bad."

Phoenix's blue eyes are glacial as he says to Ocean, "There's no time to explain now, but things might get hairy. We're going to get back to our ship as quickly as possible."

Behind him, Gemini murmurs into his comm, "We're headed back. Be ready for takeoff."

"Age before beauty." Ocean motions for Phoenix to lead the way. She has her gun out and shakes out her left arm to limber up. She passes the gun over and then rotates her right shoulder. It's stiff, as always, but nothing she can't compensate for.

Phoenix flashes an appreciative smile. "Does that mean you'll call me oppa?"

Her heart hitches, but Phoenix has already turned down the hall, so he doesn't see her falter. Although Phoenix doesn't have time to explain, Ocean's pieced together enough. Their LP was killed, his body left intact for them to find. They tripped an alarm when they came in and it's likely that the killer's watching the place. And if they're that committed to destroying evidence, they won't hesitate to dispose of the three of them too.

At the entrance, Phoenix walks to one side of the open door and Gemini sidles past Ocean to the other. She follows him, crouching down to survey the rooftops of the houses across the way. Phoenix and Gemini are also scanning, their heads darting up and around before they trade glances. Phoenix goes out first, his guns up. After a moment, Gemini touches Ocean's shoulder to motion for her to follow. They don't seem to care that their guns are out in broad daylight in the middle of a residential area. Standing at the top of the steps outside Portos's place leaves them incredibly exposed. Phoenix sticks close to the buildings, letting them shield one side of him as he stalks down the quiet street. Every whisper of air scrapes Ocean's skin. She strains to hear past the crunch of their footsteps on the gravel, the measured breath of Gemini behind her.

"Garrett," a voice calls out. Phoenix ignores it, until he stops so suddenly that Ocean almost collides with his back. The voice continues, "Why am I not surprised to find you here?"

Just ahead of them, someone steps out of the shadows. He's massive, but it's hard to tell anything else about him because he's about as wrapped up as Ocean is, only exposing the dark skin of his hands and the patch of skin around dark-blue eyes. He loosely holds out his two guns.

"Amell," Phoenix says heavily. "I can't say I share that sentiment."

"Friend of yours, Phoenix?" Gemini asks, as he and Phoenix flank Ocean.

Amell barely regards Gemini, skipping over him like a stone skimming water. "I guess you found some new playmates. Is that why you're here?" Even behind his covered face, the rumble of his voice is clear.

"What's Corvus up to?" Phoenix asks flatly.

"That's not your concern anymore, is it?" Amell replies. "You had your chance with him. Still, I can't imagine he'll be pleased when he finds out *you* sprang his trap." He slides an unconcerned scan over Ocean. "This one's wrapped up. You hiding something?"

"I'll show you mine if you show me yours," Ocean says pleasantly.

Amell's eyes widen and then crinkle in amusement. "Why don't we—"

Whatever he's about to say is lost as Gemini spins, crashing his back against Ocean's so he can reach over to kick the back of Phoenix's knee. Just as Phoenix's leg collapses and he falls, a scatter of bullets hits the ground where he was.

"Hold your fire!" Amell roars.

"Goddammit." Phoenix pushes himself off the ground, rubbing his leg. Gemini offers him a hand up. "What the fuck, Amell?"

A woman leaps down from an impossible height. She lands so heavily in front of them that the ground shakes and a ring of dirt *whumps* into the air. Ocean throws up an arm to shield her eyes from the dust and hears a faint clicking and whir. The woman straightens, pushing back the hood of her cloak. She has golden-blond hair and dark-brown eyes, her mouth a thin line. Her face is angular, starved for something other than food.

"We have clear orders, Amell," she says.

"Those orders aren't absolute, Emory," he says. "This is Garrett."

"I don't go by that anymore," Phoenix says.

"You might know him better as Phoenix," Amell corrects.

Emory disdainfully takes Phoenix in as her finger twitches over her trigger. Ocean softly pushes a step back in preparation. "Corvus said no one who goes into that place leaves alive."

"I can promise you Corvus will be *very* upset if you put a bullet into Garrett," Amell says. "He might even kill you himself."

Emory glares at Phoenix, her squint assessing him.

"I'm going to ask you one more time, Amell," Phoenix says. "What is Corvus up to?"

"You could have been a part of it," Amell says. "But you didn't have the spine for it."

"I didn't lack anything," Phoenix says coldly.

"You think your conscience has gotten you anywhere? Has it done anything for the people you loved? The planet you called home?" Amell sneers. "No. Instead, you used it as an excuse to abandon our true savior."

Phoenix's frown is a harsh slash on his face. "Savior? Do you think Corvus is capable of anything except destruction?"

"Phoenix." Gemini rubs his eyes. "I'm bored." He claps Phoenix on the back and slings an arm around Ocean's shoulder. "You can all catch up some other time, yeah?"

They manage to shamble forward a few steps away before Amell asks, "Do you have him?"

Phoenix stops. "Have whom?"

"Did you take the job? The Alliance was alerted after the ship was destroyed. But they didn't find any bodies."

"The Alliance?" Phoenix repeats with surprise as he turns around. He says scornfully, "You know I don't mess with them. If they raise my bounty any higher, I'll have to turn myself in. We only came by today to pick up a new gig. If you want to verify that, you can peruse Portos's records."

"He destroyed them all before we got to him." Emory tilts her head. "He wasn't a friend of yours, was he?"

Ocean thinks back to how carefully Phoenix closed Portos's eyes, folded his arms, and studied his body while Gemini gave him the time and space to do so. She thinks of the worry in his shoulders back at the bar and on the *Pandia*.

"He was a good LP," Phoenix says. "It's going to be a pain in the ass to find another."

"You're a liar," Amell says.

"Gasp. Me?"

"You don't deal with anyone, meet anyone, you don't immediately befriend. You're a bleeding heart, Garrett. Did you step onto that ship before blowing it up? Find another puppy dog to rescue? Even if he is the stinking prince of the disgusting Anand corporation?"

Phoenix shrugs. "I don't know what you're talking about."

Amell's eyes narrow. "Are you taking his *side*? Have you forgotten what the Anands have done to us? Did you turn your back on Mercury after you left Corvus?"

"I haven't forgotten anything," Phoenix says. "This is still my home."

But Ocean hears the tremor in his voice, and Amell spits into the dirt.

"Not if you're with him," Amell says. "What did he offer you? Money? No, that can't be it." He steps closer to Phoenix, peering up at his face. "Maybe the rumors are true, then. Corvus did try to proposition him, you know, but he didn't bite. But maybe Corvus just wasn't to the prince's taste?"

Phoenix stiffens, but Amell has moved on. He pulls down his hood to reveal his face. A scar twists up from his mouth, and his dark hair is tied back into a short bun on the top of his head. He motions to Ocean with his gun. "You next. Who are you?"

Gemini steps in front of Ocean. "You mind? I like to keep my steady's face to myself."

Amell gapes and then chuckles as Emory's face twists in displeasure. Gemini's words sounded casual, but his shoulders move with deliberate, calm breaths. His stance is wide and the hand behind his back is positioned as if he's warding her away from

Amell. He's curled his fingers, index finger and thumb extended. He leans forward, his jacket tight enough against his back to reveal the shape of the object underneath.

"We can't kill Garrett," Amell says. "But we can at least deal with the other two."

"Oh, can you?"

But even as Phoenix asks, distracting Amell and Emory, Gemini moves. The two fingers shaped behind his back outlined a position of attack, which Ocean figures out as he darts forward and diagonally to the right. Ocean dodges to the left as Emory's gun comes up, spitting laser bullets. Gemini clocks Amell in the leg, and Phoenix shoots at Emory as Ocean positions her own gun.

The last time I shot this gun, I killed someone, she thinks. But the gun is already aimed, its trigger pulled, because she's a machine, nothing if not precise, and she never misses.

Phoenix's shot hits Emory before hers. Bell-like pings answer them, and a blue shield illuminates Emory from underneath her clothes. The shots throw her back a step but leave her otherwise unharmed. A burst of bullets from Gemini's gun buffet her, and her body lights up again. She narrows her eyes at Ocean.

"You're *mine*," she says and races forward, inhumanly fast.

She whirls and brings her leg around, slamming it into Ocean. As Ocean goes flying, she feels like she's been hit by a two-by-four, a steel pipe, a tank. No one's leg can be that strong, unless—The blue shield makes sense now. She's got an augmented body. Ocean's gun is practically useless in this situation, unless the shield has a weak spot.

Emory leaps forward through the air. When she lands, Ocean hears in the crunch of her gears the same mechanical hum as when she landed from the rooftop. Emory lifts her gun, but it's a rookie error at such close range. Ocean punches up, bracing for impact as her fist connects with the metal of Emory's hand, and they both scream at the collision. Emory's shot goes wide, but pain and blood blossom across Ocean's knuckles. Using her gun as a punching glove, she chops at Emory's gun and knocks it out of her hand. Then she hurls her whole body at Emory's. It's like hitting a cement wall, but they both go down. Ocean catches a glimpse of the other fight: a blur of tangled limbs and movements. Phoenix lifts Gemini's jacket from the back just as Gemini reaches inside to pull out another gun. He shoots Amell's shoulder. Amell bellows, apparently without the same shield as his partner. Emory rolls, gathering Ocean and throwing her over her shoulder as she reaches for her own gun again.

As Ocean lands, she forces the air leaving her lungs to shape a syllable. "Gem!"

Gemini shoves Phoenix away, and the bullets light up between them. He slides between Amell's legs. He reaches up, grabbing Amell's jacket, and flips to land atop his shoulders. He presses his gun to the top of Amell's head, but Ocean sees him cock his chin at Phoenix, reading the signal there. He quickly shifts and shoots a glancing blow off Amell's other shoulder, jumping off him at the same time. Emory screams and lets loose a barrage of bullets. Gemini and Phoenix sprint for cover. Phoenix leaps down into the staircase of another unit and Gemini dashes into an alleyway, leaving behind Ocean, who's pushed herself up to a crouch. Amell and Emory spin to point their guns at her. Amell's shoulders are both bleeding and it must hurt to even hold his position, but it's Emory's face that's twisted and furious.

"It's a bad steady who leaves his girl in a lurch like that," Amell grates.

Ocean shrugs, opting for an up-and-down motion instead of the shoulder tap that would give her away as Alliance. "It's a bad shield who gets too caught up in her own anger to properly guard her partner."

Emory blanches. Ocean correctly guessed that since she's the only one with an augmented suit, it's probably her job to protect the others. Either of them can shoot her, but Ocean provoked Emory first for a reason. Ocean whips her arm around, targeting Amell, and shoots. Rather than firing off her own shot, Emory dives in front of Amell. Ocean's bullets hit Emory's shield, and it flares blue again. The force of the impact shoves her into Amell and they both fall backward. Amell squeezes his trigger as he collapses under Emory's weight, and Ocean throws herself to the ground to escape his bullets. One clips her in the leg and her blood mixes into the dust of the road.

"Stay down, Ocean!"

It's a good thing she's flat to the dirt anyway. Wind whooshes above her. A crash shatters the air. By the time she lifts her head, Amell and Emory are buried underneath layers of metal sheet paneling. Emory grips the metal and thrusts it off her body, assisting a groaning Amell upright.

"This is my turf," Phoenix says from the stairwell. "You thought *you* could set a trap for us here? You know me better than that, Amell."

Ocean sees Gemini at the same time Amell and Emory do. He's clinging to the side of a house with his knife out, having set free the paneling that crashed into them. Amell and Emory swing their guns up, but Gemini lets go of the wall in a free fall. Ocean holds her breath as he flips and lands lightly like a cat. Phoenix charges up the stairwell. Gemini slides behind Phoenix, using him to completely shield his body. That stops Amell, but Emory doesn't hesitate. Her gun's ready, and she doesn't have the same compunction that her partner's displaying right now.

Ocean props herself up on her good knee with her gun out. As her arm comes up in a straight line, everything around her seems to slow.

Then, it stops.

Every once in a while, her vision converges onto one thing. Her whole body becomes one heartbeat, an expanded thud.

Ocean's bullet pings Emory's hand. Her shield covers that hand, but the force of the shot is enough to throw her aim wide. Then, while Amell is still focused on Phoenix, Ocean aims at his back.

For a sliver of a second, Ocean considers whether or not to kill him. She feels a hand squeezing her bad shoulder, and a voice whispering in her ear, *Nice job, Headshot.*

She pulls the trigger.

The world slams into motion again. Blood jets out of Amell's back and he slumps over. Emory screams and catches him before his body hits the ground. She scrambles for her gun in the dirt.

"You don't want to do that," Ocean calls out as she carefully stands up.

"Don't tell me what to do," Emory snarls.

"He's not dead," Ocean says, and Emory halts, gun in hand.

"What?"

"He's not dead. But if you don't get him to a medic right away, he will be." Ocean stows her gun in her jacket. "I didn't hit his heart, but it's still a bullet wound, and he's losing blood. Decide quickly. You can keep fighting us, or you can save his life."

Emory stares blankly at Ocean. Then her face screws up in hatred. She hoists Amell into her arms, then gathers herself and sprints away, her gears buzzing as she leaves behind a literal cloud of dust. Phoenix has his two guns pointed after her as he edges back toward Ocean. Gemini has somehow sidled closer to Ocean during this time, too, and he flips his knife back into some hidden sheath. Both have their backs partially turned to Ocean, and as she stands beside them, lightheaded, she thinks of what that means. She takes a step forward, but her vision goes white, and when she leans on her right leg, she doesn't know what's up or down.

"Whoa, easy there."

Phoenix grabs onto her arm while her head spins. She doesn't know whether closing her eyes will help ease the sudden nausea or not, but right now, she really, *really* needs to hurl.

"Come on, put her on my back."

"You? You're barely taller than her, Gemini."

"Do you want her to throw up all over *you* then, Phoenix?"

"You make a fair point," Phoenix concedes. Ocean barely protests as Gemini crouches in front of her and Phoenix helps him piggyback her. Now that the adrenaline is leaving her body, it's limp and boneless. "Wait a second," Phoenix says. He pulls out a handkerchief and wraps it around Ocean's leg.

"Garrett doesn't suit you," Ocean says hazily as he ties the strip.

Phoenix's laugh is soft, self-deprecating. "Glad we agree on that."

She rests her head on Gemini's shoulder, her nose against his neck. As he lifts, she closes her eyes and grips her arms around his shoulders. She hopes she doesn't actually throw up all over him.

As if he can hear her thoughts, Gemini says quietly, "Steady on, Ocean."

"This isn't so bad," she says. "I was in much worse shape after I met you."

"You can't blame me for all of that."

"You made me drop into the water." Ocean tries to temper her tone. "I had to *swim*."

"I offered you a hand up. A job too. Maybe the fall messed with your memory."

Ocean's memory is perfectly fine. She remembers Gemini's body crouching over hers, the cut of his smile, and his wavy hair flattened by the rain as he held out his hand to her.

"I can probably walk just fine."

"Sure, but you don't have to, so hold on."

They'll get to the ship faster if she's carried, so she does as he says. "What's your real name, then?" Ocean asks.

He doesn't respond for a long while, long enough that Ocean's not sure if she asked the question aloud. She might have only meant to say it.

"Hurakan Castillo," he says finally. "My mom chose it."

"Hurakan," she tries it out. "That does suit you."

He doesn't answer right away, and hitches her body higher on his back. "I don't mind if you use it."

He and Phoenix move quickly, but his steps are as smooth as a fog rolling in. Ocean's lulled into a half doze and only registers that they've arrived by the sudden drop in temperature as they enter the cool space of the hangar where the *Pandia*'s waiting. She hears a commotion, then someone running. The frantic voice echoes around the garage, overloud. So loud that Ocean thinks she must be mistaken. She's never heard Sasani this agitated.

"What happened to her? *Is she all right?!*"

Ocean opens her eyes to Sasani holding out his hands. Again, she thinks something is wrong. His skin is too pale, and his expression is stricken. But despite her wooziness, she can still make out all the details of his features. His sleeves are rolled up and his hair is damp, and when he turns, she sees that a portion of his undercut has been freshly shaved. The rest looks as it did this morning, and Ocean limply reaches her hand out. She can't say if it's to confirm that his hair is only half-cut, or if it's in response to his own hands.

Gemini tightens his arms around her and steps around Sasani. "She'll be fine. Follow me and I'll take you to where you can patch her up."

They hasten aboard the ship, and Ocean closes her eyes again, tucking her head back into Gemini's neck.

TWENTY

HIS NAME IS CORVUS," Phoenix says. They're flying through space again, and almost everyone's gathered into the cockpit, although Aries is concentrating at the wheel. Ocean and Sasani are still in the infirmary. It's crowded around the table, but they're sharing the space surprisingly well. Teo doesn't know if it's everyone making the best of a weird situation or if normal is just constantly shifting. "He's . . ." Phoenix trails off. "We used to work together."

"You used to work with the person who killed my family?"

"Don't yell at him," Cass says hotly, but Phoenix holds up a hand.

"He's from Mercury, like I am." Phoenix runs his hands through his hair. "Corvus has always been angry at Anand Tech for exploiting Mercury. He hates the Alliance by extension because their contract with your father pushed Mercury to its limits. Mercury has always been completely dependent on the businesses that created us. All our resources are funneled into other planets, into Anand Tech, into the Alliance. Added onto that is the fact that your father has been extremely vocal about halting its terraforming . . ."

Had been. Teo stops himself from correcting Phoenix. Instead of addressing when or how that correction became an automatic reflex, he sifts through the tumult of his thoughts.

"Was Corvus there?" Teo asks tightly. "Did you see him?"

"No, but I recognized someone else from his team," Phoenix answers. "He was with someone new who was outfitted in an augmented suit."

"An augmented suit?" Teo's hands twitch and he has to stop them from reaching up to his ears to ward off the sound of bones cracking, Dayeon's back breaking.

"I didn't realize it then, but it's one of Corvus's old designs. He never had the funds to produce it before." Phoenix kneads his eyes. "At this point, you may as well contact your families. Corvus knows me well enough to know that I wouldn't have killed anyone on the *Ohneul*, so there's no use hiding. But there will be some restrictions—"

Teo stands, the pain burgeoning within him, as Maggie exclaims about her spouses. Von puts his hand on Teo's arm, but he roughly shakes it off.

"How could you have worked with someone like that? Did you hate us that much?"

"It wasn't about you personally," Phoenix says.

Teo laughs and Phoenix flinches. "Just generally, then? Well, what does Corvus want now, Phoenix? My family is dead. But he's still using Declan's body, his face, his image. What more could he want?"

"Total annihilation," Phoenix says. His face has gone still, and his eyes are full of hurt, but Teo can't figure out who or what for. "I shouldn't have picked you up."

His words puncture Teo's insides, letting loose an oozing nausea.

"We had a deal." Teo's voice wobbles. "You said you'd help me. I can . . ." Teo falters. He hates how pathetic he sounds. "I can pay you more."

Phoenix's face shutters. "It's not about the money." He says flatly, "There are lines I won't cross, Teophilus. Maybe you don't understand that because you've kept yourself blind all these years to the lines your family crossed. You think you can control people because of your family's money, their power? You even have Ocean pulling the trigger for you!"

Phoenix's words are more personal than any of the slings and arrows fate has struck Teo with. Teo staggers and Phoenix halts, his skin going chalky.

"Thank you for helping me get my answers," Teo coldly forces the words out. "When I get my hands on Corvus, I won't have someone else pull the trigger."

Teo pushes his chair from the table and leaves the room.

• • • • •

Ocean examines the wrap around her leg, which is neat enough to be used as a reference photo in a textbook. A cool and collected Sasani quickly stitched up her wound and then saw to her hand before leaving to get ice from the kitchen. Ocean's head is clearer now, and she's left wondering how much of what she saw in the hangar was real.

The door slides open then, revealing Sasani, who's inscrutable once again. His sleeves are still rolled up and his hair is damp. Sasani hands her an ice pack and also a can of lychee soda. When she looks up at him in surprise, he's already turned away, picking up the remainders of the bandage wrap to stow away.

"You should stay on painkillers for a while," he says. "They have plenty of those here, even if they don't have much else."

"Thank you," Ocean says. "I'm always having to thank you, it seems."

Sasani goes still, pausing in the middle of rolling the bandage. "If it bothers you, you should try not to get hurt."

"I'm always trying not to get hurt," she says.

Sasani finally looks at her, and some emotion crosses his previously unreadable face.

"Are you?" he asks. Ocean's stomach flips as if she's lost her footing. Sasani hunches his shoulder away from her again, opening a drawer to the side of the bed, but he twitches at whatever he sees inside. Ocean can guess at its state of disorder. Sasani finds comfort in the routine of taking care of his spaces. Back on the *Ohneul*, he methodically swept the small infirmary every evening. And here on the *Pandia*, he's in constant motion, absentmindedly picking up after Teo's trail of opened snack boxes, automatically straightening the pairs of shoes discarded outside room entrances. "Yet, somehow, you're the only one who got injured out there." He speaks over his shoulder, and his faint smile is more evident in his eyes than his mouth. "I guess I shouldn't be surprised."

Ocean concentrates on placing the ice pack on her knuckles, attributing the sudden wrench in her chest to the shock of its cold. She holds up the lychee soda can with her other hand.

"Is this just a bonus?"

"I thought it would make you feel better."

She cracks the tab one-handed and takes a long gulp. The bubbles fizz, popping in the silence between them. She twangs the tab a few times, a nervous gesture.

"Do you want to try?" she asks, holding out the can.

Sasani stares at her and then at the offered drink. Then, he delicately takes it from her. As he pauses with the can's rim before his mouth, she sees the angle of his collarbones, the shirt thin enough to hint at his body underneath. Ocean hears him swallow before he finally tilts his head back to take a sip. A thin stream escapes his mouth, marking a trail down his neck. She studies the spread of his tattoo on the back of his upper arms. It's her first time seeing it, other than the bare hint at the back of his neck. It must stretch across his back before ending at his elbows like extended wings. The wings are black, but the feathers are edged in silvery gray. He raises his arm to wipe his mouth and when she looks up at him, she sees that he's been watching her watching him.

"Yoon, if something were to happen to you . . ." he tries. Ocean can track his breath from how his chest expands, from the movement across his barely parted lips. It's a process that happens so naturally, without thought, but suddenly it's all she can think about, his unsteady breathing in the too-quiet room. "I don't know what I'd do," he finishes. He hands back her can and she takes it to drink from again. His eyes are dark like volcanic glass, intent on her. "And I don't know exactly what that means for me. But the thing that keeps me up at night isn't that I don't know my own feelings. It's that I don't know yours."

Her heart stops beating. He's laid himself so open, but despite the voice in her head screaming at her to answer, all she can do is hand the can back. He lifts the can, pressing his lips where hers just were. Then, he passes the drink back.

"You know, I applied to your ship after I read the *Hadouken* report," Sasani says. "I came here for you."

"The *Hadouken* report," Ocean repeats. Her heart contracts painfully, reminding her that it exists after all. "You came here because of that? Have you seen the footage?"

"No. I read the transcripts, though."

A bitter laugh fights its way out of her. Of course he hasn't seen it. She puts the lychee soda down on the side table between them.

"The *Hadouken*. Everyone seems so curious about that."

"Anand said you saved his life," Sasani says.

"That's a nice way to frame it," she says. "The reality is that I saw how it was going to unfold. The raider was going to shoot Teo in the head. The captain wasn't wrong. Dropping our weapons would result in the fewest casualties. But . . ."

"But he was going to kill Anand."

Ocean nods. "I aimed my gun at the raider next to him. A girl."

Sasani shakes his head. "I don't understand."

"I learned in Sav-Faire that you should always find out what's most important to people—what they'd save first in a fire, who means the most to them," Ocean explains.

Ocean puts the ice pack down next to the lychee can. Her cold fingers make unbuttoning her jacket an awkward maneuver. She reaches inside its lining to pull out her gun, pretending not to notice how Sasani stiffens. If someone from Sav-Faire had seen the way Sasani looked at her when they came into the hangar today, the way he looked at her just a few minutes ago, he would have been done for. She pities anyone who could look at her like that.

"Then you use it against them," she continues. "A lot of people pay attention to what others look at. But usually, what people avoid looking at is much more revealing. Not once did Tomas look at Diana. But they were constantly aware of each other. They could have been doubles partners in a tennis match." She forces herself to hold Sasani's dark, fathomless eyes. She had thought she was being honest with him last night, that she could tell him anything. "If I shot Tomas directly, there was a chance that he would still pull the trigger on Teo. So, I aimed at Diana, the most important thing to him. His primary objective became stopping me from hurting her."

"But you did it to save—"

Ocean clicks the safety off her gun, interrupting his sentence. When she clicks it on again, its sound is a dry staccato.

"Tomas moved his gun away from Teo's head to stop me. So, I immediately shot his hand, severing his trigger finger. Then, I shot him again, through the chest. Teo's head was right next to Tomas's heart, but I was confident that I could just graze Teo and still get Tomas." Sasani shudders and the sound twists in Ocean's stomach. "I killed the rest of the raiders after that."

This time, as Ocean listens to Sasani's shaky breathing, the moment elongates, awful and tinny like a rotten memory.

"You told me about your brother," Sasani says. "So how could you . . . doesn't it mean anything to you to take a life?"

But her decision hadn't been about the loss of life. It had been about not knowing the exact moment her brother died out in space, about facing a future in which Teo died because she did nothing. It had been about the certainty of that gun in her hands, the confidence that she could make something right, *be* something right.

"You read the report, Sasani," she says. "You knew I killed those people."

"Yes, but I thought—"

"You assumed I'd be more apologetic about it." Ocean holsters the gun back in her jacket. "I've thought about what their last moments must have been like. I've thought about what their friends or families must have felt. I killed them and severed all their possibilities." She mercilessly wields each word like a knife. "Does that make it better, Sasani? That I've thought about it? It's done. I can't change any of that."

"You can care about how you live now," he chokes. "You can choose differently going forward."

"I'd do it again," she says. Sasani curls his body inward, but not before she sees his awful expression. She takes the ice pack again as if they've finished the conversation and she presses it to her knuckles. She waits for it to numb her, but the cold only seems to amplify the ache. "They used to call me Headshot," she says. "It's because I don't miss."

The door slides open. Teo grips the doorway.

"Ocean." Teo's face crumbles. "I don't want to have to ask you. But I don't . . . I don't know what to do." He stumbles in and only then seems to notice Sasani. He offers out a hand as if he means to grasp his shoulder, but stops himself. "Sasani, I think our comm ban is over. We can call our families again. I thought you might want to know."

Sasani's face goes slack with relief. Teo walks forward and slumps next to Ocean. He leans his head down on her shoulder and she relaxes as their bodies find a familiar position. He wearily holds up a fist. She bumps it with her own. She doesn't watch to see if Sasani looks back at them before he leaves.

Teo wakes with a start, the stench of singed flesh stinging his nostrils, flames etched into his retinas. He scrapes frantically at himself before he recognizes the slick of his skin as sweat, not some unidentifiable goop. His breathing chafes the canned darkness of an unfamiliar room.

"You're a loud sleeper." Gemini sits cross-legged on his bed, his eyes a glimmer in the darkness. On Teo's other side, Sasani's blankets and sleeping pad are neatly folded on the ground. Teo reflexively looks to his wrist, but his comm isn't there. "It's a little after 200. It's still sleeping time," Gemini says, his voice velvet soft.

"Try telling my nightmares that."

"You're going to have those for a while. I'd tell you to get used to them, but well . . ." Gemini slips from his bed and pads over to the door. "Follow me."

The hallway holds a cool, calm quiet. Gemini hops on the ladder and slides down, landing lightly on the deck below. Teo follows Gemini down the hall to an open door. Inside, Lupus is at a keyboard. Next to them, a flat-screen plays a film Teo only recognizes as old. Some animatronic dinosaurs roam around a kitchen.

"Lupus, you have the REM band I asked you about?" Gemini asks. Lupus lifts one side of their headphones, releasing the movie's faint screaming into the room, while on-screen two kids scramble around. Gemini repeats his question, and Lupus opens a drawer, retrieving a blue wristband and tossing it over their shoulder. Gemini easily catches the band. "Thanks, Lupus."

The headphones snap back onto their head, half-lidded survey of the screen uninterrupted, fingers tapping.

"What's their story?" Teo asks as they leave the room together.

"I met Lupus after they were fired from their job at the New York Public Library."

"No kidding?"

"Got caught hacking into their own system."

"Into the *library* system? Is there anything to steal?"

"No, but it's how hackers practice. The library wasn't too pleased, though, even if there was no real security threat." Gemini shrugs. "They interested me enough that I kept tabs on them. I wanted to see if they'd get bored, if they'd get better."

"How good are they now?"

Gemini's sliver of a smile widens. He hands over the band he got from Lupus, and Teo examines the plastic wristlet.

"It'll track your sleeping. If you're having nightmares, it'll vibrate strongly enough to kick you out of the dream without waking you. Cass developed it years ago for Phoenix, and I asked Lupus to disable its comm. We're still monitoring everyone's calls."

That doesn't matter to Teo. He doesn't have anyone to call.

"Why are you giving this to me?" Teo asks.

"Not being able to sleep is its own torture," Gemini says, loping back down the hall. "It's not going to solve your PTSD. But it'll help with some of the symptoms. Phoenix told me to give it to you."

"Why?"

"Ask him. Not me." Gemini doesn't bother turning around. "Maybe he knew that your waking up every hour disturbs me. I'm a very light sleeper, you see. It's why I usually have the room to myself. It's also why I put you two in with me, so I could keep an eye on you."

Teo cranes his neck, searching the dark corridors. "Where *is* Sasani?"

"Sasani's restless, but he's polite about it. Likes to sneak around at night and listen to music."

Gemini steps so quietly, Teo might as well be walking with a shadow. Teo's booted feet land heavily even when he tries to place them more carefully. He never used to wear shoes indoors. But now when he goes to sleep, he can't help thinking about how his fingers will fumble while tying his laces if they're attacked at night. He knows it's foolish, but now that he's started doing it, he feels like something bad will happen the one night he *does* take off his shoes.

"Did you work with Corvus too?" Teo asks.

"Never met him," Gemini says. "Phoenix has said maybe two sentences about him in all the time I've known him."

"Is Phoenix going to turn me over to him?"

Gemini shrugs one shoulder like a cat avoiding an overbearing hand.

"We're headed to Venus to drop off the Alliance kids, but I'll tell you this much: Phoenix always tries to do the right thing," he says, "even if it screws him over."

Teo used to pride himself on at least knowing what the right thing was, even if he didn't do it. "That doesn't sound like the ideal sort of raider to follow."

"Eh, he's not my usual type. He's so sincere it's embarrassing. Televises all his moves. Terrible at poker." Gemini clicks his tongue, then flashes Teo a smile he doesn't understand. "But I guess I was looking for someone to break the type. You kinda wonder how he's survived this long in our business. He's so obvious, he should be long dead in a ditch somewhere, full of bullets. But that's kinda his charm, you see?" He cocks his head back at Teo. "Of course you do."

Gemini clambers back up the ladder, so Teo doesn't have to answer. Back in his room, Gemini slides under his covers, and Teo follows suit. He's surprised when Gemini speaks into the darkness.

"I'm sorry about your family. And your crew."

"Yeah. Me too," Teo says. "I'm sorry about your friend too. Your LP?"

"Portos wasn't really my friend. But he was Phoenix's."

Teo hesitates. "Have you ever lost anyone?"

"I've seen a lot of death. But I've never had anyone to lose. At least, not until the *Pandia*," Gemini says. "There's a reason I'm so careful about who we bring in."

"Why Ocean?"

"There are lots of reasons to be interested in Ocean." When Gemini doesn't continue, Teo shifts his head toward him. Gemini rolls over onto his side and props his head up on his elbow. "She's like Phoenix, in a way."

"Ocean's anything but obvious."

"True," Gemini says. "But I can stand by anyone who takes care of their own." Gemini rolls back over as if to punctuate the end of their conversation.

But after a pause, Teo says to the ceiling, "You know she's coming with me, right?"

"Not for forever, Teo," Gemini replies softly.

"I'm not forcing her to do anything."

But even as Teo says it, he knows it's a lie. Instead of answering, Gemini's breathing evens and slows. He wouldn't think it possible for someone to fall asleep that quickly, but the sound is unmistakable. Teo can't sleep, though, because Phoenix was right; it's not just that he trusts Ocean to pull the trigger for him.

When Ocean aimed her gun at him on the *Hadouken*, when that red-hot pain flared across his cheek, he thought that she had decided to shoot him in the face. And if she had, he would have thanked her for it. He would have trusted her choice more than anything he's ever decided for himself. He would have put his death, his blood, on her hands without a second thought.

When he realized, though, that the blood pooling around him wasn't his own, he couldn't be sure whether he felt relief or disappointment.

TWENTY-ONE

"EO?"

From the kitchen doorway, Von offers Teo a doe-eyed blink. He looks like he'd rather be struck by lightning than keep talking. Teo smiles while he pops open the box in his hands. Killing the messenger is pointless.

"Hi Vonderbar. Want a Moon Bar?"

"I think you should come see the news," he says worriedly.

Teo has been studiously avoiding the news after the Seonbi Embassy funeral. His parents' death is there for everyone to see, from every angle. He can't bear to watch his doppelganger plunge the blade in and out of their bodies, blood flying everywhere as a dispassionate voice-over dissects the scene. He doesn't care if that makes him a coward.

"Maybe later, hoddeok," he says.

"You'll want to see this." Phoenix appears behind Von, who whips his head around.

Phoenix's face is neutral, but Teo immediately tenses. He puts down the box of Moon Bars and motions for them to lead the way. He follows them down the hall and into the common room, where the transparent screen is on.

His brother is on-screen. Or, rather, whoever is playing the part of his brother. *God*, it looks just like him. He's so intent on his brother's features, he doesn't hear what Declan is saying at first.

"He's my brother, but I can't condone his actions. My parents are dead because of him," Declan says.

Teo sits in a chair and rests his chin on his tented fingers. Declan's wearing a white suit threaded in gold. Mourning attire, but the cut is extremely fine. It's new; Teo hasn't seen it before. The threading is subtle, but it sparks whenever a camera flashes, which is often. Declan speaks like himself, even absentmindedly tucks a curl behind his ear the way he always does. It makes Teo sick.

"Do you know who that is?" Teo asks without taking his eyes off Declan. "Is that Corvus?"

Phoenix shifts behind him. "That's not Corvus. It might be a man named Hadrian. He . . . we called him the Chameleon. He's very good at imitating people."

"This thing he's doing, this technology, you knew about it?"

"No . . . I never would have imagined this possible."

Declan looks beyond the camera, presumably at a reporter. He doesn't turn his head to listen or flinch as camera flashes go off but instead gives the reporter his full attention. It's a tactic they both learned from their father.

"Yes, I'm cooperating with the Alliance to try to bring him in. If anyone spots him, please report it. He could be harmful to others, to himself. He's clearly not in his right mind and might say or do anything to convince you he didn't do it. But I was there. I held his eyes while he stabbed me. I saw him kill—" The imposter wearing Declan's face breaks off. That's where his performance falls short. No matter what, Teo's brother wouldn't lose composure. But Hadrian's playing for the solar. If their roles were reversed, if Teo was up there, he knows it wouldn't do well to appear completely stoic. "He's the only family I have left, but he has to atone for what he's done." Hadrian directly addresses the camera and rubs two fingers on his forehead. He uses his left hand. That bastard is mocking him. "Teo. Babu, if you're watching, just come home. Please. You've harmed enough people."

Teo wants to be angry, but suddenly, all he can think about is his real brother using that same motion. All the grief he's kept at bay wells up. His parents were so *good*. His brother always took care of him, even when he didn't deserve it. But now they're just gone, not able to help anyone, leaving him with nothing but the taste of blood and revenge in his mouth. And still, he just wants to run away. His overwhelming desire is to roll over and do nothing, and he hates himself for it.

"Why am I so useless?" he whispers, and only then is he aware of the tears brimming over. Spindly arms wrap around him, and Teo lets Von hug him while he tilts his head back to let his tears gather.

"Can you give us a moment?" Phoenix asks.

Von squeezes Teo harder and confirms, "Teo?"

"Yeah. I'm fine. Don't tell Ocean I cried."

Von lets go. Teo hears him walk away, and he rubs his sleeve over his eyes.

"Here." Phoenix offers him a handkerchief, because of course he's the type of person who carries one around.

"You keep these on hand for crying damsels?" Teo asks. He presses the proffered square to his eyes, not wanting to scrub at his skin anymore.

"They're mostly for sopping up blood," Phoenix says. Teo stops and holds the handkerchief away, squinting at it. "That one's clean."

Phoenix takes a seat next to Teo and, with a fluid motion, swipes off the screen so the Declan look-alike disappears.

"If you say so. Thank you."

Teo could try to figure out what's going on behind Phoenix's vivid blue eyes, but he's exhausted with reading people.

Phoenix says, "I think I owe you an apology."

"Another one?" Teo says, but it's without venom. "We could probably spend the rest of the cycle finding things to apologize to each other for."

"Being around you . . . it's like my body is bruised and you keep pressing all the wrong spots."

"I'm flattered."

"You should be. Not everyone can get under my skin," Phoenix responds. He bites his thumb, distracting Teo. "Corvus and I . . ." Teo drops his gaze. "It's complicated. Corvus's parents were scientists, originally from Venus. Their work was used by Mercury's government to increase productivity in the mines. But when they tried to quit, they were . . . done away with." He drops his head. "My parents died working those mines too."

Something stirs in Teo. "Are you from Penelope?"

"You know about it?" Phoenix asks.

"Let's assume I don't know anything," Teo replies. He has a vague memory of an accident. He was a child and can only recall his father's devastated demeanor, the miasma of despair seeping out of his room for days after. "Most people do."

"Surely you know that Anand Tech and the Alliance have had a relationship for over twenty years now," Phoenix ventures. When Teo waves him on, he continues, "Landing the Alliance contract, becoming their sole manufacturer was, and still is, a big deal. So your father turned to Mercury. The whole solar has always seen it as a place to be stripped and plundered." Phoenix shrugs, a quick jerk of his shoulders. "Anand Tech was desperate to produce for the Alliance. My parents were part of the influx of labor. But Anand Tech didn't take the proper precautions, and one day the mines . . ." His hands mime an explosion. "The worst part is that they kept going. Even our own government just covered it up and moved on. They needed the money. Corvus and I both hated that Mercury was being controlled like that. Bled dry by people who didn't care about us."

It mixes what Teo does and doesn't know. He thought he understood the context of those business dinners with Mercurians. But their hatred had never seemed warranted from all that he researched of Anand Tech, for all that he learned about his father's work on other planets. His family was good. Anand Tech was meant to do good. It *does* good. But that doesn't mean Phoenix is lying.

"I'm sorry," Teo says.

"I can't help you against Corvus," Phoenix says slowly. "But I can at least give you some information about him. I asked Lupus to pull together a file for you."

"Do you have a picture of him?" Teo asks. Phoenix flicks open a folder from his wristband. When the photo appears, Teo's breath catches. That pale face, those unmistakable cold gray eyes. "I know him," he says flatly.

"What do you mean?" Phoenix asks.

"He approached me at a bar once. Said he had a proposal for me."

Like a fool, Teo dismissed him. Corvus sought him out, to talk to him before the *Shadowfax* left. His body flashes feverishly hot then cold. He sat at the same table as Corvus, who probably already had his plans in motion.

"Teophilus," Phoenix says. Teo squeezes his eyes shut. It should enrage him to know that Corvus sat before him. But more than that, he's consumed by guilt. He should have figured out what Corvus wanted that night, taken him seriously, taken his life seriously. But as always, he hadn't. He takes a few shallow, painful breaths and suddenly feels a warm pressure over his chest. "Teophilus, what do you need?"

Teo opens his eyes to Phoenix, who's pressed his hand against Teo's body like the last time they were in this room together. Phoenix's regard is sharp enough to feel like an actual blade. Teo struggles to backtrack, and Phoenix's expression shifts. He tentatively reaches with his other hand and Teo swears that heat is emanating from it, spreading into Teo's body. Phoenix touches Teo's chin and tilts it. His thumb grazes Teo's cheek, and Teo's breath stutters in his throat.

"Is this from the *Hadouken*?" Phoenix asks, his voice barely a whisper.

"Yes."

Phoenix has the smallest mole near the right corner of his mouth, and Teo could curse because *of course* he does. His heart threatens to thud out of his chest. He could ask why now, why *him*? But Phoenix bends closer and Teo's heartrate approximates the speed of a hummingbird's. He blames Donna and her mega-sized Phoenix poster. Both of which were burned to ashes.

Teo asks, "Do you still love him?"

The words stop Phoenix in his tracks. He searches Teo, pupils wide. They remain frozen in this position for too long, long enough for Teo to memorize the details of the moment, the exact roughness of Phoenix's fingers, and how badly he wants them to trace his skin, across his lips, down his neck. Phoenix drops his hands and leans back.

"No," he says. "But he's always going to be a part of me."

Phoenix is no longer touching him, but Teo can still feel where his hands were.

"Would you take me somewhere, as a final favor?" Teo asks.

"Where?" Phoenix responds without hesitation.

Live generously. Live well. His father's gone. His mother's gone. His brother is gone. But he's still here.

"Can you take me to Artemis?"

"To the Seonbi Embassy station on the Moon? You're turning yourself in?"

"Not necessarily," Teo says. "I'm taking responsibility."

· · • · ·

When Haven came by his room, Gemini sat up straight in bed as if he had been waiting for him, despite the late hour. Gemini's off camera now, sitting cross-legged while monitoring the call, just as he did Haven's first with his father. They could have set up in the infirmary, or in Lupus's control center, but Haven's come to like the common room best. He likes the quietness of the void outside the window as they soar through space. He also didn't want to feel like Gemini was on top of him during this next call.

"Drod, Pedar."

It's pitch black on the ship, but already the next morning on Prometheus. Haven's father rubs at his eyes.

"Haven?" he says. "Chi shode? Is everything all right?"

"I'm fine, don't worry," he assures his father.

His father relaxes back into his seat. "Good, good. As long as you're safe."

"I'm heading home as soon as I can." From the corner of his eye, Haven sees Gemini shift.

"You're an adult," his father says mildly. "But I'm allowed to worry about you. I'm the one who made you join the Alliance after all."

"You didn't make me do anything," Haven protests.

"No, but it was my strong desire you wanted to fulfill," he amends. "It was foolish of me, I know that now. If I couldn't revisit my past, I shouldn't have expected you to."

"You were not the one who chose my assignment," he says. "I don't think either of us anticipated this much excitement."

"It was very bad luck," his father says.

He considers his window again, the vastness of the solar beyond. "It has been painful at times. But I'm not sorry to be here."

His father studies him. He ruffles his hair, attempting to smooth it down. "Well, I suppose we'll see you soon."

We.

"I like your hair," Haven says. "Did Esfir do it?"

"She didn't do a bad job," he replies, putting a hand on it. "Not as good as you, though."

Haven touches his own hair, finally even after he finished it. He studies the etched feathers on his bent arm, remembering the way Yoon marveled at them.

"Is Esfir there?"

His father raises his eyebrows. "You want to talk to her?"

His father's surprise feels rightfully like a rebuke. "If she's asleep, I don't want to wake her."

"Even if she is asleep, she would want me to wake her," he says. He rises from his position without asking Haven if he's sure.

Moments later, too soon, as if Esfir was already on the other side of the door, she sits in front of the screen. Maybe that first time he called his father, she had also been waiting close by, expecting to talk to him, expecting him to ask about her.

"Haven," she says. Her face relaxes when she sees him, which he doesn't deserve. He deserves accusation, anger, disappointment.

"Drod, Esfir."

Prometheus's morning sun brings out the honey threads of Esfir's dark hair. Her feathers are of the long-billed vulture, and its gold-and-white feathers wind from the back of her wrist up her right arm. The light reminds Haven again of how she sits in the future, the next day. But Esfir has always been ahead of him, in age, in confidence. Fully formed in ways that seem unfathomable to him. They've been betrothed for only a couple of years, but the arrangement had been understood as the natural choice for much longer than that. And yet.

"We have been so worried," she says.

"I know. I'm so sorry. It was not my intention to worry you."

"Of course it wasn't." She snorts.

He relaxes. "You're the one who was always nagging me to leave our backwater moon. You and Pedar. 'See the solar,' you said. 'You won't grow properly if you stay there,' you said."

"I knew that if you experienced life beyond Prometheus, you'd understand why I was pushing you. Your pedar is the one who was hell-bent on getting you into the Alliance. I could have easily gotten you a position with me in the Norswedes. I still can."

"I wanted to thank you," he says, "for coming back to Prometheus to be with my father."

"We didn't know what happened to you," she says. "When we heard about your ship, we thought you might be dead."

"I'm sorry," he says again.

"Are you sorry that we thought you were dead, or are you sorry that you haven't talked to me until now?" she asks gently.

"I have not been good to you. Esfir . . ." Haven's hands flutter helplessly. He knows what he has to say; that's why it's so hard. "I am grateful to you for so much."

"Haven," Esfir says, the concern in her eyes now of a different sort. She slowly shakes her head.

"You made my childhood bearable," he says. "I don't think I would have survived it without you. But—"

"Wait. Haven. Whatever you're about to say, I can wait until you're back."

It would be so easy to push this conversation aside, but her pleading voice is what decides it.

"I think," he says. "It's time for you to stop waiting for me, Esfir."

One sentence. Enough to collapse a promise, a betrothal. Emotions flicker across Esfir's face before resolving into something firmer now that he's finally voiced it.

"Haven, you know I love you," she says. Gemini rises to his feet, reminding Haven of his presence. When he meets Haven's eyes, he puts a finger to his lips and slips out of the room. "You love me, too, I know it," Esfir continues. "Maybe not in the same way. I've known that for a while. But marriages have been built on worse."

Before, he might have given way to her logic, even as he felt himself sinking into sand. "It's not fair to you," he says.

"You don't get to decide that," Esfir says angrily. She stops. "Is it someone else?" The suddenness of her question startles him and to his surprise, she chuffs out a breath resembling a laugh. She smooths some wayward curls back from her face. "I see. Haven, I've always understood our relationship to be open—"

"Nothing happened," he says.

Nothing like that. He's never even touched Yoon outside of the infirmary, but he can count the number of times they've come close, can precisely measure the distance between her skin and his.

"Oh, Haven."

Esfir's leaned forward, studying his face. He wants to put his hand up, but it just reminds him again of Yoon, of how she brings her own hand to her face to hide. He still doesn't know which feelings are the right ones and which are wrong. As they passed the soda can back and forth, Yoon had slowly, deliberately taken him in. He'd wanted to close his eyes against that moment, to soak in the warmth of it, but he hadn't wanted to stop looking at her either.

To be a Mortemian is to accept death, to accept how people choose to approach it. It is to be without judgment. Who was he to tell Yoon how to feel about the lives she took? His hands are meant to heal. Her hands have taken lives. He thought he'd be able to reconcile that, but now he knows it might break him to try. It's been so easy to follow his father's wishes, Esfir's assurances, and even Yoon's unmistakable confidence as seen through a redacted report. But he has to start choosing for himself.

"Nothing happened," he repeats. He presses his hand to his heart, the heel of his palm on his sternum. "But I've been thinking about what's important to me."

"And I'm not," Esfir says.

"That's not what I mean," he says. "You are. You always will be. But I promised myself that I'd come back to Prometheus. It has always been important for me to honor my father. To carry on his ways. And I want some time back home."

He missed the last Nowruz because he was at Alliance training. Haven can picture his father in the kitchen, flour dusting his hair and a smeared white handprint on his dark-green apron. His hands deft as they fold dough over almond filling for his qottab. The hot pop of oil as he slides them one by one into the pot to deep fry.

It is a good life waiting for him. He can't spend his life chasing an absence or expecting other people to fill it. He's still forming, still learning, but he wants to value himself too.

"Will home be enough for you?" she asks.

"Yes," he replies.

"What if it isn't?"

Haven smiles. "I'll have to figure it out, then."

TWENTY-TWO

TEO HAS BEEN STANDING at the door for a while. Knock or don't knock. He should decide quickly, or else he'll be caught lurking where he shouldn't be.

The door slides open while Teo's fist is in midair, so he comes off looking like a damned fool anyway. Phoenix has his own hand up, in the middle of flattening his hair, and freezes.

"Yes?" he says. They both stand still like actors who've forgotten their next lines. "Did you forget which door is yours?"

Teo is sorely tempted to take that opening. He sighs and indicates the tabula he's holding. "Actually, I have something to show you."

"Want to come in?" Phoenix steps back. Feeling like a vampire that's gotten a lucky break, Teo moves forward, but Phoenix stops him with a palm to the chest. The sudden contact fizzles Teo's insides. "Watch your step."

It takes a moment for Teo to register the thin wire in front of the doorway.

"What happens if someone trips it?" Teo asks as he gingerly steps over it.

Phoenix flashes a grin. "Something unpleasant."

"Doesn't it defeat the purpose if you point it out to everyone who comes into your room?"

"I don't ask very many people to come into my room."

Phoenix turns away from Teo. His room is not much bigger than Gemini's. He has a bed pushed up against the far wall, and the small bookshelf next to it is jammed with books. Resting on top are a smattering of crumpled papers and a pair of spectacles. The flat-screen on the wall has a spindly crack running through it. Other than that, a small round table holds a few mugs, each filled with varying levels of liquid. Phoenix pulls out the one chair at the table for Teo and then sits on the bed, which still has rumpled covers.

"It's not—" Phoenix's head swivels around. "It's not the best it's been."

"Isn't that what you're required to say, even if you've just cleaned it?"

Teo pretends not to notice Phoenix shove an errant sock under his bed with his foot. He palms his tabula and swipes over to what he's been working on, stemming his curiosity about Phoenix's room and keeping himself from examining which titles are crammed into that bookshelf.

"Here." Teo hands over the tabula.

Phoenix squints at the screen. Then, to Teo's surprise, he grabs the glasses from the bookshelf and puts them on. He leans over the tabula and swipes to the next page, then the page after that.

"This . . . you did this?"

The screen lights up his face, showing off his intense concentration more clearly. Teo nervously knits his fingers together.

"Just some ideas."

He's been sketching, drawing mock-ups of some uniform redesigns for Phoenix and his team.

"This . . ." Phoenix trails off. "These are beautiful."

Teo's whole face goes warm just in time for Phoenix to catch it. But there's no mockery in his gaze, only a seriousness as he holds up the sketch he's currently viewing. It's of Gemini, whose uniform reflects the duality of his name, half black and half white. Teo's written some notes on the side to explain the silver stitching that will wind up his left leg, accentuating the length of it, as well as the material to use for his hood.

"I heard he's your thief, so I didn't want anything too obtrusive. I was going for subtle." Teo moves from his chair to the bed, buzzing with excitement.

"Did you learn this somewhere?" Phoenix asks. He bends over the tabula again, his golden hair in disarray.

On the bed, Teo's closer to the smell of him, a combination of some generic shampoo and, well, just Phoenix. The dull metal of his spectacles glints, and Teo has to stop himself from staring at this unexpected profile of Phoenix in glasses. He refocuses on the tabula, which is showing Lupus's design now, a voluminous, understated suit that imitates the large hoodie he's seen them hide in.

"I took a course at the Alliance. Koreans say clothes give you wings, you know. Each line, each detail, represents something significant. If you've seen Maggie's tool belt, it's a five-color knotted band designed to emulate a traditional Korean belt. Different designs can emphasize longevity, harmony, or dignity. I've studied other cultures and fashions on my own, but the Alliance uniforms are a good primer for blending function with form. Their space suits are created for more than just survival," Teo answers.

Phoenix swipes to the next page and his hand goes still. It's Phoenix's uniform. Instead of just adding a bird-shaped appliqué or embroidery to his suit, Teo's incorporated red, gold, and orange feathers into the sleeves of a long coat, creating slits along its sides for ease of movement and to imitate the fluttering of wings. Teo leans in and taps on the picture to zoom.

"These feathers aren't just for show. Eiji Nakatsu studied owls to design the Japanese bullet train, you know. Their serrated feathers allowed for not only speed, but also silence. These would also . . ." Teo trails off; he's been talking a kilometer a minute and not letting Phoenix get a word in edgewise. "I got a little carried away. They're just initial sketches." He reaches to take the pad away, fingers spreading wide to hide the picture.

"No." Phoenix grips Teo by the wrist, stopping him. "No, I love it. Don't take it back. I'm surprised is all."

"I'm not just a pretty face," Teo says glibly, mostly to keep the word *love* at a safe distance. He points his chin at the design, "Subtle isn't what I aimed for with you."

"Is that so?" Phoenix asks, amused.

"You're a completely different person out there," Teo says. Videos of Phoenix and his crew have always been popular, especially in AV. Phoenix holds himself with a braggadocious swagger, like a cartoon villain twirling a mustache. Teo saw it firsthand when he stepped on the *Ohneul*. "So, I gave you more flair. I know what it's like to play for the cameras, after all."

Teo examines the design anew now that someone else has seen it. He forgot that he colored in Phoenix's eyes for the sketch. He looks up and now Phoenix's actual eyes are too close, vivid in a way that Teo could never have captured no matter how long he agonized over color options. He's all too aware that Phoenix is still holding on to his wrist. Phoenix slides his thumb into Teo's palm. He lifts his other hand to Teo's cheek.

"I've noticed you too," Phoenix says. "In photos, you always tilt your head away to hide your scar."

Teo closes his eyes. Draws in a deep breath. He steers the conversation back to safer waters. "I've written out all the instructions, but I'm sorry I can't tailor these suits myself. Make sure your tailor measures you accurately, though. That's crucial."

"Is it?"

Phoenix releases Teo, much to his almost unbearable relief. But then he reclines on his bed, and everything about this scene—his posture, the unmade bed—screams at Teo. What is it about Phoenix that reverts him back, more than a decade, to the skittish colt sneaking out to meet Elisabet Rawn?

"Exceedingly," Teo says, marveling at how even his voice sounds. "I don't want false measurements messing up my design."

"Why don't you take them now?"

"Now?"

"Sure." Phoenix stands, his hands resting at his waistband. "Do you need me to take off my shirt?"

Teo sees Phoenix's hands clutching the hem of his shirt, and his mouth struggles to shape words. "No. That won't be necessary."

"Suit yourself."

Teo finds that his hands have gripped Phoenix's covers. He relaxes his fingers. "I don't have a tape measure."

"But surely you have a measuring function on your band?"

Phoenix would know better than Teo.

"Relax your arms," Teo says as he inspects the wristband that used to be Phoenix's own.

Teo finds the measurement tool and then starts at Phoenix's shoulder. He traces it down his arm. The band beeps every time a centimeter is added, and he drags his wrist just past Phoenix's. He marks down the measurement on his tabula and then repeats the same motion for Phoenix's other arm, slowly drawing a line down the length of it. More slowly than he needs to, but it's not like Phoenix is hurrying him along. The only noise in the room comes from the wristband, sounding for all the world like a heartbeat monitor, except that its regular blips have no bearing whatsoever on the erratic state of Teo's heart.

"Arms up," Teo instructs, and Phoenix obliges.

Teo traces his wrist around Phoenix's chest, and Phoenix's muscles bunch under his shirt. They're solid, of course. Teo would, should, joke about Phoenix's physique, but it takes everything in him to note down the measurement with a neutral face.

"Next is your waist," he says.

He touches his wrist to Phoenix's waist and knows he's not imagining it when Phoenix inhales sharply as his fingers not-so-accidentally brush the indent of his hip. He takes his time here, bringing his body around Phoenix's. Teo's breath falls softly on Phoenix's neck, and he shivers in response, the sound reaching its way inside Teo. He lifts his band and jots down the number.

He examines his writing as if it holds some innate secret and asks casually, "Shall we continue?"

Teo lifts his eyes but isn't prepared for the onslaught of Phoenix's full attention. His cheeks are crimson, his hair tousled, and his shirt untucked from when he offered to take it off earlier. Teo wants to curse.

"What's next?" Phoenix asks.

Teo eases closer to him, then closer still. Phoenix backs up into his bed and then sits down as Teo steps forward yet again. He parts Phoenix's legs with his body, standing in between them. Keeping his eyes locked on Phoenix, he leans down until they're eye to eye, nose to nose, lip to lip. If Teo tried to measure the distance between them using his wristband now, how many beeps would blip? Teo pulls off Phoenix's glasses and puts them to the side, and his eyes close. Then, slowly, giving Phoenix every opportunity to pull away, he places his hand in Phoenix's. He presses their hands together, palm to palm. A holy palmers' kiss. Their fingers interlock. Teo remembers that hand on his face, and he wants it there again, that flutter of fingers over his scar. But then he remembers whom that hand belongs to.

"Are you just using me?" Teo whispers. Phoenix's eyes fly open and Teo catches panic flickering in them. Even if he was expecting it, even if he provoked it, he has to tamp down the disappointment building in his stomach. "Is this some elaborate ploy to finally get your revenge?"

Phoenix's eyebrows knit together. "That's not—"

Teo pushes Phoenix down onto the bed, cutting him off. He stretches their interlocked hands high above his head, pressing them into the sheets. Teo plants his other hand next to Phoenix and holds himself over his body.

"Don't mistake me for a fool. I've been seducing people to further agendas for a long time."

He lowers his body tantalizingly close to Phoenix's, just barely not touching. Phoenix's body is taut underneath his, trembling. Phoenix nervously licks his lips, and Teo homes in on the beauty mark next to the corner of his mouth.

"Teophilus." Phoenix's voice is strangled, and Teo's body flushes hearing his name, even though he doesn't want to. "Teophilus, just kiss me."

They lock eyes, and Teo slowly, deliberately, touches his lips to the corner of Phoenix's. He draws back only enough to exhale on his skin, to catch the gust of Phoenix's panting. He leans in for another and Phoenix meets him halfway. His arms wrap around Teo, and their bodies slam together. Phoenix's mouth is on his and Teo has the chance to breathe in how good Phoenix smells, to slide his hands into that damn hair. They grasp each other greedily, hungrily. Teo slides his tongue into Phoenix's mouth and Phoenix moans, bunching his hands into Teo's shirt. He holds Teo tight against him, as if trying to fit Teo into his every groove. Teo breaks away to gasp for air.

"Teophilus—" Phoenix groans into his ear, and Teo wants to hold that voice close, burrow deep into it because it feels so good.

He's already memorizing this moment, even if there's no way he'll be able to recall the memory in the future without it hurting him. He's being used, he's using himself, he can't keep it straight. The hand he puts up to push Phoenix away clutches a fistful of his shirt and brings him closer instead.

Then, everything lurches.

Teo goes flying off the bed and, for one disorienting moment, thinks that Phoenix has thrown him off. But around him, mugs are rolling on the ground. Some lay shattered in puddles. Another crash reverberates across the room and the lights above flash crazily. Phoenix's wrist mirrors the same rapid blinking, and a shrill alarm goes off. Phoenix pushes himself off the bed. He blinks at Teo, sits up, roughly hand-combs his hair, and bumps his comm. A minivid of Aries pops open.

"We've been hit!"

"Obviously," Phoenix says. He clears his throat and stands, tucking in his shirt. "By what?"

"Another ship! Phoenix, you better—"

"I'm on my way."

Even as he's speaking, Phoenix's hand is on the side panel. He hardly waits for the door to slide open enough for him to squeeze through the gap. And then, he's gone. Teo's left in the room with the lights flashing and the piercing alarm ringing, and all he can do is put his hands against his ears and crouch on the floor with his knees pulled into his chest. He can smell the burning, hear the crackling flames coming for him.

"Teophilus, you coming?" Phoenix is framed in the doorway. Before Teo can answer, Phoenix's hand is in his, helping him up. "Come on."

He keeps his hand in Teo's as they leave the room together, carefully stepping over the trip wire, only letting go when they reach the ladder and clamber down. Teo lands moments after him and sees Ocean and Sasani hurrying down the hall.

"You jake?" Ocean asks as they stride toward the cockpit together.

"Yeah, marv." The alarm peals overhead and he cringes.

"They're hailing us!" Aries exclaims.

"Who is?" Phoenix asks as they enter the cockpit.

Aries is at the controls, one hand on the wheel and the other on the keyboard in front of him. Gemini is perched at another console, bringing up a viewfinder of their surroundings.

"The ship attacking us," Aries answers. "I can't see them, though. They must be using some sort of cloaking."

"Lupus?" Phoenix says into his wrist. Their picture pops up. "Run diagnostics? How long do you need to home in on their location?"

"You'll know when I know."

Aries sighs. "My least favorite answer."

"Cass is ready on your word," Gemini announces. "I'm going to do some damage control on the ship."

"Maggie can help with that," Ocean says. "If you need it."

Gemini nods at her and runs out of the room.

"Now's as good a time as any," Phoenix says to Aries. He points to Ocean, Sasani, and Teo. "You three stay out of sight of the cameras."

Teo points behind him. "We're already in its blind spot."

The screen in front of them blinks on, revealing a large dark-skinned man with a scar across his mouth. "You like that shot across the bow, Garrett?"

"You've never had good aim," Phoenix says mildly. "What's this about, Amell?"

"Could have shot you dead in one go," Amell says. "But Corvus wanted to give you one last chance."

"One last chance for what?" Phoenix asks. Then Teo notices his whole body solidify.

Someone steps into the frame next to Amell. Pale hair and paler eyes, as if he's been wholly washed of color. He takes a seat and his lips spread in a bodhisattva smile.

Corvus.

"Garrett. I meant to contact you earlier, but I got caught up. As you can imagine."

"Actually, I can't," Phoenix says, his voice strained. "That's the problem."

"That was your choice," Corvus says laconically. He studies some far-off point, and Teo remembers that even at the bar, he always focused his attention elsewhere. "You were the one who left."

"You always acted like you were better than us," Amell sneers. Corvus places a hand on Amell's shoulder and he immediately quiets.

"We wanted different things," Phoenix says and Teo hears the tautness in his voice.

Corvus says Phoenix is the one who left, but he's the one drifting closer to the screen, caught in his former partner's gravitational pull. For the first time, Corvus looks directly at Phoenix.

"Not from each other, we didn't," he replies. His words aren't directed at Teo, but they electrify him. Teo bites his lip hard enough to draw blood as Phoenix averts his gaze, as if blinded by trying to look directly at the sun. "Do you have him, Garrett?"

"You'll have to specify," Phoenix says. His hand clenches into a fist at his side. "How did you find us, anyway?"

"Ship ID zero-one-eight-seven-eight-four-zero-eight-two-three," Amell reads off a side screen.

Phoenix shakes his head. "You said Portos destroyed all his files."

"We didn't get it from him. It's your turf, Garrett. Of course, we'd find someone else you left your ID with. You know, *in case of emergency*. Took a couple of tries, killed a few locals, but we bled it out from a bartender, eventually."

"You didn't," Phoenix chokes.

Phoenix hunches over the console. Teo rises from his seat, but Ocean's hand comes down on his shoulder. She shakes her head at him.

"Not now," she says quietly.

"Whatever he offered you for his freedom, I can double it," Corvus says. "I'm amply funded now."

"I surmised as much." Phoenix squeezes the words out. "You'd need it for the augmented biosuit. Did you come up with the clone tech too?"

"It's not clone tech." Corvus settles comfortably into his seat. "It's a skinsuit. A deepfake skinsuit."

"Deepfake skinsuit?" Phoenix repeats. "As in . . ."

"The more images available of the subject, the easier it is to construct. And nothing is easier, of course, than finding photographs and videos of the Anand family."

"You got Hadrian in the suit."

"He just needed a little oomph. You know he's always been uncanny at picking up mannerisms and vocal inflections. A voice modulator, a light lift in his boots, that was all he really needed." Corvus examines his fingernails. "I can explain the compounds that went into creating the human torches, too, if you'd like."

"Was it worth it?" Phoenix asks bitterly. "Your revenge?"

"What is revenge except a plea for empathy? When you seek revenge, the thing you want most is for the other person to acutely experience your pain. But that doesn't mean I won't enjoy the journey." Corvus shrugs. "My focus isn't limited to personal vendetta, though, Garrett. Consider who strengthened the Anands: the Alliance." Corvus smiles. "Then after that, who knows?"

As Corvus laughs, Teo thinks of his crew, his brother, his mother, his father. He rises, and Ocean's hand comes down hard on his shoulder once more. He whirls to face her, to rip her hand away, to snarl in defiance, but she's already left her spot behind.

Ocean strides directly into the camera's viewpoint. Aries and Phoenix gape at her, and Corvus narrows his pale eyes.

"Who are you?" he asks.

TWENTY-THREE

WHO ARE YOU?" Corvus repeats.

"You haven't had the pleasure of meeting me," Ocean says as she brings out her gun from its side holster, flashing its handle at the screen. "But Amell has."

"Oh, it's you." The scar at Amell's mouth twists as he frowns. "Had your chance, but you missed."

"I never miss," Ocean says.

Corvus has been eyeing their interaction from the side of the frame and says, "You're Korean."

"Thanks," Ocean says.

"It wasn't a compliment," Corvus says. "You must be from the *Ohneul.*"

"And you must be the one who ordered its destruction," she says. "Is your plan always annihilation?"

"Garrett knows I can never have just a piece." Corvus tilts his head toward Phoenix. "Will you give me Teophilus?"

"No." The answer tumbles out of Phoenix immediately, as if in spite of himself.

"You never were good at lying." Corvus's mouth tugs downward, a deep indentation.

"If I had been better at lying to myself," Phoenix says softly, "I might have stayed with you."

Corvus unfolds from his gathered position, and Ocean recognizes that calculated control used to disguise emotion.

"What do you think you'll accomplish by holding him, Garrett?" Corvus asks icily. "He'll just die with your whole crew because of your false sense of morality."

"God, I never thought this day would come," Amell interjects, laughing feverishly. "I never got what Corvus saw in you. And now I can finally turn your ship into a raging inferno."

"So, it's come to this?" Phoenix holds Corvus's gaze, ignoring Amell's outburst. "Will you pull the trigger?"

"There'd be an intimacy in dealing your death," Corvus says. They stare at each other as if no one else exists. Phoenix is the first to break again, and he lowers his chin.

"If I give you Teophilus," Phoenix draws out the words slowly. "Will you let the rest of my crew go?"

Ocean goes cold. Teo makes a noise from behind them and Corvus cocks his head. He doesn't have a chance to respond, though, because Ocean snaps her weapon to Phoenix's head.

"Phoenix." She imitates the warning lilt she's heard Gemini and Cass use, making sure to drag out her words. "Over my—"

"Over your dead body, yes." Phoenix's hand gently closes over hers. He turns his head to her, repositioning the gunpoint to his forehead. "But Ocean, I just need a little more time."

Before she can say *I know*, the cockpit lights up with a brilliant flash.

For a fleeting moment, Ocean thinks Amell tired of their conversation and decided to blow up their ship with the vidlink still on. But the beam of light comes from off in the distance.

"How's that for a shot across the bow?" Phoenix says wryly as he turns back to Amell and Corvus. Ocean holsters her gun again.

"How—" The lights in the room behind Corvus and Amell flash wildly and alarms wail.

"I never liked you either, Amell, you pompous enabler. You were always too dazzled by the blazing torches of your fanaticism to discern that it was hellfire guiding your way."

"Corvus isn't the devil," Amell growls.

"No." Phoenix directs his words to Corvus. His mouth wrenches to the side as he speaks with a self-deprecating rasp. "He's the morning star," Corvus flinches. "I wasn't sure this day would come either. Now's your chance; you better not miss."

"*Garrett—*"

Phoenix swiftly turns off the call in the middle of Corvus's howl. When he whirls around, his face is pale and his blue eyes are glittering. He flings up screens left and right, moving almost too fast for Ocean to process.

"Nice shot, Cass," he says as he sticks up her vidscreen on the wall. She's in an unfamiliar room, at another set of controls.

"Gemini told me to do it!" Cass says quickly.

From his screen, Gemini lazily flips her off and says, "I take full responsibility. But all credit goes to Lupus for narrowing down their location."

Phoenix throws up another screen with Lupus, who salutes with two fingers. "Thanks for buying me time."

"Lupus, excellent work," Phoenix says. "Cass, keep on it. Things are about to get hairy."

"I hope that's not my future I'm staring at, Phoenix," Cass quips. "Don't expect that shot to slow them down much. Their central control is probably buried deep within the ship, like ours."

The ship shakes as it's hit. Phoenix hops to the side to find his balance. "Aries!"

"I'll do my best," Aries grunts and jerks the wheel over. "But it's not going to be pretty."

"Just get us to the Moon in one piece. It's the closest place we can go to take cover."

"Ocean, run backup," Gemini says.

Phoenix gestures to the seat next to Aries, and even then, his motion doesn't register right away. Ocean shakes her head. "I can't—"

Maggie's head pops up in front of Gemini's. "Ocean, you would not *believe* what a task driver Gemini is. No time for test runs, but you'll just have to trust my work."

Ocean sees then, for the first time, the new pedals installed underneath the panel. Her chest tightens.

"She's ready for you," Phoenix says.

"I just had a *gun* to your head," she finally manages.

Phoenix blinks at her. "Your safety was still on."

"How could you have possibly known that?"

Phoenix smiles and pats the seat. "We could use your help," he says.

Sliding into that seat is like coming home. When she stretches her feet forward, the pedals are at the exact right distance. She rests her right hand lightly on the wheel and her left hand travels to the shift at her side. It has all been waiting for her, and this time, she's not begging a hand in a lap to be raised, not hoping on someone else's choice.

"How far are we from Artemis?" Phoenix asks Aries over Ocean's shoulder.

"It's not getting there that will be hard. It's getting past the barrier once we arrive," Aries says placidly.

"Shall I blast it?" Cass asks.

"Even if it would break their shield, that's *not* a good first impression to make," Phoenix says.

Aries dodges and weaves, making them a more difficult target while Cass fires off shots behind them. Ocean can't see the other ship in the window—its cloaking device is still in effect—but Lupus has thrown an amorphous blob of a target on the screen. Gemini is right; without it, they'd have no idea what to aim at or fly away from.

"We'll have to hail Artemis once we get closer," Phoenix says. "I'm sure we have their attention by now. Teophilus, any chance your contact's on standby?"

"After this commotion, she might wash her hands of me. She did *not* want to involve the Seonbi."

"Well, we always keep it interesting, don't we?" Phoenix mutters. Aries grunts in response. He throws his body against the wheel as if that will somehow sharpen his turn. A laser shot skids off their side, proving him wrong. "One piece, Aries! One piece!" Phoenix groans from his new position on the ground.

Sitting copilot to Aries is like sitting passenger seat to a crazy uncle careening wildly around steep mountain curves, although it may be harsh of Ocean to judge him when a murderous Mercurian's in hot pursuit.

"I've established comms with the Seonbi Embassy," Lupus says from their screen. "Ready?"

Phoenix raises a hand to wave, but the screen to the left of them has already switched on. A Korean man wearing a pale-gray hanbok peers at them.

"Please move your skirmish away from the Moon," he says.

"We'd actually love permission to enter your airspace, particularly through the shield guarding your troposphere." Phoenix pulls himself up from the ground, grasping the back of Ocean's chair.

"We want no part of your dispute. You're Phoenix, aren't you?"

"Guilty?"

"Indeed."

The *Pandia* is hit again and the panel beeps loudly, in a different cadence from the alarms overhead. Even if Ocean isn't yet versed in the *Pandia*'s language, she can guess what that means.

"Homing missiles?" she asks.

"Yup," Aries says.

Behind her, Teo's probably still sitting at the table, the same tense set to his body, the one that took over when Corvus started talking. But she can't think about soothing his shaking hands right now, or slowly bringing color back to his white fingertips.

Ocean commands, "Let me take over."

Aries nervously glances at Phoenix. "You sure?"

"Do it," Phoenix chimes, his attention on the vidlink unwavering.

Aries's fingers fly over the keys while Ocean places her feet on the pedals.

"All yours," he says with the final click.

"Hold tight."

She swivels her right heel down and to the side while adjusting for the thrusters, then spins the wheel, spiraling the ship into a tight barrel roll. People yell as items go flying. The *Pandia*'s a heavier ship than she's used to and judging by the other ship's maneuvering, theirs is lighter and faster. Two missiles sail by them and hit the shield surrounding the Moon instead, inciting a cuss storm from the Seonbi still on-screen.

Manual flying is a lost art. Automated controls keep the ship from crashing and stabilizers keep it flying straight, but neither allow its pilot to get within three meters of anything before trying to fishtail a close landing. If they wanted to crash-land on the Moon, Aries could have done it. But Ocean has to keep them alive while they're between its shield and a much nimbler ship hell-bent on destruction. Aries brought the *Pandia* into the Moon's exosphere, though, the perfect starting point for Ocean. Artemis's engineered density is far lower than Earth's, but it's enough to work with. She tilts the ship on its side and flies adjacent to the Moon. Then she cuts directly perpendicular and away. The ship in pursuit whizzes past while Cass fires, crowing into the air. The *Pandia* is bulky, but not when its pedals are under Ocean's feet. The ship is an extension of her body, responding to the point of her toe and lift of her wrist as they complete their pas de deux in space.

Ocean scans the screen again. If she wants, she can ram forward and maim Corvus's ship enough to joust it into Artemis's shield, turning everyone onboard into the inferno that Amell threatened them with earlier. But she remembers Phoenix's strangled voice after hearing about Hector, his hands sliding over Portos's eyelids, and the expression he wore as he renounced Corvus. She glances back at Sasani and at Teo next to him. Teo shakes his head at her, but it could mean anything: a denial of whatever's on her face or an acknowledgment of what will happen next.

It's always been easy for her to aim and pull the trigger. Aim and push the pedals. Facing the wheel again, Ocean sets the *Pandia* on a collision course with the other ship. Her heel swivels in tandem with her left hand shifting gears. She flies straight ahead, gaining speed.

And then, at the last moment, she tilts sideways, narrowly avoiding the blob on the screen. They zip past each other, and Ocean loops the ship around as if they're on a roller-coaster track.

"Cass?" Ocean calls.

"Whatever you got, wild child, I'm ready."

Ocean slams the brakes and uses that momentum to swing a 180. As the ship is facing its opponent, she aerobrakes. It's the same principle used in old-school landings on planet surfaces, utilizing an aerodynamic decelerator. It leaves them completely exposed for a moment, but as promised, Cass goes full throttle, opening fire. The space before them flickers as their shots hit Corvus's ship and their cloak drops away completely. Ocean swivels the *Pandia* back and forth to cast off Amell's bursting missiles. Despite her efforts, one of them slips by and explodes into them. Ocean gusts forward and his ship agilely leaps to the side, hitting her once again. Yet another cadence of alarms joins the fray.

"What do we have, Maggie?" Ocean asks.

"Good news and bad news, chief," Maggie shouts, the shrieking alarms accentuating her words. "Good news is he hit our brakes, so it won't affect us in the air."

"Why you gotta give her the dessert first?" Gemini yells off-screen.

"Bad news is we're pretty much shot for our landing?" Ocean asks.

Maggie's affirmation is overlaid with Phoenix's voice at her side.

"You're just going to let us die out here?" Phoenix accuses the Seonbi.

"We don't negotiate with terrorists," he replies primly.

He's going to leave them to fight among themselves, to die or to be forced to kill. Ocean knows the *Pandia* can't outrun the other ship, and she can't keep this up forever.

"I need an in!" she says through her teeth.

"Now if you'll excuse us," the Seonbi says with a note of finality. He raises a hand to cut off the transmission.

"This is Teophilus Anand," Teo announces over Ocean's left shoulder, and relief rushes through her. "You're going to want to bring me in. Alive."

"Teophilus Anand?"

"Alert the Alliance," a different voice instructs the Seonbi who answered their call. Ocean doesn't have the luxury to check who it is.

"You're not going to call the Alliance, and I'll tell you why," Teo says coolly. Even while wildly distracted, Ocean recognizes that tone—it's his politician voice, a solar leader's son's voice.

"Oh really? Why are you here then if not to turn yourself in?"

"You're a Diplomat, aren't you? Then surely you know that the Alliance regularly sends an embassy to Mars to keep the peace." Ocean could laugh at Teo calmly condescending to the Diplomat. But a spatter of missile fire makes her swallow her amusement as she focuses again on the controls. "The last thing Mars wants is to stir up trouble. They just want to be left the hell alone." He pauses. "I was there when the *Shadowfax* was boarded. And if you've thought about it at all, you know it wasn't Martians who attacked us. I know who they actually were, and I know they're not done killing Koreans. If you let us die out here, that information will die with me."

"What's to stop us from turning you in?"

"Lim Eunkyeong," Teo says. "Oh Haneul. Choi Hwanhee, Cho Gina, Kang Min, Park Minkyu." Ocean bites her lip. Teo is listing the names of the Seonbi who died while being escorted by the *Shadowfax*. "I was supposed to protect them. I failed. But I can do something to atone for it. If you hand me over to the Alliance, whatever I say will be swallowed up in their politics, their red tape, their haste to show that they've taken care of the problem."

The pause in their negotiation is punctuated by a hiss of the transmission.

"I'm guessing you want access, but don't want the other ship to follow you in?"

"That would be ideal," Phoenix says.

"It'll be quite a small window."

"Ocean?" Phoenix asks.

"I can do it," she replies. "I'll take whatever you can give me."

"You heard her," Phoenix says.

"I'm sending you the coordinates."

Ocean scans them after they load onto the screen. She almost laughs. The window is so tiny she might have to angle the ship diagonally to fit through it. But it isn't surprising at all. The Seonbi are making her prove that the *Pandia* is worthy of help.

"How's that?" the Diplomat asks, his voice impeccably smooth. "We want to attract as little attention as possible."

"Call it a done deal," she says.

The *Pandia* darts through space under her controls and she brings it close to the Moon's shield again, its left wing teasing a kiss. But Ocean knows if she touches the shield, it'll jolt the ship away. She keeps an eye on the ship behind them.

"Cass, let him come in close, yeah?" she says.

"You got it."

Appreciation for Cass's confidence flickers through her. She knows exactly what Ocean's asking for. Ocean rotates the wheel gently to the left. She's got the coordinates up on a map overlaying the steering window. She guns the accelerator while turning the wheel sharply to the left before steering in the opposite direction. The back part of the ship loses traction and slingshots parallelly around the curve of the shield, keeping her wing as close as possible to it. Amell struggles to regain control of Corvus's ship, unprepared for Ocean's precise maneuver. Cass shoots him while he's free-spinning in the air.

Ocean's already dovetailing, spinning the ship sideways. The opening in the shield is in front of them. She hits a bump in the air and for one brilliant moment, her body lifts from the seat. She's weightless, a thousand skeins of light threaded through one sliver of time. Then her body slams back down. The ship shivers as its wings scrape through the narrow opening. As soon as they're through, the shield closes behind them. Shots from Corvus's ship rebound off it ineffectually. Ocean watches the display as Amell dives to follow them in but slams into the shield and is forced back.

"Ocean, we're burning up!" Aries yells.

They made it in, but that raging inferno might still be in their future. Her hands are white-knuckling the wheel and her back is slick with sweat. Her body's so hot, she could be liquifying.

"I need a touchdown with a delay hook," she says tersely. "Maybe you have training grounds?"

"What does that mean?" the Diplomat asks.

"She's coming in hot." Maggie jumps in. "And our brakes are shot. Do you have a training area for this kind of thing?"

"Hangar B," the first Korean says.

"Lead them there," the Diplomat orders. "Discreetly."

Their landing will be anything but discreet, but there's no use explaining that. She directs the ship's nose upward, coasting as close to the shield as she can while she waits for the coordinates to pop up on the screen. When they do, she considers them.

"Maggie?" she asks. She's never done a hard landing like this outside of simulations.

"Send me specs for Hangar B," Maggie commands the Seonbi. After less than a minute, she reports, "Seventy-eight knots."

"Seventy-eight?"

Aries leans forward and taps the keyboard, bringing up another screen that shows the ship's current speed. They're at ninety-three.

"How much wiggle room do I have?" she asks.

"Do you want the truth?"

"Always, Maggie." Ocean allows her lips to curl into a smile. "When it's time, can you drop the tailhook?"

She's going to need to concentrate on the ship's speed.

"I'm on it!"

Ocean curves the ship around, scouring the horizon. She sees it at the same time Phoenix does.

He cusses and yells, "Hold on, everyone!"

Ocean grits her teeth and the ship dives. She darts forward into a nearby forest and the ship's belly clips the treetops. It shudders and she steadily brings it up. 84. She dips it down into the forest again.

"Do you know what discreet means?" one of the Seonbi yells.

Ocean's body bounces around her seat. 70. She checks the location of the hangar. They can make it. One hand on the wheel and the other on her gearshift.

75.

84.

Her hand is slippery against the gearshift, but her movements are automatic as she eyes the ship's speedometer as well as the approaching hangar. She noses down into the trees again, then pulls up.

76.

82.

Ocean spots it, the long runway that leads into Hangar B. An enormous pool demarcates its end, along with a titanium drawline that extends across its diameter. Everything depends on Ocean's incoming speed, and Maggie's ability to drop the tailhook at the right moment. At 80 knots, Ocean slams the ship down into the ground. The road explodes before them, carving the earth and throwing sand into the air. The ship skids forward.

"Hold on!" she yells, hopefully for the last time.

At the last possible second, Maggie drops the tailhook, and it snags on the drawline. The ships dumps into the pool and a tsunami crashes out of it onto the hangar. Waves subsume Ocean's vision, like she's drowning all over again. She thinks about how she's had it wrong this whole time. Despite her attempts to run away, despite the attempts to *push* her away, maybe she was always meant for the water.

The whiplash of the hook throws everyone out of their seats and sends them slamming against walls and the floor. Ocean's flat against the ground, panting. She tastes blood in her mouth and her ears are ringing shrilly. She presses her palms against the floor to push herself up.

"Is everyone—"

Someone rams into her, and yells jumble together as Teo hugs her. Phoenix piles on top, and Ocean flattens even farther when Aries collapses onto the heap. Cheers erupt from behind them, raw and weak from the tension, and Ocean twists to see Von and Dae crowding the doorway. Von's cheering, his arms tight around Dae, whirling them both around. Ocean's at the bottom of the dogpile, but she's riding high on relief and an even stronger exhilaration. She holds up her hands so she can see how much they're shaking.

"I'll see you all very soon," the Diplomat on-screen says, but they're all too preoccupied to answer him. When Ocean is able to swivel her head toward the screen, it's already blank.

"Ship status report?" Maggie asks.

"No, please no," Phoenix groans from the ground. "Just get your ass up here, Maggie. We need to give you a medal or something."

Ocean pushes herself up onto her elbows and meets Sasani's eyes. He's still lying on his stomach under the table, and he props his chin up as he gives her a soft, slow smile. But before Ocean can respond, Gemini plops down on the ground between them, blocking her view.

"Ocean," he says. "It was good flying."

He holds out his hands to her and she grasps them as he slides her toward him. The precarious pile topples apart, and he helps her to her feet. He flashes her his heartbreaker's smirk, a fraction of the dazzling smile she received on the bridge. Ocean's answering smile is too large to contain, spilling over into a laugh made of something bright and fierce.

"Hurakan," Ocean tries the name. "Thanks."

Hurakan's fingers tighten around her arms and his hands are warm against her skin. The two are still facing each other when Sasani stands on the other side of the room. He nods once at Ocean and then turns his head away, holding his elbows.

"I always wanted an ace pilot," Phoenix remarks, spreading his limbs across the ground in a snow angel position. "A thief, a hacker, a fighter, an accountant, and now a pilot. My ultimate party is almost complete."

"Your idea of an ultimate party has an accountant?" Teo teases. He's lying on his stomach and rests his hand on Phoenix's shoulder.

"Hey," Aries protests weakly.

"They jailed Capone for tax evasion," Phoenix says. "And I'm not made for a cell. Speaking of which, we'll need your particular set of skills to keep us out of one."

Teo props himself up, smiling first at Phoenix and then at Ocean.

"I'll take care of it."

ACKNOWLEDGMENTS

My sister and I always talk about what a good driver our mom is. She's not a downhill specialist who can drift around steep mountain curves, but her parallel parking is a thing of beauty. I doubt it came naturally to her. I think she became one of the smoothest drivers I know by accruing experience. My mom raised us on her own. She sacrificed so much to provide for us in every way, driving us to the library, to auditions, and to school when we missed the morning bus.

All this is to say: I owe everything to my mom. She wanted me to succeed in life, and she knew how vital art is. So, whatever I write is thanks to you, Umma. *Ocean's Godori* is indebted to you. Thank you for your painstaking work translating haenyeo songs and always being a phone call or katalk away when I wanted the best bugeo guk recipe or needed to check hangeul. But thanks most of all for raising me.

Every day, in a million different ways, I feel lucky to have izmeister as my sister. Izzy's largely responsible for getting me back into writing books, and I think I'm always writing for her, trying to create worlds for her to enjoy. We have a large age gap, but early on, she became someone I looked up to because of her constant thoughtfulness and her side-splitting wit. For *Ocean's*, thank you specifically for further translation help, for checking over Maggie's Glossary, and for forever being my go-to when I want to know what the cool youths are up to.

No matter how good (or bad) you feel about a finished piece, you never really know if it will connect with anyone. Enter Amy Bishop-Wycisk, agent extraordinaire, who took a chance on me, and saw through *Ocean's* sci-fi trappings to the beating heart of it. Thank you for your expertise every step of the way—from all your work within *Ocean's* to all the nitty-gritty details outside the story—and for being the best champion. I don't know how many times I've expressed to others how marvelous you are and how thankful I am that you're my agent.

Sareena Kamath is a phenomenal editor and really just a joy to work with. Thanks to her and the Zando team, this has been the best possible debut author experience. I always felt like I was in good hands with you, Sareena. Thank you for creating *Ocean's Godori* with me, for shaping it into the best possible story it could be, and for understanding its characters and what I was trying to say from the get-go. Working with you has been a dream.

I'm particularly grateful (and have so much admiration) for Tiff Liao and TJ Ohler. Thank you for taking up the baton and bringing me over the finish line. I'm indebted to you for all of your care.

When I first saw the gorgeous cover, crafted by Jee-ook Choi and Evan Gaffney, one of my first thoughts was that I hoped my story would do it justice. Thank you both for your beautiful work. I've also been such a fan of Jee-ook for years, so having her illustrate it was a dream come true.

Thank you to the Hillman Grad family as well: Lena, Naomi, and Rishi. I'm so appreciative of all the work you do. Thanks for celebrating and making space for artists like me to not only express ourselves genuinely, but also to never feel like we have to justify our place or what we have to say. I'm truly honored to be on this journey with you.

Thank you to Elliott Bay baes Sage Cruser and Lara Kaminoff. Sage, for our numerous walks and talks about life and art and for being one of the first people to read *Ocean's* when I was at the "what even is this?" stage to assure me that it indeed *was* something. Lara, for your encouragement and precisely slicing away at a draft to make it sparkle for querying. Thank you both for just generally inspiring me (and others!) with your creativity and your generous spirits.

Matt Choi, thanks for the late-night drives and for your humor and kindness. Being related to you always felt like a privilege, spending time with you always a special gift.

Thank you to Y. Zin, whose beautiful book *Haenyeo: Women Divers of Korea* was an invaluable resource as I researched for *Ocean's*.

Many, many thanks to Whitney Bak, for your meticulous and thoughtful copy editing to bring *Ocean's* to a polish.

Thank you to Yuki Hayashi, whom I've never met, but whose wonderful music has fueled 95 percent of *Ocean's* writing and editing. What would I have done without you?

And finally, if I'm grateful to my mom for raising me, I'm grateful the most to Sam for who I am today. Thank you thank you to my husband, Sam, who has been the greatest believer in *Ocean's* from the beginning. Thank you for your unfailing support, for being the best partner in life I could have ever hoped for. Thank you for being my first reader and cheerleader. You always knew what I needed, whether I wanted help working out story beats, technological what-ifs, geopolitical ramifications, or the hearts of the characters. Thanks for believing in my characters, but most of all for believing in me. *Ocean's* would not be what it is without you. Thank you for making it better, but more than that, thanks for making me better, and for your love that has always allowed me to be more, not less.

MAGGIE'S GLOSSARY OF ALLIANCE PARLANCE

So, you've just signed up for a stint at the Alliance! Congrats! As the leaders in space, Korea really has the best program for anyone wanting to see a little bit of the solar, even if you're not a full-fledged Alliance member! But you may have found that even though everyone claims to speak in Common, people use a lot of words you may not be as familiar with. Ever the good Samaritan, I, Margaret Thierry, have put together an unofficial* little guide for you so you won't come off like a complete uncouth bumpkin.**

aigo (아이고): Can mean something like "Oh no" or "Oh geez." As with most things, tone has a lot to do with it. There's a big difference between when someone trips and falls and another person goes "Aigo! Are you jake?" and the times when you do something a little foolish and someone

---

* I have been reminded to tell everyone that this has not been authorized by the Alliance in any shape or form.

** I have gotten all hangeul spell-checked by Ocean Yoon, so if you have a problem with it, you can take it up with her.

gives you the side-eye with an "Aigo . . ." I have an older crewmate who sighs "Aigo aigo aigo" to himself whenever he settles down into a seat.

aish (아이씨): I know many of you may have come to this guide expecting a primer on swear words. I did have a few colorful ones included, but was told very firmly to remove them. But rest assured, a few weeks with the Alliance, and you'll probably be as well-versed as I am! Anyway, this one is a very mild word of frustration that isn't even a cuss but still probably shouldn't be used around your superior. On the shoot to shit scale, it veers closer to shoot.

ajumma (아줌마): This is a term for a middle-aged woman, but I'd be careful where/when you use it. I've found some people get really offended when you call them that . . . Oh and I would *not* call your captain that. That's not respectful at all.

anju (안주): Drinking food—either main dishes or snacks to go with your alcohol! But listen, there's a science to it, if you know what I mean. Like fried chicken should go with beer, and fish stew should go with soju . . . Anyway, it's too much to get into here, but I have a whole other guide to that and if you want to know more, message me on AV (contact info at the bottom).

bab (밥): You're in the Alliance, so you'll probably hear words like jeong and han being thrown around as what is the most important to Korean identity, but I'm not well-equipped to talk about what those mean. This word though is probably my favorite. Bab is the word for rice but can just stand for speaking about food generally. I've found that when Koreans are asking after each other, rather than asking "How are you?" the more general "Bab meogeoseo?" or "Have you eaten food?" is more meaningful. Koreans, like all quality people, understand how important food is to the body and soul.

banchan (반찬): Properly following our bab entry is banchan, which are the side dishes that come with the meal. They typically come in small portions, are shared with your table, and accompany your rice before the main meal. My favorite banchan is kkagdugi or radish kimchi, but specifically the kind made by Ocean's mom. I also like the seasoned spinach banchan. Or maybe the anchovies? Or . . . Well, you get the point.

Bangpae (방패): One of the three training schools of the Alliance. This one is for the main corps or soldiers. It means "shield," and I feel like they got shorted. I mean, the other schools are Dragon and Tiger. And they got stuck with . . . shield?

call or kol (콜): Along the lines of "Deal" or "I'm in!" If someone says "Hey, let me buy you a beer" or "Let's go to see a movie" you can respond with "Call!" I mean, if you actually want to.

daksal (닭살): Chicken skin. Although this means chicken flesh, it's also slang for something akin to goosebumps. You can use it whenever something has raised the hair on your skin, whether it's from someone scaring you or when you're an awkward third wheel to a couple steadies being very touchy in public.

dangyeol (단결): This is what you say when you're saluting in the Alliance. It means "unity" or "unification." I've heard other words were more commonly used for saluting in the Korean army before North and South Korea reunified, but this is now the standard.

gamsahamnida (감사합니다): Formal way of saying thank you.

geonbae (건배): Oh, this one's important! You use it to say "Cheers" when drinking with others in Korean. Also important, when you're pouring alcohol for a seonbae (a geonbae with your seonbae, as it were), *always* pour with both hands. And when you drink, make sure to rotate your head or upper body away from your seonbae as if you're hiding your action from them. If your seonbae pours for you, always hold out your glass with two hands. This is how I remember it: anytime you're interacting with your seonbae and there's alcohol involved, consider the honor to be very heavy, so you need two hands for it.

gisuksa (기숙사): Dormitory. As you know, Alliance houses their dormitory in Seoul proper! It's actually pretty great. Students occupy the bottom five floors and the top levels are for alumni who can stay for free. Not to mention that Alliance has their own convenience store on the third level (A-Mart), and a sublevel that connects to the Seoul subway system.

Horangi (호랑이): One of the three training schools of the Alliance. This one is the command, or leadership school. Horangi means tiger, and the animal has been an important figure in Korea for hundreds of years. They had tiger statues guard royal tombs and a tiger mascot when they hosted the 1988 Olympics!

hwatu (화투): A popular Korean card game, also known as go-stop (고스톱) or godori (고도리). The cards have very distinctive illustrations with red backs. Commonly called go-stop because when a player wins a round, they have the option of continuing the game for the chance to win more points (and they say "Go") or ending the game then and there (saying "Stop"). You'll almost certainly see this played around the Alliance barracks, and I am now being reminded to tell you that gambling is strictly illegal in Korea. At least for Koreans. Did you know that casinos and hwatu parlors are set up so foreigners can gamble in Korea even though natives can't? Wild. Not that I would partake . . .

injeong (인정): This is a word of acknowledgment, and can be used to say "Yes, I recognize you're right" or "I accept." A lot of times on the AV board or in messages, you might see it reduced to the letters ㅇㅈ. Sometimes someone might say "Injeong halggeh," which is a longer way that can mean something like "Geez, fine, you're right" or like "I acknowledge and accept you." Again, like most things in life, I've found it's about tone.

insa (인사): Insa is a large umbrella term for greetings. This is something I wish I had known before joining the Alliance! Koreans are big on respect, courtesy, and hierarchy (more on that later). There are proper ways to greet someone, but a large part of that is bowing. You should always bow when greeting someone who's above you on the Alliance chain, but most Alliance kids have had this ingrained in them since they were kids, so you'll find them bowing when meeting new people or even ducking their head when calling for the ajumma in a restaurant. The angle of the bow, the positioning of the arms, or the duration of the bow can vary. And then they have more formal bows known as jeol (절). Different kinds of jeol are specific to weddings, funerals, and more. It's too much to get into, but I might upload a video later with examples. Stay tuned!

jal meokkesseumnida (잘 먹겠습니다): I will eat well. Remember what I said about Koreans and food? Alliance members will say this before a meal (obviously), or you can say "Jal meogeoseumnida" (잘 먹었습니다) after eating, which means "I ate well." If someone has served you food or made you food, it's very important that you show your appreciation in this way. Either sentence can mean a general "Thank you for this meal," which I think is a nice sentiment to have about every meal we eat.

jansori (잔소리): Nagging, basically. Like, "I hate calling home because I get so much jansori from my parents." Or, "Can you believe the jansori I got for showing up late?" But listen, maybe sometimes that jansori is deserved? Call your mom more often!

namisa (남이사): I wouldn't recommend using this because it's not very polite, but you should make your own judgment calls, I guess. It basically means: "Mind your own business" or "What right do you have to care?"

The "nam" part of it translates to "person," or more accurately "person I have no connection to."

nongdam (농담): A joke. But don't take it personally if people in the Alliance don't laugh at your jokes, or when you tell one, they say in a kind of mean voice, "Was that supposed to be a nongdam?" I've learned that sometimes people just don't laugh at the same things I do, and I respect that.

noonchi (눈치): I'll try to explain this, but I've been told I don't have a good grasp on it. Literally, it means something like "eye feeling" and it has to do with how good you are at picking up vibes or perceiving social cues. If you're told you have good noonchi, or fast noonchi, that's a compliment, and you're probably good at reading the room. But seeing that you're reading this guide, maybe you, like me, are someone who needs to work on their noonchi . . .

noraebang (노래방): If you're in the Alliance, chances are you've already experienced these karaoke rooms. If you're worried about how badly you sing, don't worry . . . noraebang always have these perfectly engineered mics to make your voice sound 76x better than normal. But if you *really* don't want to sing, that's fine, just be prepared to brandish a tambourine and at least keep a beat. The Alliance is big into group mentality and supporting each other, after all.

***Ohneul* (오늘):** This is the ship I fly on! Which I guess might not be that useful to you, but this is my guide so . . . it's captained by Dae Song and the word means "today," which is a play on Captain Dae's name too! Today, or "to Dae." Anyway, the *Ohneul* is Class 4 and she's seen better days, but I think she's got a solid crew.

Oori Da (우리 다): This is one of the best KBBQ places in Seoul. They don't use charcoal, but they do artificially emulate the smell of it and that infuses into the meat. I was talking to the ajumma who runs it, and Oori Da translates to "all of us" in Korean. So when you say "Oori Da Gaja," it can either mean "Let's go to Oori Da" or "Let's go, all of us!" I thought that was cute.

pa-seu (파스): You'll know this by smell if not by name. These are medicated patches you can throw on any aches and pains. My ship's doctor swears by them, although I'm not sure how well they actually work. When you watch old serials, you'll see old Korean men putting big white pa-seu on their shoulders at the end of the day.

Savoir-Faire (Sav-Faire): You haven't heard of Sav-Faire? You really do need to get out into the solar, don't you? Where did you think all our Diplomats come from? Sav-Faire, or Diplomat school, is this big fancy boarding school on Neptune where kids are shipped off to at age eight and train until they graduate ten years later. Officially, you learn politics and culture. But unofficially, I've heard they're not very nice.

Seonbi (선비): A lot of people mistakenly think that the Seonbi, or Scholars, are part of the Alliance, but they're a separate entity. The Seonbi tradition dates back to the Goryeo and Joseon dynasties, and refers to virtuous, learned men who lead lives of study and integrity. Similar to haenyeo, they experienced a resurgence in the last couple centuries, especially since Korea was trying to honor their traditions while moving into the future. That's the reason why the solar's tenth seowon was built on the Moon at Artemis! I don't know much more about it, other than that they fulfill a lot of diplomatic duties for Korea now because of their neutral status. Oh, and they wear cool hats.

steady: If you don't know what this means, you probably don't have to worry about it. But out of pity, I'll fill you in. Steady refers to a relationship of yours, typically of the romantical kind. Can be used as a verb or as a noun.

Yong (용): One of the three training schools of Alliance. This one is for the flight program. Yong means dragon, and it refers to those that have become true dragons and can fly. In Korea, dragons are known to bring rain, and are generally all right mythical beings when compared to some other legendary dragons that pillage and hoard their treasure.

yeokshi (역시): Of course, or as expected. For example: "Yeokshi, Kim Minwoo won the best actor award this year."

A word about honorifics:

The Alliance is very big on rank and age. If someone is above you in rank, you should always speak to them respectfully and by title (Captain, XO, etc.). Someone who is a similar rank to you, but older or more experienced, should be called **seonbae** (선배).

Now, if you've watched any serials at all, you may be familiar with some other more casual tag-ons. I'll give you a quick rundown:

- If you identify as a female, you may refer to an older female as **unni** (언니), an older male as **oppa** (오빠), and an older nonbinary person as **ilssi** (일씨).
- If you identify as male, you may refer to an older female as **noona** (누나), an older male as **hyeong** (형), and an older nonbinary person as **reunsaeng** (른생).
- If you don't identify as solely/either female or male, you may refer to an older female as **keunnim** (큰님), an older male as **joji** (조지), and an older nonbinary person as **noinna** (노인나).

You'll find that the Alliance tends to be a bit more conservative than the rest of Korean society. But generally, how you identify and how who you're addressing identifies is fluid. Honorifics can be fluid as well. For instance, I'm female and my XO Ocean is female, but I often call her hyeong, because she's always giving me older brother vibes. (Or I sometimes even call her hyeongnim for fun, which is what gangsters call their mob boss in serials.)

Ultimately, the use of any of these words signifies closeness, so really you should just ask what people prefer to be called or if they're comfortable being called different honorifics interchangeably, because there's no right/wrong answer. (Although I guess the wrong answer would be calling someone something they don't want to be called . . . so never mind, I guess there is a wrong answer.) Some people identify both as unni and reunsaeng, or noona and hyeong. Some people don't. And some people would prefer not to be categorized at all.

ABOUT THE AUTHOR

ELAINE U. CHO may have moved to the Pacific Northwest for the rain. If you spot her in the wild, she'll most likely be among books, in a movie theater, or pointing out the best dogs (all of them). She has an MFA in Flute Performance from CalArts and is a kyūdō practitioner. *Ocean's Godori* is her debut novel.